IT C

IT CAME FROM ON HIGH

ANDREW HARMAN

ORBIT

An *Orbit* book

First published in Great Britain by Orbit 1998

A CIP catalogue record for this book
is available from the British Library.

ISBN 1 85723 678 5

Typeset by Hewer Text Ltd, Edinburgh
Printed and bound by
Mackays of Chatham plc, Chatham, Kent

Orbit
A Division of
Little, Brown and Company (UK)
Brettenham House
Lancaster Place
London WC2E 7EN

For true believers everywhere.
And in memory of James (Seamus) Gill.
Have a Guinness ready for me.

Acknowledgements

There is an old adage which says that the best place to hide a lie is between two truths. I couldn't agree more. Except that here, I like to call the lies fiction. Well, they're pretty much the same after all, stuff made up between the facts to get you out of trouble. But actually there *are* a whole stack of truths in this novel, honest, and I must thank some people who made their (unwitting) massive contributions in helping me get the truths as correct as I wanted.

First there's Peter Hebblethwaite, whose invaluable book *In the Vatican* (Oxford University Press, 1987) gave me an immensely valuable peek behind those walls.

Then there's Paul Davies, Professor of Natural Philosophy and author of the small but perfectly formed *Are We Alone?* (Penguin, 1995). If there was one sentence destined to start me off thinking, then surely it had to be, 'It's hard to see how the world's great religions could continue in anything like their present form should an alien message be received.' Miss out the word 'message' and you've got the germ of a novel! Thanks, Paul.

And then, slap my wrists, there's a whole bunch of folk who I really should have thanked before: they're the teams that bring me stacks of science, technology and sometimes just downright weirdness in ways I can understand. All you people responsible for *New Scientist* and *Focus*, please, take a bow! But before the more particular of you start telling me that papal astronomers don't think that way, (*New Scientist*

21, Dec. 96, p. 30) or that it was ESA who reported the black hole in galaxy 3C390.3 (*Focus*, Aug. 97, p. 11) and Hubble would never be able to see it real time, anyway, I know – but hey, telling lies is always more fun!

Finally, there are two other folk I want to thank. John Parker, my agent, whose comments and objective help throughout the (oft brain-wrenching) editing of this novel helped enormously. Thanks, John!

And, saving the best 'til last, my final Rolo goes always to Jenny, my wife, who has to put up with it all after a hard day's work. I love you.

Contents

A Great Escape

Five small time periods prior to curfew. Narcteenth of P'yoon. Space

The semi-sentient globes of a neo-silicate chandelier tweaked their refractive indices another six points and flung calming motes of light around the darkening room. In moments, harmoniously soothing wavelengths bathed the room and scattered across the interlocking tile floor with the power to calm the most fevered of brows.

Much to the disappointment of the chandelier, the figure pacing restlessly below didn't miss a step. The overlarge kneepads, which were currently the fashion thereabouts, rustled with every pace, echoing off the sparsely tapestried walls. She reached down tensely, snatched the complex chronometer from a pocket and scowled at it, the tension showing across every scale of her mustard-yellow forehead. Already the nightly ritual of curfew was being bolted down. The sun was setting across the banks of projector screens and the power to the cloudy skylights was being turned down. Soon, very soon, it would feel like night. And soon, if he didn't show up, it would be too late. Anything that moved without the luxury of a triple-signed pass and a large wad of ready bribes didn't move for long. Just as it had been every night since the war ended so spectacularly.

'Where is he . . . ?' she breathed nervously to herself and

risked another glance around the curtains of the neo-silicate window. 'Where is he?'

'He'll be here, my lady,' whispered her faithful maid, brimming with the terminal overconfidence of the romantically inclined.

'Ohhh . . . How can you be so sure?'

'Trust me,' she smiled. 'The look in his eyes when I delivered your last letter said it all.'

'Really?' whispered the Lady Kh'Xandhra, her eyes lighting up. 'What did that look say?'

'It said, "I shall be there at the appointed time, even though it shall be a risk. No security force can stand in my way for my heart is burgeoning with the newfound joys of all that is the ancient force of love. Love for my one true heart's desire. The Lady Kh'Xandhra!" '

'Wow!' whispered Kh'Xandhra, pirouetting with delight, 'All that in one look.'

'Well . . . er, yes. He has *very* expressive eyes.'

'Ohh, you've noticed, too? And aren't they such a gorgeous shade of puce? I want him here, now. Where is he?'

'Fear not m'lady, he knows the plan.'

It was true, they'd been through it a hundred times. A hundred covert meetings had covered the timing, the route, the signals, the way out of his territory. He knew the drill. There was no excuse for sloppiness. The window of opportunity was narrow enough without him being late. If he'd stood her up his excuse had better be very good. After all, it would be his last. She'd see to that, personally.

And suddenly the left ventricle of her heart fluttered as a terrible thought struck her. What if he wasn't late? What if they'd captured him? Found him scrambling over the wall to reach her? What if even now he was being beaten to a pâté at the merciless tentacles of her sworn enemies? A small gasp of lovelorn alarm slithered between her lips.

But, no, it couldn't be that, could it? She would've heard the distant alarms by now. She would've heard the hot pursuit. She would've heard . . . well, something. Wouldn't she?

Desperately, she stared at the chronometer again, annoyed that it had barely moved. But then, scant moments before the final bolts of curfew were screwed down for the night, there was a small buzzing of Attom-Pak thrusters and a silhouette descended gracefully on to her balcony. She dashed excitedly across the room, her mind a whirl of anticipation. She took a breath and quivered with helpless excitement.

The silhouette stepped off his trusty Hovva-Thruster and nervously approached the reinforced neo-silicate window.

'What's he waiting for?' quivered Kh'Xandhra, her heart pounding out paradiddles against the ridge of her pronounced sternum.

'The password,' prompted the maid. 'Give him the password.'

Kh'Xandhra's lips squirmed into an 'o' of alarm.

'The password!' whispered the maid urgently.

Kh'Xandhra took a breath. 'But soft, what laser through my window breaks?' she called.

'Mine!' answered her long-awaited lover. 'Please, take cover, darling. I wouldst not want to dent a scale on your delicious dermal layer.' Silhouetted by one of the thousands of setting sun-screens he swung a military grade laser blaster out of a suitable holster and lined up on the pre-stressed neo-silicate in the window.

With one squeeze a focused pulse of high-energy photons shattered the translucent barrier separating the two lovers. Shards of neo-silicate blasted into the room, spun through the air and embedded themselves in the stellar tapestry adorning the far wall. It was the first casualty of the night, shredded irreparably.

'Come, my sweet, Kh'Xandhra,' he crooned, beckoning sweet encouragement through a cloud of de-ionising silicates. She needed no further bidding. In a flurry of kneepads and gossamer scarves she sprinted towards him, skipped over the windowledge and landed in his young strong purple tentacles.

'Oh, Kh'Vynn, you came for me!' she gushed, all heaving sternum and fluttering compound eyes.

'Of course,' he answered heroically, clutching her tightly to his scaly chest. And he would have smothered her in passionate kisses on that very spot if it hadn't been for the tell-tale whine of Attom-Pak thrusters at ten o'clock.

'It seems, my dear, I have underestimated my people's security systems and my escape has been noticed. They are on to us,' he announced and, exhibiting the subtle blend of forceful urgency and acute tenderness for which eloping lovers in mortal danger are famed, he helped her on to his idling Hovva-Thruster. 'Hold tight, my darling,' he ordered, settling heroically on to the front of his escape vehicle.

'But . . . my perch-belts?' squeaked Kh'Xandhra.

'There is no time for such safety precautions. Hold tight around my midriff,' he commanded and shoved the pair of Attom-Pak thrusters into *drive*.

'Halt!' shouted a heavily amplified voice from one of the pair of security Hovva-Thrusters screaming towards them.

'Never,' shouted Kh'Vynn defiantly and powered his Hovva-Thruster off the balcony. It plunged fifty feet into the darkening gloom before he looped it around on to level flight. A million balconies flashed by them in a blur of carved stonework. The purple security guards screamed after them, sirens wailing.

Alone in the palatial room, the tentacle-maid wiped at a moist eye and watched them vanish into the roseate sunset and wished that he had used a slightly lower setting on the laser blaster. Scorched neo-silicate was such a pain to get out of tapestry.

Far too close for the comfort of the fleeing lovers a pursuing security guard flicked on his attention-grabbing speaker. 'Running away is useless!' he bellowed in amplified tones.

Kh'Vynn slewed his Hovva-Thruster around a corner, barely missing a slow-moving delivery blimp and clipping his rear fender against an overlarge balcony. The first guard around the corner wasn't quite so lucky. He grazed the reinforced hull of the blimp, ricocheted into a distant wall and tumbled out of sight in a small supernova of fusing powerpacks. Cursing, the guard floated gently down into the gloom safe in the protection of his air-bag. The second guard swooped around the corner, performed a vengeance roll and slammed on his afterburners. He was going to catch these renegades. He was determined to. Eloping wasn't allowed thereabouts, oh no. Six hundred and thirty-sixth law of the Council of Decent Behaviour, everybody knew.

Kh'Vynn swerved his Hovva-Thruster expertly through dozens of ornately hewn back streets, judging his angles to perfection. His fifty-three separate practice runs were undoubtedly paying off. He swooped into a rapidly darkening cavern and headed for a distant exit, secure in the knowledge that it would take fourteen point three tiny time periods to cross, just long enough to really involve his beloved Kh'Xandhra in their desperate escape.

'Take this, my sweet,' he shouted over the rushing atmosphere and passed her a small device that bore an uncanny resemblance to an Earth-style video-remote. 'Enter our password, my dear.'

'You mean you remembered?'

'Of course.'

Delightedly, she entered the name of her favourite planet

with a quivering tentacle tip and together they flashed into a dark chasm.

Across the cavern the security guard locked on to the fleeing lovers and pressed harder on his accelerator. He glanced at his chronometer and grinned evilly. In moments he'd have them under any of the forty-seven different curfew laws.

'It hasn't done anything!' shouted Kh'Xandhra, staring at the remote as the balconies flashed past. 'It . . . It hasn't worked!'

'Fear not, my love. Its effects are not directly within our line of sight,' reassured Kh'Vynn. 'I requested that you activate it since it appears that time is of the essence.'

'The guards?'

'One is still in pursuit, desperate to sentence us to a life apart. And, as you know, curfew is approaching.'

Kh'Xandhra clutched tighter around her lover's midriff as she heard this news, her heart pounding ever faster.

Suddenly Kh'Vynn switched down two power settings and spun the Hovva-Thruster to the left in a very neat wind-brake turn. 'Duck!' he shouted and swooped them beneath a slowly rising corrugated door. Inside, the unmistakable sound of warming Type-23 Ytterbium Collider Drives could be heard, revving within an unfeasibly shiny spacecraft.

With deft flicks of the controls, Kh'Vynn skittered his Hovva-Thruster to rest in a shower of sparks and helped his beloved off the passenger perch. In a flurry of gossamer scarves and kneepads they sprinted across the storage room towards the idling craft and the chance of freedom. Freedom together.

At that very instant, the pursuing security guard swooped through the door at full throttle and opened fire with far too much gusto.

Understandably, Kh'Xandhra screamed. But with one leap

Kh'Vynn was on the case, tugging his beloved into the relative safety of the ship. Already the gull-wing door was closing, blocking off the green death rays of the guard, sending them ricocheting dangerously throughout the garage. A stray pulse hit Kh'Vynn's trusty Hovva-Thruster, instantly reducing it to a puddle of smouldering fudge.

'Everything will be fine. Trust me,' reassured Kh'Vynn, staring imploringly into his lover's compound eyes.

'Of course,' she answered, forcing a desperate smile.

'Strap yourself in, my sweet,' he said and squirmed on to the tiny flight deck of the craft. Not even pausing to buckle himself in, Kh'Vynn wrapped a determined tentacle around the main power control and pushed forward. The ship quivered, fought with gravity, took to the air and accelerated towards the back wall of the garage.

One deftly aimed positron pulse took that out in a shower of gravel.

The security guard followed, already realising he didn't stand a chance of effective pursuit. It was a well known fact that a pair of Attom-Pak thrusters was no match for a set of recently serviced Type-23 Ytterbium Collider Drives. The shiny craft shrunk rapidly into the distance and, watched by the fuming guard, it smashed through the barrier of the Royal Lepton Space Port and Sports Club.

Before any of the idly snoozing mustard-yellow guards had noticed, Kh'Vynn had powered his trusty craft through baggage check and was accelerating up a long tunnel towards a shimmering ellipse of space and freedom.

'Oh, darling, do hurry!' shouted Kh'Xandhra risking a glance at her chronometer. 'We have not long to escape our underground world of artificial light and cruel separation . . .'

Suddenly, alarm klaxons blasted into life, flashing gaudily down the narrow exit tunnel.

'Unauthorised craft, you are under orders to return to your landing bay until correct flight planning is filed and membership details are—'

Kh'Vynn snarled as he flicked off the video screen and thrust the main accelerator forward.

Ahead of them, a set of blast-proof doors began to creak inexorably shut across the exit tunnel, eclipsing the smattering of stars which glittered encouragement. Chewing nervously at his lips, Kh'Vynn angled the craft towards the centre of the closing gap, took a breath and powered through. In a wrench of metal he lost the radio antenna and a wing-viewer. But deep down he knew it could have been worse. Far worse.

And suddenly they were free, flashing through the remnants of their planet's war-destroyed atmosphere and powering off into the barren wastes of space; two star-struck lovers eloping towards their favourite planet.

'Oh my darling brave, brave love,' cooed Kh'Xandhra, her tentacles caressing the back of Kh'Vynn's purple scaly head. 'You did it. We have escaped that tyrannical world which so cruelly endeavoured to keep us eternally parted. Now, freed from those divisions, we can truly be happy.'

'My beloved, I have one more task to complete before I take you into the aft quarters and begin exploring the delights of those regions which decorum dictates one keeps covered.'

'Decorum be damned,' cried Kh'Xandrha. 'From this moment forth we can make our own rules.' She stepped back from her lover, unravelling her tentacles with the slightest of slithers, and snatched at the clasps of her cloak and decorative kneepads.

'No, my darling, I really must . . .'

His jaw dropped as she removed her cloak with a flourish

and stood clutching it before her, enticingly exposing glimpses of the delights which lay beyond.

'. . . I . . . I . . . er, the auto-pilot . . . er . . . course and stuff . . .' gagged Kh'Vynn, his mind far from the intricacies of astrophysics. 'I really must . . .'

'Tarry not too long with the controls, my darling, for I shall be waiting . . .' She fluttered a triplet of eyebrows in his direction and vanished into the aft cabin with a demure flash of inner thigh.

That day, Kh'Vynn programmed the auto-pilot faster than he had ever done in his life.

As he slammed the door to the aft cabin and began fiddling desperately with the hooks of his undergarments, the unfeasibly shiny ship increased power to its Type-23 Ytterbium Collider Drives, accelerated to maximum and slid into the boundaries of hypercorrugated morphospace on a glorious streak of gleaming ions.

09.23 Twelfth of April. Los Angeles

The Bishop of Los Angeles fidgeted uncomfortably in the back of the motionless cab as the fare clicked over the psychologically distressing hundred-dollar mark. Feeling the back of his neck tensing with the frustration of one trapped in a traffic jam he tapped on the glass behind the cab driver.

'Look, what's the hold-up? We've hardly moved in the last half hour.'

'Search me,' shrugged the cab driver, chewing boredly on his fifth stick of nicotine gum and staring at the acres of gridlock ahead. 'Hollywood Boulevard ain't normally this bad. Must be another one of them star dedications.'

'What? Whose plaster handprint are we waiting on today? George Clooney?'

'Nah. Doubt it,' muttered the cab driver. 'He's lost

box-office clout since the disappointing takings from his last few outings on the big screen. If you ask me he shoulda stuck to *ER*.'

'I'm not asking you.'

'Could be Kate Winslet,' mused the cab driver. 'I mean, okay, she's English but, Hell, she can act. I mean ever since that starring role in *Titanic* she's gone from strength to box-office strength, especially . . .'

'Are you a cab driver or a mobile movie critic?' asked Bishop Gianelli impatiently.

'Hell, driving folk 'round Hollywood some knowledge rubs off, y'know?'

'And that knowledge doesn't include short cuts?'

'Short cuts? What? Like back streets?'

The Bishop nodded in the rear-view mirror and scowled in a surprisingly unholy manner.

'Nobody ever likes the back streets,' tutted the driver. 'You don't ever see any stars down the back streets.'

'But you get across LA faster. There's less traffic.'

As if to illustrate the Bishop's point the fare clicked over to one hundred and ten dollars.

'Hmm, you could be right,' conceded the driver. 'But, c'mon, admit it, ain't you just a bit curious about who's big enough to cause all this chaos?'

'On any other day I might be,' admitted Bishop Gianelli. 'Right now I've got other things on my mind.'

'Uh-huh. What's that, then?'

'Oh, just the election in Italy,' offered the Bishop with enforced nonchalance.

'They lookin' for a new president then?' asked the driver, showing his complete grasp of events happening in the world outside Tinsel Town. 'When did they get rid of the last guy? Er . . . Mussolini, wasn't it?'

'No. *The* election,' frowned the Bishop, the LA heat

prickling under his collar. 'The one for the new Pope. You know, the one in Rome?'

'What? You tellin' me Italians get to choose the Pope?'

'You're not Roman Catholic, are you?' said Gianelli wearily.

The Bishop's question floated unnoticed past the driver's ear. For at that very instant his attention was grabbed by twenty-five feet of *Tyrannosaurus rex* strolling casually down the road towards them.

'That's the cause of this hold-up,' muttered the driver matter-of-factly, as a pair of press helicopters circled above the theatrically roaring monster. 'I shoulda guessed.'

'What . . . what's that doing on Hollywood Boulevard?' choked Bishop Gianelli reaching for the door handle.

'Pawprints of the Stars.'

'What? You're not telling me that . . . that thing has just . . . ?' His voice trailed off as he mimed making a palmprint in a patch of freshly poured concrete.

'Sure. Next to Lassie I shouldn't guess.'

'But it's just a dinosaur,' gasped the Bishop, staring in amazement at the white flashes of drying concrete on its right claw.

'*Just* a dinosaur? That's an Oscar-winner. Best Supporting Reptile in *Jurassic Park VIII: Not the Valley of Gwangi. Honest.* I shouldn't be surprised if some of these folks have been waiting all night just to get a glimpse of this moment. You don't know how lucky you are.'

'A cab fare of a hundred and thirty dollars and rising? You call that lucky?'

'Small price to pay to witness a moment of movie history.'

'Just get me out of here,' growled Bishop Gianelli.

'Er, where was it you wanted to go?'

'The Bishop's Residence,' tutted Gianelli. 'Just next to that big churchy thing with a cross on top.'

Reluctantly, the cab driver screwed the steering wheel hard to the right, mounted the sidewalk and slid off down a side street away from the biggest star in Hollywood.

Twenty-three small time periods after end of curfew. Sintellienth of P'yoon. Space

As usual, the hundreds of screens outside the neo-silicate windows of the Imperial Palace showed a thoroughly glorious sunrise. Thin layers of high cloud shimmered ephemerally before the purplish sun and were picked out in a tasteful violet. As sunrise programmes went, it was one of the Regal Commander's favourites. But this morning he was in no mood to enjoy it.

'Where is she?' he demanded, the tip of his Dijon-hued tentacle pounding out irritation on the gleaming polymarble dining table. 'How dare she keep me waiting.'

'Why don't you start, dear?' offered another mustard-yellow creature at the far end of the table. 'You know how you hate to eat scuffler when its cold. And it's your favourite cut, too. Irradiated buttock.'

'What's keeping her?' hissed the Regal Commander, ignoring his wife.

'It's just her age, dear. They do sleep a lot at her age.'

The Regal Commander kicked at the table leg, sending the beryllium acrylate cutlery rattling noisily in their holders. 'Sleeping? I didn't send my finest troops into a hopeless series of interminable battles just so she could sleep in!'

'Of course not, dear. That would be a silly thing for a Regal Commander to waste all those millions of tax yesheks on, now wouldn't it?'

'Twenty-three small time periods past curfew,' he growled, furrowing the scales on his brow in an impotent

12

demonstration of his annoyance. 'She should be here instead of frittering away her days in that bed.'

'Now I hate to be the one to say "I told you so", but you really shouldn't have bought her that Strato-Snoozer Deluxe. A simple bail of topak would've sufficed until she was married off. That's twenty-eight thousand yesheks wasted, that is.'

'Married off? My daughter? Never!' bellowed the Regal Commander, his cheeks flushing towards the darker shades of the rougher cut farmhouse mustards. 'There's no one on this planet good enough.'

'Now what about that Kh'Vynn? He's nice enough.'

'Are you mad? I'm not having that purple-skinned oaf getting his dirty tentacles on my Kh'Xandhra.'

'Oh come now, you're just saying that because he doesn't believe wealth and land and all its associated power should remain the preserve of those born into it,' said the Regal Commander's wife, nibbling gently on the irradiated buttock of a lightly grilled rodent.

'How can he possibly not believe in it when it's here for all to see? Why, that daughter of mine is the living embodiment of sintellien generations of inbred aristocracy. And, speaking of whom, where is she?'

This time the Regal Commander didn't wait for an answer from his wife. He launched himself upright and stomped off in the general direction of Kh'Xandhra's private chambers.

The squeals of fury which echoed down the corridor gave his wife the slightest hint that something was amiss.

'Look at this!' shrieked the Regal Commander, pointing at the shards of scattered neo-silicate and the scorchmarks around the edge of the polymarble window frame. 'I don't call this sleeping in. Do you?'

'Oooh dearie me,' whispered his wife, as she began to wonder if there was perhaps more to Kh'Xandhra's late appearance at table than first met her eyes. One of those teenage moods perhaps?

'Military spec laser-blaster marks,' growled the Regal Commander slamming an angry limb against the shattered frame and receiving a nasty little nick in one of his suckers for his trouble. 'This can mean only one thing. She's been kidnapped!'

'Oooh, do you think she'll be all right? I mean, she'll have to go without her breakfast and that's no way to start the day, is it?'

Fuming, the Regal Commander whirled on his heels and stormed out of the room, a curled tentacle slapping against the pad of another. 'General Elite!' he bellowed. 'Fire up the Strato-Fortress, the War is on again!'

In a matter of minutes the tectonic plates above the Regal Palace split along a series of lines which were far from natural and two vast rafts of scorched rock hinged into the dead sky. Three hundred and twenty Type-98 Ytterbium Collider Drives roared to full power as a single enormous Strato-Fortress arced into view and swung off on a low planet orbit, cannons powering up.

At almost exactly the same time, on the far side of the planet, a unanimous waggling of purple tentacles declared a tactical referendum a resounding 'Yes'. Moments later, and humming the Creatures' Republican Hostility Anthem, the Council of War jogged off side by side to set themselves to the task of democratically piloting their Tropo-Nihilation Engine against the common enemy.

09:53 Twelfth of April. Los Angeles

Two hundred and fifty dollars lighter of pocket, Bishop Gianelli burst in through the front door of his Residence and scurried towards his office.

'Oh, there you are,' began his housekeeper in a curiously broken Scottish accent. 'What kept you? It doesn't normally take all morning to do a Last Rites.'

'It didn't. I was held up. Dinosaurs on Hollywood Boulevard,' hissed the Bishop and cannoned on into his office. 'Have I missed it?'

'Dinosaurs?' whispered the housekeeper to herself. 'Did you say dinosaurs?'

'Yes. Of all the days twenty-five foot of *Tyrannosaurus rex* chooses to go walkabout, why today? Is there any news?' He clicked a button on his remote and a thirty-inch TV screen crackled into life. Expertly he thumbed it on to CNN and the oak-panelled room was filled with the earnest chatter of an overeager reporter.

'. . . latest addition to the collection of Pawprints of the Stars caused traffic chaos today as an estimated thirty thousand people turned out to see the world's most famous dinosaur leave his mark.' The screen briefly showed a vast lizard towering above crowds of cheering fans, swatting at circling helicopters and roaring, before it clicked back to the reporter holding a microphone threateningly under the nose of a bushily bearded man.

'And you, sir? Have you travelled far to witness this moment of cinema history?'

'Sure have. I hitched in from Kansas and slept on the sidewalk last night.'

'So for you it's been kind of a prehistoric pilgrimage?'

On screen the bearded one nodded. Bishop Gianelli shook his head. 'Pilgrimage? You don't know the meaning of the word. C'mon, tell me what's going on in Rome.'

Suddenly, as if in answer to Gianelli's impatient request, the reporter jammed a finger in his ear and looked straight at the camera. 'Er . . . ahhh, well, it seems I've got to hand you back to the studio now for some other news. Er, Fraser?'

'Thanks, Ike, now it's over to Rome, Italy, where it seems there's been some developments in the papal elections of the Pope.'

Bishop Gianelli sat forward on his chair as the screen filled with a rooftop view of a remarkably insignificant-looking chimney pot. In the top right hand corner hung the CNN logo and the crucial words 'Live Via Satellite'.

'Er, hello, Kelsey Cox, over in Rome, Italy. Just tell us what we're seeing here? It kind of looks like a chimney pot. Is that right?'

'That's spot on, Fraser. It's the chimney of the Sistine Chapel.'

'That's the one with the nicely painted ceiling?'

'It sure is, Fraser. You've been doing your research . . .'

Gianelli found himself grinding his teeth as the anchorman and reporter traded banality via the miracle of satellite technology. 'Get on with it,' he growled under his breath.

'. . . and, wait, Kelsey, can I see smoke there?'

'Er . . . I'm just checking on my monitor and . . . yes, that's smoke, Fraser.'

'Black smoke,' grumbled Gianelli. 'Haven't they made their minds up yet?'

'That's black smoke, Kelsey. Is there any significance in the colour?'

'Well, it's interesting you should ask that, Fraser, you see if the smoke was to turn white . . .'

'Er, like it's doing now, Kelsey?'

'Why yes. Just like that, Fraser! That means the Cardinals in the Sistine Chapel have decided on the name of the new Pope.'

Bishop Gianelli sat forward on his chair. 'Oh, my God!'

'Well, Kelsey Cox, over in Rome, Italy, just when will we be finding out who that new Pope is?'

'It's difficult to say, Fraser, but I'll wager that even now the Papal Secretary, a Cardinal Tardi, will be on the telephone to the lucky man, even as we speak.'

'Viewers, stay tuned to CNN and we'll bring you that name just as soon as we can.'

Suddenly, behind the Bishop the door opened and his housekeeper hurried in. 'Er, telephone call for you, Bishop,' she announced, holding out a mobile.

'Not now, can't you see I'm busy,' whispered Gianelli.

'Er, this is urgent,' said his housekeeper.

'So's this. They've just chosen a new Pope.'

'Yes. I know,' said the housekeeper, waggling the telephone significantly.

'Well, if you know, why are you bothering me? Take a message and . . .'

Suddenly there was a flurry of excitement on the TV and CNN's Kelsey Cox ran across the screen and thrust a microphone underneath the nose of a grey-haired Cardinal shimmering in crimson vestments, a telephone tight against his ear.

'Er, Cardinal Tardi, Papal Secretary to the Pope, Kelsey Cox from CNN. I understand you've just elected the new Pope?'

'Take a message? Is he busy?' muttered Cardinal Tardi into the phone and looked up in confusion. 'A new Pope, yes that is correct. I'm having a little difficulty getting hold of him at the moment.'

Bishop Gianelli stared at the live broadcast from Rome and turned slowly round to his grey-haired Scottish housekeeper as he heard her say into the phone, 'Busy? Er . . . yes, he's . . .'

In seconds, Gianelli was on his feet and across the room pointing frantically at the phone.

'It seems he's free now, Cardinal,' she said and handed over the Motorola.

'Bishop Franco Gianelli?' asked the TV and the telephone almost simultaneously.

'Er . . . yes?'

'Are you sitting down?' asked Cardinal Tardi. 'I have some news for you.'

'Oh, my God . . .' whispered the ex-Bishop of Los Angeles as he sank into his chair and stared at the TV screen.

One hundred and sixty small time periods after curfew. Sintellienth of P'yoon. Space

Three hundred and twenty Type-98 Ytterbium Collider Drives burned at full throttle, coughing plumes of toxic smoke from the exhausts of the Strato-Fortress. Mottled mustard tentacles worked hard at the helm, straining to keep the vast ship on a tight low planet orbit as it hopped over a ridge of battle-scorched mountains. With the inevitability of an eclipse it soared on towards a date with revenge.

'Regal Commander, I have sensor contact!' shouted the Prince of Sensors above the growl of the engines. 'A Tropo-Nihilation Engine in low planetary orbit.'

'Steer immediate pursuit vectors, now,' hissed the Regal Commander from the Throne of the Battle Bridge.

'I don't think that'll be necessary, Your Imperiosity,' answered the Prince of Sensors.

'What? Not necessary? Are you questioning my orders?' shouted the Regal Commander, slamming a clenched tentacle on to the side of his throne.

'No, no, no, no. They're heading straight for us!'

The Regal Commander ground his teeth in deep thought for a moment before barking a series of orders. 'Forward cannons to full charge. Hold course. Let's blow them out of the sky!'

'Er, Your Imperiosity, is that a good idea?' asked an incautious Tactical Strategy Minion who was within Regal range.

Hard on the heels of the sound of vertebrae shattering beneath the might of angry tentacles, the Regal Commander cleared his throat and announced, 'Now, that is a very good question.'

The Tactical Strategy Minion saluted feebly and, with a final gurgle, expired on the bridge floor.

'A *very* good question. Should I give the order to vaporise the enemy's Tropo-Nihilation Engine and in so doing risk my beloved Kh'Xandhra within the ensuing fireball? Or do I refrain, allowing them to complete their kidnap plans and sentence my only daughter to an unknown and certainly unpleasant future? But . . . if they are indeed Hell-bent on snatching the remaining Daughter of the Regal Line for their own evil ends, why are they flying the wrong way? Is this a cunning ruse to provoke a head-on collision which will destroy the entire war fleet of both our armies, setting the glories of warfare back to the dark days of tentacle-to-tentacle combat? Gunnery Minion, focus all forward cannon batteries on their engine pods and fire . . .'

'Your Regality, I have audio contact,' declared the Communications Serf.

'. . . on my mark,' finished the Regal Commander, raising a tentacle proudly.

'Er . . . I really think you should hear this,' suggested the Communications Serf waggling his headphones desperately.

'Cannons to full charge,' growled the Regal Commander.

'Your Regality . . . !' Suddenly, the Communications Serf flicked a switch on his console and the entire Battle Bridge echoed with the monotone voice of the enemy.

'. . . in short, if you steadfastly continue this refusal to

19

return our Kh'Vynn safely to us, then we, as duly elected representatives of the Council of War, shall shortly pass a motion to blow you out of the sky. Is that clear?'

'What? What is this? Give me audio, now,' shouted the Regal Commander, glaring at the Communications Serf. And, with one flick of a switch, words were flashing across the ether.

'You shall not have a chance to vote on any motion if you don't return the eldest Daughter of the Regal Line to me, now!'

For a brief moment the only sound was the roar of Ytterbium Collider Drives, but suddenly the speakers crackled once more into life. 'On behalf of the duly elected representatives of the Council of War, I, as Comrade Communicator, do ask the following. Er, what makes you think we've got your daughter?'

'Well, isn't it obvious?' hissed back the Regal Commander, turning more mustardy by the minute as anger rose inside.

'No.'

'Well, look. She's not anywhere in the Palace, right? So . . .'

'So you automatically jump to the conclusion that she's been kidnapped by us, eh?'

'Oh, don't try that guilt trip on me,' shouted the Regal Commander. 'You lose track of your Kh'Vynn and blame us, the Royal Line, just as quickly. Well, we wouldn't stoop so low . . .'

'As Comrade Communicator it has been pointed out that it is my duty to ask the following question in the moments prior to our imminent head-on collision. If they are not in your so-called Palace and they're not here with us in the Republic, then . . ?'

At that instant the two ships shuddered to an inertia-damped halt and hovered above the planet's surface, inches apart. The mustard-yellow Regal Commander stared out of his viewing hole at the purple-hued Comrade Navigator of the enemy Tropo-Nihilation Engine. As one, they both stared up into the distant wastes of recently vacated space.

'Uh-oh,' they mouthed in shocked motionlessness.

It didn't last long.

'After them! Now!' screamed the Regal Commander, pointing upwards into the blackness beyond.

In moments three hundred and twenty Type-98 Ytterbium Collider Drives were powering the Strato-Fortress out into the cold dark reaches of space, a screaming Tropo-Nihilation Engine hard on its tail.

'I have something, Your Regality,' shouted the Prince of Sensors, tapping excitedly at his screen.

'What is it?' snapped the Regal Commander.

'An ion trail from a pair of Type-23 Ytterbium Colliders. And it's fresh!'

'Lock on and pursue!' declared the Regal Commander. 'And the Gods help the creatures giving them sanctuary. Let us hope they will enjoy their forthcoming annihilation!'

'Course locked on, Your Regality,' offered a Navigation Knave.

'Well, get on with it!' hissed the mustard-yellow leader.

The Navigation Knave stabbed a willing tentacle at a large red button and, almost instantaneously, the Strato-Fortress blurred into a screaming smear of space technology and slid through the boundaries of hypercorrugated morphospace on a stream of gleaming ions.

'I propose an urgent motion to follow that Strato-Fortress,' announced the Strategic Comrade of the Council of War.

A unanimous waggling of tentacles carried the motion and, even before it had been correctly minuted for future

21

Council of War meetings, space quivered and the Tropo-Nihilation Engine vanished in an explosion of shimmering plasma.

The emptiness of local space paused pregnantly and awaited the roll of cinematically correct opening titles.

They never came.

Trouble with Miracles

22:59 Twelfth of April. The Vatican

Shimmering in the Roman sky like some curious levitating porpoise, a white Sea King helicopter flashed through the floodlights illuminating the dome of St Peter's. It arced sideways on a churning column of lightly dieselled air and made its final approach towards the Vatican helipad.

No sooner had the chopper's suspension taken the load than the side door was slid open by two burly Swiss Guards in full Michelangelo designer uniform and a bewildered looking Los Angelino was led out.

'This way, Your Holiness,' shouted Cardinal Tardi, pressing his crimson biretta to his head beneath the decelerating rotors.

'Er, don't I have to kiss the ground or anything?'

'No time,' tutted Tardi with a terse flick of his silvered head. 'Besides, that's only for state visits. Have you forgotten already, you live here now. Come.'

And, with a rustling of crimson vestments, the Papal Secretary strode off towards the papal palace, His Holiness jogging behind.

'Arms up, please,' cried a voice at Gianelli's ear and jammed a tape measure under his armpit.

'What the . . . ?'

'Oh, come, come, do behave,' tutted the man with the tape.

23

'Twenty-six,' he barked to his assistant. 'Anyone would think you'd never been measured up before. Forty-four. Hmmmm, diet needed I think.'

'Ahhh, my inside leg's twenty-eight,' spluttered His Holiness, feeling certain he didn't want that being measured in the nether reaches of the Vatican gardens.

'I'm sure it is. But that's no concern of mine. Its long flowing robes for you from now on. Now, what about these?' He tucked his tape into a suitable pocket and flipped open a glossy magazine covered in natty white papal robes. 'Any three to be going on with.'

'Er . . .' spluttered Gianelli, staring blankly at the almost identical garments under the fading Roman evening.

'Oh, come, come. The Gucci and the Versace. Fine? And the Armani. They can do next-day delivery. Finishing won't be as good, but as long as you're covered that's all that matters. Got to look the part for all those meetings tomorrow.' And with that the Vatican Apparel Liaison Officer leapt on to a waiting Suzuki and screamed off to place three orders for sets of designer vestments.

'Meetings?' gasped the new Pope.

'Now, what about your name?' asked Cardinal Tardi as he whisked them through a small archway. 'Must get that sorted quick sharp.'

'I was a bit excited in the helicopter, I . . . I couldn't make up my mind.'

Tardi frowned but somehow managed not to lose any momentum. He swept on around a small border of geraniums, the foot of his cloak stirring up a tiny whirlwind of leaves.

'I thought, well, seeing as I was brought up there, how about Angeles. Pope Joshua Angeles.'

'It will do,' conceded Tardi, ducking in through a high arched door and heading off down a marble-floored corridor. 'Doesn't have the classic ring of Ignatius, or Pius, but I'm sure the people will like it. Now, here we are.' Tardi skittered to a sudden halt and pushed open a heavy wooden door. 'Best way to familiarise yourself to a new set of challenges is to get right in there, don't you agree?'

'Er, well . . . I . . .'

'Excellent. I'm sorry the paperwork's piled up a bit more than usual but, well, what with electing you and all that I've hardly had a chance to see to any of it.'

'Paperwork?' gulped the Pope, staring at a desk groaning under a mound of unopened letters. 'Where did it all come from?'

'Ten billion followers do produce a tidy mound. They're just the ones marked "Personal". Anyhow, I'll bring some coffee in later and we can start writing your first papal address. Ciao.'

And with that, Cardinal Tardi was gone, his feet clattering away down the corridor.

Resigning himself to the fact that even the Son of God had to get his hands dirty and clear up after the picnic following the Sermon on the Mount, he rolled up his sleeves and slid in behind the desk. As his thumb ripped into the first envelope his curiosity pricked. Just what did people write to the head of the Roman Catholic Church in letters marked 'Personal'? Eagerly he smoothed the sheet of Basildon Bond out before him and began to read.

Chapel of St Tibs
St Naimhe's
Atlantic

Dear Your Holiness,

After all the weeks of trying, it's finally happened. I haven't seen a single scorpion on the island. It's a miracle. It must be. My prayers and fastings have finally . . .

25

Pope Angeles rubbed his eyes and stared once again at the letter.

'Scorpions?' he muttered and, somewhat at a loss what to do with it, he filed the letter to one side. Taking a breath he reached out and attacked another.

> Chapel of St Tibs
> St Naimhe's
> Atlantic

Dear Your Holiness,

Sit down. Are you sitting down? Well, I've got some news. It's a bit sad really, but, as they say, only through real suffering can we reach true understanding. I think it was Henry Cooper that said that. Anyhow, it's about Satan. I think he's given me a message.

The Pope's eyes bugged out as he stared at the thinly scrawled letter.

No, honestly. See, there he was fetching sticks when one bounced funny and fell down the old well. Quick as a flash he was after it, yapping as he fell.

Shaking his head the Pope skipped down a few paragraphs.

. . . so I've rechristened it Satan's Well after its miraculous healing powers. I mean, any other terrier, any other well and it would've been over in an instant, but I hauled him out with barely a scratch. And d'you know, he fetched the stick, too. Shame the pneumonia had to get him, though.
Yours,
Fintan O'Suilleabhain. Father.

Pope Angeles looked up from the letter and stared at the malevolent pile on the desk. A trickle of sweat oozed between his shoulder blades.

'Jet lag,' he muttered to himself. 'That's all it is. Bit of fresh air and they won't seem so bad.' Heading towards the door and giving no truck to a sprig of nagging doubt which was sure it was impossible to get jet lag from a helicopter, he headed off down the corridor and hoped he would be able to find something approaching a garden.

23:15 The Vatican

A smiling pair of fifteenth-century cherubs cavorted amongst a ceilingful of fluffy clouds and listened in on the conversation going on below.

'Well?' asked Cardinal Alighieri, sipping Napoleon Brandy from an overlarge crystal globe. 'Will he do?'

'I believe so,' smiled Cardinal Tardi with far too much relish. 'He'll require work, but nothing I can't handle.'

'Are you sure there's enough time to be certain? I mean, the world will be watching his address. There's only four days to get him ready.'

'And whose fault is that?' tutted Tardi, scowling through the swirling contents of his glass.

'Is it my fault the Russians wouldn't stop voting for the Bishop of Cuba?' whined Alighieri.

'You should have had them under control. It was touch and go for too long.'

'We got our man in the end,' offered Alighieri with more relief than confidence. 'Two thirds plus one majority. The vote went our way, that's all that matters.'

'You have heard of the skin of teeth?' mumbled Tardi and sucked forty-year-old brandy between his incisors.

'That's irrelevant now. Gianelli's in.' Cardinal Alighieri raised his glass, attempting to steer the conversation on to firmer ground. 'A toast, dear Cardinal. The Bishop is dead, long live Pope Angeles the Pliable.'

'Pope Angeles the Pliable,' mused Cardinal Tardi, his face creasing into the kind of expression a dozen evil despots would kill for. 'Oh yes. A few weeks' time and he'll be convinced he's running the place.'

23:24 The Vatican

Still wearing the brightly coloured jogging suit he'd slipped into for the flight, Pope Angeles swung open a door and stepped into the vast expanse of perfectly tended acreage that was the Vatican gardens.

Rubbing his neck and strolling along a pea-gravelled path, he stared up into the night sky and idly attempted to pick out small clusters of stars. The distinctive 'W' that was somehow supposed to be Andromeda's mum swam into view and hung at an odd angle. For a moment he stared at the skewed Cassiopeia, slowly the truth dawning on him that Los Angeles was now a good third of the planet away.

He was here for the duration now. The head of the Roman Catholic Church. Quickly, he made a mental note to start sending out change of address cards. If he got his finger out he could probably get them done before Easter.

Suddenly he stopped in his tracks. Easter. A quiver of chronic stage fright slithered up his spine as he calculated dates on his fingers. Now, assuming he hadn't crossed any date lines, which he felt certain he hadn't, then . . . He took a quivering breath as it dawned on him that in four days' time, count it, four, he would have to stand on a certain balcony high above the massed crowds in St Peter's Square and deliver his first papal address. To the world!

'Oh no, public speaking,' he whimpered. 'What am I going to say?'

His mind filled from corner to corner with a sea of expectant faces waiting for his words of wisdom.

'Er . . . Love thy neighbour?' he floundered, his voice echoing inside his mind. 'No? What about covet not thy neighbour's ass?' Somehow he had the overwhelming feeling that spouting a commandment or two wasn't going to cut the mustard. He needed something a bit more substantial. Something to get his teeth into.

Just one question. WHAT?

For the briefest of moments every atom of his psyche wished he was a Zen Buddhist. That way if he didn't come up with anything half decent he could blame the Being That Is The Universe.

His mind whirling desperately, he trudged off through the cicada-infested jungle of the Vatican gardens.

He didn't get far.

Just behind a building which was one of the finest examples of Mannerist architecture thereabouts, a pair of Cardinals talked in hushed tones and watched a figure in traditional Galilean fishing robes as he wobbled precariously on the edge of a vast concrete fountain. Suddenly, without fanfare or the flashing of warning lights, the Galilean fisherman stepped delicately off the edge.

'Oh my God! He's . . . he's walking on the water!' gasped His Holiness as he watched the figure stroll gingerly across the pool, his heels a scant three quarters of an inch above the largest of the ripples.

'You? What are you doing here? These gardens are out of bounds to the public,' snapped the tallest Cardinal, who was sporting lab vestments and a chiselled English accent formed in the days when Formula 1 racing cars were round at the front.

'He's walking on the water,' whispered the jogging-suited Pontiff, waggling a bewildered finger at the Galilean as if the very act would make it somehow easier to comprehend. 'It's a miracle!' he squeaked as a possible

29

subject for a certain papal address shimmied into sight.

'Miracle? Oh, no, no,' shrugged the Cardinal, scowling at the inconvenience of his unexpected audience. 'Nothing that exciting. The Turin Shroud, now *that's* a miracle. Walking on water's just simple physics really. Now if you could just buy your tickets for the garden tour tomorrow . . .'

'This is part of the tour?' asked the Pope.

'Well, no,' tutted Cardinal Holridge, pointing towards the exit. 'As a matter of fact we're out here in the middle of the night to make sure the general public *don't* see us.'

'Of course, what would they make of us if they saw folks walking about on any handy expanse of water.'

Cardinal Holridge looked quizzically from the man in the jogging suit to his Japanese assistant and back again. Somehow he didn't like the sudden and unignorable feeling that he had just got off on several wrong feet. 'Er . . . Us?' he said. 'You're one of us? Let me guess. The new Cuban Missionary for Cultural Affairs?'

'Do I look Cuban? Franco Gianelli,' he began, holding his hand out. 'Bishop of Los . . . Damn. I suppose I'll get used to that when I get my tiara.'

'Oh, my God. I didn't recognise you without your clothes on . . . er . . .' The Cardinal flushed and attempted to backpedal on to firmer ground. 'I'm Cardinal Holridge, Head of the Congregation for Icon Authentication.' He glanced at the Pope's knuckles searching for a ring to offer a quick peck to. There wasn't one. 'Er . . . this is my assistant Cardinal Kotonawa and . . .'

'Let me guess. Jesus Christ?' asked the Pope, pointing to the Galilean fisherman performing little pirouettes on the surface of the water.

'Ahhh, hah, no, no,' winced Holridge. 'No one so, er, important. Luigi, come over here will you and meet the P . . . Pope?'

With only the slightest shrug of disappointment the fisherman stepped on to the edge of the pool and threw his cloak back over his shoulder.

'Now, Your Holiness, if you'll just look at the items strapped around Father Luigi's waist . . .' A winking array of LEDs, ultra-high-performance lead-acid batteries and a stack of supercooled electromagnets hung around his midriff from a dozen webbing belts. 'Pulsed nuclear magnetic oscillations,' explained Holridge in the way he had of leaving one as much in the dark as before he started. 'Leads to dipolar repulsion from the water molecules,' he babbled in a way that would have made Raymond Baxter cringe. 'Bit like the Maglev trains the Japanese have.'

'But what's he doing walking on water?'

'Ohhh, that's part of our Pre-emptive Research Programme.'

Still metaphorically dripping behind the ears, the new Pontiff scratched his head.

'We, er, got a bit of a sniff of a chance that there could be a paper coming out very soon with categorical proof that Jesus never could've walked on water,' explained Cardinal Kotonawa in a clipped Japanese accent.

'What? But that's in the Bible and . . .'

'Exactly,' chimed Holridge. 'That's just what I said. D'you know, if it's not the Muslims trying to rubbish one of our miracles it's the Mormons, or someone else. It's a constant battle for us just keeping ahead of them, keeping a lid on it all.'

'But I've never heard of any of this.'

'Works then, doesn't it? Of course, we have to time our counter-leaks precisely otherwise it does tend to get a bit messy. Lourdes got a bit out of hand, if you want my opinion.'

Angeles looked at Holridge, a picture of complete

31

confusion. 'But, er . . . you and Cardinal Kotonawa here, you *can* prove that Jesus walked on the Sea of Galilee. I mean, Father Luigi there, he just did a width before my very eyes . . .'

'Ahh, now that's the snag. Luigi there can hang about on that pool all night but it doesn't really help prove that what happened two thousand years ago was a miracle, does it?'

'Why not?' struggled the Pope, the grip on his address slipping.

'Son of God's omnipotent, isn't He? Knows everything, right?'

The Pope nodded.

'So what's to say He wasn't a dab hand at high energy physics and just happened to have knocked together a couple of pulsed dipolar super-cooled electromagnets?'

'Ahhh . . .' deflated the Pope, feeling a migraine coming on.

'But then again . . .' mused Holridge as another thought occurred to him, 'if we can find real evidence of pulsed dipolar super-cooled electromagnets being used on the banks of the Sea of Galilee about two thousand years ago, now that *would* be a miracle.'

Angeles massaged his temples.

'There's an awful lot more to proving miracles are real than people think, you know. You don't need just positive proof, you need anti-negative proof, too. Deny the deniers their denials and all that. I tell you, I can spot a fake icon a mile off now. Chicken thighs passing themselves off as the index fingers of some long-dead saint. Red lead primer masquerading as the blood of a martyr. They don't get past me. Take the Turin Shroud, I'm this close to proving that's the real thing,' announced Cardinal Holridge, proudly holding his thumb and forefinger a scant millimetre apart.

'Oh really?' said the Pope, suddenly feeling the unmistakable ignition of a light bulb in his brain.

32

'Yup, the very cloth worn by Christ two thousand years ago when He came back from the dead.'

'You can *prove* that?'

'As soon as the results are all in, it's in the bag.'

'How would you like to tell me all about it?' smiled Pope Angeles. 'It could make an interesting Easter address, don't you think?'

Holridge and Kotonawa's jaws dropped. 'You're serious?'

The Pope nodded. It was all the confirmation Holridge needed. He was spinning on his heels and heading off towards the Papal Academy of Sciences in milliseconds.

'Er, just one thing,' called Angeles. 'A favour. That walking on water device . . . Er, can I have a go? See, it's not often you get the chance to be elected Pope *and* walk on water in the same day.'

Thirteenth of April

08:59 The Vatican

The morning sun skipped gaily across the rooftops lining the Via della Conciliazione, bounced off the brows of a couple of the statues lining St Peter's Square and rattled through the window of the papal office. It beautifully highlighted the white-vestmented figure squatting behind the Louis XIV writing desk, sending coronas of wonder off the Holy ring and painting a picture of ostensible beatific calm.

At least it would have, if His Holiness hadn't been hiding behind a large Ming Dynasty dressing screen.

'Yes, thank you, I can fasten that up myself,' came his voice over the acreage of delicately painted storks.

'Your Holiness,' tutted the sibilant tones of the Vatican Apparel Liaison Officer, 'I have known grown men dissolve into sobbing wrecks when faced with the complex intimacies

33

of papal vestments. Now, whilst I feel certain that life in Los Angeles has prepared you for some of the more colourful undercassocks, it is more than my job's worth to ensure that you are correctly garbed. The Muslims would never let you live it down if any of your seams were crooked.'

'Yes. I see.'

'Now this goes here and fastens up behind . . .'

'Is this going to take much longer?' hissed Cardinal Tardi, his hands crossed squarely in the small of his back, his eyes restlessly patrolling the boundaries of St Peter's Square.

'Perfection is a virtue,' called back the Apparel Liaison Officer. 'Now don't worry about this, it'll ride up with wear.'

As a Roman pigeon casually evacuated its bowels on the head of a nameless saint, Cardinal Tardi took a breath and turned away from the window. He had to try again. Time was slipping away. He cleared his throat. 'What about sex?' he asked suddenly.

The Apparel Liaison Officer squeaked.

'What?' gasped the Pope, peering around the screen in shock at the tall, greying Secretary.

'Sex has always gone down well in the past,' added Cardinal Tardi.

'Er . . . I'm sure it has,' mumbled the Supreme Pontiff nervously. 'But . . .'

'I'm certain it would be good for you, too, Your Holiness. Fornication always hits the mark.'

'Er . . . It does?'

'Oh, yes, yes. Most rewarding. In fact, I'm surprised you haven't already considered it.'

'Er . . . You are?'

Tardi stalked across the room and slithered into a high-backed leather chair, tucking his crimson vestments demurely around his thighs.

34

'Oh, yes. Normally it's the first thing any Pope thinks of. You shouldn't be shy about it, you know?'

'I shouldn't?' asked the Pope, beginning to wonder if he hadn't been elected on account of his rugged good looks.

'Not at all,' encouraged Tardi, tugging a notepad out from his tunic pocket and licking the tip of his pencil. 'Now, how d'you wish to go about it? Let's establish some ground rules shall we? One. "No" to bondage?'

'That's enough!' squeaked the Apparel Liaison Officer erupting from behind the screen. 'You can fasten up your own Armani. I don't want to know!' Blushing, he fled the room, his hands fluttering like handkerchieves from his wrists.

'Was it something I said?' asked Tardi as the Pope emerged, straightening his chain and settling his tiny biretta on his head.

'Something about bondage, I think.'

'Whatever. Now how do we feel about contraception?'

Pope Angeles raised his eyebrows. 'Er, I hadn't really thought about it.'

'Hadn't thought about it?' gasped Tardi dropping his pencil with expert theatricality. 'Why, it's your *duty* to include something about it in your address.'

'Address . . . Ah, oh, yes, yes. My address. Of course.' A wave of relief washed across Pope Angeles's face. 'Ha, what was I thinking?'

'I don't know. What were you thinking?' frowned Tardi.

'Er . . . Never mind. I've got a lot on my mind,' hedged His Holiness uncomfortably. 'Didn't sleep too well. Funny dreams about walking on water. Nerves, I guess.'

Tardi's frown deepened visibly. 'Your Holiness, may I point out that it is only three days to The Big Day?'

Pope Angeles heard the capital letters hovering in the Vatican air. 'You think I don't know?'

'Three days and, unless one has just popped into your head in the last five seconds, you haven't a topic upon which to base your first papal address. I need something quick. The translations take time, you know. Go with sex,' insisted Tardi. 'You'll feel better for it, believe me. You can have sex before marriage, or sex tourism . . .'

Pope Angeles shook his head and hooked his index finger around his chin thoughtfully. 'No. I want something original. Something new. Something to make people sit up in the aisles and pay attention.'

'Your Holiness, may I remind you that you aren't Whoopi Goldberg sent to perform Sixty Gospel Greats?'

'No.'

'But as Papal Secretary, I . . .'

'You can have my address this afternoon once I've finalised all the details.'

'I beg your pardon,' coughed Tardi, wind exiting his sails.

'This afternoon's all right, isn't it?'

'Well, yes, but . . .'

'Good. Now, if you could just make sure that everyone is present at this morning's meeting, that'll be marvellous. There's a little something I think everyone should hear. The details are here.' Angeles handed Tardi a sheet of paper. 'I know an hour and a half's a bit short notice but . . . well, I'm sure you can cope.'

'Er, yes,' murmured the Papal Secretary and found himself backing out of the papal office with a distinct feeling of his grip loosening tangibly.

Pope Angeles admired his Armani vestments in the mirror for a few minutes, sighed happily and reached for the pile of envelopes. Somehow this morning they didn't look quite so daunting. He flattened a letter out before him and began to read the now familiar spidery script of a certain Fintan O'Suilleabhain, Father.

Dear Your Holiness,

After weeks of praying it's finally happened. I just added potatoes and water and one mouldy apple and it worked. Okay, so it took a little longer than at the wedding feast and it tastes a sight more like poteen, but it was mostly water and now it's mostly spud wine. Boy, has it got a kick . . .

Pope Angeles groaned. Maybe he had spoken too soon.

09:53 The Vatican

A pair of smiling fifteenth-century cherubs cavorted amongst acres of fluffy clouds and blatantly eavesdropped on the one-sided conversation going on below.

'I tell you, I don't like it,' said a particularly squat Italian around a mouthful of tepid chocolate croissant. A blizzard of pastry flakes settled gently on to the ancient Chinese rug beneath his sandalled feet.

'Uh-huh,' grunted Tardi, licking his thumb and turning over another sheaf of paper, his reading glasses poised on the tip of his Julius Caesar nose.

'"Uh-huh"'? Is that all you've got to say?' protested Alighieri around a slurp of steaming cappuccino.

'Uh-huh,' answered Tardi predictably, his finger halfway down another page of tightly scrawled notes.

'I don't understand you sometimes. I really don't.'

'Hmmm?'

'In less than half an hour that damned Holridge stands up in front of the entire Vatican Council and delivers the speech he's been waiting his entire life to give. And the new Pope invited him!'

'Hmmmm,' answered Tardi, hoisting his reading glasses over the bridge of his nose and turning another page with his ink-smudged thumb.

'Are you listening to me?' whined Alighieri, his voice liberally seasoned with panic. 'We're thirty minutes away from the Pope being handed scientific proof that the burial cloth long thought to have wrapped the body of Christ, the Son of God, after His untimely crucifixion . . . Proof that cloth is genuine! Have you any idea what that means?'

'Hmmmm,' grunted Tardi, devouring another paragraph.

'Look, I've thought this through. If the Son of God is real, then, by definition His Mum and Dad are too. Thus, science says God exists. Fact. Scientific truth. No one'll need faith any more. Tardi, if that happens then . . . d'you realise we'll . . . we'll be out of a job!'

'Hmmmm.'

'Is that all you can say?' shrieked Alighieri, close to hysteria. 'I haven't worked my way up to Cardinal for it all to be taken away. I like it here in the Vatican. It's quiet, the tax breaks in the bank are good and there's some fine views in the height of the tourist season. The bikinis those Scandinavian students insist on wearing can be quite pleasing to the eye, y'know. I tell you, He certainly knew what He was doing when He put sixteen-year-old Danish girls together . . .'

'You worry too much,' said Tardi, settling a pair of high-powered binoculars on to the bridge of his nose and starting to scan St Peter's Square. His eyebrows twitched irritably as he pulled focus on a scruffy-looking tourist settling a violin case on to the pavement before him. The busker tossed a few coins on to the tattered velvet interior and, with minimal consideration for the social niceties of tuning, launched straight into action.

Tardi was stabbing numbers into his mobile phone in

seconds, disgust written large across his brow. Just by looking at the dubious bowing action he could tell the busker was definitely of the less aurally pleasing type. Right now he was in no mood for begging in his territory. Pavarotti himself could be belting out 'Nessun Dorma' in all its football-tainted glory, but if he hadn't cleared it with Tardi first he wouldn't reach the second coda.

A connection was made in Tardi's telephone. 'Fifth ring,' he tutted irritably into the mouthpiece. 'Where were you? . . . That was rhetorical . . . *Rhetorical*! Look it up in a dictionary. Undesirable in Sector 27. Deal with it, man. Immediately.' He clicked a stopwatch, disconnected the phone and continued his surveillance of St Peter's Square. Suspiciously, he watched a group of trigger-happy Japanese tourists exposing yards of film at each other.

Behind him Cardinal Alighieri was tucking into the fourth security cappuccino of the morning.

'You haven't heard a word I've said, have you?' he accused, aerosoling a thin film of froth over the high polish of the Louis XVI desk. 'I'm not worrying *enough*. We've got a Pope that listens to scientists! Where d'you think that'll end, eh? He'll . . . he'll put us on the Internet!' squealed Alighieri in a spasm of technophobia.

'Get a *grip*,' hissed the Papal Secretary. 'Are you forgetting my position? Decisions of that nature must come through me first.'

'But he's bound to want to set up a Vatican home page . . . I'm certain . . . Freedom of Speech and all that. If the FBI have their own home page then . . .'

'It's already been done. I took the liberty between votes in the Sistine Chapel,' grinned Tardi behind his binoculars. 'HTMLs aren't that hard, you know.'

Alighieri almost choked. 'What are you saying?'

'Blessed are the computer literate for they shall Internet

the world,' preached Tardi, his binoculars still fixed to the violining busker.

'What?'

'Microsoft 2:34.'

'Are you serious?' Alighieri trembled, a croissant twixt plate and mouth.

'Joke,' grinned Tardi. 'You know, you really *should* learn to relax.'

'Relax? What happens when Holridge proves the Turin Shroud is real? You think the Muslim extremists are going to be pleased about that, eh? You think we'll be safe?'

'My dear Cardinal Alighieri,' began Tardi turning from the window for the first time, 'I have been Papal Secretary now throughout the terms of three Supreme Pontiffs. All of them have wanted to change things. Pope Angeles is not going to get the better of me. This is just teething troubles. Clear?' insisted Tardi enigmatically and turned his binoculars out of the window just in time to see a pincer movement of Swiss Guards appear from behind four different pillars. Moving like pike-toting yellow, blue and red Exocets they crossed St Peter's Square on target for a certain music-torturing busker.

'Alighieri, in your panic you seem to have forgotten just one small thing.'

'And what's that. The blessed release of imminent armageddon?'

'The possibility that Pope Angeles might just *not* like Holridge's theories.'

'What?' gasped Alighieri.

'A few well-chosen words in the papal shell-likes and . . .'

Outside, the Swiss Guards swooped on the busker, confiscated the takings and herded him towards the Via della Conciliazione and the rest of Rome.

'He could be out on his ear,' finished Cardinal Tardi clicking his stopwatch again. 'Hmmm, three minutes twenty-two. Not bad, not bad. One good thing about the Swiss Guard being Swiss, makes them damned efficient.'

'What well-chosen words?'

Tardi pointed a casual finger at the report he had so recently been reading. 'What d'you think I've been reading all this time?'

'You . . . you've got Holridge's notes? But how?'

'The Swiss Guard,' grinned Cardinal Tardi as warmly as a pike in winter as he stood and headed for the door.

'Time for that meeting, I think.'

And, as he followed, for the first time that morning Cardinal Alighieri began to realise that perhaps he had been panicking just a little too much.

10:27 The Vatican

In a corridor simply decorated with fifty-two assorted alabaster saints, a clump of Cardinals and Bishops shuffled into the ornate theatre which was to be used for this morning's Vatican Council meeting.

Moving with the stealthy purpose of a starving wolf, Cardinal Tardi slipped through the crowd and headed for the figure in the gleaming Armani vestments.

'Good Morning, Your Holiness,' he said and delivered a cursory peck on to the papal ring of office. Tardi moved closer to the papal personage and lowered his voice. 'Ahhh, I'm glad I caught you before Cardinal Holridge actually said anything. Your Holiness, do you think it's wise to allow him to speak?'

'Of course, Tardi. This is an exciting day. He assured me his discovery was utterly foolproof, cast iron.'

'Dear old "Premature" Holridge, he does get a trifle engrossed in his work.'

Pope Angeles looked quizzically at his secretary.

Tardi, pretending not to notice, continued in the same casual manner. 'When you congratulate him after the talk, er . . . a word of warning, Your Holiness, don't say anything about the Miracle of the Milanese Molars. He's still a little sensitive about that.'

'I haven't heard about that one,' whispered the Pope, raising an eyebrow of acute intrigue.

'Probably for the best it doesn't go too far outside these walls. Reputations can be so easily damaged, you know. After all it wasn't his fault. The evidence *was* very convincing.'

'Evidence?'

'Oh yes. A quite miraculous decrease in gum disease and tooth extraction among twelve- to fifteen-year-olds in the Milanese parish of St Apollonia, which coincided exactly with the construction of a brand new shrine dedicated to that very saint.'

'St Apollonia? Isn't she the patron saint of . . .'

'Dentists, yes,' confirmed Tardi before the Pope had finished. 'But I can't blame Holridge for making the connection. The dental evidence was rather overwhelming, after all. He was ready to go to the press with it, you know. CNN, the works . . .'

'What stopped him?'

'It seemed the miracle didn't coincide with the construction of the shrine. It was something a little more secular. Milan County Council built a fluoridation plant upstream. Well, it nearly ruined him. Threatened to hand in his collar, everything.'

Pope Angeles stopped in the aisle and turned to Tardi, his brow furrowing with concern. 'So are you saying I *shouldn't* let him speak? Cancel his talk?'

'Er, no, no, not at all, it's just, well, pinches of salt . . . and all that.'

42

'Nonsense,' tutted His Holiness. 'He should be given the opportunity to put such a traumatic incident behind him. He must speak. It'll do his confidence the power of good.' He turned and began shuffling sideways between the stage and the crimson rectangle of tiered seating, heading for his front of house seat.

'But, Your Holiness . . .' began Tardi, a squeak of pleading in his voice.

'No, he made the decision himself. He's obviously ready. I've spoken to him this morning, he's positively brimming with enthusiasm. This is just what he needs.'

'Yes, Your Holiness,' mumbled Tardi, aiming his backside for the folding seat on the right of the Pope.

Before he was settled, the scathing voice of Cardinal Alighieri rattled harshly in his ear. 'Well, that went well!' he hissed from the second row as the lights began to dim and a hush of expectancy began to rise like morning mist.

It wasn't the only thing rising at that precise moment. Cardinal Holridge's blood pressure was going ballistic. Standing in the wings and peering nervously through a gap in the velour curtains he suddenly felt as if his collar was a good six sizes too small. He turned three washes paler as the sound of important bottoms shuffling uncomfortably in brushed velvet seats rustled into earshot. Suddenly a voice was added to it.

'And now, before the main business of today's council, we have an extra item,' announced the Pope. 'Here to announce the very latest in theological findings, Cardinal Frank Holridge.'

A polite ripple of bemused applause fluttered around the auditorium.

'I . . . I can't do it,' whispered Holridge, close to panic behind the curtains. 'I can't go on. One night's preparation just isn't enough, especially without my notes. God only

43

knows where they've got to. No, I can't do it.' He turned and aimed himself at the door. There was a sudden flurry of limbs and he found his exit blocked by Kotonawa adopting the type of karate stance which no one with a European tongue could ever pronounce properly.

'Look, I didn't take this job to deliver lectures to . . . to all them!' pleaded Holridge, jerking a thumb over his shoulder.

'Keep your voice down,' hissed Kotonawa. 'They can hear you.' His eyes darted towards the auditorium.

'Fine. I'll do my talk from here. They'll never even notice. It's dark out there.' Holridge was babbling.

'And who will point to the slides, hmmm?'

Holridge adopted an oh-so-reasonable pose. 'Harry, old chum . . .'

'They're expecting *you*. The Pope asked you.'

'Come on, you're a dab hand with the laser highlighter . . .'

In a flash, Kotonawa had three of his fingers at Holridge's neck, carefully arranged in a triangle around his voice box.

'You go. Give that talk or, three seconds from now, I'll make very sure you never sing plainchant again,' hissed the Oriental one with more than a little nod towards his nation's Samurai past.

Holridge swallowed and felt the unwelcome resistance of a triplet of Japanese digits.

'No, no, not the plainchant . . .'

With his left hand, Kotonawa pointed towards the auditorium. 'Your choice. Three . . .'

'That's no choice.'

Kotonawa's teeth shone in the gloom as his grin widened. 'Two . . .'

'For a man of the cloth, you're enjoying this *far* too much.'

'One . . .'

'I'm going, I'm going!'

Much to Cardinal Kotonawa's satisfaction, the Head of the

Congregation for Icon Authentication adjusted his biretta and stepped out through the purple velour curtains.

Fifty pairs of eyes tracked Cardinal Holridge's professorial entrance as he stalked across to the lectern, cleared his throat and leaned towards the microphone. 'Gentlemen of the . . .' It was as far as he got before the customary squeal of feedback assaulted everyone's eardrums. Wincing, he tried again, attempting to avoid the combined weight of fifty scowls. He leaned gingerly forward, 'Gentlemen of the Cloth . . .'

'Skip the intro,' interrupted Cardinal Tardi from his seat next to the Armani-upholstered Pope on the front now. 'We all know who we are. Am I right?' Forty-nine red skull caps nodded in silent agreement. 'Now hurry up, Holridge, we do have a schedule . . .' He flicked a glance at his gleaming Rolex and appeared to be consulting a clipboarded time-table.

Cardinal Holridge glanced at his three sheets of tightly typed introduction and stifled a whimper of nerves. He'd been on this case for the best part of six years, he couldn't just launch into his talk without the backing of his notes, could he?

Tardi coughed and tapped his watch significantly.

'Er, first slide please,' muttered Holridge, feeling stress tighten around his throat. As if by magic, a photograph slid on to the screen behind him.

Holridge snatched his laser pointer out of his pocket and thumbed it into life. 'As you can see, here we have a white, male Caucasian in his early thirties. Er . . . I believe His face is somewhat familiar to most of you?'

A ripple of derision oozed its way towards him, its epicentre firmly fixed in the vicinity of a certain Papal Secretary in the front row. 'Of course we're familiar with Him,' tutted Tardi. 'We didn't get where we are today *without* being familiar with Him.'

Swallowing nervously, Cardinal Holridge signalled to the projectionist and his second slide sidled on to the screen. He pointed to the X-ray-like image, his laser picking out ghostly details as he spoke with forensic authority. 'Signs of acute trauma to the cheek-bone. Here. Severe bruising to left patella, here, indicating a fall at, or near, time of death. A hundred and twenty-three visible sub-dermal haematomas across back, shoulders and buttocks suggestive of malicious whipping. Major abrasions across the shoulders, here and here, pointing to the victim being forced to carry a heavy cross-shaped object. Penetration wounds between fifth and sixth ribs, here, and at wrists and ankles. And, gentlemen, the clincher . . . arterial and venal blood flow patterns indicative of post-mortem relocation of the body.' He paused, waiting for a gasp of surprise, or even mild shock. It didn't come. The audience of Vatican heavy-weights stared back implacably.

'Er, in short, He was moved, after the time of death.'

'Course He was moved. You're the professor. Think about it. Would you have left Him there in that heat?' Tardi waved a beringed hand under his nose.

'No, I suppose not, er, post-mortem decomposition would have started to set in with some rapidity,' conceded Holridge and filed the remains of his talk into a small waste basket behind the lectern. 'Er, but that's not all. Er . . . using the latest state-of-the-art temporal assessment equipment we have pinned down the time of death to . . .'

'Good Friday A.D. 33,' chorused the entire audience.

Holridge was stunned. 'You . . . you knew? But, how?'

'Eye-witness testimonies,' derided Tardi. 'Gang calling themselves the Apostles. You heard of them? Wrote gospels, preached to the masses, that kinda thing.'

'Yes, but . . .' began Holridge with the distinct feeling he was losing grip. 'Don't you want to hear about the latest carbon-dating findings?' he asked, a squeak of pleading showing around the edge of his vowels.

'Yes, about these latest findings,' began Tardi. 'Who actually gave you permission to . . .'

'I am the Head of the Congregation for Icon Authentication. The Shroud is an icon, therefore I gave myself permission,' blustered Holridge. 'Now about these new findings, Your Holiness . . .'

'We don't *need* new findings.' dismissed Tardi. 'The Turin Shroud dates back to 1460, give or take. Just like they found in 1988. Case closed.'

'Er, not necessarily,' announced Holridge and, in a triumph of improvised sign language, he desperately signalled the projectionist to skip to slide twenty-three.

'The 1988 findings *don't* actually prove categorically that the Shroud was somehow drawn on cloth dating back to 1460.' A host of images flashed momentarily on to the screen behind him as the projectionist fast forwarded through the carousel of slides.

'Let him speak,' hissed the Pope into Tardi's ear with the air of the Godfather. 'It's the only way he'll get over the Milanese Molar Miracle.'

'This better be good,' grumbled the Papal Secretary, settling back into his chair. 'Best labs in the world agree on 1460. This better be *very* good!'

Slide twenty-three settled into place behind Holridge's head showing the hastily drawn decay curves for carbon-12 and its heavier brother, carbon-14.

'I take it you know how carbon dating works?' asked Holridge, still miffed that he hadn't been able to give his introduction. All this would've been so much easier if he'd primed them first. He knew the average Cardinal's attention span when listening to anything too scientific. Thirty seconds, on a good day.

'Remind me,' answered Pope Angeles before Tardi could speak.

'Well, Your Holiness,' struggled Holridge, wiping a bead of sweat from his brow, 'carbon-14 is an unstable isotope of the naturally occurring carbon-12.' Still draped in his coffee-stained lab vestments, he highlighted the steeper of the two ski-slope graphs behind him. 'Being unstable it decays faster, so, by measuring the ratio of 14 to 12, and assuming a predictable rate of decay and a normal starting ratio . . .'

Pope Angeles coughed theatrically through his ringed fingers.

'Ahem, in layman's terms . . . er, as it were,' winced Holridge as he glanced away from the graph and cast a quick look at the bank of Cardinals, 'we can calculate how old anything is by measuring the ratio of carbon-14 to carbon-12. The fewer carbon-14 atoms present, assuming a normal distribution at the time of manufacture, the older it is.'

'And that is precisely what they did in 1988,' pointed out Tardi helpfully.

'Well, that was their mistake, you see?'

'What mistake?' asked His Holiness, sitting forward in his seat sensing a real address opportunity approaching. If he just lost a bit of the science and presented it as fact . . . He quivered with anticipation.

'They assumed a normal distribution at the time of the cloth's manufacture,' spelled out Holridge in a way that left everyone utterly confused. 'It wasn't surprising they didn't see it, I mean, it took even me weeks before I figured it out.'

'Figured what? Holridge, what are you trying to say here?' tutted Tardi.

'Isn't it obvious? They failed to consider "The Inherent Miracle Hypothesis",' declared Holridge. He was greeted by the ominous silence of an audience deafened and blinded by science.

'Uh-oh. Miracles again,' whispered Tardi into the Pope's ear.

The stage beneath Holridge's feet suddenly began to have about it the feel of extremely thin ice. It was time for some desperate explanation. 'Look, the Shroud of Turin is the cloth that wrapped the body of Jesus Christ after He was taken down from the cross, right? So that very same cloth was in direct contact with a body which – and we have sworn affidavits to this from the Apostolic Four – a body which rose from the dead, right? Now I'm sure everyone here would be most willing to agree that resurrection is a *far* from common occurrence. In fact, "miraculous" would probably be a more suitable word.'

Tardi sucked his teeth noisily and tapped the side of his head.

'So . . . so, there's no way that the Shroud of Turin could ever be considered a *normal* piece of cloth after it had been in direct contact with an event which you yourselves have agreed was nothing short of . . . well, miraculous.' Holridge scoured the audience for any sign that anyone was following his argument. 'That's . . . that's the whole basis of . . . of my "Inherent Miracle Hypothesis", see? The $^{12}C/^{14}C$ ratio was bound to be stuffed up. In fact, er . . . on the next slide I have calculated that the radiation generated during the resurrection of a recently crucified thirty-three-year-old, twelve-stone male Caucasian would be sufficient to cause an error of just over fourteen hundred years in the date given by carbon dating.' He turned to the graph behind him which showed a decay curve swept backwards through the x origin. 'Thus placing the *real* date of the Turin Shroud as . . . as there!' His finger stabbed at the slide behind him, right next to a date scribbled on the margin. 'Spring A.D. 33!'

The silence that greeted this revelation was as stony as Death Valley and twice as unwelcoming.

'What is it?' spluttered Holridge staring imploringly at the Vatican heavyweights. 'Don't you see? I've just proved, by scientific means, that the Shroud of Turin is real!'

Cardinal Tardi stood. 'Holridge, when it was agreed to set up the Congregation for Icon Authentication, within the bounds of the Pontifical Academy of Science, you said you'd get proof. Real scientific proof? That my dear Cardinal is just statistics! Come back when you've got something to get excited about. Now, there are plenty more items on the agenda, if you don't mind . . .' Tardi pointed to the exit.

Miserably, Holridge picked up the remains of his papers and began shoving them into the waste-paper basket. Right on cue Kotonawa emerged from the wings and sidled into the spotlight, blinking. 'Well, that could have gone better.'

'Shut up,' hissed Holridge and trudged miserably off across the boards to a deafening roar of apathy.

'Item one on the agenda . . .' declared Tardi officiously, railroading all thoughts of Holridge's lecture out of the collective short-term memory. 'Proposed by our old friend Father Fintan O'Suilleabhain of the Parish of St Tib's, another innovative suggestion if I may say so. Way up to his usual standard.'

A ripple of amusement scurried around the inside of the theatre.

'I think a brief show of hands will sort this one out fairly quickly. Now, all those in favour of Father O'Suilleabhain's suggestion for providing a range of altar dips, such as taramasalata, hummus and herbed olive oil, for those who feel the communion hosts are a little on the dry side, er . . . please, raise your hands.'

Pope Angeles shuffled uncomfortably in his seat as he watched Holridge slip off the stage, wrestling with vague feelings of . . . of what? Guilt? Disappointment? Confusion?

Yup, they were all there singing barber shop in his mind. And the one with the loudest voice was Panic.

In the time it had taken for Holridge to deliver his lecture all chances of using the Turin Shroud as the subject of the Easter address had gone out of the window, across the road and halfway out of town. He was, in common parlance, up a certain creek and paddleless. But then it wasn't his fault if he didn't understand a word of it all. Was it? Science was like that sometimes. Confusion sang a solo as he wondered briefly how come Cardinal Tardi understood it all.

11:45 St Naimhe's

Four and a half miles off the south-west coast of Eire, on the little-populated island of St Naimhe's, Father Fintan O'Suill-leabhain poured himself the first of his post-mass sherries. He leaned back in his chair and stared at the ceiling admiringly. Twenty-seven different spacecraft from a host of movie and TV sci-fi spectaculars hung there in full matchstick splendour. A Bryant and May *Babylon 5* swung in a gentle breeze and faced off against a Swan Vesta Klingon *Bird of Prey*. Behind them, a strangely wooden *Alexei Leonov* creaked ominously and looked as if it was on a final approach vector to dock with his latest pride and joy – a 1/72nd scale *Spectrum Cloudbase* built entirely from the little cardboard matches that come in twenty-fours from restaurants. He crossed his heels on the desk and dreamed of all the meals he'd forced himself to have just so he could collect the matches for that. And almost instantly he wished he hadn't. Seven years he'd been on this island and he hadn't set foot in a restaurant in all that time.

Still, he could cope. It wasn't as if he was completely alone out there in the Atlantic. He had his congregation, after all. Okay, so there were never more than three of them including the goat, and it was a rare day indeed if any of them stayed awake throughout the whole evening service, but there was no denying they came. Father O'Suilleabhain took a gulp of sherry and wondered just how much longer they'd be gracing his services. Surely the Vatican wouldn't really close him down for having such a small congregation, would they? Size shouldn't matter, it was what you did with them that counted, surely?

But there had been that letter a few weeks ago ... Nervously, his eyes drifted to the far wall and a six-foot-square noticeboard covered entirely with other letters bearing Vatican postmarks. Fintan sighed as he took another sip of Jerez's finest. It would be nice if those letters actually said something a gnat different once in a while. The refusals were getting a little monotonous.

Office of The Papal Secretary
Città del Vaticano
Roma
Date as Postmarked

Dear ... Fr O'Suilleabhain,

After careful consideration of your proposal, The Vatican Council has regretfully to inform you that it is unable to grant miracle status to The Chapel of St Tib's at present. This rejection in no way occludes you from offering other suggestions you may have.

Your Brother in Faith,

Cardinal Tardi

But still, it *was* nice of them to write. If they chose not to adopt his suggestions then, well, it didn't matter too much.

After all, he had his creature comforts. A tepid glass of Amontillado after a hard mass, a shedful of donated matchsticks and a stack of spare time to glue them all together. Saluting the small but perfectly formed posse of Angels he firmly believed inhabited the bridge of his 1/72nd scale *Cloudbase* he raised his glass once more to his lips and began wondering just how many books of matches it would take to get a really good *Millennium Falcon* going. If he had the time, of course.

He had barely taken a sip when he heard someone unbarring the door of his chapel. Rolling his eyes heavenwards he looked at his watch and tutted under his breath. 'Early,' he muttered and drained his measure of Jerez's finest with pleasure. If they were here for twelve o'clock confession they could wait, he was busy. Besides, they couldn't really object. Anyone who turned up early for confession was bound to be either such a religious fanatic that the extra quarter hour of quiet meditation on the evils they had perpetrated would be welcomed wholeheartedly or, alternatively, they must have notched up a bulging catalogue of sins from which they were desperate to be absolved. In which case the extra fifteen minutes of quiet soul-searching would do them the power of good.

Happy with his reasoning, Fintan drained his sherry, reached for the bottle of Amontillado and refilled his glass in the snug vestry of the Chapel of St Tib's.

At that same instant, the main doors of the chapel were pushed open and, echoing a hundred spaghetti westerns, a man stood silhouetted in the arch of the door. Silently he peered around the darkened interior trying not to let it show he was waiting for his eyes to adjust.

Had this been any of the major pasta-producing regions of Italy trying to pass themselves off as old El Paso then there was no doubting the piano player would have stopped in the middle of a chorus, several holsters would have been surreptitiously unfastened and a distant roulette wheel would have clattered into stony silence. Sadly, as this was a tiny chapel perched atop a tiny lump of basalt four and half miles off the south-west coast of Eire, nobody batted an eyelid.

Adopting the type of unholy expression suitable for a frustrated man of the press out for a story, Seamus Killarney of the *Cork Herald* stomped down the darkened aisle, eyes peeled, pencil at the ready.

He was five rows from the altar when suddenly he saw it. The parish register. A spasm of desperate excitement writhed in the pit of his stomach. In a flash he was over at the leather-bound book flicking backwards and forwards through the lists of weddings, births and deaths. There had to be something here, he could smell it. On an island this size and this far from the mainland with only one ferry a week, there had to be some signs of wife swapping, or babies born to widows . . . or something. A glint of madness showing at the corner of his eye, he searched for a killer story. Or at least something to give his editor when he got back.

'Can I help you?' asked Father Fintan O'Suilleabhain from the vestry door.

Killarney spun around and glared at the priest. 'Well, as a matter of fact, I believe you can,' he growled and advanced on the clergyman. 'You can give me a story.'

'Ahh, now are you still on about that?'

'A week I've been here now,' hissed Killarney. 'A week without a story! You got me here under false pretences telling me I could have an exclusive interview with Mel Gibson.'

Father Fintan feigned innocence. 'Ah, now you can't still be convinced I said *Mel* Gibson . . .'

'Why else would I be here?' hissed Killarney, beginning to feel sure that his days in the *Cork Herald* were sorely numbered. 'You called me on the ferry radio two weeks ago and told me that Mel Gibson, famous Australian actor and director, star of three *Mad Max* movies and object of many a female fantasy, was coming here to direct the St Tib's Easter Passion Play.'

'Nell Gibson,' corrected Fintan for the fiftieth time. 'It's not my fault there was a lot of static that day. And I didn't say a word about *Mad Max*.'

'But you didn't deny it either.'

'Well, now you're the journalist . . . You're bound to know more about people than me,' countered Fintan limply. 'How was I to know if Nell had starred in *Mad Max* or not?'

Killarney's jaw fell open. 'How? How? Because she's never been off this island in the last thirty years, that's how.'

Father Fintan looked at his shoes. 'Ahhh, well . . .' he said.

'Is that all you've got to say for yourself?'

Fintan looked pathetic. 'Fancy a bottle of wine? It's a bit sweet but the Vatican doesn't agree with serving Cabernet Sauvignon at communion.' Fintan, in need of some rich red sustenance himself, headed back into the vestry and reached for a handy bottle.

'I suppose that's the best I'm going to get out of you, isn't it?' grumbled Killarney and followed.

'Well now, I'd offer you a snifter of poteen but I'm fresh out. A gallon doesn't last as long as you'd think, you know,' said Fintan as he slopped wine into the reporter's glass.

'Look, Father, I want something to show my editor when I get back to Cork. Go on, admit it, you made this story up in a pathetic attempt at swelling the congregation.'

'Made it up? Me? Of course not. Well . . . Not all of it

anyhow. Nell Gibson really is going to . . . er, well she *would* be directing the passion play if . . .'

'If St Tib's Chapel wasn't in imminent danger of closure. Lack of congregation I believe.'

Fintan looked up. 'You know?' He clutched his glass tightly.

'Oh yes.' A smile of malicious victory licked at the edges of the reporter's mouth. 'It didn't take me *too* long to figure everything out.' His voice echoed with a strangely conspirational tone, almost begging Fintan to ask the next question. Naturally, he obliged.

'Er . . . figure what out?'

'Of course, it took me a little longer to get hold of the documentation,' answered Killarney in as unhelpful as a manner as he could. He was going to make Father Fintan O'Suilleabhain suffer for sentencing him to an unscheduled week's stay on the rocky nasal protuberance that was St Naimhe's.

'Documentation?' gagged Fintan.

'The Pilgrim's Charter does make for fascinating reading,' gloated Killarney.

'What?' Fintan's eyes darted across the vestry towards his filing cabinet. 'How did you . . . ?'

'Has nobody ever told you to lock the vestry door during confession? You never know who might wander in.'

'You stole . . .'

'Borrowed,' grinned Killarney, reaching inside his jacket. He pulled out a large brown envelope and handed it back to Fintan. 'Returned.' He took a triumphant swig of wine and leaned back against the wall with the air of a Hollywood Nazi interrogating officer having lightly grilled an enemy spy. 'An audacious little plan. You should be congratulated,' added Killarney, completing the picture. 'Clever of you to spot Clause 58 . . . Er, now how did it go? Oh yes.

"The term congregation refers only to attendees present at functions or events with a significant theological element, brackets, jumble sales are right out, close brackets." Tell me, how long did it take to hatch your little plan? Minutes?'

Fintan's shoulders slumped. It seemed Seamus Killarney of the *Cork Herald* had ferreted out the truth behind his desperate plan to boost St Tib's congregation figures and so keep his chapel open.

A spasm of melodrama welled inside Fintan's heart, fuelled, no doubt by almost half a bottle of Amontillado.

'But what was I supposed to have done?' he pleaded to the man of the press, feeling himself painted into a defensive corner. 'Accept defeat and abandon my three parishioners to the spiritual desert that is the Atlantic?'

'Well . . .'

'No!' snapped Fintan feeling a surge of evangelism coming on. 'Should I have stood my ground and directly defied the Vatican's Pilgrim's Charter?'

'Er . . .'

'Of course not! There was only one thing I *could* do,' he declared. 'Use any available means to save the chapel, put the island of St Naimhe's on the map and come out of the whole thing smelling of chrysanthemums.'

'Ahh, now that's what I thought you'd say,' said Killarney, finally managing to get a real word in.

'You did?' Fintan stared at the reporter. He hadn't expected a cynic of the press to actually agree with him.

'Well, I might have said roses, or Chanel No 5, but chrysanthemums are fine by me.'

'They are?'

'Sure. Anyone who can almost get the press to work the way *they* want them to can smell of anything they desire as far as I'm concerned.'

'A top-up?' asked Fintan and, amazed, he glugged a good few hundred grapes' worth into Killarney's glass.

'Nobody would have suspected it was your doing if the *Cork Herald* just happened to say that your passion play was being directed by none other than Mel Gibson.'

Despite himself, Fintan's ears reddened. 'Nell Gibson,' he offered.

Killarney scowled. 'And if this mistaken report just happened to catch the public's attention by mentioning the presence of said antipodean star and so result in your passion play being a massive sell-out? Well, it wouldn't be your place to turn the crowds away now, would it?'

Fintan shook his head guiltily.

'And, being a fine upstanding member of the Roman Catholic Church who obeys all the doctrines of the Vatican Council, including a certain Clause 58 of the Pilgrim's Charter, well, you'd just have to count all those attendees at the sell-out play as members of the congregation, now wouldn't you?'

A priestly nod.

'And so, miraculously, and through absolutely no fault of your own, the tiny Chapel of St Tib's upon the Island of St Naimhe's can legitimately claim a massive congregation thus saving itself from imminent closure and thus proving that He does indeed function in mightily strange ways.' He pointed heavenwards.

Sheepishly, Father Fintan nodded, his shoulders sagging as he stared into the face of defeat. His last-ditch attempt had failed. Okay, he would be the first to admit that it had been a million to one shot, but, hey, they work in the movies. Right now there was only one thing that would keep his tiny chapel open. And that was a miracle.

A twinge of an idea wriggled at the edge of his consciousness.

'You only made one mistake, you know,' smirked the reporter. 'You never should have let me set foot on this damned island.'

'I know,' sighed Fintan, glancing forlornly at his notice board. A six-foot-square patch of Vatican notepaper shone back at him, challenging, daring him to find another way to skin a proverbial kitten.

And suddenly it happened.

Shocked by the abrupt change in his voice, Fintan heard himself say, 'And of course, now that you know all about my failed plan, I cannot allow you to leave . . .' He felt his lip curl in a way that would have made Peter Lorre proud. In a flash, he realised there was in fact just one more chance.

'What? You can't keep me here.'

'I must. It's my duty.'

'Oh, come on. The ferry goes in a few minutes.'

'You cannot leave!' shouted Fintan leaping to his feet and frightening himself almost as much as he surprised Killarney.

Under the heavy duvet of silence that slithered curiously into the vestry, Fintan broke first.

'Well, not without me first telling you about the miraculous properties of Satan's Well out there.' He pointed out of the vestry window to an ivy-encrusted column of collapsing stones.

Sceptically, Killarney narrowed his eyes. 'Satan's Well?' he asked, still horribly aware that he hadn't a scrap of story to offer his editor.

'Named after my wire-haired terrier,' said Fintan.

'You had a dog called Satan?'

Fintan nodded, milking the situation for all it was worth. 'The water in that well saved his life. I tell you it's holy water, it is. If he'd fallen that far down any other well he would've . . . It would've been all over, instantly. But no, he survived.'

'Uh-huh? And where is he now?'

'Ahh, well, he succumbed to the pneumonia after I dragged him out but . . .'

Seamus Killarney tutted as the veneer of belief shattered. He stood, headed for the door and a date with the weekly ferry.

'Look now, with the correct marketing this could be a place of pilgrimage. St Tib's Shrine. What a story, eh? Look, there was a time when people hadn't heard of Lourdes, you know? They don't close down chapels out there. And they're French!'

Killarney lifted the latch and stepped into the tiny chapel. His heels were dogged by Fintan.

'Well, how about if I gave you an exclusive on something else I've been working on? The biggest change in Holy Communion since . . . since the Last Supper.'

Despite himself Killarney was interested. 'Biggest change in two thousand years?'

'*Nearly* two thousand.'

'Yes, yes. All right, what is it?'

Fintan grinned, leaned forward and whispered confidentially in Killarney's ear. The reporter leapt backwards and stared incredulously at the priest. 'Are you serious?'

Fintan nodded proudly. 'That'll put me on the map, eh?'

'No, no,' spluttered Killarney, shaking his head and heading out the door.

'What? What's wrong with it?' called Fintan.

'I'll tell you what's wrong with it,' hissed Killarney, swinging around the door. 'Pepperoni pizza is not the Body of Christ!' The door slammed shut with a resounding echo.

'Oh,' answered Fintan. 'What about tortilla chips?'

The only answer he received was the horn's report from

the ex-trawler-cum-ferry as it made its approach to the island.

Miserably, Fintan trudged back to the vestry and a date with a half-finished bottle of communion wine and a quarter-inch imaginary Angel.

12:17 The Vatican

Deep within the perfectly tended expanses of the Vatican gardens, in a laboratory somewhere in the bowels of a splendid example of Mannerist architecture, Cardinal Frank Holridge was feeling rather sorry for himself. He slouched across a desk strewn with papers, head in hands and stared miserably into the expanses of distant space.

'Six years' work on the Shroud,' he moaned to no one in particular. 'Six years and they just dismissed it as . . . as statistics!'

'Yes, but, it could have been worse,' offered Cardinal Kotonawa, pulling what he hoped was a reasonably sympathetic face.

'Worse than statistics? How?' sulked Holridge.

'Well . . . er, they could have laughed at you.'

'And you think they aren't?'

'Ahh . . . well, at least you can't actually hear them.'

'Oh, thank God for all His small mercies,' grumbled Holridge, his chin sinking on to the desk, readying himself to get the most out of this disaster. It had been a long time since he'd had a good sulk. But, just as he was drawing the duvet of darkest moods over himself, a thought struck him that sent everything a good three shades darker. 'Oh God, the Pope!' he moaned. 'Great first impression, eh? What's he going to think of me now?'

'Er, well . . . I'd ask him if I were you,' said Kotonawa.

'Ask him? Oh sure. What d'you expect me to do? Crawl

into his office with a smile on my face, casually bring up the subject of the biggest farce ever to hit the Vatican and ask him what he thinks about it and my future as the Head of the Congregation for Icon Authentication?'

'I don't actually think you need to go that far.'

'What? Why not?'

''Cause he's here. Look.' Kotonawa pointed through a window at the approaching Armani-clad Pontiff.

Holridge leapt to his feet, alarm writ large across his forehead. 'What's he want?' he squeaked in panic, running around the lab in a manner normally ascribed to the more headless varieties of poultry. 'He's going past. Please, tell me he's going past! Tell him I'm not here!'

'Well, if I could I . . .'

At that very instant the door handle turned and Pope Joshua Angeles entered the lab in a flurry of blazing white.

'Aha, Your Holiness . . .' squeaked Holridge, his fingers fidgetting at chest level. 'I was just, er . . . busy, er . . .'

The Pope looked across at the paper-strewn desk. 'Now that's what I like to see in a man. Getting right back in the saddle again. It's always the best, you know.'

'Er, yes, yes, of course,' whimpered Holridge guiltily.

Kotonawa shot him a dirty look.

'Always the best. Take Babe Ruth,' said the Pope, carefully avoiding Holridge's eyes. 'Where would Babe Ruth have got if he'd quit after his first strike out, eh?'

'Is this a trick question?'

'No, not at all,' muttered His Holiness uncomfortably. 'I just er, popped in to . . . Well, after this morning's presentation . . . Er, look, you haven't got anything miraculous *without* the science, have you?'

'Without?' gagged Holridge.

Angeles nodded. 'It doesn't really go down too well with some of the folk around here. Why else d'you think Darwin was dead a hundred and fourteen years before anyone really listened?'

'And it was a good three centuries before anyone said sorry to Galileo,' added Kotonawa helpfully.

Holridge was shaking his head. 'But *without* the science? What's the point? I mean, a scientific proof that the Turin Shroud is real without the sci— Well, it's like a rabid dog with a colander.'

Pope Angeles stared desperately at Kotonawa for an explanation.

'Can't hold water,' shrugged the Japanese Cardinal and shook his head apologetically. 'Don't ask, it's a long story.'

'What's wrong with the science anyway?' challenged Holridge. 'Six years that took me. I don't know how many times I've checked the results. It's perfect!'

'But, er, don't you think it's a bit . . .' Pope Angeles passed the palm of his hand slowly across the top of his head.

'What? It's simple. Reinterpretation of the $^{12}C/^{14}C$ breakdown ratio with respect to the skewed parameters arising from the Inherent Miracle Hypothesis couldn't be any easier. Any fool can see that, even a cursory glance using all the widest error bars shows it's the genuine article! The Shroud of Turin!'

'All I'm asking, Frank, is, well, what have you got that doesn't need *thinking* about? You know, something you can show people that they don't have to understand but they just *know*. Something a bit more miraculous.'

'Like making the Eiffel Tower disappear?' sulked Holridge, his scientific pride smarting.

'Er, I think you're missing the point here,' soothed Angeles as delicately as he could. 'I want to prove that *God* exists, not David Copperfield.'

'So, what have you got in mind?'

'I don't know. Er, something you can point at,' floundered

His Holiness. 'Er, Noah's Ark? The Ten Commandments, you know the original stone things? Er, the Star of Bethlehem?'

Holridge looked up and rubbed his chin thoughtfully, a glimmer of interest sparkling behind his eyes. 'The Star of Bethlehem, hmmmmm. Harry, where's that chart we found hidden in that secret compartment in one of the Dead Sea Scroll vases?'

'I'll just get it!' called the Japanese one, already halfway through the door.

Cardinal Holridge was already staring into space, his train of thought spinning its wheels eagerly. 'Now, there's no guarantee I can do this, but, if I remember all the facts from the ancient chart then, bearing in mind changes in calendars and slight incongruities in their astral plane alignment calculations . . . When d'you say you want this?'

'Easter Sunday.'

'Leave it with me,' grinned Holridge as Kotonawa re-appeared with a papyrus star chart. In seconds the two Cardinals were poring over the ancient sheet, rubbing their chins and 'humming' and 'hawing' like the best of them.

Pope Angeles breathed a sigh of relief and headed towards the door.

12:19 St Naimhe's

Father Fintan O'Suilleabhain rocked on the back legs of his chair in the way he knew he shouldn't and looked admiringly at his ceiling. Or rather he looked admiringly at his matchstick model of the *Spectrum Cloudbase* and let his sherry-fuelled imagination run free. His mind's eye floated in past Colonel White, nodded casually to Captain Scarlet, zipped around a corner and entered the haunt of the Angels. There they were, his own private harem of deadly female fighter-pilots lounging on banks of sixties-style sofas.

Beaming to himself, he settled down next to his beloved Melody and admired the highlights glinting off her white skin-tight PVC'd thigh. Ahhh, if only he could have really been there, it would have been Heaven. Heaven in *Cloudbase*.

And then, suddenly it hit him. Before his very mind's eye a dozen fragments of thought blurred together. They swirled into a multi-coloured idea and, in moments, had coalesced into the very essence of a concept.

Fintan was on his feet and running, his trusty sherry glass falling shattered on the floor. If only he could catch Killarney before the ferry left for the mainland . . .

He clattered out of the door of St Tib's and sprinted off down the hill, the concept expanding inside his head.

Why couldn't he have seen it before? It was all so obvious. This was the way to get the congregations in – cult TV masses. Already he could see it all. The Bible according to Captain Scarlet. It was perfect. *Cloudbase* was Heaven hovering above the world, watching, led by the God-like Colonel White. At his side were the Angels, shimmering-white, ready to avenge the slightest transgression. And Captain Scarlet himself, he who fell off a car-park and rose again, the immortal saviour of mankind fighting the fallen-angel of Captain Black! And then there was Captain Blue . . . Ahhh, okay so maybe he didn't fit, but what the Hell.

Fintan dashed on after Killarney, his mind spinning with admiration for Gerry Anderson. 'So everyone's dead impressed by C.S. Lewis and his Christian morals in Narnia, eh? Well, world, you ain't seen nothing yet. Nothing at all.'

Unfortunately for the world at large, certain events were already unfolding which would somewhat delay the announcement of Fintan's revelation. A strange cloud formation appeared one hundred and fifty miles out over the mid-Atlantic and began spreading with unnatural haste. It was the type of cloud formation for which no Earth-based meteorology text book would have a name. An unsurprising detail really, since it showed all the distinctive signs of being the sub-ether bow-wave of an incoming Type-23 Ytterbium Collider Drive recently decorrugated from morphospace. Just ask any student of Interstellar Hyperspace Displacement Physics.

Down at the lump of concrete piling which passed as the St Naimhe's ferry-port, Seamus Killarney of the *Cork Herald* was wobbling his way up the gang-plank and on to the weekly ex-trawler-cum-ferry. And he was muttering to himself, partly from relief that the ferry had actually come, and partly from the frustration of a wasted week.

'So how soon do we sail?' he hissed to a bearded man in an oil-stained sweater and Captain Birdseye hat.

'You're the last one comin' aboard,' answered the Captain in a voice cracked through an overdependence on low quality rum.

'But I was the only one.'

'I told 'em they should have a duty-free shop but they wouldn't listen.' The Captain hauled the gang-plank up and dropped it on the deck.

At that very instant an interstellar two-door sedan, with twin Type-23 Ytterbium Collider Drives and Full Galactic Converters, blasted through its bow-wave signature and erupted into Earth atmosphere with a perfectly normal flash of static discharge. It was followed by a wild eruption of highly charged ions and a fizzing flare the like of which Industrial Light and Magic would have given their eye teeth to get on the big screen.

'Looks like a storm front coming in,' mused the Captain, trying his best to look every inch the old sea dog he wasn't.

66

'Time to weigh anchor.' In minutes various ropes were unhooked and, riding a cloud of diesel the size of a small zeppelin, it pulled away from the pier and off into the relative shallows of the Atlantic.

Seamus Killarney punched the air and invented a new sea shanty on the spot. 'Time to weigh anchor.' The words rattled deliciously in his mind as the truth settled in. He was free of the island of St Naimhe's.

Grinning, he looked back, savouring the delicious sight of land slipping away. It was then he noticed that Father O'Suilleabhain had come to see him off from the quayside. Animatedly, the priest leapt up and down, shouting.

Killarney waved back, unable to hear a word above the thrumming of ancient diesel engines. O'Suilleabhain stamped an impatient foot and looked around him in desperation. In a flash he had it and dashed off across the quay to fetch a large sheet of cardboard and a handy pot of paint.

From two hundred yards out of the harbour Killarney strained his eyes to read the message Fintan was holding up.

'I have a story for you!' proclaimed the sheet of corrugated card in dripping red letters a foot high. Killarney raised a thumb and Fintan spun the placard around.

'Captain Scarlet is God!' shouted the second message silently across the ever-widening gulf of Atlantic.

Killarney semaphored gestures of acute disbelief, tapping the side of his head to suggest that perhaps Fintan was in fact several choruses short of a hymnal. A suggestion which was borne out by the priest's sudden adoption of a variety of offensive gestures which wouldn't have looked out of place in a medieval archery field.

A hundred or so miles away an unfeasibly shiny spaceship plunged wildly towards the Atlantic on a streaming vapour trail of toxic fallout, which, according to all the manuals, was quite normal for any Ytterbium Collider driven vessel suddenly entering a nitrogen/oxygen environment. With a scant fifty feet to spare the spaceship pulled out of its death spiral and, barely noticing the fifty-three-g turn, flashed towards the stratosphere at a velocity speeding bullets can only dream of.

It was only as it reached forty thousand feet that the first signs the pilot knew little of aerobatics began to show. Any decent interstellar traveller would tell you that for the finest powered turns within semi-saturated nitrogen/oxygen atmospheres, you need your Galactic Converters set to tepid, otherwise . . .

Simultaneously, both ion inlets glowed crimson, went terminal and, with a sickening cough that spelled imminent write-off, the alien craft stalled. In a perfect demonstration of the hovering skills possessed by the average coral atoll, it slid Earthwards.

On the quayside of St Naimhe's, Father Fintan was stamping on his hastily prepared placards and wailing about the unfairness of it all. 'Just get it all figured out and . . . Why me?' he sobbed, raising his eyes to Heaven as a dozen tons of red-hot alien technology dropped gracelessly out of the afternoon sky.

Approaching a velocity which would make any passing Concorde green about the gills, the interstellar craft hit the chapel roof on a comet-tail of vaporising atmosphere and kept going. Slates, rafters and puffins went everywhere. They were followed by a dozen pews, a ton and a half of rubble and a cupboardful of *The Big Blue Book of Hymns*, slightly foxed.

Whether it was Him working in His traditionally Mysterious Ways, or simply the fact that sixteenth-century builders knew a thing or two about putting a chapel together in a remarkably blast-proof manner, no one will probably ever know, but somehow, the cone of destruction was focused almost straight up. A shower of slates, pews and cupboardfuls of hymnals flew several hundred feet into the air, arced gracefully in the afternoon sky and landed in a neat circle of debris around the island. Most of the puffins, though startled, found their wings and fluttered safely to roost several minutes later.

Three hundred yards out from the harbour of St Naimhe's, Seamus Killarney was still wondering if the world would be hungry to know that the parish priest of St Tib's was barking mad when suddenly, above the growling diesel, the sound of the biggest story he had ever missed clattered into earshot with a percussive report.

'I'd get that engine seen to if I were you,' shouted Killarney not looking up. 'Anything that backfires that badly needs a damn good overhaul.'

Open-mouthed in shock, the Captain of the ex-trawler peered over the bow and steered onwards through a growing slick of blue hymnals.

Stars and Streaks

12:42 Thirteenth of April. The Atlantic

Much to the extreme irritation of the resident game fisherman of the Florida keys, the ninety five thousand tons of the USS *Indiscriminate* was out on manoeuvres.

'Thirty degrees starboard!' yelled Rear-Admiral Rosenschmirtz excitedly, his binoculars jammed up against the bridge window. In instant response, the white-gloved helmsman swung on the wheel and sent the Schwarzenegger Class warship heeling dangerously into the grey swell.

'Full ahead!' shouted Rosenschmirtz around the Havana cigar which was almost as thick as his Village People moustache. 'And, you, get me targeting!'

The Captain of the *Indiscriminate* picked up a handset and handed it to the Rear-Admiral, his nose somewhat out of joint. He hated it when the Rear-Admiral was on board. Especially when he was trying to show off to the other brass.

'Call this full ahead?' sneered Major-General Hiram J. Gelding III, his steel-grey two-millimetre hair bristling in a way that would've made Bruce Willis proud. 'Even a Stallone Class tank can move faster than this. Through a Korean swamp. In reverse.'

Rosenschmirtz clamped his molars hard around his cigar and barked into the handset. 'Fifteen degrees elevation. 045 by 122. Full barrage in tight formation. And throw in a couple of Exocets.'

'Is this going to be much longer?' yawned Major-General Gelding. 'Only I find sea battles so tedious.'

'And how excited d'you think I feel?' complained Major-General Isenheimer, the head of Speculative Intelligence, peering over his glasses and trying to look as intellectual as David McCallum. 'I trained on F-18s. Call this slow? You don't know the meaning of the word.'

'Target achieved,' crackled a speaker on the bridge console. 'Weaponry locked and in "go" mode.'

Rear-Admiral Rosenschmirtz squared his shoulders and made sure the sun caught his heavily braided shoulders to full effect. 'Fire!' he commanded around his cigar.

Instantly the entire side of the USS *Indiscriminate* erupted in a seething cloud of smoking vapour trails as the entire defence budget of several third world countries was launched seaward.

'Wake me up when they're about to hit,' grumbled Major-General Gelding, stifling a yawn and picking at his thumbnail.

Half a dozen Sidewinders powered across the bright Florida sky and slammed into the side of a disused oil tanker. They were followed a fraction of a second later by fifteen Exocets.

The rusting ex-Iraqi ship buckled, was consumed in smoke and finally ignited in a satisfying deep red ball of flame.

'Three . . . two . . . one . . . Boom!' muttered Major-General Isenheimer over the eerily silent eruption, counting down the gap before the dull rumble of marine destruction hit.

'Look at that!' shouted Rear-Admiral Rosenschmirtz, binoculars jammed tight against his forehead. 'Direct hit! Target destroyed!'

'Woopie-do,' tutted Gelding. 'What d'you expect? If you

can't hit a half-mile-long rusting tanker moving at three knots, side on, it's a sorry look out.'

Rosenschmirtz ground his teeth.

'Still, it was a nice explosion,' admitted Isenheimer, crimson flames licking at his binocular lenses. 'Good flames, lots of smoke, annoys the civilians. Just what you want. Could've been three miles closer, but what the Hell. Beggars can't be . . .'

'Well, that's gratitude,' hissed Rosenschmirtz, his cheek muscles flexing, his fists settling petulantly on to his hips. 'I arrange for us to have our monthly Global Threat Assessment Meeting out here, on my old ship, on manoeuvres. I pull a few strings, lay on a couple of Exocets, throw them at a handy tanker and that's the thanks I get? I mean, I thought you'd appreciate a bit of action, you know, remind us what warfare looks like, bring back a bit of the good old days? Don't know why I bothered. Next time we'll stay back at the Pentagon shall we? Your office or mine?'

'Finished?' tutted Gelding examining his thumbnail again.

Rosenschmirtz nodded feebly.

'Good. Let's see if we can't find us a decent zone of unrest then, eh?' grinned Gelding, punching the Rear-Admiral in his decorated chest.

Rosenschmirtz swung a playful punch back but the Major-General was already halfway across the bridge. 'Carry on,' he muttered to his Captain and slid off in hot pursuit. With the vague sniff of possible military intervention somewhere in the world spurring his heels he left the bridge.

At that very same instant, just above the waterline, a spotty seventeen-year-old marine by the name of Private Tyrone was sat in front of an unfeasibly large tonnage of cutting-edge microchip technology. Banks of cooling fans whirred like impatient Harriers under camouflage netting. Racks of parallel motherboards spat whirls of electrons in countless different directions, processing data at a speed that would have made Bill Gates verdant with envy and hurling it all on to an eighteen-inch circle of radar screen.

Idly, Private Tyrone stared at his particular circle of phosphorescent sky, tapped his foot to the country strains of Garth Brooks and wondered precisely what it was that he was supposed to be looking for. As a slide guitar wailed forlornly in his ear, against regulations, he compared the number of green spots on his radar patch to the number of redder ones upon his chin. So far he was quite clearly up by two dozen blackheads and a galaxy of acne. By the time he'd polished off the ten pack of doughnuts on his lap he'd be well out in front.

Suddenly, a twinge of excitement tingled at the back of his neck as, without fanfare or public announcement, a small pimple of greenery slithered on to the bottom right of his screen. He sat up, staring at the new and unidentified arrival to his patch of airspace, his heart starting to beat faster. Could this be the one . . . ? The screen refreshed itself and the new arrival lurched a good quarter inch further west. Private Tyrone's index finger wriggled closer to the alert button, rearing back, cobra-like, ready to strike. It was instant promotion to the private who alerted Mother America of First Contact. That, and a free copy of the *Independence Day* trilogy on VHS, signed by the President himself. Well, it was enough to keep anyone alert.

Private Tyrone held his breath as his screen updated itself again. Tiny pixels shuffled a step sideways, dragging their flags of identification across the screen with them. He ignored them, his attention was fixed on the new arrival in the bottom right-hand corner. His chest tightened. The screen flickered. The pixel moved a fraction west and . . . A flag appeared claiming it to be Concorde flight BA 357A Heathrow to New York.

Private Tyrone deflated miserably and, not for the first time, cursed the British Airport Authority. If the Brits were going to have the busiest airport in the world they could at least have the decency to upgrade their identifier software. A three-screen refresh period is too damned slow.

Mentally waving adios to his copy of the *Independence Day* trilogy Private Tyrone pressed the eject on his cassette player and turned Garth Brooks over. Settling himself back into his chair and turning the volume in his headphones up a notch, Private Tyrone readied himself for a gentle daydream of the fun he could have with the blonde babe in the middle of Mr Brooks's backing singers.

He didn't get far.

At that precise moment a small and very unidentifiable flying object plunged on to his radar field, swooped towards the bottom left-hand corner of Eire, crashed into an innocent chapel and vanished from view.

Private Tyrone blinked, rubbed his eyes and stared dumbfounded at the screen, his finger poised above the alarm. Milliseconds away from alerting the entire crew of the USS *Indiscriminate* to First Contact, he hesitated, suddenly unsure. The screen refreshed itself . . . And showed no sign of anything but scheduled transatlantic flights.

'What the . . . ?' he whispered, doubt mounting in his mind. Alien atmospheric entry had never looked like that in training simulations. They'd hung about on screen for at least two refreshes. Well, nothing could possibly move that fast, could it? Straight across the Atlantic in under a second and a half?

In an uncharacteristic spasm of efficiency, Private Tyrone flicked back through back-up memory and pulled up an image labelled '12:43.15'. The streak appeared in eerie green ghostliness amongst the crisp spots of neatly labelled air-craft. And questions reared their ugly heads.

Could he possibly be looking at real evidence of First Contact recorded on his radar set? Or was it some kind of artifact of static electricity? Could he ever live it down if he alerted the Pentagon chiefs to a spark off his jumper?

There was only one way he could find out if that image was real. Glancing quickly over his shoulders to make sure no one was watching, he began tapping away at the keyboard in front of him. In seconds a modem was linking him to several of the more nerd-attracting reaches of cyberspace.

12:59 St Naimhe's

Four and a half miles off the coast of Eire it looked as if Bonfire Night had come several months early. Tongues of fresh oak smoke curled into the sky above St Naimhe's as sets of pews spontaneously erupted into showers of flame. Stained glass windows slithered from their mullions like psychedelic fountains and congealed stickily on the stone floor. And already the water in the baptismal font was well hot enough to poach eggs.

Panting desperately with the effort of sprinting up from the quayside, Father Fintan O'Suilleabhain breasted the top of the hill and stared at the shattered and burning remains of the Chapel of St Tib's. In that instant two things struck him. One was the wave of intense heat emanating from the spacecraft lodged in the aisle of the gutted building. The other was an overwhelming feeling of deep, deep dread. Miserably, he slunk down against a handy gravestone and stared at the tongues of flame.

Suddenly from around the back of the vestry there was a sharp detonation and a cunningly converted zinc dustbin launched itself into the air on a vapour trail of 100%-proof spirit.

'Ahhh, now that's bein' a mighty shame, that is,' came a voice from behind him as Fintan's poteen still looped out into the nether reaches of the Atlantic. 'Mighty shame. That was for brewin' a nice drop of the spud, that was,' mourned Fergus Ni Correaghan, local sheep farmer and part-time inebriate, his chin on his crook. 'Was it not myself that was warnin' you 'bout stokin' the fires too high?'

'What? No, no,' gagged Fintan. 'You think I . . . ? My still . . . ?'

'And a waste of a good drop, too,' tutted Fergus Ni Correaghan, trudging away. If he'd had a handy black armband in his pocket he would've certainly slipped it on and headed off down the pub to break the news to all. As it was he just headed off down the pub anyway. After all, the heat had given him a thirst.

Helplessly, Fintan stared at the crimson flames chewing hungrily at the backlit shell of sixteenth-century masonry. Silently, a small snowstorm of shredded and charred hymnals began settling around him.

'Why me?' whimpered Father Fintan as the third verse of 'Faith of Our Fathers' settled on his head. 'Why me?' A fragment of Vatican notepaper fluttered on to the grass between his feet and stared up at him accusingly.

Despite the intense heat, a sudden shiver of terror slithered down Fintan's spine as a dread question formed in his mind. It swooped out of the sky, circled once and settled on the gravestone behind him, as black and foreboding as a raven in a Hammer film.

What would Papal Secretary Cardinal Tardi do about all this when he found out?

Nervously, Fintan swallowed. It was a well-known fact that Tardi despised any damage to Church property and had made it his very own personal crusade to ensure everything remained as intact and spotless as the very day it was made. Many was the number of six-year-olds who had suffered decades of poverty, their confiscated pocket money financing the purchase of new oak pews for the Sistine Chapel after being caught slipping gobs of chewing gum under the ends of the old ones.

A crate of recently bottled poteen exploded noisily in what was left of the vestry.

'Oh, God. Tardi'll kill me. He'll bring back the Inquisition. Iron maidens. Guillotines . . .' wailed Fintan his head in his hands. 'I'm a dead man as soon as he finds out. Dead, dead . . .' His voice trailed away as the tiniest glimmer of something which could just possibly turn into hope slid into view.

'*As soon as he finds out,*' whispered his more secretive side. '*As soon as he finds out . . . Who's to say he ever needs to know, eh?*'

Fintan looked up guiltily. 'No,' he breathed with a certain fundamental lack of conviction.

'*Ask yourself this . . . How often does Tardi just happen to pop in unannounced for a quick snifter of afternoon sherry?*'

And so, mourning the almost certain loss of the collection of matchstick spacecraft in his vestry, and wishing he had a few King Edwards and a roll of foil handy, he settled down to wait for the bonfire that was the Chapel of St Tib's to cool. Now, if he could just get in there by tomorrow morning. . . . And if the mop and dust pan wasn't too melted . . . Then maybe, just maybe . . .

Somehow Fintan didn't feel very confident about any of it. Cardinal Tardi had a very unnerving knack of finding out about things. Especially the sudden and untimely destruction of an ancient chapel.

Already the lab in the fine example of Mannerist architecture, deep in the Vatican gardens, was beginning to look as if it had been recently hit by a very large bomb. One whose warhead had been tightly stuffed with papyrus star charts and computer printed astral calendar projections, that is.

'Damn that Pope Gregory,' cursed Cardinal Holridge once again as he tried working a date backwards through time. 'Why did he have to mess the calendar up?'

''Cause he reckoned the Julian one was screwed up,' offered Kotonawa helpfully.

'And he thought this would be better? Ask the Russians what they think about it now. D'you think they're happy about celebrating the October Revolution on the seventh of November?' He scowled impatiently at a host of densely scribbled figures and cross-referenced them against a small fraction of the Bayeux Tapestry. 'Divide by four hundred, carry twenty from the fifth of April and . . . Damn, damn!' He flung the cross-stitched comet across the lab. 'And it's not Halley either.'

'You sure?'

'Oh yes,' scowled the head of the Congregation for Icon Authentication, jabbing his finger at fifteen sheets of A4 covered in calculations. 'Jesus Christ would've had to have been born in a barn in Jackson, Illinois in the early half of 1910 to get the right elevation for that one.'

'What about Shoemaker-Levy? Have you tried that?'

'Ulan Bator, the seventeenth of February, 1543,' grumbled Holridge, unearthing a small Post-it note from beneath a vast pile of workings. 'It's hopeless. No comet comes any-where near.'

'Er . . . who says it was a comet? It is called the *Star* of Bethlehem after all.'

'No, it couldn't be,' frowned Holridge rubbing at his chin. 'Something from another galaxy?'

His eyes started misting over as he tried to comprehend what devious trick of intergalactic geometry could possibly arrange for a certain star to appear over the Middle East two thousand years ago, and stay there just long enough to allow a triplet of local kings to go hiking across the desert. 'Makes perfect sense,' he conceded and snatched at another well thumbed astral projection.

'It does?' asked Kotonawa, shrugging.

'Absolutely, my dear Harry. But in order to be anywhere near the right place, it would have to be out in the vicinity of the lower quadrant of the outer edge of . . .' His voice drifted away as he flattened a deep blue star chart across the lab desk and swept a vast curved ruler across a couple of dozen galaxies.

14:59 The Atlantic

The board room on deck 2 had been perfectly kitted out as an exact copy of Rear-Admiral Rosenschmirtz's office back in the headquarters of the US Department of Defense, Arlington, Virginia. Arrays of the world's most advanced tracking equipment nestled in racks around the walls and hummed contentedly to themselves. Vast boards of perspex geography hung from the ceiling, sporting flotillas of sticky shipping and scrawls of chinagraph pencil. As a copy of his Pentagon office it was spot on, right down to the smallest details. Even the walls met at seventy-two degrees.

Major-General Gelding rubbed at his two millimetre fuzz of hair and scowled at the perspex map of Japan. 'So you're telling me that we know exactly the whereabouts of all their Sushi Class destroyers?'

'That's an affirmatory yes,' answered Rear-Admiral Ro-senschmirtz, proud of his information gathering as he pointed to the Tasman Sea. 'And the Aussies have got their four Keating Class destroyers and the *Sir Les Patterson* exactly where they said they'd be.'

'Hmmmm,' grumbled Gelding suspiciously.

'C'mon then, Isenheimer. You must have some good news for me?'

The Head of Speculative Intelligence brushed at his quiff of incongruously boyish blond and pulled a face that he hoped evoked images of *The Man from U.N.C.L.E.* 'There's the Kenya Capability Scenario,' he announced enigmatically.

'That the nonsense about damn Africans going nuclear by the end of the year?' grumbled Gelding.

'How did you know about . . . ?'

'Should change your password,' tutted Gelding. 'Anyway, it'll never happen. They'll never have the cash to feed a five-kiloton capability.'

'Of course they will,' flustered Isenheimer. 'The price of rhino horn will go through the roof once the FDA report comes clean and backs the Chinese claims about it being *the* best aphro-disiac. Have you any idea how many rhino are in Kenya?'

'There won't be an FDA report,' said Gelding with a slight smirk of pride playing at his lips.

'I've seen it,' countered Isenheimer. 'It's amazing, graphs, statistics, everything . . .'

'Never happen.'

Isenheimer glared suspiciously at the other Major-General. 'You buried it?'

'Can't have Africans going nuclear. That's dangerous. Now gimme some good news. There's got to be someone somewhere looking to start a war?'

Isenheimer looked at Rear-Admiral Rosenschmirtz. They both shrugged.

'A coup? Border dispute?' begged Gelding. 'C'mon, tell me that Saddam's got bored with diplomacy?'

'The only thing I've got of any mayhem potential, believe me, you wouldn't like,' tutted Isenheimer.

'Don't tell me. The "R" word,' cringed Gelding.

'All of it. Religious. Middle-East type stuff. But even that won't last the week if my sources in the Vatican are correct,' said Isenheimer.

'What?' coughed Gelding incredulously. 'An end to religious wars? Never.'

'They'll down tools in a second if what I hear's true.'

'What? If what's true?' repeated Gelding, a slight twist of concern edging into his voice.

'That the Pope's about to prove God exists. Scientifically!' announced Isenheimer.

A shocked silence snuggled into the pentagonal room and began making itself comfortable.

'Well, goddamn it, what's that got to do with us?' blurted Gelding, setting the silence off on its toes. 'Hell, a job in the military's a job for life.'

'Not if the military doesn't exist any more it isn't,' said Isenheimer.

'You cannot be serious? Tell me he's not serious, Rosenschmirtz?'

Isenheimer leaned forward and fixed his Army colleague with a disturbingly confident stare. 'I'm perfectly serious. I've had my best Speculative Extrapolation Officers go over this a dozen times with all the best AI programmes and it comes out the same every time. Three years after the Pope proves God exists, we're history.'

'No, no. They can't . . . People need us,' squeaked Gelding, his world starting to unravel. 'Look what we've given them. Satellite TV, non-stick pans, antibiotics, microwaves. TV dinners wouldn't exist if it wasn't for us having wars.

And what about global warming? If we hadn't invented nuclear reactors the whole planet would be a real mess now. How can they get rid of the military?'

'The Flock Coagulation Scenario,' answered Isenheimer. 'As soon as the Roman Catholics prove God exists, they claim him as their own and . . . bingo, all the floating faithful flock to join them. Within two years the whole planet are on the same side, singing the same hymns and calling each other "brother and sister" and we, gentlemen, are out of a job.'

'But . . . but are you certain of this?' whimpered Rosenschmirtz, staring into a rapidly bleakening future. A future without ships to command, without aircraft to carry, without explosions to warm the cockles of an aging heart. 'How good are your sources?'

'A Vatican Cardinal. He wouldn't lie now, would he?'

Major-General Gelding picked at his thumbnail, a scowl deepening across his forehead.

'All right, so he wouldn't lie too much,' Isenheimer corrected himself.

'But how sure are you that the Pope'll go public with this?' begged Rosenschmirtz desperately.

'Have you ever known an Italian-American keep quiet about something this big?'

'Goddamn it,' snarled Gelding suddenly, his fists clenching angrily as thoughts of continent-spanning congregations of smiling brethren crowded into his head. Cheerfully they rattled tambourines at him, trilled endless verses of 'Kumbayah' and skipped barefoot across acres of daisy-spotted fields, beads rattling from a million tie-dyed kaftans. 'We can't let this happen!'

The floor seemed to lurch beneath his feet and a film of sweat bubbled coldly across his brow. 'I haven't dedicated myself to the glory of the US Army for the last forty-two years for that kind of peace! To the War Room!' he declared and lurched for the door. 'Tambourines!' he snarled angrily. 'Only good for one thing. Target practice!'

Rosenschmirtz looked at Isenheimer. 'Tambourines?'

The Head of Speculative Intelligence shrugged.

15:43 The Vatican

Cardinal Holridge's index finger did what its name determined and wriggled its way down yet another magazine index. A grunt of extreme dissatisfaction rang around the lab as this proved to be as wholly unsuccesful as all the others.

'I don't believe it,' snarled the Head of the Congregation for Icon Authentication and tossed the final volume of *New Spaceman* on to a heap of several hundred glossies. 'You'd think that would have had *something* about it. How can they have the nerve to call themselves "The Premier Guide To Astrophysics For All The Family" when this is all the mention they give to galaxy 3C390.3?' He prodded the bottom left-hand corner of a three-foot-square wallchart of 'A Hundred Great Galaxies'. 'How are you supposed to spot the Star of Bethlehem in that lot?'

'Nobody said it was going to be easy,' offered Kotonawa, poring over a remarkably well-thumbed copy of last August's *Amazingly Unfeasible*.

'I've a good mind to cancel the subscription.'

Kotonawa looked up in alarm. 'Cancel? But . . . but what about "The Cut-Out-And-Keep Eagle Nebula Mobile" which starts next month and builds to produce a realistic ceiling decoration that will entertain and inform?'

'What about it?'

'Well, I thought it would look nice up there,' suggested Kotonawa pointing at a bare patch of Mannerist ceiling next to a balsa pterodactyl.

Holridge scowled and pointed to the magazine in front of his Japanese colleague. 'Found anything useful in there?'

'Er, in a word? No. But . . . er, are you sure that galaxy 3C390.3 is the one?'

'Of course, I've been over the figures a thousand times.'

'I know, but you are putting quite a lot of faith in those manuscripts. Are you sure the ancient Jordanians were as precise as you would like?'

'You've seen the cross-correlation with the sightings. Royalty don't travel that far across the Middle East on a whim, you know. And then there's the triangulation with the shepherds. I'm telling you, it's right. I know it. And if I could only get a better view than this the world would see it too.' Once again he squinted forlornly at the two-inch patch of fuzzy colour on the wallchart. 'I can't give the Pope this and call it proof.'

Hopelessly Kotonawa turned the page in *Amazingly Unfeasible* and entered the nether regions of the classifieds. It was then, out of the corner of his eye, that he saw it. Jammed between an advert extolling the virtues of a correspondence course for the illiterate and a fortnight's potholing holiday in the tunnels of the Viet Cong lurked the answer to Holridge's prayers.

Nightmares with your Nebulae?
Grief over those Galaxies?
Confused by Cosmic Constellations?
Then let NETWORK NERDSCAPE help.
Log on to the combined intellect of the World's Scientists now!
http://www.network.nerdscape.com
Help is only a Modem Away!

'Er, just how desperate are you?' asked Kotonawa, turning the page around and pointing up the tiny box.

Cardinal Holridge's expression hovered for a moment at extreme suspicion, quivered towards absolute incomprehension and eventually plumped for a shrug of 'what the Hell, nothing ventured and all that'.

Minutes later, the modem in Kotonawa's pc was flexing its virtual fingers and logging on to the intellectual forum that was Network Nerdscape.

Before the eyes of the two Cardinals the screen filled with hastily scanned-in images of random cosmic phenomena. Galaxies gyrated around wildly, moons merengued and a whole host of stars salsa'd with the gay abandon not normally associated with stellar masses. In the bottom right-hand corner a small grey alien waved stiffly before evaporating in a scatter of pixels leaving the Network Nerdscape cover page.

'Question or answer?' asked the screen and in a second Kotonawa had clicked on 'question'. He flexed his knuckles excitedly and readied himself to type in their conundrum.

'Wait, wait, not so fast,' panicked Holridge suddenly, gripped in the scientific equivalent of stage-fright. 'This has got to be phrased right. You know, rubbish in, rubbish out. Er . . . let's see. The Star of Bethlehem is in the galaxy 3C390.3. Discuss? Hmmm, no, no. Too exammy. How about . . . A long time ago in Bethlehem, so the Holy Bible says . . . Nah, too Johnny Mathis. Er . . .'

Kotonawa fidgeted impatiently at the keyboard and, whilst Holridge wrestled with the complexities of phraseology, he clicked on 'Answer'. With only the slightest flick of static the most recent of Network Nerdscape's pleas for help slid into view.

Calling all ufologists! Anybody out there got any idea what this is?
Answers to www.tyrone.indiscriminate.navy.com

And beneath it was the unmistakable view of a radar trace of the Atlantic taken at 12:43.15 that very day. Cardinal Kotonawa rubbed his chin and peered at the screen pock-marked with scheduled flights. Across it all shimmered a single brush stroke of green which ended abruptly four and a half miles south-west of Eire. 'Weird,' he mumbled to himself and began scrolling down to look at some of the answers.

Just as he was getting into the finer details of the proofs from a group of Manchester University students who were certain the trace was made up entirely of the intestines of an innocent greenfly smeared across the screen, Cardinal Holridge tapped him on the shoulder.

'Got it,' he said happily and handed over a scrap of paper.

Kotonawa stared at the heavily crossed out query in his hand. 'That it?'

Holridge nodded. 'Oh yes. That's perfect, simple and secretive. Nobody'll figure out why we're so interested in that particular fragment of space. The Muslims won't get suspicious.'

'True,' shrugged Kotonawa. 'Let's just hope it gets you the right answer.' And without further ado he typed it in.

I need a decent picture of galaxy 3C390.3.
Anybody know where I can get one?
Answers to www.holridge.icon.vat.

'What happens now?' asked Holridge, eagerly hopping from one foot to the other.

'We wait.'

'Wait? How long?' asked Holridge, sounding as impatient as a five-year-old on the twenty-third of December.

'As long as it takes,' shrugged Kotonawa and flicked back to the other side to see if anyone else had grave doubts that

86

greenfly intestines had anything to do with a smear over Eireann airspace.

17:25 The Vatican

Cardinal Tardi's voice echoed around the inside of the dome of St Peter's as he continued explaining the choreography of a forthcoming ceremony to a small group.

'. . . and then, after you receive the tiara and another blessing you stand and . . .'

'Will that need more incense?' asked Cardinal Alighieri.

'No,' hissed Tardi. 'There'll already be three banks of four over there and two rows of six behind those pillars. Any more and the OB units will need extra lighting rigs.' He turned back to Pope Angeles who was perched on a particularly ornate-looking pew.

'Now, Your Holiness, you then rise and make your way across to the lectern where . . .'

'You didn't say anything about him going to the lectern,' interrupted a stocky man in check plus-fours who looked for some reason as if he should have been wearing headphones and microphone. He glanced at a clipboard. 'If you'd said anything about him going to the lectern I'd have it here. Look, nothing.' He tapped the clipboard officiously with his pencil and began looking around the basilica through a tiny viewfinder. 'No, he'll be out of sight. He can't go to the lectern.'

'Well, you'll just have to get another cameraman,' said Tardi, counting to ten under his breath.

'Another cameraman?' gasped the plus-foured director from Reuters News Agency. 'It's not that simple, you know. We're already pushing the receiver board to full, you add another view-feed and you'll need another board, and an extra vision-mixer and . . .'

'If that's what it takes . . .' began Tardi.

'. . . and that's expensive. Triple time on Easter Sundays,' finished the director.

'Triple time?' squeaked Tardi.

'On Easter Sunday?' coughed Pope Angeles. 'Er, Cardinal. A word about scheduling, please?'

Reluctantly, the Papal Secretary crossed to the still un-crowned Pontiff. 'I know what you're going to say,' began Tardi in his finest pre-emptive placatory manner, 'but look at it as an opportunity. He's up for the whole package. Corona-tion plus address. Now, we throw a couple of hymns in, a few processions and we're talking about a three-hour special.'

'Three hours?' gasped Angeles.

'World-wide! Billy Graham would kill for that.'

'Yes, I suppose he would . . .' gasped the Pope, trying to keep up with the movement of goal posts.

'So, if you cross in front of this pillar here,' said Tardi, 'and move to the lectern round here then . . .' Slickly delivering the three hours as a *fait accompli* he headed back towards the director. He picked up on Tardi's lead.

'Then we can cover that from Steadicam 2,' smiled the plus-foured one, walking crabwise down the aisle. 'Perfect! Then we hold for a couple of lessons, turn and we're set for the exit procession down that way.'

Not sure that he would be able to remember all of that, and for the first time having a certain amount of sympathy for rehearsing wedding parties, Pope Angeles stood, genu-flected and headed off down the aisle, his mind filling with clouds of mounting dread.

'Er, Your Holiness,' called Tardi. 'I need a word about your address.' He made a move to follow but the man from Reuters had other ideas.

'Power feeds?' he insisted. 'Where do I get them? And what about cable ties? Where can I run cables?'

Tardi was ensnared.

Pope Angeles failed completely to notice; the cloudbanks of dread swirled greyly inside his head. Three hours in front of the world's news agencies! And then delivering his address at the end! Even Moses hadn't had it that bad, had he? His left knee suddenly began to feel disturbingly weak and he knew there was only one solution. He needed a healthy dose of fresh air.

Well, fresh air and some news of the LA Raiders. He looked at his watch and tried his best to calculate time differences and Sky Sports Channel schedules.

While he couldn't actually be one hundred per cent certain of it he felt pretty confident that if he hurried he could just catch the rerun of last night's *MidNite FloodLite Special*.

Minutes later, he burst into his papal quarters, a sheen of perspiration glistening on his brow and collecting in the small of his Armani-upholstered back.

In seconds, remote control in hand, he was on the Renaissance chaise-longue at the far side of the room, pressing controls as if there was no tomorrow. With a whirr of motors a 42-inch Sony LCD TV slid out from behind a mahogany bookcase and powered itself up.

'Where is it? Where is it?' he muttered desperately, stabbing out combinations of numbers. Suddenly the screen flashed up a familiar logo and filled with a gridded stadium. 'Yes, yes, yes! Just in time,' he cheered and settled down to watch the slick-haired announcer.

'Good Evening, football fans! And welcome to this afternoon's rerun of the *MidNite FloodLite Special* played last night, live, at the home of the LA Raiders where they faced up to their arch enemies the San Francisco 49ers at midnight and under floodlights. Coverage and commentary will be brought to you by Zack . . .'

Suddenly, the grinning commentator was obliterated by a silver blizzard of static and a speakerful of white noise hiss.

'What the . . . ?' began Pope Angeles, his index finger flashing reflexively towards the remote. The screen beat him to it. It flashed once, turned black and then crackled violently for a few unnerving seconds until a nervously grinning Italian anchorwoman appeared, pressing an earphone firmly into her right ear.

In thickest Roman she announced, 'Er . . . Hello there, football fans . . . Er, looks like we kinda got a few problems with our satellite link for this afternoon's *MidNite FloodLite Special*. Er . . . on your behalf I'd like to reassure you that we will be on to our lawyers immediately and will be suing for full compensation. I mean, they had a contract, right? Er . . . in the meantime, in place of the scheduled game we'll be bringing you . . . er . . .' She pressed her ear and frowned in concentration, listening. 'Oh . . . right . . . yeah. Everyone's favourite alien movie. *ET: The Extra-Terrestrial* . . . er, enjoy.'

Slouching despondently in his Armani vestments, His Holiness Pope Joshua Angeles watched as his home team was replaced by a screenful of Spielberg-lit spacecraft descending from on high into a handy patch of American woodland.

17:47 The Atlantic

Major-General Hiram J. Gelding III was pacing up and down inside the chart-strewn war room of the USS *Indiscriminate*, his hair bristling like an incensed Bruce Willis.

'What d'you mean?' he demanded for the fifth time. 'What part of "no" means we can't invade?'

'Nix. Nein. Nyet,' began Rear-Admiral Rosenschmirtz before he was cut off by Major-General Isenheimer.

'All of it! You can't just go invading the Vatican,' said the Head of Speculative Intelligence.

'Of course we can. It's easy. Park this ship anywhere in the Med and any of the choppers can airlift us direct . . .'

'That's not what I meant and you know it,' hissed Isenheimer. 'You can't invade because the repercussions will . . .'

'But they're a threat. You said so yourself,' insisted Gelding, fists pounding on a map of Bolivia. 'And a threat needs . . .'

'A *possible* threat,' reiterated Isenheimer. 'We don't know for certain that they have proof damaging to our position.'

'And by the time we find out it'll be too late! There's only one way to stop them using any information they have. Gentlemen, have you forgotten the "P" word?' growled Gelding.

'Please?' asked Rosenschmirtz.

'Pre-emptive!' barked Gelding, rolling his eyes.

'No. We need something more before we can . . .'

Suddenly there was a sharp rapping of knuckles on wood and the door burst open. A marine swept in with a piece of paper and slapped it on the chart-strewn desk. 'Sirs, something of interest, sirs!' He spun on his heel and hurried out, sensing that he had just placed something flammable next to a blue touch paper,

'What the Hell . . . ?' blustered Gelding, staring at the sheet.

'Radar trace,' mused Isenheimer. 'But of what? Nothing I know can move that fast. Halfway across the Atlantic in under a second. That's bound to be top secret.'

'Atlantic?' barked Gelding sniffing something interesting. 'Who owns bases in the Atlantic?'

'Er . . . Ireland,' answered Rosenschmirtz, picking a coloured chart of the area out from underneath Bosnia.

'Ha. I knew it!' shouted Gelding, leaping several tall buildings of logic to get to a conclusion that suited him. 'Ireland . . . And they thought they could fool me with that! C'mon, Rosenschmirtz, set course! We're wasting time!'

'What?' spluttered Isenheimer, clutching at his head as the train of Gelding's thought turned to dust on the horizon.

'Do I have to spell it out?'

The Head of Speculative Intelligence nodded.

'Word association,' grinned Gelding dangerously, the whites of his eyes glowing. 'Fill in the missing one. Roman . . . ? Irish . . . ? Is the Pope . . . ?'

Rosenschmirtz was trying to find something to do with legions and stew when Isenheimer whispered the word 'Catholic' in awe-stricken tones.

'You wanted more. That's it! They're gearing up for action!'

Isenheimer shook his head in disbelief. 'You can't possibly think that . . .'

'Er . . . he might have a point,' said Rosenschmirtz, looking up from the chart in his hand.

'Look.' He pointed to the tiny outcrop of rock that lurked four and a half miles off the Irish coast and dwelt under the name of St Naimhe's. 'That radar trace ends directly here.' His fingernail hovered under the tiny symbol for a church.

Major-General Hiram J. Gelding III punched the air with delight. 'Gentlemen, today is a great day to be a soldier and a great day to be an American.'

Somehow Isenheimer didn't feel quite so sure.

Within ten minutes, and much to the satisfaction of Rear-Admiral Rosenschmirtz, the USS *Indiscriminate* was steaming full ahead towards the Mediterranean.

Slouching on the Renaissance chaise-longue in his Armani vestments, His Holiness Pope Joshua Angeles stared at the 42-inch Sony screen and was closer to tears than he had been in years. Emotions writhed inside his intestines as, almost halfway across the world, with a minute and a half of the rerun to go, the LA Raiders were well on target not to repeat their 1984 38–9 hammering of the Redskins. Thirteen points down, they were almost certain to be ejected from the Superbowl in less than ninety seconds and nothing, but perhaps the swiftest administration of intravenous chemical assistance, could do anything to stop it. For anyone who had lost their heart to the team from the City of Angels it was set to be the biggest upset of the decade. Again.

But of this Pope Angeles knew nothing. The satellite link which should have been feeding him the repeated closing moments of the *MidNite FloodLite Special* was still charting the adventures of a small extraterrestrial with a glowing finger.

As His Holiness watched, a flock of cyclists pedalled casually past a full moon and disappeared into a suitable few acres of American woodland. Minutes later the Supreme Pontiff watched through rapidly moistening eyes as the eponymous hero was carried up into the Heavens in a shimmering blaze of halogen lamps. And the credits rolled.

'And they all lived happily ever after,' he muttered as he stabbed the remote and shut off the screen. 'Well, at least until the sequel, *ET II: The Second Coming.*'

And suddenly he stopped, catching his thoughts as the 42-inch screen slithered behind the Renaissance bookcase.

'The Second Coming? What made me think of that?' he wondered almost guiltily. 'It was only a movie.'

And in that moment a small fraction of his short-term memory began flicking back through the slice of sweet-but-engrossing cinematic pie that is ET. It didn't take long before he realised the truth. A cold shiver of excitement slithered down his spine as he recalled the arrival from on high of a small vulnerable being upon this world. He gasped as it died, rose again and, carried to the right spot by faithful bicycling disciples, left this Earth and retook its rightful place in the Heavens above.

Suddenly, he was on his feet, across the room and shakily dialling a number on the phone.

'Hello? Heliport? Is Vatican 1 fuelled and ready? . . . It is? Excellent! I'll be there in five. What? . . . It's me. The Pope!' And so, dropping the receiver into the white telephone's cradle, Pope Joshua Angeles whirled out of the office in a flurry of Armani, ideas already hatching for the most amazing papal address this century. This was going to be one the world would remember.

19:43 St Naimhe's

With a handkerchief wrapped around his nose, like some extra from a low budget western, Father Fintan O'Suilleabhain edged his way towards the blackened mess that had once been the vestry of St Tib's. He braced his shoulder against what had once been the outer door and pushed. Clouds of choking ash erupted everywhere as it collapsed into just so much carbon, leaving Fintan looking forlornly down at the latch in his hand.

Miserably, he pushed on and began to start praying that it would be a mighty long time before the likes of Cardinal Tardi ever wanted to pay a visit. He had the distinct feeling it was going to take some little while to clear this up.

The door of the broom cupboard turned to powder before him and revealed a small puddle of orange goo that had once been the chapel's dustpan and brush.

'Why me?' he whimpered as he re-estimated time scales up towards the more hopeless end of the spectrum and his mind filled with the dread curse of all financially strapped parishes: the Church Roof Repair Fund. Thoughts of endless tombolas, fêtes and underpopulated bring-and-buy sales writhed ominously in the recesses of his mind. Behind them stood a tackily painted red and white cash thermometer, steadfastly showing zero.

Hopelessly, he drifted through the black vestry and out into the smouldering mess of the chapel, ticking off the mounting catalogue of destruction. One sixteenth-century roof – destroyed. Fifty-three second editions of *The Big Blue Book of Hymns* – shredded. Eighteen sixteenth-century stained-glass windows – melted. Ninety-eight classic oak pews with matching kneelers – tinderised.

And it was then that he really began to doubt that all this had been somehow his fault.

Well, it didn't seem overly likely that an erupting poteen still, no matter how large and however rapidly it was travelling, would cause the chapel roof to implode. And then there was the matter of the fifty-foot-wide hole in the centre of the aisle and the way it was glowing in an oddly greenish metallic sort of way. Pulsing.

Somehow, Fintan felt sure that even the most dangerous of brews didn't do that. Surely?

Finding himself thinking of old science-fiction movies he edged nervously towards the hole, expecting at any moment to hear the eerie sound of theremins.

'Er . . . hello. Is anybody alive in there?' he called into the dark pit. 'Do you want me to call an ambulance?'

Cardinal Holridge's heels clicked to a halt, squeaked on the tiles as they changed direction and, with nary a pause for rest, set off again.

'Nervous?' asked the Oriental gentleman at the computer terminal, an inscrutable grin shining in the screen glow.

'Of course I'm nervous,' snapped back Holridge, pacing the floor. 'I've never had to do anything like this.' He flicked a glance at his watch and winced. 'Kotonawa, you . . . you *are* sure you can get us in, aren't you?'

'You are sure the calculations are right, aren't you?'

'Of course,' snapped back Holridge, biting his bottom lip.

Kotonawa swivelled around on his chair and looked at the feverish Englishman. 'Promise me you won't be disappointed if we . . . well, don't get anything. I mean you are putting quite a lot of faith in those manuscripts.'

'Faith is something I have a lot of and I'm telling you this is it. It is! C'mon, get busy. Now.'

'But nobody's seen it for nearly two thousand years,' reminded Kotonawa. He glanced at his watch. 'What difference is ten minutes going to make?'

Holridge almost slapped his forehead with frustration. 'We've been through this. Galactic oscillations, remember?'

Kotonawa shrugged. 'Never was very good with all that heavy cosmological stuff,' he confessed.

'Now he tells me,' snorted Holridge under his breath. In a second he was across the lab, both hands firmly on the back of Kotonawa's chair, staring intently into his face. 'Black holes, right? You know them, massive gravity wells that suck in light and anything else that happens to be within arm's reach? Well there's one weighing about two hundred million times more than the Sun slap in the centre of galaxy 3C390.3, out there.' He pointed in a vaguely easterly direction. 'And it's wobbling. One thousand years this way, one thousand years that. Tonight, it changes direction, tonight! And for ten minutes we will just . . . *just* be able to see around the edge of it to what lies beyond.' Holridge, not normally given to such pagan gestures of luck generation, crossed his fingers.

'And you're *sure* that's the star?'

'No. That's why I need the proof. The *world* needs the proof. That's why I need you to . . . Oh God, look at the time! Get to it! Now!' Holridge spun Kotonawa back to his keyboard and pushed the chair under the desk. Oriental fingers clattered feverishly on tiny keys as Holridge resumed his pacing, his hands wringing around each other like greased eels. 'If we miss this we can say goodbye to any mention of science in the papal address,' he muttered. 'If only there was another way.'

'Something more legal, you mean?'

'Just shut up and work,' hissed Holridge as he scowled at the printout of the answer to their plea on Network Nerdscape.

If you want a look at 3C390.3 hijack yourself a bloody big
telescope.
Luv Barney Hubble

And not for the first time did he find himself thinking about the mysterious ways in which God worked. The faith of millions depending on two Cardinals stepping across the invisible boundaries of the law. If only the two-metre Vatican Advanced Technology Telescope at Mount Graham, Arizona had been just a bit more powerful then none of this digital skullduggery would have been necessary.

Behind him, like a trained narcotics beagle with a sniff of a cocaine haul, Kotonawa eagerly hunted for the opening he

97

needed. His digital fingers prodded here and pushed there and suddenly . . .

The terminal screen flashed blue and flung a glittering starscape at him.

'Aha! Gotcha!'

Holridge was across the lab in two bounds and peering at the screen. 'Is that it?'

The logo of the North American Space Agency hovered above a rather fine picture of the Horsehead Nebula and answered his question. 'Well go on, do like it says. Enter the password.'

'Aye, Captain,' answered Kotonawa and typed in 'Buzz Aldrin is King'.

The screen blinked and tossed back a terse 'Access Denied'.

'Woops. Must've changed it,' mused Kotonawa and scratched his chin. He flicked through a file on the desk next to him, spied another command and inputted that quickly.

'Are you serious? *That's* a password?' gasped Holridge as he watched the box fill with 'To Infinity and Beyond'.

'Trust me, I know what I'm doing,' grinned Kotonawa. 'It worked last month. Well, at least that's what the Hacker's Website said. NASA are big fans of *Toy Story* you know. We'll be in before you can say . . . Ahhh, maybe not.'

'Access Denied' answered the screen.

'Oh God, oh God!' panicked Holridge, staring down at his watch.

'Don't worry. It's three strikes and out,' consoled Kotonawa, flicking back desperately through the file of downloaded passwords.

'Exactly. Three strikes. One left!'

'You really ought to calm down . . . Aha, here we go.' He cracked his fingers noisily and typed 'My God . . . It's full of stars!' With unnecessary theatricality he spun his index finger three times around the return button and jabbed it.

'You're enjoying this far too much.'

The screen shimmered and dissolved into a series of menus. Kotonawa was on it in seconds, bashing strings of unfathomable commands into the keyboard. Barely glimpsed title pages flashed across the terminal in blurs of colour and neatly arranged typefaces, graphics whirled headily, until . . .

The screen crackled, turned black and filled with waves of tiny white letters that certainly weren't Times New Roman 12pt.

'Pass those co-ordinates, would you?' smiled Kotonawa.

'You're . . . you're in? That's it?' He handed over the co-ordinates and attitude correction calculations. 'I thought it would be more, well . . . it's just text.'

'That's operating systems for you,' mused Kotonawa. 'You were expecting Windows?'

Holridge blushed and once again showed his ignorance of all things computery as Kotonawa's fingers clattered across the keyboard.

Meanwhile . . .

In the chilly wastes of local space, just beyond the outer edges of our atmosphere, a long dormant computer heard its name being called. Digital ears pricked up and listened in the near vacuum as strings of commands whispered its way. After a few milliseconds of rapt attention the computer saluted and, with devastating efficiency, began handing out its own cascade of orders. Fuel pumps whirled, electronic ignition systems powered up and simultaneously a whole host of attitude thrusters sparked into life. In that instant, the world infamous Hubble Space Telescope drifted away from Earth and angled itself towards the distant galaxy known romantically as 3C390.3. Motors whirled, gyros spun and within moments brand new fields of view were being harvested of every tiny detail.

Back in the darkened laboratory, Kotonawa sat back and clicked a stopwatch. 'That's it,' he said. 'Forty-five seconds before they track us. Let's hope it's long enough.'

'Seconds?' shrieked Holridge, incredulity shimmering at the edge of every consonant. 'Forty-five *seconds*?'

'Yeah, NASA are good at tracking hackers.'

'We're . . . we're sat here waiting for galaxies to align themselves in a once-in-two-thousand-year arrangement and you tell me we've got forty-five seconds to see it happen?'

'Said your calculations had to be good, didn't I?'

'But that's . . . that's imposs—'

'Ooooh, hold on. Something's coming through,' interrupted Kotonawa, his attention suddenly grabbed by images assembling on the screen. 'Oh my God . . . look at that!'

They stared as something strange appeared around the edge of a black hole slap-bang in the middle of galaxy 3C390.3. It shimmered eerily at the edge of blackness; a distorted blob of light twisted by the equivalent of two hundred million suns. Slowly it rose, a feeble Mediterranean sun above an endless inchoate sea. It grew to a minuscule glowing comma and, almost before they had the chance to take it all in, it set again.

'Well, was that it?' asked Kotonawa, looking away from the screen into the awestricken face of Holridge.

'Th . . . that was it,' he whispered and sat down feeling flushed with wonder. 'That was it! I knew it! Exactly where I said it would be, exactly on time. The Star of Bethlehem in all its glory . . .'

'Er, just one thing,' said Kotonawa. 'Shouldn't it have been a bit, you know, more spectacular?'

Holridge frowned. 'What are you saying?'

'Well, shouldn't it have been a bit brighter? How many shepherds d'you suppose saw that just then?'

'What?'

'And it didn't really hang around for very long, did it?'

'Meaning?'

'Look, I don't want to be seen as being *too* picky . . . but if I was a wise man I think I'd've found it a bit hard to follow that for very long. Even Hubble can't see it now. Look!' he pointed to the screen.

'Are you suggesting that *wasn't* the Star of Bethlehem?' challenged Holridge. 'After I gave you the co-ordinates and . . . What the Hell is that?'

The two Cardinals stared in wonder at the screen as two blobs of local space writhed uncomfortably, twisted into a vortex of unfathomable complexity and spat a pair of alien ships into view. The Imperial Strato-Fortress flashed out of hypercorrugated morphospace scant nanoseconds before the Republican Tropo-Nihilator, blazed a shimmering ion trail past Hubble's field of view and raced on towards Earth atmosphere.

'What the . . . ? Did you see that?' gasped Holridge. 'What were they?'

But Cardinal Kotonawa didn't get a chance to answer. At that very instant the screen of the terminal flashed a host of warning signs and began warbling alarms. 'They're on to us!' he squeaked and leapt for the power switch. The screen crackled black and the fan in the main terminal died.

'Safe,' breathed Kotonawa. 'They won't find us now.'

Holridge stared numbly at the blackened and deathly silent screen squatting behind Kotonawa.

'Tell me . . . *Please* tell me you saved those pictures,' whispered Holridge.

'Saved them?' asked Kotonawa, shifting uncomfortably on his chair. He winced as Holridge began sobbing pathetically.

'You . . . you could've lied to me. Just once you could've lied.'

At that very instant, far out on the edges of what is considered our solar system, an ion emission detector homed in on the trail of a Type-23 Ytterbium Collider Drive, orders were barked and numerous capable tentacles swung a pair of vast intergalactic craft in on an intercept course with Earth.

Faith: The Final Frontier

20:45 Thirteenth of April. Ten miles south of Foggia, Italy

In the thin triangle of evening shade offered by a sun-bleached shell of a block of flats, an international guerrilla checked her ammo clip. Twenty-three armour-piercing rounds grinned up at her like half a jaw of deadly dentistry. She spat a clichéd Middle American curse at the sand and thumped the clip back into the gun. It was low, dangerously low. But then, that was par for the course. There wasn't much about this job which wasn't dangerous.

Behind her, half a dozen others, dressed in the same desert camouflage and matching thigh-length boots, took stock of their ammunition situation. Gloved hands stroked gunbelts and double-checked their boot-tops for balanced throwing knives.

'Enemy!' barked their team leader, falling to her knees with an enticing flash of camouflage suspenders. In seconds, sandy balaclavas were tugged over faces and the guerrillas slunk into motionlessness, seeming to metamorphose into slabs of shattered concrete. Of course, not every slab of steel-reinforced building thereabouts gave the appearance of being quite as armed to the teeth, but, hey, there were limits to field camouflage.

The street beyond rumbled and squeaked as an enemy assault cannon caterpillared its way towards them. The turret swivelled in watchful arcs, menacing. In a way that would have made James Cameron proud, half-bricks and helmets crunched sickeningly beneath the tracks as its laser sight searched for suitable targets.

The guerrilla leader coughed another command and held out an impatient and delicately manicured hand. A beige drainpipe of a bazooka was slapped into her open palm. With a grunt she hefted it on to her shoulder, flipped up the sight and braced herself against a handy wall.

Unheard over the rumbling of the alien assault cannon, a Vatican Sea King swooped in. A member of the Swiss Guard reached out a white gloved hand and rocked the shoulder of the sleeping Pontiff. 'We are almost nearly being here now,' announced the boy from Basle in a confusion of European vowels.

At that very instant a guerrilla attack was launched on a patrolling enemy. A bazooka coughed a titanium-tipped armour-piercing round across the street, scored a direct hit on the assault cannon and blew its head clean off. The turret spun a hundred feet into the air on a crimson plume of destruction and the pilot of Vatican 1 leapt into evasive action.

A hundred and fifty feet below, the alien crew scrambled out of the decapitated vehicle and glistened in heavily sculptured silicon armour. Sadly, their freedom was somewhat curtailed by a sharp peppering of .303 rounds in to vital organs.

Far too close for comfort, and for no apparent military reason, a large office complex exploded. As if in the grip of appendicitis, it buckled over, coughed fire from every orifice and swiped the legs out from underneath a row of innocent water towers.

The helicopter swooped low over acres of carpet-bombed chaos, whacked to a halt and settled on to the shrapnel-littered sand.

In seconds it was pinned and mounted on the laser cross-hairs of an alien assault cannon. Suddenly, a desert-cream jeep leapt into the street on a vapour trail of sand and diesel, its engine over-revving dangerously. It performed a neat handbrake turn and powered towards the gleaming Sea King, the cargo of long-legged assault aliens screaming wildly, waggling the Alpha Centaurian equivalent of Kalashnikovs and removing their safety catches.

'Cut! Cut!' screamed a man with a megaphone, erupting from behind a gutted block of flats.

'Jesus. I don't believe it! Who the Hell's that guy think he is landin' a chopper on my set?'

And in that instant the world around Vatican I changed completely. Bodies rose from the decapitated remains of a smouldering tank and brushed themselves off. The jeepful of angry Alpha Centaurians ripped their heads off, turned into Italian film extras and lit up a host of cheap cigarettes. And, showing no respect for the more normal laws of physics, the row of water towers rebuilt themselves before the Pope's very eyes as he stepped out of the helicopter.

The one with the megaphone stared open-mouthed at the spotless figure in Armani vestments as he drifted amongst the scenes of mass intergalactic destruction. 'You're . . . You're . . . Your Holiness,' he squeaked.

'Hey, Giorgio. It's me, Franco,' declared the Supreme Pontiff, spreading his hands wide and advancing through the rubble. 'You don't recognise me?'

'Franco? Franco Gianelli of East 54th Street?' spluttered the man with the megaphone.

Pope Angeles smiled. 'The very one. Quite an entrance, eh?'

'Jesus, what's with the helicopter and the . . . the vestments? This another one of your scams?'

Pope Angeles stared quizzically at Giorgio Scipioni,

infamous director of well over fifty less-than-historically-correct war movies. 'You mean you haven't heard? Where've you been for the last two days?'

'Filming this. *Gazan Dolls*. Jesus! Location shoots, I hate the goddammed lot of 'em!'

Nervously, a fidgeting producer leant towards Scipioni and whispered in his ear. The director whirled impatiently and grabbed the producer firmly by the epaulettes. 'What d'you mean "cut the blasphemies?" Jesus, it's a free country. I can say what I damn well like . . . What d'you mean "not in front of the Pope"? What Pope? Him? Nah, that's Franco Gianelli from East 54th Street, me an' him grew up together in LA. He was always pullin' jokes and games an' . . .'

It was only when a remarkably grubby copy of *The Times* was slapped in his hands that Scipioni was silenced. He looked up from the two-day-old photograph and swallowed nervously. 'You? For real?'

Pope Angeles nodded, his gleaming white biretta flashing in the sun.

'Jesus, I know I've been out of touch filmin' around the world, but . . . Hell, I'll be damned!'

'You will if you keep that up,' smirked the Pope.

Scipioni's eyes narrowed as a small clump of neurones in the back of his head reminded him that time was indeed money and, due to the unfortunate arrival of a gleaming white helicopter in the midst of a very pricey scene, an awful lot of sponsor dollars were gurgling uncontrollably down a drain. 'You came here just to tell me that?' he muttered. 'Nah, don't believe it. Why you here, eh? C'mon Franco, what's that pilot of yours doin' droppin' you off in the middle of my warzone?'

Behind him his producer winced. That was no way to address the leader of the Roman Catholic Church, even if he had just ruined a rather pricey piece of cinematic history.

Pope Angeles spread his arms and stood with his palms towards the sky. 'Giorgio, please, it's only a film.'

'You tell that to my distributors,' snapped back Scipioni. 'I've gotta reshoot that whole battle 'cause of you. And that ain't cheap. You any idea what these explosions cost, eh? Three fifty each. And that's dollars, not lire. And then there's the rigging charges, technicians and actors. This isn't a cheap scene, not cheap. I'll be running into overtime I'm sure of it and what with that and the unions and . . .' Suddenly, he slammed the megaphone to his mouth and yelled at the idling alien assault cannon over by the helicopter. 'Hey, Sophia. Hey!'

The lid of the turret flipped back and a well-upholstered woman appeared, sporting flak jacket and combat suspenders. She tossed her black hair over her shoulders and stood, hands on hips, displaying a cleavage that could kill at a hundred yards.

'Sophia, that was great, y'know, swervin' round the rubble there. Loved the cloud of diesel. Great, great, nice touch. Now, next take I just wanna see a bit more pathos, y'know what I'm sayin'? Pathos. That's not just an alien assault cannon you're drivin' there. It's an icon. You know, a symbol of alien's inhumanity to man. I wanna see that comin' through in your drivin', y'hearin' me, Sophia?'

Sophia waved a uniquely Italian gesture at her director and slammed the captured alien caterpillar into reverse with a very unmilitary stiletto.

'It's her first big movie,' apologised Scipioni.

'Sure. Her first with most of her clothes on anyway,' frowned Angeles.

'Don't tell me that's what this little visit is about. You don't approve of the movie?' The Pope opened his mouth to reply but Scipioni was in there like a shot. 'Well, let me tell you, this is valuable cinema I'm makin' here. Nobody's ever fully explored all the aspects of women tank commanders in their role as saviours of the world. Feminity and macho retaliation wrestling in the same body as society collapses under an all-out alien assault. This is virgin territory, as seminal as *Full Metal Gymslip* I made a few years back.'

'And it's all as factually correct as that, eh? Thoroughly researched?' asked Angeles.

'Every last detail,' insisted Scipioni, his hand hovering over his heart. 'Hey, I make sure I get everything just right!'

'Funny, I never saw tank commanders wearing bikinis and flak jackets on CNN.'

'Ahhh . . . er . . .' Scipioni looked around desperately. He leaned closer to the right ear of the Head of the Roman Catholic Church. 'Well, between you and me, there was a news blackout. Hush, hush. CIA, y'know?'

'Three Hail Marys for that one I think.'

'All right, all right. Call it artistic licence. But that's what the punters pay for. Give the audience what they want that's what I always say. And believe me Sophia's got a lot to give.'

'Forty-two inches, if I'm to believe the press. And all natural.'

'Yeah, yeah. Silicon's natural, isn't it?'

Behind them, the producer's eyes widened and wondered if living in the midst of a warzone for the last few months here in southern Italy hadn't just affected his sanity a little. I mean, this last conversation. The Pope didn't really have conversations like that, did he?

'Giorgio,' smoothed Angeles, changing tack, 'I'm sure *Gazan Dolls* will be well up to your usual high standards. But I didn't fly out here to discuss the acting ability of your leading ladies.'

Scipioni took a step back and narrowed his eyes. 'So why *are* you here?'

'I have a proposal for you.' Pope Angeles slid a

companionable arm around Scipioni's shoulder. 'Something right up your street. Let's walk and talk.' The Pontiff led the director off towards a patiently waiting white helicopter and, with a flick of a beringed finger, signalled for the engines to begin revving.

20:53 The Vatican

Cardinal Holridge looked up from a printout of a patch of the Atlantic, expressions of excitement, terror and sheer confusion vying for overall control of his facial muscles. 'Twenty-three thousand two hundred and twelve miles an hour?'

'I got it up nearer twenty-five,' nodded Cardinal Kotonawa. 'But whatever way you look at it, that's fast.'

'Too fast. Man cannot live at such speeds,' whispered Holridge, looking up towards the outer edges of the solar system.

It was a look which Kotonawa recognised instantly. Holridge had worn it for a whole month when fossilised bacteria had been found inside a certain Martian meteorite. It was a look that said 'They're here!'

'Oh, no, you can't possibly think . . .'

'What other explanation is there?' insisted Holridge. 'You saw those ships on Hubble.'

'I *glimpsed* something . . .'

'Spaceships!'

'They could've been anything. Optical distortions, er . . .'

'Spaceships!'

'All right, all right, so what if they were spaceships. You'll never find out for certain. Let's just forget about it and start doing something useful like trying to find out if this hole in St Aubert's head was really made by the Archangel Michael's finger.' He waggled a Japanese digit out through a hole in an ancient-looking skull.

'Yes, yes, good idea. You can tell me all about it when I get back,' said Holridge, heading for the door in a flurry of crimson.

'What? Get back from where?'

'I need to check out a claim about the return of an ancient saint to rid her island of woodworm. It could be a miracle, you never know. Could be perfect for the papal address . . .'

'Where are you going?' called Kotonawa, but Holridge was already out of earshot and dashing down the corridor.

The Japanese Cardinal's eyes settled on a map casually discarded on the desk. A circle of red crayon ringed a tiny island four and a half miles off the south-west coast of Eire.

'St Niamhe's, surprise, surprise,' tutted Kotonawa and he began clamping an ancient skull into a handy vice.

20:59 Ten miles south of Foggia, Italy

A pair of Swiss Guards, clad in the standard-issue Michelangelo designer uniforms, snapped to crisp attention as Pope Joshua Angeles appeared around the end of the revving Sea King helicopter.

'At ease, men,' murmured the squat Italian-American Pontiff, flicking a fat finger in the general direction of the door. Fumbling only slightly with a seven-foot pike, the taller of two blond guards wrestled the door open and pulled out the steps. Barely slowing his pace, the Pope scurried up the red-carpeted treads and disappeared into the interior of the remarkably well-appointed chopper, the Italian director hard on his heels.

'Well, what d'you think?' he asked, settling himself into the heavily upholstered throne squeezed against the far wall.

'Nice,' whispered Giorgio Scipioni, taking in the decor of the tiny, air-ready papal palace.

'No, I mean my proposal,' corrected the Pope, sweeping an Armani'd arm towards a suitable chair.

'Well, what do *you* think I think?' smirked Scipioni and looked at the ceiling. Much to his surprise it sported a small but perfectly formed copy of part of the roof of the Sistine Chapel.

'I think you need some refreshments,' smiled His Holiness and pulled open a small mahogany cupboard close to his left hand. Two heavily ensaladed platters of sandwiches appeared. 'Er, sea bass or caviar?'

'Got any BLTs?'

'Come, come, it's Friday, mustn't have meat,' tutted the Pope setting the platters on to a table and wheeling it forward. Scipioni frowned and scratched at his ear.

In a matter of seconds, the Pope was holding out a pair of wine bottles, offering Scipioni a glimpse of the labels with the casual air of a professional juggler. 'Red or white? I must say, the Pinot Noir does go especially well with the caviar, the unpretentious fruitiness countering the saltiness of the beluga with nonchalant charm.'

'Got any Bud?'

'Third drawer down in the ice-box behind you. Do help yourself.'

Scipioni needed no second bidding. It had been a thirsty day, what with recreating a dollar-hungry alien invasion of the Gaza Strip for the demanding master that was cinema and then having it ruined by the untimely arrival of folk dressed in Armani vestments and Michelangelo designer military uniforms. He turned to the table, two Budweisers in each hand.

The Pope smiled at him, his hands together, a glass of crimson wine waiting patiently before him. 'For what we are about to receive . . .' he began.

'All right, all right, that's it Gianelli, c'mon what's the

111

game?' hissed Scipioni, slamming the quartet of Buds on to the table.

'Game?'

'Yeah. Don't come the innocent with me. The vestments, this helicopter? What gives, huh?'

'Er, that won't be necessary, men,' smoothed His Holiness.

'What kind of an answer's that?' snapped Scipioni.

Angeles pointed to a spot three inches behind the producer's head. Scipioni whirled around and found himself staring down the shafts of a pair of glinting pike, hovering scant inches from tender flesh.

'Swiss Guard,' offered Angeles as Scipioni slowly raised his hands. 'Very efficient, don't you think?'

'Very,' he whimpered and produced the type of smile which some of the less scrupulous cheesemongers would kill for. Two pairs of crystal blue eyes stared back from beneath blond eyebrows, fixing Scipioni for just long enough to make absolutely certain who was in charge. Then, suddenly, and without a word of command, they spun on their heels and marched out, somehow managing to spin the seven-foot pikes around within the confines of the mahogany-panelled Sea King. In moments they had repositioned themselves either side of the door, ears pricked.

'. . . may God make us truly thankful,' whispered Angeles underlining the prayer with the distinctive burst of white noise that normally accompanied the opening of a perfectly chilled bottle of Budweiser. 'Now then, Giorgio, you were saying?'

Scipioni drained half of the bottle in one mouthful and pressed the frosting glass against his forehead, hoping it would somehow give him some sense of reality. 'Look, Gianelli . . . What's going on here? I mean, you turn up unannounced, after all these years, after runnin' out on the best scam we'd dreamt up, dressed in a white frock and you ruin my film. C'mon, tell me, what d'you want?'

'I told you, out there,' answered the Pope around a mouthful of caviar sandwich. 'I need you.'

'You need me after all these years? No way, man. This is some new scam of yours, ain't it?'

'Not at all. This is real. You're perfect. Exactly what I want.'

'Exactly what you want? Hey, I gotta admire your nerve, man. Comin' back to try and pull one on me. How long's it been? Twenty years?'

'Twenty-five.'

'Twenty-five years since you blew the Antarctic farming franchise out of the water and hightailed it to . . . to . . . where the Hell did you get to, anyhow?'

Pope Angeles pulled at his vestments. 'Take a guess. It backfired.'

'Backfired? Geez, how could it backfire? That was the perfect scheme. Guaranteed success. Who could possibly refuse to invest one hundred dollars an acre for prime Antarctic grazing land?'

'Or the special offer price of three hundred dollars a head to stock it with thoroughbred low-fat Himalayan ice-ostriches? The miracle of evolution which nature has specially selected to thrive and grow in a pre-frozen, oven-ready manner . . .'

'. . . thus significantly reducing any processing and shipping costs, and so maximising return on capital investment all across the board. Yeah, perfection. How could that backfire?'

'Well, you remember that big house? The one with the big gardens and the religious-looking statues on the lawn?'

'The one owned by "some geek with way more dollar-potential than brains"?'

The Pope nodded sheepishly and busied himself with another caviar sarnie.

'Sure, I remember it,' tutted Scipioni. 'How could I forget? That's the last place I saw you. "Stay right there," you said, all smart like. "I'll be back with a million bucks before you can say Kentucky Fried." Twenty-five years is a Hell of a long 'Tucky, pal.'

'Well, like I said, it backfired,' said Angeles. 'How was I to know the Bishop of LA lived there?'

Scipioni stared at the Pope, his eyebrows jumping into a 'V' of shrewd suspicion as he scrutinised the Armani vestments. 'The Bishop of LA?' he muttered around the neck of his second Bud. 'Ohhhh, I get it,' his face creased into a conspirational grin. 'Backfired. So, where d'you bury him, eh, Gianelli?'

'What?'

'When it backfired,' he repeated, folding his fingers into a handgun. 'Where d'you hide him? Under one of the statues, was it? In the baptismal font? You can tell your old buddy.'

'No, you've got it all wrong. He didn't have a gun. I didn't . . .'

'Geez, I didn't know Bishops handled so much cash. I ain't stupid, I know these things ain't cheap.' He swept his arms around the interior of the helicopter. 'Damn clever that was. Wish I'd thought of it. Knock off the Bishop of LA, step into his shoes and inherit a flock that always gives generously.'

'No, no. This is real,' protested the Pope, tugging at the collar of his vestments. 'That's what I mean by it backfiring. He sold me on God.'

'Jesus . . .'

'Yeah, Him too. Well, at first it was either that or a quick call to LAPD. But, after a while I . . . well, I got to like it.'

'You're sayin' this Pope thing's real?' gulped Scipioni.

'That is exactly what I'm saying. Look,' he pulled open a mahogany drawer and tipped out a host of photographs. 'There's me taking my vows, see? Now, that's my first

114

church, little place in Vermont. That's me and the Arch-bishop at the Synod . . .'

'Whoa, whoa . . . now I get it,' said Scipioni, backing away from the table in the grip of sudden theophobia. 'Now you've come for me. Well, thanks for the beers, but no thanks. Count me out . . . See I got a million things I should be doin' right now. Er, movies don't just make themselves, y'know?'

'I know, I know,' nodded Angeles. 'Technicians to order about, special effects to rig, dollies to grip . . .'

'Sure . . . And that's not even the half of it. Believe me, unless you know what you're doin' it all gets so outta hand . . .'

'And that's precisely why I'm here,' smiled Angeles. With a flourish, he whisked a sheaf of papers off a shelf and slapped them into Scipioni's palms. 'Ever considered a change of artistic direction?'

The director looked at the title page, then looked up at the Pope, a smirk prowling around his face. 'This is some kind a joke, right? *Faith: The Final Frontier*? C'mon, you cannot be serious,' he spluttered. 'Nobody does Holies any more. No call for sequels, see? And Charlton Heston's too old. Besides, who wants to go see a movie that's over three hours long, sports a massive cast and you already know how it ends?'

'That's what they said about *Titanic*,' countered Angeles.

'Look, Franco, it's been great seein' you after all these years, but like I said, movies don't make themselves.' He handed the sheets of paper back and made a move towards the door of the helicopter.

'Well, if you aren't interested in an audience of ten billion . . .' began Angeles, taking back the draft screenplay.

'T . . . ten billion? Whoa, that's way up with *Baywatch*.'

'Almost unlimited budget. CGI . . .'

'CGI?' said Scipioni, one foot dangling out the door, his attention pinned and mounted by the three initials of modern cinema his budget just wouldn't stretch to. He'd already had to cut several of the more complex scenes and resigned himself to *Battlestar Galactica* lasers. But, with just a bit of CGI . . .

'Oh, yeah,' offered the Pope, waggling a vast technical carrot. 'You'll need the latest computer graphics kit to get the Four Horsemen of the Apocalypse looking just right and it'll make Sodom and Gomorrah a bit easier. I'm still not quite sure if we've got enough tech to get the Parting of the Red Sea looking spot on.'

Scipioni rubbed his chin thoughtfully. 'Let's see, now, you got the Four Horsemen, plagues, Partin' of the Red Sea, and that's just act one. Now a paintbox could handle that if you can wait for the full rendering of backgrounds and wire-frames. But, you're still gonna need a couple of parallel-ported Render-Benders for the real tricky stuff.'

'Not a problem,' smiled Angeles.

'Not a problem? You . . . you've got the budget for that?' he asked, with not a small hint of envy.

'Nope. We can go one better. We've got the kit,' offered the Pope proudly. 'Had it for years, apparently.'

Scipioni looked at the Pope. 'What does the Vatican want with CGI?'

'You promise not to tell?'

Scipioni nodded, trying to figure the answer.

Angeles leaned forward in his favourite chair. 'Papal addresses,' he whispered. 'You don't think I've really learned to speak thirty-five languages do you? I'll do the Italian and the English versions and all the others are done by translators behind the scenes. Then we do post-production lip-sync with CGI and send the videos all over the world. Easy. Well, now I've got something to tell the world, it should be. You in?'

'You've got a pair of parallel-ported Render-Benders just for that?' spluttered Scipioni.

'Don't get used enough, though,' sighed the Pope. 'Easter and Christmas is their main busy time. The rest of the year they just sit there. Doing . . . well . . . nothing.'

'Nothing,' whimpered Scipioni, imagining what he could do with a few hours on that kit. Half a day with the right technicians and he could have the most spectacular laser fire from Sophia's alien assault cannon. And maybe that alien sex scene he had to cut due to physical impracticalities of multi-tentacled sex . . . maybe that could be done in the digital domain. He was certain Sophia would be grateful for that.

'Nope, they're doing absolutely . . . nothing,' grinned the Pope, tugging the carrot again with an eager feeling of nostalgia.

Scipioni wiped his palms on the thighs of his trousers. 'Absolutely nothing?' he whined, saliva rising in his mouth at the thought of a digitally composited Sophia having it away with a black shiny-backed invader from Alpha Centauri. 'Er . . . Your Holiness, I was wondering if perhaps I could get my hands on . . . Er, look, this film . . . d'you need a director?'

The Pope grinned and tapped on a bulkhead. In seconds, Vatican 1's engine coughed into life and the rotors began spinning up to take-off speed.

'Look. You serious about an audience of ten billion?' asked Scipioni as the Swiss Guards pulled the door shut and the Sea King lurched into the air.

'Would I lie?' grinned Pope Angeles.

'That's what I thought,' nodded Scipioni and reached for his mobile phone. It would seem that his producer was about to get a sudden and unexpected promotion.

21:05 The Atlantic

A hundred and three nautical miles off America's eastern seaboard in the war room of the USS *Indiscriminate*, Rear-Admiral Rosenschmirtz pointed to a wall. Upon this wall, for the benefit of an extremely terrified Private Tyrone, a vastly enlarged projection of his screen was being displayed. He stood in his best approximation of full attention and began to get the distinct impression that he wasn't in here for his back to be patted.

'You remember this screen, huh, Private?' shouted Rear-Admiral Rosenschmirtz in his best hoarse-drill-sergeant voice.

'Sir, yes, sir,' answered Private Tyrone feeling pleased that he had remembered the correct way to answer. And sure enough the as yet unidentified Concorde flight BA 357A from Heathrow to New York slithered on to the bottom right-hand corner of the screen in a replay of the events from that morning.

'Our guys in Surveillance plucked this off the airways at eighteen three thirty this evening,' growled Rosenschmirtz.

'Get on with it,' barracked Major-General Gelding. 'Just court-martial him. Give us all a laugh.'

Suddenly an unidentified streak of alien technology zipped across the screen and vanished just off the south-west coast of Eire.

'Comments, Private?'

'Er . . . well, at first I thought it was a First Contact scenario but I sometimes get interference like that on satellite when there's too many sun-spots about.'

'Interference . . . hmmm. Shame the rest of the world didn't think it was interference. What about this, Private?' The Rear-Admiral flicked a switch on his remote and the screen changed. It showed a strangely familiar region of the Earth's surface with a similarly familiar selection of civilian aircraft cluttering the sky.

'Oh, sir, that's bad, sir. I can hardly read any of it now, sir.'

Rosenschmirtz reddened. 'Never seen Russian before, Private?'

An unidentified streak of alien technology zipped across the screen and vanished just off the south-west coast of Eire.

'Then what about Iranian, Private?'

The wall flicked to a screen labelled with squiggles of fluent Middle Eastern. It had an unnervingly familiar look to it. Even down to the streak of alien technology which flashed across it and disappeared off the coast of Eire.

'Still think it's sun-spots, Private? Still think you've got a job, Private?'

But, with Private Tyrone's future career progression within the US Marines dangling in the balance above a future of latrines, the door burst in and a marine flicked a swift salute.

'Sir, channel twelve, sir. I think there's something you should see.'

Rosenschmirtz jabbed the appropriate button. Almost instantly the wall flashed up images of the inside of Ground Control at JPL and framed two technicians in grainy black and white.

'Wayne? That you doin' that? Over,' asked Flight Co-ordinator Dwight D. Vecchio on screen as he watched the Hubble Space Telescope telemetry go haywire.

'Er . . . Hell no, Dwight. Thought it was you. Over,' came the crackled reply through the headphone feed.

'Now why would I be firing thrusters, Wayne? Over.'

'Bored maybe? Face it, Dwight, you ain't done much flight co-ordinatin' for the past few months,' answered Lieutenant Wayne T. Fishburne Jnr, in his distinctive Texan drawl, his quarter inch fuzz of military hair glistening under the artificial lights. 'Sittin' there, day after day, watchin' Hubble sittin' up there in geostationary. Hell, that ain't exactly excitin'. I'd understand if you flicked a little switch, just now. Over.'

'Wayne. It wasn't me. Over,' said Vecchio as his screen flashed red warning messages at him. Telling him things he really didn't want to know. Things like the fact that Hubble wasn't under their control any more. 'I didn't do it. Over.'

'Straight up? Over.'

'Straight up. Over.'

'Well, if *you* didn't do it and *I* didn't do it, then . . .'

Two figures leapt up from their stations at opposite ends of the ground control room. They looked at each other for a second, military meerkats on the brink of panic. Simultaneously, they slammed their palms on to their alarm buttons.

'Look at that!' said Major-General Hiram J. Gelding III around a thumb-thick Havana. 'That's military efficiency that is.'

'And what d'you call that?' hissed Isenheimer as the screen changed to show the position of the Hubble Space Telescope.

'My God,' choked Gelding. 'Three hundred clicks off course. What's goin' on? Why wasn't I informed? It's them goddamned Russians? Ain't it?' He exhaled two lungfuls of choking blue smoke at Isenheimer as if this was a new form of interrogatory procedure. 'Bound to be. Those commies have never forgiven us for tellin' the truth about Mir.'

'Referring to it as "a rusting tub not safe to keep a dead dog in", wasn't exactly the most diplomatic of statements,' said Isenheimer.

Major-General Gelding clenched his teeth tight around his cigar. 'So what're those Russians hijacking American space hardware for, huh?'

'Two theories,' offered the Head of Speculative Intelligence. 'Either they're trying to re-enact the waltzing space-station scene from *2001* . . .'

'Or?' growled Gelding, sending a cloud of partially combusted Havana to inhabit the same airspace as Isenheimer's head.

'Or they're looking at some as yet uncharted part of space. There. Look.' He pointed an awestricken finger at a large central video screen as image telemetry was assembled.

'What the Hell is that?' drawled Gelding, elequently capturing everyone's thoughts in five little words.

They all stared as something strange appeared around the edge of a black hole slap-bang in the middle of galaxy 3C390.3. It shimmered eerily at the edge of blackness; a distorted blob of light twisted by the equivalent of two hundred million suns. Slowly it rose, a feeble Mediterranean sun above an endless inchoate sea. It grew to a minuscule glowing comma and, almost before anyone had the chance to take it all in, it set again.

Gelding stared at the screen, the grip on his cigar the loosest it had been in decades as images of the Hacker–Tracker programme filled the wall and chased down the culprits.

'No, no, that can't be . . .' began Isenheimer, staring at the screen showing a map of the world. A small patch glowed on the kneecap of Italy. 'The . . . the hackers were in the Vatican!'

'I told you!' shouted Gelding joyously. 'You didn't believe they were dangerous. This just proves it! The Vatican is full of Russians!' He grabbed a radio off a handy clip and bellowed into it. 'F-18s scramble. Scramble!'

Much to Rear-Admiral Rosenschmirtz's irritation his crew obeyed. Along the full length of the USS *Indiscriminate* klaxons began to sound alarm stations, men in flight suits scurried in all directions and those whose job it was to

121

ensure the steam launch catapult was ready to hurl several million dollars' worth of Eagles into the Atlantic sky bit their fingernails and set to checking operating pressures.

21:12 The Vatican

A pair of cherubs stared down from a frescoed sky and were mighty pleased they weren't in Cardinal Holridge's shoes right then.

'No. N.O. Absolutely not!' insisted Cardinal Tardi.

'But how am I supposed to determine if the legend of St Naimhe is true . . . Oh, bless her hessian socks!'

'For the fifth time you cannot "borrow" Vatican 2.'

'But . . . but this is important. You think St Patrick's legendary ridding Ireland of snakes was innovative? Well I've got news for you, Naimhe of Kilfergus did it first. In A.D. 345, so the legend goes, she completely banished woodworm from the entire island she was living on. The island which now bears her name.'

'Woodworm?' frowned Tardi. 'What did she have against woodworm?'

'She considered them to be the very work of Satan himself since they were the only creature not to have been given a ticket by Noah. Stands to reason, doesn't it? I mean, ask yourself what was the ark made of, eh?'

'You can't have it,' said Tardi and continued with his paperwork.

But Holridge wasn't for turning. 'Naimhe's dying words took the form of a single solemn vow. A vow to return from her final resting place if ever her beloved island was plagued with woodworm again. Now if I can just find evidence that there are still no woodworm on St Naimhe's then . . .'

Suddenly he was cut off by the warbling of Tardi's telephone. 'Don't you have anything better to do?' asked the Papal Secretary, reaching for the receiver and glaring at Holridge. 'Something elsewhere?' he added. 'Hello? Ahhh, Your Holiness . . . A meeting, tomorrow morning. Er . . . yes I'm sure I can arrange . . . Everyone? Yes, Your Holiness.'

Fuming, and having run out of even the most far-fetched reason for getting his hands on Vatican 2, Cardinal Holridge finally got the message and trudged out of Tardi's office.

21:21 The Jet Propulsion Laboratory

The President of the United States of America blinked as the wallscreen he was looking at stopped showing images of the patch of space around the black hole in the centre of galaxy 3C390.3. A small comma-shaped star set into oblivion.

'Hmmm, pretty . . . but I don't see why that got you guys so excited. You didn't bring me all the way out here to JPL to show me that?'

Trembling with terror in a darkened corner Flight Coordinator Dwight D. Vecchio and Lieutenant Wayne T. Fishburne Jnr looked with wonder at their country's leader and knew why he was President. He was so astute.

'Er, no, sir,' answered Professor Olenburger, the Chief Science Officer for the Pentagon Advisory Committee Regarding Entities of a Non-Earth Origin. 'That's all we're releasing to anyone not in this room, sir. Look at this.'

He signalled to the folks in the projection booth and the screen sprang back into life.

'I've seen this already,' observed the President.

In the corner Dwight D. Vecchio sighed with admiration.

'Please continue to watch, sir,' said Professor Olenburger and almost instantaneously the screen filled with two shimmering craft from the far side of the universe as they unfolded from hypercorrugated morphospace.

123

'Oh, my God!' choked the President. 'They're not weather balloons, are they?'

'Wow!' whispered Vecchio. 'Sharp!'

'No, sir,' answered Professor Olenburger. 'And they're heading directly towards us.'

'They're coming here? Here? To Earth?'

'Yes, sir,' nodded the exobiologist.

'Oh, my God, we've got to get ready to welcome them to our planet,' flapped the President. 'We need bunting and ticker-tape and limousines. T-shirts, we need to get those printed up. God, how long have we got before they arrive?'

'Sir, that is the good news. The two craft have just entered our solar system and, at their current velocity, it will be three and a half weeks before they will require our hospitality.'

'Three and a half weeks? It's not long. Not long at all,' said the President and headed for the door of the viewing room, an overwhelming urge to get back to the White House and start painting the dome with a star map rising within him. At the door he stopped and turned back to the Professor. 'Er, this . . . information . . . Nobody else knows about it do they? No foreigners?'

'No, sir, absolutely not, sir. These walls are completely impenetrable to hostile ears.'

Unfortunately, their telephone system wasn't.

At that moment, in several of the more powerful countries around the globe, heads of state were grabbing caption writers from every advertising agency to come up with the most perfect greeting in time for their arrival. Something a little more twenty-first century than 'Hi there. Nice of you to drop in!'

Unfortunately, the arrival wasn't going to be twenty-four days away.

Out on the edge of the solar system, two ships shimmered into invisibility and, completely ignoring all the rules of physics known to modern man, overtook an awful lot of very miffed photons.

Fourteenth of April

03:43 The Vatican

In a small, artificially darkened room somewhere in the lower reaches of the Radio Vaticano building, an unfeasibly large amount of technology hummed to itself as it crunched an inordinately large quantity of seemingly random numbers.

Amazing himself at just quite how fast he was getting the hang of it all, Giorgio Scipioni commanded the parallel-ported Render-Benders to begin compositing surface textures on to the wire-frame models he had spent the early hours of the morning creating. He watched in rapt delight as a metallic skin congealed across the digital skeletons, turning them into three-dimensional entities before his very eyes. Grinning, he reached out towards the large ball set in the middle of the desk and rotated the images through a full three sixty, admiring every line with the pride of a dress designer weighing up a freshly togged supermodel on the catwalk. It was good, he knew it. Okay, not a patch on the stuff Industrial Light and Magic were knocking out, but hey, it *was* still early days. Now, once he ran it all through the Fractalising Engine and polished it with GizmoLight v 6.4 well, all that would be left is a bit of motion-capture movement simulation and Ezekiel himself wouldn't be able to distinguish his babies from the real thing.

Flexing his knuckles, he reached out towards the touch-screen, selected the Fractalising Engine from the menu and headed off towards a small booth in the back corner of the room.

Several minutes later he emerged wrestling with the zip of a strange black woollen jumpsuit. Reflective silver discs glinted at each of his major joints, reflecting the light from the screens of the parallel-ported Render-Benders humming behind him. With a final grunt of satisfaction, Scipioni tugged the hood up over his head and adjusted the dotted silver strip down the line of his centre parting.

'Ready for action,' he chuckled to himself and nonchalantly tweaked the angle of a small video camera perched on a tripod. An image of himself slewed into the centre of one of the screens and a message declared, 'Motion-Capture Movement Simulation Ready.' Instantly, the shiny metallic figure which he had created jerked into life and began matching every move he made.

Chuckling to himself, he watched as the computer-generated image waggled two fingers back at him, raised a single index finger and happily began exploring the inside of its right nostril. Grinning like a seven-year-old on Christmas morning he turned his back on the camera, folded his arms and began rubbing his hands up and down. On screen a shimmering golden statue writhed in delight and appeared to be in the grip of a passionate embrace.

In the instant he saw the gyrations of those golden hips, Giorgio Scipioni knew that he was looking at the tool that would give *Gazan Dolls* the essential ingredient it was currently lacking; the multi-tentacled alien sex scene with his pneumatically enhanced heroine, Commander Letitia D'Sighren of the Stiletto Corps.

Even as that thought rose in his mind, he began filling in the very details of it all. Helping his beloved Sophia into that skin-hugging woollen jumpsuit and . . . No, wait. For that essential added degree of accuracy he could dispense with any unnecessary layers of clothing. He rubbed his hands together in delight, his palms beginning to sweat as he imagined applying a host of small silver disks to the relevant portions of Sophia's exquisite anatomy.

And that was only the start. Once she was scanned into the Render-Benders he could have her do whatever his wildest fantasies could imagine. He could have her march into an alien hive, wearing nothing but a pair of holsters and a webbing belt, toting a pair of Uzis, safety catches removed . . . But why should digitised extraterrestrials have all the fun? What was to stop him joining in, taking her exquisitely pixelled waist firmly in his CGI'd arms and tangoing away across the universe? Eyes closed in rapt imagination, his arm shot out horizontally, his head flicked to the left and in moments he was stalking across the room in a crabwise tango of delight. A gold figure on the screen followed his every move.

'So you've discovered the motion-capture facility, I see?' observed Pope Joshua Angeles clicking the door shut behind him.

Scipioni froze in mid-step.

'Funny though, I don't remember there being a tango scene in the Bible,' said Angeles.

'Ahhhh . . . It's for Adam and Eve,' bluffed Scipioni, his right foot dangling eighteen inches above the floor.

'Hmmmmm, I see.'

'And I've got the perfect Eve in mind,' grinned Scipioni. Over his shoulder, a gold figure turned and walked towards the edge of the screen.

'Yes, well, I didn't come to discuss casting just yet. How long before we've got anything to show?'

'Ah well, I'm really just starting to get to grips with the cinematic intricacies of . . .'

'Let me rephrase that. The first screening is set for this morning at nine.'

'Nine?' gasped Scipioni. 'But . . . but there's so much left to do. I'll have to work non-stop, all night, without a break.'

'Oh, don't worry about that. You'll be fine,' smiled His Holiness.

'I . . . I will?' spluttered Scipioni. 'How can you be so sure I'll stay awake? Is it a message, from Him?' He pointed towards the ceiling.

'Nah. I'll send coffee,' grinned the Pope and ducked back out of the door.

On the screen the golden figure slumped and shook its head.

Ezekiel in CGI

It was exactly the type of place which camels would hike
miles to reach. Desert dunes rolled into the hazy horizon,
sweltering beneath a burning sky. Dromedaries of all
demeanours gathered expectantly, looking for charters as
ships of the desert. Bactrians stared out from beneath their
richly curling eyelashes and set imaginary courses across the
copper-coloured dunes. Lizards gasped, their tongues scraping the sand while green beetles toasted to a golden brown.

In short, it was a scene that would have made Luke
Skywalker homesick in seconds. A day much like any
other. Well, except for the sandstorm approaching from
the north.

Streaks of lightning flashed and zipped within as it
devoured the desert, humming wildly to itself as if driven
by a couple of Rolls-Royce Merlins. An aura of light
surrounded it, fixing the eyes of all who watched, nailing
their attention.

And, as it neared, details began to form within, betraying
the very source of the sandstorm as far from natural. Far
from normal. Four golden figures floated within the centre
of the maelstrom, each with four wings, each sparkling like
unearthly crystal. Each looking like the product of countless
millions of dollars of computer graphics engines.

And suddenly, blasting through a copper curtain of sand,

129

a quartet of gleaming discs erupted into full view. Around their edges were high rims dotted with eyes and sat atop them were shining figures each with four wings and each with highly decorated helmets.

The lead ship arced over and frisbeed through a petrified herd of camels, sending them spinning in all directions. Then it plunged through a sand dune, pulled a fifteen-G loop turn and ended up hovering twenty-five feet above the desert, staring down at the gathered audience. Oddly, the golden figure bore more than a passing resemblance to a certain director of less-than-historically-correct war movies.

'Son of Man,' it bellowed above the sound of straining antigravity engines. 'Stand up on your feet and I will talk to you.'

Suddenly, the lights came on around the tiny auditorium and the projected image faded.

'Well, what d'you think?' asked Pope Joshua Angeles, leaping up from his front-row seat and standing in front of the screen.

Cardinal Tardi was on his feet evincing total outrage. 'What in the the Name of All That's Holy was that?'

'Ezekiel, I believe,' offered Cardinal Holridge from the second row.

'Ezekiel? And since when has Ezekiel looked so . . . so Spielbergian!'

The Pope grinned and raised a covert thumb to a fawn-suited man in the corner who looked as though he had been up all night fiddling with computer-generated images. He had.

'And when has Ezekiel mentioned anything about camel tossing?' shouted Tardi.

'That, I believe, is called artistic licence,' offered Pope Angeles. 'Besides, the kids'll love it. Hmmm, maybe we could even CGI in a few more. What d'you say, Mr Scipioni?'

The man in the fawn safari suit shrugged wearily. 'Sure. I can even have the ship smash one of their skulls. Killing camels always goes down a storm, nobody likes camels.'

'Arabs do,' offered Cardinal Alighieri.

He was ignored.

'All right, all right. Apart from the camels,' began Pope Angeles again. 'What did you think of it all?'

'It's a complete outrage,' hissed Cardinal Tardi, adopting a stance not unlike that of a chief inspector after uncovering a child pornography ring. 'It's a good job it was confiscated when it was, who knows what damage that could have done to the more vulnerable of imaginations. Very sensible of you to bring it to our attention in this way, Your Holiness. After all, we can't allow just *anybody* to steal from our Bible and turn it into cinematic drivel.'

'Er, Cardinal Holridge, your opinion?' asked His Holiness.

'Where . . . where did it come from?' gasped the Head of the Congregation for Icon Authentication. 'It's all so . . . so . . . wow.'

'Factually correct?' asked the Pope.

'Er . . . well, apart from the guys on the spaceships sitting rather than standing, er . . . yes. But, where did it come from?'

'I made it!' announced Giorgio Scipioni, tapping his chest proudly.

'You!' snarled Tardi, his lip quivering as he stared at the fawn-suited film director. 'What possessed you to turn our beliefs into . . . into . . . ?'

Pope Angeles turned to Cardinal Tardi and fixed him with the type of hard stare it was difficult to ignore. 'Because I asked him to.'

'What?' shrieked Tardi, grabbing at the back of his chair to steady himself.

Angeles stood before the audience of Vatican luminaries,

his hands crossed in the small of his Gucci-upholstered back, feet slightly apart. 'Gentlemen, you have just been looking at the very genesis of the centrepiece of my first Easter address.'

Cardinal Alighieri jabbed Tardi in the ribs and nervously whispered, 'What's he on about? What's he talking about? You told me you had him sorted! "Nothing controversial," you promised! "Sex before marriage," you said.'

Tardi's molars gnashed together. He'd known that an American Pope would be a mistake. He'd told them all in the Sistine Chapel, but had they listened? Still, it was probably better than the Cuban.

'Gentlemen, it's time for a change!' declared Pope Angeles, the fire of evangelism shimmering in his eyes. 'Yes. The time has come for us to fight back.'

'Fight back? Er . . . against what?'

'Against a creeping menace which threatens to steal an entire generation of followers from under our very noses.'

'Buddhism?' said Tardi.

'Ecstasy?' suggested Alighieri.

'Nintendo?' offered Holridge.

'No, gentlemen, our fight must be directed against something more sinister, more deadly to our beliefs, something that has been stealing from us for decades. Dear brethren, our enemy is . . . science fiction!' declared Pope Angeles, striking a pose of exquisite evangelism.

Cardinal Tardi raised his hands in despair. 'No, no, no. We fight sin and evil. You know, Satan? Remember him? He's the important one, not . . . not aliens.'

'Are you really sure about that?' challenged the Pope. 'It's a fact that more teenagers believe in the existence of extraterrestrials than believe in God.'

'Oh, come now. How can that possibly . . . ?' began Tardi.

'How? Because they see them every night on cable, that's

how,' interrupted Scipioni. 'They believe because they can see! In Wide-screen, Technicolor, Loudsound and Director's Cut!'

'And that belief runs deep,' continued the Pope. 'Driving them on pilgrimages across the world, seeking out apostles and icons . . .'

'Never heard of conventions?' insisted Scipioni.

'Thirty thousand people turned up on Hollywood Boulevard just to see a dinosaur leave its footprint in the sidewalk,' added Angeles.

'But what's that . . . that snippit of Ezekiel we've just seen got to do with any of this?' struggled Holridge, trying to tie the pieces of the jigsaw together.

'That, my dear Holridge, is the newest weapon in our Holy War,' declared Pope Angeles.

Tardi stared intently at the Supreme Pontiff and shook his head in utter confusion. In the three short days he had been Head of the Roman Catholic Church, Joshua Angeles had suggested some strange things to him. The Gospel on CD-Rom, the New Testment Chat-Line, signing up Ice-T to mix the rapBible on CD. Those he had successfully nipped in the bud. But this . . . ? Nothing had prepared Tardi for this latest news.

'Right now we're getting the Word of God to pygmies in Brazil,' continued the Pope, 'to untutored herdsmen in the wastes of Mongolia, to the nomadic tribes in the Negev Desert. But there's still millions we're missing. We aren't getting to the Paramount pilgrims, the worshippers of Warner Bros, the Buena Vista brethren. You follow?'

Cardinal Tardi shook his head.

'Well then, observe,' declared the Pope flicking a switch on the TV remote in his hand. With the briefest hiss of hydraulics a 42-inch Sony LCD TV swung out from behind the projection screen. He punched a password into an ergonomic keyboard which appeared from a drawer in the lectern.

The LCD screen flashed into life welcoming them all to Vaticanet. Angeles bashed out a few more commands and in seconds the screen was filled with the type of graphical representation a million marketing managers would kill to get their hands on. Two shimmering curves seemed to float in 3D above a gently rippling turquoise background.

'Pretty,' observed Scipioni. 'Got "Sonic the Hedgehog" on that? Or "SimMaggedon 2000"? . . . oh, er, I guess you wouldn't like that one.'

The Pope frowned briefly and ignored him. '*This* is a line showing the average congregational attendance at Sunday masses since 1977.' Angeles thumbed his keyboard and a rapidly decending ski slope flashed red and black. 'Now this is the average cinema attendance over the same period.' A blue and gold line sky-rocketed towards the top of the screen. 'You see, gentlemen? In short, we're losing people to the movies.'

A couple of crimson birettas nodded comprehension.

'Good. So name the most successful movies of all time,' challenged Pope Angeles.

'Er . . . *Gone With the Wind*?' answered Holridge.
Scipioni winced.

The Pope shook his head and gestured upwards. 'Higher?'

'*Alien 5: This Time It's Really Wipe-Out* has just over-taken *ET II: The Second Coming*,' answered Scipioni triumphantly. '*Cutesie's Return* grossed fifty million dollars in the first weekend!'

'Don't tell me this is all to do with money?' sneered Tardi.

'Course not,' countered Scipioni. 'He's talkin' about bums on seats. Millions of people pour into the movies every day. Now why do they do that?'

'Er . . . Popcorn?' spluttered Tardi who, despite the in-sistently throbbing blue and gold line soaring skyward on the screen, was really losing track of where the Pope was going with this.

'Geez, you really ought to get out more. They go to be entertained. You know, damn fine story lines. Good versus evil, armed with lasers and explosions courtesy of Industrial Light and Magic!'

'Gentlemen, it's time we took the Word of God to the cinema,' preached the Pope.

'What, with leaflets and tambourines?' asked Alighieri.

'With 80mm surround sound and CGI,' announced Angeles, sounding more presidential as the minutes went by. 'We go 3D if we have to. Look, science fiction's been stealing all our best ideas for long enough. It's time we fought back.'

'I'm sorry, you've really lost me there,' confessed Holridge. 'Best ideas?'

The Supreme Pontiff was on his question in a second, pulling it down like a cheetah on a chihuahua. 'Who came down from the Heavens in a blaze of glory, "died" and rose again before being taken back in a halo of light?'

'That's a bit obvious isn't it. Jesus.'

'Yeah. And?'

'And no one.'

'ET!' declared the Pope.

Cardinal Holridge was stunned. He ran through the story quickly in his mind and, despite some odd things with kids on flying bicycles, he had to admit there was a nub of truth there.

'And there's more,' continued Angeles. '*Star Wars*. Luke Skywalker. Luke. Third Gospel according to . . . And let's not go forgetting *Star Trek*. Captain Kirk. Kirk, church! You seein' this? *We* had all the ideas first.'

'And what about, "To boldly go where no one has gone before"?' suggested Scipioni.

135

'Didn't Moses say that?'

Suddenly Tardi cleared his throat and, clutching his chin as if in deep thought, asked, 'Er, I really don't want to wreck this entire scheme, Your Holiness, but, isn't there a teensy problem here? What is it exactly you are proposing to fight back with?'

'That's what you've just been watching,' said the Pope, waving a Gucci-upholstered arm towards the screen. 'Ezekiel!'

'It's a bit short to get the entire message of God across, isn't it?'

'Hey, there's only so much one guy can do in one night, all right?' said Scipioni, frowning at the Papal Secretary.

'Gentlemen, the snippit of Ezekiel you have just witnessed is just the start of *Faith: The Final Frontier*. And that's what my first Easter address is going to announce. Mr Scipioni assures me that he will have a full ninety-second trailer ready for broadcast to the world on Easter Sunday.'

The gathered audience of Cardinals leapt to their feet, shouting in either rapturous delight at such an innovative and interesting idea, or in utter damnation of the entire scheme.

'Gentlemen, gentlemen, please, please,' soothed Angeles, laying his hands over the boiling sea of debate filling the plush theatre. 'It seems there is a touch of disagreement here. I suggest that you go away and think on what you have seen and heard. We shall reconvene here at two this afternoon and put my ideas to a vote. If you are in favour we go ahead and set about winning back a generation of youth who, if we are not careful, will be lost to *The X Files* and *Star Trek* and a whole lot more.'

'A vote? But, Your Holiness . . .' began Tardi.

The Pope raised a beringed hand, silencing him in the aisle.

'Until this afternoon, gentlemen,' he declared, leaping off

the stage and breezing out of the theatre in a flurry of Gucci vestments.

'A vote,' cringed Cardinal Tardi as the door clicked shut. 'What does he think the Vatican is? A democracy?'

Alighieri tutted sympathetically.

'I warned them about Americans, I did,' insisted Tardi, heading towards the exit shaking his head.

09:32 The Vatican

Under the unblinking gaze of a pair of cavorting cherubs, Cardinal Tardi burst into his office, closely followed by Cardinal Alighieri.

'What's got into him? "Our enemy is science fiction"!' snarled Tardi, kicking his Clarice Cliff Bizarreware waste-paper basket across the floor. It hit the far wall and exploded in a very expensive eruption of pottery flowers. 'Have you ever heard anything so ridiculous? Have you?'

'Well, I must admit . . .'

'What does he think he's playing at? *Faith: The Final Frontier*? He's mad. Mad! I'm, telling you, we'll be the laughing stock of the world's religions!' wailed the Papal Secretary. 'You don't see the Jews, or the Buddhists going for such gimmicks, do you? Never see the Hindus resorting to such cheap . . .'

'Er, actually, if I recall it right, I think the Mormons tried something similar a few years back,' offered Alighieri.

'What? Are you sure?'

'Yeah, The Osmonds. D'you remember them? Donny and Marie and Little Jimmy . . .'

'Oh, God! That's it, we've got to stop him!' gasped Cardinal Tardi as the strains of 'Puppy Love' began baying in the back of his mind. 'I must be losing my touch. Three Popes never got anything past me that I didn't want and now in days this guy comes up with the most radical idea to hit the Roman Catholic Church in decades. It can't happen. I can't let it. It'll ruin my reputation.'

'But how? What can we do? You know as well as I that a papal decision cannot possibly be overturned. It's the rules. What he says goes,' panicked Alighieri as several choruses of 'Crazy Horses' stampeded around the inside of his brain, whinnying in a most distracting manner. 'Once he's made his mind up it's law within the week. We're doomed!'

Tardi crunched his heel angrily on one of the larger fragments of his shattered 1931 waste-paper basket and hung his head in despair. But only for a moment. 'Doomed? Not necessarily.' A glimmer of inspiration tugged at Tardi's eyebrows.

' . . . ? . . .' said Alighieri.

'This is one decision where he *doesn't* make his mind up,' explained Tardi under his breath, ideas congealing in his head. 'I heard him. You heard him. *We* decide! Us! Now, paper!'

The Papal Secretary pulled out a handy sheet of Basildon Bond and began scribbling names under two columns. In a surprisingly short time he was standing back surveying the list.

'No! No! I don't believe it!' he hissed and counted up again. 'Twenty-seven for, twenty-six against!'

'Are you sure?'

'Oh yes. I saw who was nodding back there,' insisted Tardi, his brow furrowing as he recalled the inside of the auditorium with photographic accuracy. 'One vote short. We're doomed . . . unless . . .' He stared hard again at the list of Cardinals and grinned a grin that could freeze helium in seconds. 'Oh yes. Yes indeed. Beware the sword of democracy for it cuts both ways!' He declared as he leapt to his feet and headed out of the room.

'Sword of democracy?' called Alighieri around the slamming door. 'Shouldn't that be Damocles?'

09:35 The Vatican

A lipless grin reflected in the shiny melamine of the laboratory workbench of the Congregation for Icon Authentication as a long-dead skull was clamped securely into a carefully padded vice.

'Careful, careful. Not *too* tight,' reminded Kotonawa as Cardinal Holridge wound angrily at the steel handle. 'We don't want to crack it. It wouldn't be a fair test then, would it?'

'Fair test?' asked Holridge, shaking his head.

'Of course. I don't think the Archangel Michael was in the habit of carrying vices around with him.'

'Hmmm, suppose not,' mumbled Holridge, staring at the skull which bore an uncanny resemblance to a certain Papal Secretary.

'You seem a little distracted. Do you want me to do it?' offered Kotonawa, reaching for the Bosch drill already fitted with its 12mm trepanning bit.

'No, no,' tutted Holridge snatching the green power tool from his Japanese lab manager. 'Head of Department's privilege,' he added and squeezed the switch. The Bosch growled contentedly. 'I don't think we need hammer action, do we?'

'Well, I wouldn't know. I've never been on the receiving end of an archangel's index finger. Or any other miracle for that matter.'

Holridge ignored him, approached the aged skull clamped in the vice and, his mind filling with Tardi's stubborn refusal to loan him Vatican 2, he pulled down his goggles and advanced.

'You feeling all right?' asked Kotonawa as a lick of a grin twitched at Holridge's mouth.

'Ohhhh, yes,' whispered the Cardinal, flicking the power switch with the impatient relish of Damon Hill on pole position. Spreading his feet, he grasped the drill tightly and, with the air of a maniac brain surgeon, fired up the Bosch. In seconds, fragments of skull were scattering in all directions as he bored through the right parietal lobe.

'Done,' he announced a few moment later and stepped back in a strangely relaxed manner. Appraising the punctured skull with critical eyes, he compared it to the far older cranium standing patiently on another bench. 'Two long deceased skulls, two identically placed holes. What is wrong with this picture?'

'Apart from the fact that the eighth-century skull belonging to St Aubert is mounted on a rather tasteful gold-wired pedestal and this other's in a metalworking vice, you mean?'

'Of course,' tutted Holridge and placed the drill back on the bench.

'The holes are completely different shapes.'

'But does that prove, as is commonly believed, that this hole in St Aubert's skull here was made by the index finger of the Archangel Michael in order to remind him to go off and build Mont St Michel?'

'Well, it certainly proves it wasn't done by a Bosch and a 12mm trepanning bit.'

'Pass me that hammer,' ordered Cardinal Holridge, picking up a cast iron replica of an index finger. Kotonawa obliged and Holridge once again approached the skull in the vice, carefully positioning the tip of the finger against the bone of the left parietal lobe. One swift blow left the skull as destroyed as a chocolate egg on Easter morning. 'Hmmm, the Miracle of St Aubert, Bishop of Avranches, two, modern science, nil.'

'The French Tourist Board will be pleased,' observed Kotonawa.

Before Holridge had a chance to launch into a lecture on the pros and cons of using sights of ancient religious significance to sell plaster gargoyles and a variety of crêpes, the door burst open and Cardinal Tardi swept into the lab. He cast a brief glance at the shattered remains of a long-dead skull. 'Bad morning?'

'Average,' answered Holridge warily.

'Well, it's about to get a lot better,' announced the Papal Secretary, forcing a smile. 'About your proposal of last night, well, I've been thinking about it and I may have answered in the negative a little too hastily.'

'Meaning?'

'The body of research currently gathered regarding the status of the modern miracle is sadly thin.'

'Is that a criticism?'

'No, no. Ha, of *course* not. It is merely a reflection of the difficulty you have in securing transport for your studies,' oozed Tardi. 'Cardinal, how would you like a little trip to St Naimhe's?'

'What? Really?' squeaked Holridge, looking as expectant as a beagle in the butcher's.

'Do you need any other equipment than what is in this bag of yours?' asked Tardi, grabbing a large black case from under the bench.

Holridge was taken aback. 'Well, no, I don't think . . .'

'Then come with me,' he urged, snatching Holridge around the shoulders and sweeping him towards the door. 'We mustn't keep them waiting.'

'Keep who waiting?'

'Why, Vatican 2, of course,' answered Cardinal Tardi, his voice echoing out of earshot down the corridor.

Cardinal Kotonawa stood in the centre of the lab, his

jaw sagging with amazement, not believing his ears.

It took Tardi the best part of five minutes to half push, half drag the bewildered Cardinal Holridge through the Vatican gardens and on to the helipad. Barely stopping for breath, he swung Holridge's black case in through the door of the idling Sea King and pushed the clerical scientist after it.

'Bon voyage!' he shouted above the roar of engines and grabbed at the handle of the door.

'No, wait!' yelled Holridge as he picked himself up off the carpeted floor. 'I . . . I can't go. Not now!'

'Nonsense, of course you can. You're already on board. The helicopter's fuelled.'

'Yes, but the Pope. He needs me for the vote this afternoon!'

'He won't mind. Believe me he can be very forgiving,' insisted Tardi, both hands sliding the heavy door shut.

'Wait, wait!' cried Holridge, rummaging inside the pocket of his lab vestments and grabbing at a piece of paper. 'Give him this. It's a few notes on why I think he should go ahead and make *Faith: The Final Frontier*. If I sign it will it count as a postal vote?'

'Now that's an *excellent* idea.'

Holridge smiled, leaned against the back of a suitable Swiss Guard and scrawled an incomprehensible signature on the sheet, registering a resounding 'Yes' vote well ahead of the close of polling.

Tardi grabbed the paper, swung the door shut and leapt away from the gleaming white Sikorsky, whirling a definitive finger above his head. The pilot revved the engines and, in an eruption of leaves and dust, Vatican 2 clambered laboriously into the Roman sky and hopped over a distant wall.

Smiling contentedly to himself, Cardinal Tardi screwed

142

the sheet of paper into a tight ball and flicked it into the depths of a suitable rhododendron.

13:23 The Atlantic

One hundred and twenty miles off the west coast of Eire an example of state-of-the-art Eastern Bloc sonar pinged into the grey nothingness of the Atlantic. The pulse scattered in all directions, irritated a few dolphins, got right up the noses of a couple of courting sperm whales and, without warning, hit metal. In seconds it was wriggling its way back through the chilly waters, joyously ready to announce that an enemy vessel had been detected.

'Enemy vessel detected,' announced the subtitles below the angular features of the Russian marine at the sonar screen.

'Bearing?' snapped back the terse script of a man with an awful lot of stripes on his shoulder.

'127, heading 075. Twelve knots.'

The one in charge turned to a chart, pulled out a handy protractor, a pair of dividers and a long ruler with silhouettes of American destroyers on. In moments he had drawn a line straight towards a tiny island four and a half miles off the south-west coast of Eire. He smoothed his beard and turned on a youth with bulging headphones. 'Sonar ID?' demanded his subtitles.

'USS *Indiscriminate*.'

'Helm, one hundred and twenty metres and hold.'

'*Da, da*,' said the helmsman and, just to make things that little more difficult to see, he flicked all the lights to red.

Forward stabilisers dipped ten degrees and, displaying all the grace of an overgrown elephant seal, the SS *Denisovitch* slipped off silently towards a depth of one hundred and twenty metres.

Twenty-two thousand three hundred miles above, a final flare of manoeuvring thrusters settled a highly secret lump of space hardware into a nice new geostationary position. Precision stepper-motors wound infra-red and thermal imaging cameras a few degrees to the left and pulled focus. Cloud-piercing lasers flashed out of tiny orifices and, in a matter of seconds, the top secret military satellite was cheerily gathering data, bundling it up into heavily coded packages and hurling it back to Earth with consummate digital efficiency.

Two hundred and forty-seven miles due west of a clot of tourists buzzing around the terracotta army of Xian, a youth of the Chinese intelligence service watched as the first gobbet of data was decoded and flung on to his screen. He shovelled a last mouthful of prawn-fried noodles into his mouth, wiped it with the back of his hand and squinted at the cluster of flares before him. In a second he had identified and dismissed four innocent international transatlantic flights. Moments later he was chuckling to himself as a flotilla of Spanish trawlers were rounded up by a British coastguard frigate and escorted out of Cornish waters.

And then, after flicking to the decoding package, he found what he was really looking for. Nonchalantly steaming like the clappers towards the south-west coast of Eire was the unmistakable trace of the USS *Indiscriminate*. Almost directly north of it, at a depth of a good hundred metres or so, was the shady figure of Soviet Submarine *Denisovitch* and, masquerading in the unlikely guise of flight IA 666 to New York, an aging Iranian MIG spy-plane circled at thirty-nine thousand feet.

The youth of the Chinese intelligence service praised his good fortune at having such fine equipment to work with, resettled his cap on his head and, pausing only to hide his noodle bowl, he pressed the alarm button.

144

Halfway across the world, deep in the bowels of the USS *Indiscriminate*, a marine leapt to attention and only barely missed knocking himself senseless on an awkwardly sited bulkhead.

'Sir, Chinese Geostat is online. Expect Heightened Oriental Alert Status in five . . . four . . .' A pale-green satellite-shaped cursor hovered in the midst of the cluttered trans-atlantic air routes. It flicked to red and, just to get its message across, started flashing 'Three . . . Goddamn it, sir. Guess they've upgraded their software. Heightened Oriental Alert Status achieved. The Inscrutables are watch-ing.'

'Some party this is turning out to be,' mused Rear-Admiral Rosenschmirtz, his eyes roving across the fields of informa-tion technology arrayed before him. Casually, he watched the Iranian MIG trying desperately to conceal itself behind a handy cloudbank whilst the Russian sub strafed the area with radar emissions and tried to pretend it was in fact a large blue whale Hellbent on beaching itself on the coast of a small island called St Naimhe's.

But even though Rosenschmirtz had all the technology he needed to see through any disguise the enemy chose to hide behind, hack into the Civil Aviation Authority database and interrogate every coastguard within a thousand miles, there was one small spot of worry on his mind. And it was heading almost due west, losing height on a final approach vector.

'What *is* that?' hissed the Rear-Admiral, stabbing a finger at a large screen.

'Speed, height and trajectory would seem to indicate a helicopter, sir.'

'Japs coming to join the party?' interrupted Major-General Gelding around a vast Havana.

'No need, sir. They've got the Chinese satellite bugged, sir.'

'Then who could it possibly . . . ? Oh God, no,' panicked Gelding suddenly biting his cigar.

'Jesus. Arm warheads and lock on. Be prepared to blow them out of the sky on my mark.'

'Ahem. *My* mark,' reminded Rosenschmirtz. 'I'm the Rear-Admiral.'

'Sir?' asked the marine at the alarm station. Rosenschmirtz nodded and a klaxon blasted dramatically into life, resonating hoarsely throughout the ship.

'So who is it?' challenged Rosenschmirtz. 'Iraqis?'

'Worse,' spat Gelding. 'CNN. Our President paid good money for us to be out here, I'm not having civilians getting in the way, stealing our thunder and . . . Hey, who turned the alert off?'

'You can't just blast civilians out of the sky!'

'They're no civilians,' growled Gelding. 'They're parasites, scum of the Earth, the scrapings of . . .'

'Sir, they're not CNN, sir,' offered a promotion-hungry marine. 'We have visual coming in from the F-18s and, well, sir, the helicopter's the wrong colour.'

The marine tapped a computer keyboard and the screen filled with a gleaming white Sikorsky Sea King whacking low over a medium Atlantic swell.

'What the Hell?' spat Gelding past his harassed cigar. 'It's the God Squad. That's Vatican 2!'

At that very instant, the Iranians, Russians and Chinese observers realised exactly the same thing. The rest of the world was only moments behind.

13.25 St Naimhe's

Charred oak beams lay across the heaps of charcoal that had once been ancient pews. Puddles of congealed stained glass lurked below windowframes, set into the type of psychedelic

146

paperweights Caithness Glass would kill for. And through the gently smouldering wreckage of the Chapel of St Tib's, Father Fintan O'Suilleabhain picked his way carefully, a makeshift broom of suitable branches in his hands.

Grunting with the effort, he hefted a vast trunk of rafter out of the way and piled it with the others in the corner. Already he'd worked out that if there were enough of them intact he could rebuild some of the pews. Okay, so they'd need about ten coats of paint to hide the scorchmarks but it *could* work. Maybe.

If only he could be so sure about what to do with the fifty-foot hole in the middle of the aisle. Now, if he were just to fill it with water, it could be a giggle come the next baptism. Hmmmmm, maybe not. Perhaps this was his chance to actually fulfil a long-term dream and start a terrapin farm? Nah. What about floating a small-scale model of Noah's Ark on it? Or maybe . . .

Suddenly his thoughts were shattered as a cloud of dust erupted behind him and swirled into a wild whirlwind. 'Oh no, not again,' whimpered Father Fintan as the air above St Naimhe's was shredded by something immensely heavy trying to float. Snowstorms of mangled hymnals were whipped up and blizzarded towards total whiteout.

Fintan dived behind the blackened remains of an up-turned pew as a Sea-King-shaped shadow drifted over the chapel and slowed to a hover.

'Oh God,' whispered Fintan. 'He's here. Tardi's come for me!'

As if in confirmation, two ropes dropped into the aisle and a pair of gaudily uniformed Swiss Guards abseiled out of the sky, their pikes tucked under their armpits.

'No, no. Excommunication for sure!'

In seconds the guards had stationed themselves either side of the hole and Vatican 2 was sliding away over the nave to settle itself carefully on to the graveyard.

'Bell, book and candle! No, I don't want to be a civilian!'

On a cloud of swirling dust that would have completed any Spaghetti Western entrance, Cardinal Holridge skittered to a halt in the main archway. With his lab vestments flapping theatrically around his knees he paused for a moment, raised his wrist and briefly wound his Timex back an hour. It was obsessive, he knew, but somehow he never actually felt part of the landscape unless his watch was showing the correct local time. It was all something to do with a near-terminal attack of jet-lag brought on by flying from Beijing to Rio and then on to Moscow in the space of one day. He was sure he'd lost more than his hand luggage that day. Five hours of his life had vanished, too. Somewhere.

Happy now that his feet were planted firmly on *tempus firma*, he pulled out a large magnifying glass and peered at the large expanse of oak next to him. 'Hmmm, no sign of woodworm holes here,' he muttered to himself as he examined the ancient wooden door slouching from its hinges. 'Right that's that done. Now to business.'

'Er, is this what you're looking for?' asked one of the Swiss Guards, waggling his pike helpfully towards the fifty-foot chasm.

'Too right,' grinned Holridge and hurried up the aisle towards the trembling priest huddling behind the blackened pew.

For Fintan it was too much. He knew it was better to come clean, turn himself in, it would be easier. At least that's what they always said on TV.

'Look, it wasn't me. I didn't do it. My poteen still wasn't even on. Honest. It just fell out of the sky,' babbled Fintan, emerging in a cloud of dust from behind the pew, hands high. 'In fact, I wasn't even here at the time.'

'And you are?'

'Father Fintan O'Suilleabhain, priest of the Chapel of . . .' he stopped and looked around him. 'Well, I was. Look, this isn't my fault. Would I lie?' he pleaded.

'Fell out of the sky, eh?' mused Cardinal Holridge, his gaze fixed on the hole where the aisle used to be.

'Yes, yes. I just turned around and all of a sudden it just hit the roof and . . . well, this happened. It wasn't me. Honest.'

Holridge turned to one of the Guards. 'Bring the rope,' he ordered.

'Rope?' spluttered Fintan, watching as the Guard double-timed it out of the chapel. 'You won't need that. I'll come quietly.' He held out his wrists like a forlorn criminal caught in the act.

Holridge clicked open his black case, tugged out a bright orange climbing harness and began struggling into it. Baffled, Fintan watched as the Swiss Guard returned with a tightly coiled rope and began lashing it around the scorched baptismal font.

'You're not going down there?' gasped Fintan.

'And why not?' smiled Holridge, excitedly screwing closed the gates of his carabiners.

'Why not? Haven't you seen *War of the Worlds* or *Invaders from Mars* or *The Day The Earth Stood Still* or *Them!*?'

'Yes.'

'Well then . . .' Fintan looked towards the glowing hole. 'First one down there never comes out.'

'Nonsense,' tutted Holridge completing his final harness check. 'Besides, *The Day The Earth Stood Still* is the one with that big shiny robot. Nobody goes anywhere near any holes.' He switched on his helmet lamp and, his pockets stuffed with a variety of scientific-looking tools, he disappeared backwards down the hole.

'Nobody goes down any holes in *War of the Worlds* either,' offered the larger of the Swiss Guards paying out the rope. 'The Martians come out of that spaceship, you know, the one with the screw lid.'

'Ja, and no one goes down holes in *Them!* . . .' began the other guard before his colleague turned on him.

'Course they do. That's the one with the ants.'

Forty-eight feet below, Cardinal Holridge was descending jerkily into the depths of the crater, slabs of virgin basalt sliding past his nose.

'Are you there yet?' shouted Father Fintan, his voice echoing in the gloom.

'Another couple of feet,' he gasped from breathless lungs.

'What? Can't hear you.'

'Two feet!' he yelled.

And then, much to the acute relief of the more vertiginously challenged side of his psyche, his toes touched down.

'What can you see?' shouted Father Fintan down the hole, straining his eyes to see what was being picked out by Holridge's helmet lamp.

The voice from below sounded distant and not a little shaky. 'Well, there's something hard that looks like met—'

Suddenly Holridge's voice was replaced by a muffled but insistent warbling.

Fintan took a breath. 'What is it? What's that noise? Get out of there!' he warned, knowing for certain that warbling noises heard in the proximity of recently grounded spacecraft meant only one thing: a messy and sticky end at the tentacles of a compound-eyed beast from beyond the stars.

He peered over the lip of the chasm, heart in his mouth, focusing on the tiny spot of lamplight.

'I warned him. You heard me warn him!' panicked Fintan over the shrill warbling of high technology.

Unconcerned by the priest's mounting alarm fifty feet above his head, Holridge tugged his portable Motorola out of his inside pocket. 'Hello? Ahhhh, Kotonawa, good to hear from you . . .'

Halfway across Europe, Cardinal Kotonawa sketched the larval stage of the furniture beetle *Anobium punctatum* on a scrap of paper. 'Well, any sign of woodworm there?'

'Bit difficult to tell after the fire.'

'Fire?' coughed Kotonawa, sitting up and dropping his pen. 'Is that how St Naimhe gets rid of woodworm?'

'This isn't anything to do with her,' chuckled Holridge.

'And what Earth-shattering observation leads you to that conclusion?'

'Well, apart from the fact that I'm currently fifty feet below the central aisle of St Tib's in a hole carved out of solid basalt and there aren't any pneumatic drills kicking about, there's this. Listen.' The thin tinkle of sound which came out of Kotonawa's earpiece really didn't do the hollow metallic boom the sonic justice it so richly deserved. 'Did you get that? Shall I hit it again?' asked Holridge, ten pounds of virgin basalt in his mitt. 'I'm telling you, you don't get resonance like that just anywhere, now do you? And it's so shiny,' he enthused, seeming to have forgotten entirely about phobias beginning with 'c' and small dark holes. 'And . . . oooh, now would you look at that!'

There was the unmistakable sound of fingers brushing rubble off a large metallic object of extreme shininess. 'Wooooow.'

'What is it?'

'It's amazing . . . Utterly incredible . . . I'll call you back. Bye.' With a small click, the phone went dead.

Cardinal Kotonawa wasn't the only one who growled as the connection was cut. Deep in a small room in the bowels of the Radio Vaticano building, Cardinal Alighieri muttered an ancient Italian curse or three and began rewinding a cassette. This, he was certain, Tardi would be most interested to hear. He grabbed the cassette, glanced at his watch and hurried out of the room towards a two o'clock meeting with the Pope.

In the bottom of the fifty-foot hole, Holridge was angling his helmet lamp and staring at a foot-long lozenge of metal which had somehow become detached from its rivets. It shone with the polished pride normally only seen on the gleaming belts of world champion boxers. But this was no WBC prize for pugilism. This was worlds away from that. Galaxies, in fact. He stared at the etchings on its surface, devouring every detail. A fine tracery of intergalactic cartography glistened in diamond-laser clarity. A ring of unrecognisable script snaked around the edge looking like something from a seventies Yes album. But the image that held his eyes tighter than Kaa ever held Mowgli was in the centre of the gleaming trophy.

Two vaguely humanoid figures stood outlined in embarrasingly frank detail. Naked as the day they hatched, holding tentacles delicately, pointing wistfully to a highlighted star, first left after the Pleiades and straight on till morning.

13:42 The Vatican

'Oooh, now would you look at that!'

A state-of-the-art Sony surveillance tape-recorder confidently reproduced the unmistakable sound of fingers brushing rubble off a large metallic object of extreme shininess.

'Wooooow.'

'What is it?'

'It's amazing . . . Utterly incredible . . . I'll call you back. Bye.'

For a few seconds the Sony hissed professionally on the Battle Bridge of the USS *Indiscriminate* before Isenheimer's finger switched it off.

'And that's it?' mumbled Major-General Gelding around a thumb-thick Havana.

'Every word,' answered the Head of Speculative Intelligence in his best David McCallum voice.

'Damn them, what are they up to?' growled the Major-General, staring at the disappointingly uninformative pictures which the F-18s had radioed back. So far he had at his fingertips a total of four facts. One – something unidentified had caused something strange to happen on the transatlantic radar systems. Two – a small chapel was now missing a roof and the vast majority of its insides. Three – the Vatican was involved. And four – quite simply he had to get closer.

'Where are those maps?' he shouted around his cigar. 'Bring me the maps of that island!'

Rear-Admiral Rosenschmirtz nodded wearily. There was a brief rustling of paper and a vast expanse of extremely detailed ordnance appeared on the photo-strewn table. Gelding leaned forward, the palms of his hands in the blue of the Atlantic, his jaw working away at his Havana.

Suddenly his index finger whistled out of the sky and landed on a small cove to the south of the island. 'We go ashore there,' he growled.

Nervously, an ordnance marine looked to Rosenschmirtz.

'Yeah, yeah. Whatever,' muttered the Rear-Admiral, playing with his Village People moustache moodily.

The marine cleared his throat. 'Sir, I don't think we can, sir.'

'What?' roared Gelding, wheeling on the marine. 'Of course we can go ashore there. We are Americans, we can land a seaborne squad anywhere we choose. No geographical feature can stand in our way. Is that clear?'

The marine nodded. 'Sir, yes, sir. But . . . that island, sir. It's Vatican territory, sir. We've got to be invited to invade.'

'Shitshitshit! Goddamit,' shouted Gelding, slamming his fist on to the map and causing Rosenschmirtz no end of delight.

153

Complete silence filled the Battle Bridge for a few endless seconds as the Major-General's cheeks reddened dangerously.

'There is another way,' offered Isenheimer and whispered in Gelding's ear.

Suddenly the Major-General straightened up, smoothed down the front of his tunic, took a long hard drag on his cigar and declared, 'Who said anything about invading, hmmm? We're just going to watch. American observers. Break out two landing craft immediately. Have them ready to launch in two minutes!'

A flock of marines scattered in all directions, snatching at communications devices and barking orders into them.

14:03 The Vatican

The expectant murmur of a collection of Cardinals rose in the well-appointed lecture theatre as they awaited their chance to vote on the subject of the papal address.

Pope Angeles strutted restlessly across the front of the stage, his hands crossed in the small of his back. 'Still two missing,' he muttered to himself. 'Where can they be?'

Cardinal Tardi hid a wry smile and casually observed for the benefit of all present, 'That, of course, is one of the problems of democracy. Everything waits for the vote.'

'Right now everything is waiting on two Cardinals,' frowned the Pope, glancing at his Rolex and rolling his eyes.

As if in answer to a silent prayer of impatience, the door at the back of the auditorium creaked open and, panting, Cardinal Alighieri hurried down the aisle. In seconds he was settling himself behind Cardinal Tardi, grinning feebly up at the Versace-clad Pope.

'Where've you been?' whispered Tardi sternly over his shoulder.

'Something came up . . .'

'You should've been here. What if he'd insisted the vote was on time?' hissed Tardi in a way that would've made many a ventriloquist proud.

'This was important. A phone call from . . .'

Suddenly His Holiness cleared his throat and announced, 'Gentlemen, we have waited long enough. It's time for business.'

Cardinal Tardi's hand shot Heavenwards, ignoring Alighieri's insistent prodding of his shoulder. 'Your Holiness, apologies for absence have been recieved from Cardinal Holridge. He was called, er . . . unavoidably away. However, he has instructed me which way he would have voted and therefore I shall be casting his vote.'

'And it never occurred to you to mention this earlier?' asked the Pope.

Tardi shrugged noncommittally. 'Religion and democracy. Can't quite get used to it. The old ways were much simpler. Whatever you say goes.'

'Yes, well, I say it's time to vote on the subject of *Faith: The Final Frontier.* Now, all those in favour of fighting to save the souls of a generation by reaching out and talking to them in a language they understand, raise your hands.'

There was a rustle of crimson cloth and a forest of hands ascended bravely into the air. Allowed a brief respite from his work on the Render-Benders, Giorgio Scipioni was on his feet and counting.

The Pope looked out over the congregation and barely hid a frown of concern. It was a far thinner crop than he had hoped for. It would be close. Very close.

'And those against?' he asked, a slight quiver in his voice.

Both of Cardinal Tardi's hands shot into the air followed by those of the more conservative members of the gathering.

Scipioni's finger bobbed over the hands, counting quickly

and writing down the result on a clipboard. Almost reluctantly he handed it to the Pope.

'And the result is . . .' began Angeles nervously. 'Those for, twenty-six. Those against . . .' He looked at the figure and his face turned pale. 'Twenty-seven.'

Cardinal Tardi was on his feet in moments, hiding his delight with remarkable assurance and ignoring the scowl from Cardinal Kotonawa. 'Oh, Your Holiness, what a shame. A radical and innovative idea such as that defeated by the very narrowest of majorities, run aground upon the most unfortunate of reefs of misfortune . . .'

Behind the Pope, Scipioni was looking up from his clipboard in confusion. Suddenly he began counting up all those present.

But Cardinal Tardi was in full flow. 'It has long been known, Your Holiness, that democracy can be the very cruellest of discriminators. Consider not that this vote was in any way a personal slight . . .'

Scipioni finished counting, scratched his head, looked at the total on the clipboard and smiled. In a flash he was whispering in the Pope's ear.

Of this Tardi saw none as he sermonised to the gathered Cardinals. '. . . or that this vote reflects upon your undoubtedly fine leadership skills which, though as yet naive and unhoned in many ways will, I feel certain, soon start to shine in both a secular and magnificently clerical manner . . .'

'I am very pleased that you feel that way,' said the Pope in a surprisingly cheerful tone of voice.

Cardinal Tardi's monologue stopped in a dropping of his jaw. Nervously, he turned around. 'Er . . . Your Holiness . . . ?'

'It seems that in my, ahem, "naive and unhoned" way I forgot to include everyone relevant in this vote.'

'You did?'

His Holiness smiled as he nodded, his white biretta shining victoriously. 'It has been pointed out by Mr Scipioni here that I failed to consider two other interested parties.'

Tardi glared at the Italian-American film director. 'What? He can't vote! He's not ordained, or . . .'

'Who said anything about Mr Scipioni?' asked the Pope. 'I'm referring to me. And since I am in favour that means the vote stands at twenty-seven against twenty-seven. One vote either way will decide it all.'

'Ahhh,' breathed Tardi feeling a touch unsteady on his feet. 'Two votes, I believe you said. Who . . . who's the other?' Somehow he wasn't sure he wanted to hear the answer.

Pope Angeles smiled and, by way of answer, pointed Heavenwards.

'Oh no, no. Not Him? He can't,' struggled Tardi. 'He's not here.'

'Tut, tut. He's everywhere,' corrected Angeles, feeling sure he shouldn't really be enjoying seeing Tardi squirm quite so much.

'I mean He's not, er . . . Well, how's He going to vote?'

Angeles held his hand out towards Scipioni and, obligingly the director flicked a fifty-lira coin into the air. It arced gracefully across the stage, landed in the Pope's palm and was instantly slapped on to the back of his hand. 'Heads or tails?' he asked Cardinal Tardi.

'Er . . . tails,' whimpered the Papal Secretary, bewildered.

Angeles revealed the coin with a grin. 'Oh, it's heads. Motion carried in favour of the proposal,' he declared and tossed the coin back to Scipioni.

Feeling like the victim of one of the more subtle fairground con-artists, Tardi bowed with as much grace as he could muster and headed for the door, Alighieri close on his heels.

On the stage, Scipioni was shaking his head in wonder. 'You took a chance there, didn't you? What if it'd been tails?'

'Ahhh, you forget,' grinned the Pope and he looked Heavenwards. 'He's on my side now.'

'You're telling me it had nothing to do with heads I win, tails you lose?'

'Would I?' grinned the Pope and skipped off the stage with only the slightest chuckle. 'C'mon, we've got a film trailer to make.'

14:12 The Vatican

It came as little surprise to the pair of cavorting cherubs on the ceiling that it was Cardinal Tardi who kicked open the door and stormed in on a wave of frustration. They stared down knowingly from their frescoed vantage point and decided that it really was time the Papal Secretary took a holiday.

'It's time you took a holiday,' suggested Cardinal Alighieri, much to the satisfaction of the cherubs.

Tardi strode across his office and glared out of the window. Much to his disgust, a small group of tourists was playing cricket in St Peter's Square. Fuming, he snatched a mobile phone out of his pocket, stabbed a single button and began rattling away in fluent Italian as a baseball-capped youth bowled his travelling companion a googly and was acutely disappointed when it was returned at double the delivery speed. Almost instantly a lissom teenager, wearing both the biggest hat and smallest bikini top Tardi had seen in a long time, set off in hot pursuit. The Cardinal folded his mobile back into his pocket, noted the time and observed that the fielder's bikini was definitely not of the supportive sports variety.

'You know, a holiday. Couple of weeks on one of the lesser known Maldives, recharge the batteries and all that,' offered Alighieri. 'I mean, it would be churlish of me to suggest that you were actually slipping, but . . .'

158

'What?' snapped Tardi, rounding on Alighieri. 'Are you suggesting I'm losing it?'

'Well the vote didn't go precisely the way you expected,' said Alighieri, wincing as Tardi's fists clenched angrily.

'The vote. Never seen anything so underhanded in all my time spent serving the wishes of three Popes,' growled Tardi staring into the middle distance. 'That showed flagrant disregard for all the rules.'

Tardi turned back to glare out of the window as six Swiss Guards burst simultaneously from three different doors on intercept courses for the cricketing tourists. In seconds the blue and yellow Exocets had them surrounded and contained. Their team leader looked up expectantly at the window and, with a flick of Tardi's wrist, the heathen cricketers were banished for ever from Vatican soil.

'That wasn't democracy,' grumbled the Papal Secretary. 'He had two votes.' He looked at his watch. Thirty-five seconds. At least he could still depend on something.

'He wasn't the only one with two votes, was he?' reminded Alighieri.

Any trace of satisfaction vanished from Tardi's face as he spun around. 'That was completely different, mine was a proxy vote. A *legitimate* proxy. Holridge couldn't be there in person, so I put my hand up for him. Simple. Now what Angeles did was . . .'

'More successful,' interrupted Alighieri.

'What? You turncoat traitor . . .' began Tardi, protesting a little too forcefully.

Alighieri ignored him. 'Look, that's all history anyway. Now, *this* is far more important.' He waved a cassette in front of Tardi's nose.

'What can possibly be more important than . . . ?'

'Just listen, will you?' Alighieri slammed the cassette into a state-of-the-art Sony surveillance tape-recorder and pressed

159

'play'. The office filled with the unmistakable sound of a recently recorded telephone conversation between Cardinals Holridge and Kotonawa. Much to Alighieri's satisfaction Tardi's jaw sank further open as the sound bite progressed.

'*Oooh, now would you look at that!*' declared the disembodied voice of Holridge as the tape-recorder confidently reproduced the unmistakable sound of fingers brushing rubble off a large metallic object of extreme shininess.

'*Wooooow.*'

'*What is it?*' begged Kotonawa.

'*It's amazing . . . Utterly incredible . . . I'll call you back. Bye.*'

The Sony hissed professionally for a few seconds before a plump Italian digit switched it off.

'What the Hell was all that about?' gasped Tardi, staring fixedly at the tape-machine.

'I was hoping you were going to tell me,' confessed Alighieri. 'After all, it was you that sent him off in Vatican 2.'

Tardi's eyes showed a ring of terrified white. 'That was just to get him out of the way. I didn't know he was going to find . . . What has he found?'

Alighieri shrugged. 'Haven't a clue. But he sounds very excited about it. And with Holridge that's always a bad sign.'

Tardi shook himself. 'It's all right, it's all right,' he insisted through clenched teeth. 'Nothing to worry about. Bit of damage limitation when he gets back and no one will ever know. Whatever it is, we'll bury it.'

'Er, it might not be quite that easy,' offered Alighieri.

'What? What d'you mean? Why not, it's easily contained. Just Holridge and Kotonawa to deal with.'

Alighieri shook his head.

'Don't concern yourself with the Swiss Guard. I control them whatever anybody else says . . . What? Why are you shaking your head? There *is* no one else.'

160

Alighieri took a bundle of radar traces out of his inside pocket and dropped them on the desk.

'I took the liberty of stopping off at the office of the Head of the Surveillance Division.'

Cardinal Tardi stared at the rapidly growing international interest amassing off the bottom left-hand corner of Eire and dearly wished that right then, at that very instant, he was in the middle of a very, very, long holiday on one of the lesser known Maldives.

14:22 St Naimhe's

Half powering, half surfing in on the back of a restless Atlantic breaker, a pair of US Marines landing craft ground on to the St Naimhe's beachhead and dropped the bow doors. In seconds a crack squad of fifty troops was splashing through the shallows and terrifying the local puffins.

'Up there!' yelled Major-General Gelding, pointing to the white-streaked cliff ahead. 'Fire when ready!'

'Sir, yes, sir!' rattled off two marines and stretched a vast expanse of rope netting between their shouldered bazookas. One nod between them and the net was arcing towards the cliff-top on a pair of flaming trails, acres of rope mesh paying out behind. With a dull pair of thuds two explosive bolts riveted it securely to the summit and the squad of fifty surged forward.

In seconds the newly formed USS *Indiscriminate* Multi-Disciplinary Observation Force was swarming up the hundred-foot cliff as if it was just another training mission.

14:23 St Naimhe's

Above the whacking of the Sea King's rotors it was almost impossible for Fintan and the Swiss Guard to hear Cardinal

Holridge's shouted commands. But somehow, between them, via a mixture of repetition, miming and the odd small gobbets of complete guesswork, they had managed to attach three magnetic hausers to the unfeasibly shiny hull of the spacecraft.

'Lower!' yelled Holridge, his throat raw with the effort, as the fourth pad headed his way. Quickly he offered a swift prayer that this wouldn't take too much longer. Another few minutes of shouting above the downdraft from a hovering chopper and his days in the Vatican Plainchant Society were surely numbered.

Looking like something from the finest of fifties sci-fi movies, the magnetic-tipped hauser snaked towards the hull of the ship and, with a final leap, clamped itself firmly in position.

Holridge turned, grabbed at his rope and, with a workmanlike spit on his hands, began hauling himself out of the claustrophobic confines of the chasm.

In moments he was standing in the shattered aisle of St Tib's Chapel, waving frantic directions to the hovering chopper. Juggling rudder and throttle with consummate skill, the pilot took up the slack on the hausers and began to struggle into the air. Whirlwinds of charred wood battered around the nave, kicking up blackened vortices of unusable hymnals. And, much to the mounting concern of all present, the spacecraft of unfeasible shininess refused to budge an inch. Gritting his teeth, and with a keen eye on the fuel gauge, the pilot twisted the throttle. A couple of dozen more revs per minute spun into the rotors and with a squeal of metal on basalt, things began to move.

And not just inside the chapel, either. Sprinting over the horizon like cavalry hungry for revenge came fifty of the USS *Indiscriminate's* hand-picked marines. Barely resisting the temptation to duck and dive between all available cover, they dashed towards the skeleton of the chapel.

Complaining in no uncertain terms that tugging crashed alien spacecraft from the midst of shattered chapels was not in its job description, the helicopter did exactly that. With a final squeal of grating metal and a sickening change of the helicopter's altitude, the basalt gave up its strangely alien filling. And, for the first time, human eyes beheld properly the craft from on high.

'Thought it would be bigger than that,' tutted the larger of the two Swiss Guards with a hint of disappointment. 'It made enough of a mess.'

'Tell me about it,' grumbled Father Fintan.

Thirty feet above, the pilot wrestled with the swinging payload, fighting to keep the helicopter steady and, surely using more limbs than was humanly possible, he pressed a button to lower a rope ladder.

'It's incredible . . . utterly amazing . . .' was all Holridge could say as he stared at his own reflection swinging slowly above the aisle. But he wasn't allowed to stare for long. With business-like efficiency the Swiss Guards flung a tarpaulin over the alien craft, settling the dark cover snugly down around the hausers and even tying it together neatly underneath.

'Don't you think it's incredible?' asked Holridge, his voice dripping with awe.

'Think what's incredible, eh?' asked Major-General Hiram J Gelding III, suddenly appearing through the remains of a chapel window.

Father Fintan turned to the cigar-toting intruder. 'Oh, hello. Er, I'm afraid you've come at a bit of a bad time if you want a mass or anything. And baptisms are a bit sticky. Weddings I could do at a push but . . .'

'No, no that's all right, we just came to have a bit of a look around. Now what was it your friend there thinks is so incredible, hmmm?' asked Gelding, gesturing orders for his commandeered marines to surround the chapel.

'I haven't a clue what it is,' confessed Fintan with an expansive shrug. 'There I was minding my own business when all of a sudden . . . nyaaaaoooowkaboooom, it just fell out of the sky.'

'Straight out of the sky?' pressed Gelding. 'Weird, huh? Now you wouldn't be mindin' too much if me and my boys were to just peek under that tarpaulin and have a closer look now, would you?'

'No!' squealed Holridge suddenly as the conversation trickled into his awestricken mind. 'No, you can't have a look, no, not at all, it's . . . er, it's boring . . . you wouldn't be interested.'

'I'm interested in all sorts of things,' smiled Gelding through the window in as disarming a manner as he could muster. 'Especially things that just fall out of the sky.'

'Fall out of the sky,' whimpered Holridge. 'Hah, all sorts of things fall out of the sky. It's not that rare you know.' Frantically, he gestured to the Swiss Guards to get back in the helicopter. They headed off towards a rope ladder which dangled conveniently by the side of the door.

'All sorts of things,' continued Holridge nervously. 'Er . . . blocks of ice out of aeroplane loos . . . plagues of locusts . . . frogs . . . they've been known to, er . . .'

'Spaceships,' offered Fintan helpfully.

'Ha, no you don't mean that,' gabbled Holridge. 'He doesn't mean spaceships at all, he means satellites and Mir and stuff like that. Don't you?'

Fintan looked from the Cardinal to the row of military types lined up in the empty windows and his face cracked into a smile. 'Oh, I get it. No silly me. It wasn't a spaceship at all,' he admitted and winked at Gelding. Holridge breathed a sigh of relief.

'It was a weather balloon, right?' added Fintan, getting into the spirit of all things conspirational.

Holridge screamed and grabbed Fintan firmly around the mouth, hustling him away towards the rope ladder dangling from the Sea King.

'No, no, Fintan. *Hot air* balloon,' insisted Holridge for the benefit of the gathered marines. 'He always gets mixed up with that one. It's the Pope's attempt at circumnavigating the world in a hot air balloon. Can't let Richard Branson have all the limelight, can we?' With difficulty Holridge began shoving Fintan up the rope ladder. 'I don't know how many times I've told him it's a hot air balloon,' insisted Holridge, stepping on to the bottom rung as marines swarmed in through the chapel windows.

To Holridge's immense satisfaction the pilot leaned on the power, dipped the chopper's nose and swooped off towards Vatican Hill.

'Well?' barked Gelding as the gleaming white Sea King shrank in the afternoon sky. 'Anybody get that on film?'

An embarrassed silence descended on the ruined chapel.

'I said, anybody get that on film?' repeated Gelding a little louder. 'Will the marine who thinks he's got a decent video-enhancable shot of that chopper's payload take one step forward.'

Not an army-issue boot shuffled.

'Didn't anybody bring a camera?' begged Gelding as a slightly scorched manuscript of 'Faith of Our Fathers' settled gently on the toe of his right boot. 'Sketch pad?'

As Cardinal Holridge scrambled up the last few rungs of the swinging rope ladder, it was odd, but he felt certain that faintly, in the distance, he just caught the sound of the screams of the officer in charge of the USS *Indiscriminate* Multi-Disciplinary Observation Force. Either that, or a startled puffin.

Activate Agent Rublev!

At first glance, the scene in the Piazza Risorgimento, now that it had finally been pedestrianised, was real tourist Rome. New antique statues thrust marble genitalia into the air with almost the same gusto as their other weaponry. Circular tables were scattered everywhere, looking like an explosion in a tiddlywinks factory. Multicoloured sunshades flittered their tassles at a variety of angles anywhere between jaunty and rakish. Newly opened trattorias spilled waiters in all directions. It was a picture which any wannabe travel photographer would give his favourite wide-angle lens for. Well, at a first glance he would.

Only on closer inspection did it become blindingly obvious that there was indeed something wrong with this picture. Dark-grey-suited men sat one to each table, peering suspiciously out from newspapers in a variety of languages.

The man behind the *Financial Times* pressed an earphone deeper into his right lobe, took a sip of tea and almost choked. He peered at the surface of his darjeeling and groaned. Why did the Italians always insist on sprinkling chocolate on top of everything in cups? He cleared his throat in a way that was impossible for any waiter to ignore and pointed at the offending particles melting into a chocolate slick. A greasy-haired Roman in a pesto-stained apron slouched up to the table and removed the offending beverage.

166

'Bring me a beer, there's a good chap,' said the Englishman in an accent that could only have come from years as an RAF Wing-Commander. '*Without* the chocolate, if you don't mind.'

The waiter grunted something vaguely in the affirmative and stomped away between the terracotta pots. The man from MI5 rustled his paper and checked on how his Halifax shares were doing.

'May I?' came a voice from beyond the *FT*. The Englishman looked up over his bifocals.

'Agent Olevski, what a pleasant and hardly unexpected surprise. Please *do* join me.' With quaintly old-fashioned politeness, the Englishman rose, folded his newspaper over his high-powered binoculars and welcomed the Russian to his table.

All across the piazza, grey-suited men tried to appear to be looking the other way whilst they adjusted a host of high-powered microphones.

'Do forgive the interruption, Agent Etheridge-Willis, but I appear to have arrived at a time when no other tables were available,' offered Agent Olevski with a slight burr to his rounder vowels.

'That will teach you to linger with the daughter of the Canadian minister,' smiled Etheridge-Willis.

'You know about me and Jolene?'

'Of course, dear Oleg. It *is* my job, you know.' He leaned forward and added in a whisper. 'By the way, were you aware she was originally christened Julie, but Dolly Parton inspired a change by deed poll.' He leaned back and raised his voice a little. 'Shocking the effect country music can have on impressionable minds, don't you think?'

Much to his satisfaction, a wave of baffled expressions rippled across the piazza as a cluster of intelligence agents tapped microphones and attempted to fathom what coded secrets the Brit was passing the Rusky.

' "Achy-Breaky Heart",' said Oleg, happy to be able to supply another infamous country song for discussion.

'Hmmm? What's that, old man?' said Etheridge-Willis, distractedly taking his finger from his flesh-coloured earphone and scanning the skies over St Peter's.

' "Achy-Breaky . . ." Never mind,' muttered Agent Olevski, his eyes following his opposite number's gaze.

Across the piazza, a Chinese gentleman played excitedly with his binoculars and edged his chair a few inches to the left. Satisfied that he had an uninterrupted view of the evening sky above Vatican Hill, he took a sip of cold cappuccino and waited.

Another soundbite of air-traffic-control information crackled in the privacy of Agent Etheridge-Willis's ear. Nonchalantly, he opened a packet of breadsticks, broke one in half and dipped it in the garlic-flavoured pot of olive oil sat on the table. 'Care for one?' he asked Oleg.

'No thank you.' He waved his hand across his mouth and pulled a face. 'It's Jolene, you understand.'

'Of course, I was forgetting your evening at the opera. How remiss of me.' He sucked noisily at his breadstick and casually pressed a lump of it into the plastic carnation decorating the table centre. Behind a particularly well-endowed statue of a Roman centurion, an Iranian agent waggled his finger in his ear and cursed as his audio went dead.

Agent Olevski frowned. 'Is there nothing you don't know?'

'Hmmm, well, as a matter of fact I believe there is.'

Oleg raised an eyebrow. 'Oh, do tell.'

'I hate to confess it, comrade, but, try as I might, I've never been able to find out what Helen Mirren's taste in undergarments is.'

Oleg raised both eyebrows.

Etheridge-Willis sucked dreamily on another garlic-oiled

breadstick and stared into space. 'I think it was *2010* that did it for me. The combination of delicious feminity wrapped in countless million tons of spaceship and topped with that Russian accent of hers . . . Simply divine.'

'I'm sure I could get you pictures,' offered Olevski, wondering which MI5 secrets he could exchange for a couple of dozen skin-flicks of Ms Mirren.

'Oleg, are you trying to insult me? I don't want to be *told* if she prefers basques to high-leg bodies. No, no. I want to make it my own personal mission to find out for myself.' A glint of delight flashed in his eyes.

In the background the distinctive sound of labouring rotor blades hammered into earshot. Etheridge-Willis popped a final chunk of breadstick into his mouth, wiped his fingers on a handy napkin and sighed. 'But, in the meantime, I suppose I have other duties.' He peeled back the *Financial Times* and picked up his binoculars.

Olevski took an admiring breath and stared enviously at the perfectly moulded grips settling into the Englishman's palms. 'New?'

'Hmmm, what's that?' muttered Etheridge-Willis, expertly pulling focus with a finely knurled thumb wheel.

'The binoculars, are they new?' Olevski looked at the chunky Practika bins in his own hands. They were trusty old friends, he'd watched the whole of the Vietnam War through those. But, like the best of trusty old friends, they didn't see things as well as they might these days. Especially around dusk.

The sound of Sikorsky rotors thrummed towards the helipad on Vatican Hill.

'Hmmm, I do believe I need nightsights,' tutted Etheridge-Willis. With a flick of his left thumb his viewfinder exploded into stunning clarity. 'Ahhh, that's better.' The eyes of the pigeons roosting on St Peter's turned suddenly green. So did Agent Olevski's.

'I hate you Westerners,' tutted Oleg, trying to focus on where he expected a certain white helicopter to appear.

Etheridge-Willis looked at the Russian intelligence officer. 'I say, Oleg, old chap, that's a little strong, don't you think.'

'Pah. You sit there with your brand new MI5 issue binoculars as if nothing is wrong in the world . . .'

'MI5 issue? These? I think not.'

'Then where did you . . . ?'

Etheridge-Willis put a finger to his lips and looked around at the piazzaful of world intelligence agents. As he expected, they were all staring at a blank bit of sky just to the right of the dome of St Peter's. Much to his amusement the Iranian was taking full advantage of the local artwork. His four-inch reflecting telescope was propped upon the erect marble manhood of a rather miffed-looking Roman centurion.

'Oleg, allow me to give you a piece of advice.' He reached into his inside pocket and pulled out an A3 brochure printed on glossy paper. 'In there you'll find everything you need for international covert operations. Be the envy of your colleagues with tomorrow's products today.'

Agent Olevski stared at the folded brochure, excitement rising as he saw hand-held video rewinders, security switches to time lights on and off, twelve-volt palm-sized tyre inflators, devices to locate keys by simply whistling. Every page was filled with devices just waiting to find something to use them for. 'Tell me,' he whispered. 'What is "Innovations"?'

Etheridge-Willis tapped the side of his nose meaningfully and focused his binoculars on the rapidly approaching chopper that was swinging into view. Olevski stuffed the brochure into his pocket and followed suit.

'Fascinating,' muttered the Englishman as he stared at the gleaming object slung beneath the angel-white Sea King.

'What is it? What is it?' pleaded Olevski with the urgency of a gopher.

'Remarkable.'

The helicopter swung low and with a peculiar sense of anticlimax, vanished behind the roof of the Vatican museums.

'What was it? What was it?' gasped Oleg.

Etheridge-Willis, like the rest of the grey-suited men in the Piazza Risorgimento, rubbed his chin and wondered the very same thing. It was a bit of a conundrum, that one. Roundish, covered in tarpaulin and slung on the end of a quartet of heavy-duty hausers. There was only one thing he had seen the Church use that was anything like that, but surely it couldn't be . . . Not that big?

'Did you see?' begged Oleg. 'What was it?'

The Englishman nodded. 'Incense burner,' he answered.

'That big?'

'You know this new Pope, he's likes things big. Probably his American upbringing.'

'Yes, but, what would he possibly want with an incense burner that big? I mean they're normally . . .' He cupped his hands into a sphere about the size of a partially deflated basketball. 'And they produce *plenty* of smoke.'

Etheridge-Willis shrugged and stood. 'Well, I've heard he's planning to pull the crowds in St Peter's Square on Easter Sunday. Maybe he wants to bless them all at once. Imagine that, eh? A fifteen-foot incense burner swinging over St Peter's Square on the end of a helicopter. That would put Pink Floyd to shame for sure.'

Agent Oleg Olevski stared open-mouthed at the Englishman.

'Enjoy the . . . er, document,' smiled Etheridge-Willis and began to stroll away.

The greasy-haired Roman waiter suddenly appeared at the

171

table and called, in broken English, 'Sir, you're a beer.'

'Oleg, do help yourself,' called Etheridge-Willis and disappeared around a handy corner.

Agent Olevski shrugged, glanced at his watch and decided that maybe he did have time for a quick lager. He reached for the beer and recoiled in horror. There, floating innocently on the frothy head, was a good teaspoon of chocolate gratings.

'Urgh, the English,' winced Oleg, 'no sense of taste.'

19:23 The Vatican

In a darkened room in the depths of the Radio Vaticano building, the newly hired director of *Faith: The Final Frontier* leaned back in his chair and yawned expansively.

'Okay, Franco, what d'you think of this?' asked Scipioni.

The Pope, clad in his favourite Versace lounging vestments, grabbed his coffee and settled down to watch the latest digital edits.

A screen on the parallel-ported Render-Benders crackled into life and filled with the very type of place which camels would hike miles to reach. Lizards gasped, their tongues scraping the sand, while green beetles toasted to an appetising golden brown.

Suddenly, as if driven by a couple of Rolls-Royce Merlins, a sandstorm whirled in from the north.

The Pope took a bored sip of his tepid coffee. 'I've seen this before, haven't I?'

'Yeah, the new bit's coming up in a minute. Keep your eye on the second ship, okay?'

Right on cue a quartet of gleaming discs erupted into full view. As usual, sat atop them were shining figures each with four wings and highly decorated helmets. The lead ship arced over and frisbeed through a petrified herd of camels.

'There, there, watch!' enthused Scipioni, pointing excitedly at the second ship as it broke formation, pulled a spectacular loop and plunged towards a solitary camel on a distant rock.

'What's that in his hand?' asked Angeles. 'It looks like a . . . Oh no, you didn't?'

Scipioni just giggled as the forty-foot-long croquet mallet whistled through the air and casually removed the head of the solitary camel.

'Oh, that's disgusting,' winced Angeles.

'No wait, keep watching. This is the best bit.' The camel's head spun forward and flashed off to the right, peppering the screen with glistening globs of digital blood as it vanished.

'Was that *really* necessary?' frowned the Pope.

'Trust me, the kids'll love it!'

'I'm sure they will, but what theological message does that portray?'

'Message? Er . . . don't mess with anything wielding a forty-foot croquet mallet?'

Angeles shook his head.

Scipioni tried again. 'Be sure your sins will find you out?'

Angeles frowned and shook his head.

'Okay, okay, I've got it. Camels are ships of the desert, right? Captains order ships about, right? Heads order camels about, yeah? So the message is . . . don't let your head rule your . . . er, camel!' The silence of the papal response was overwhelming. 'I'll . . . I'll take it out then, hmmm?'

Angeles nodded.

Carefully saving it for a possible future in a more personal venture, Scipioni cut the scene.

'Sorry. I guess I got a bit carried away. But there's lots to get excited about in here, you know?' He patted a copy of the Bible which was lying on the console.

'You've started reading it?'

'A good director always reads his source material,'

grinned Scipioni. 'And what a story! Murder, sex, alien invasions . . .'

'And the theological messages. Don't forget them.'

'I've been thinkin' about some of them and d'you know I've got *the* perfect Eve lined up and ready to start. She's been in movies before and she's well talented, if you know what I mean,' grinned Scipioni, his cupped hands hovering a good ten inches in front of his chest.

'Let me guess. Sophia?'

'You thought of her too. Hey, we're still on the same wavelength. I'll get her up here right away and we can start . . .'

'No, no, she's too . . . er, how can I say this. I want Michelle Pfeiffer.'

'Hey, don't we all?' grinned Scipioni.

'For Eve.'

Scipioni rubbed his chin and imagined the scene. 'Hmmm, Michelle Pfeiffer and Sophia together . . . Nice.'

'No, no. I want Ms Pfeiffer to play Eve. She would bring a perfect sultry and seductive vulnerability to the role. Combining childlike innocence with a smouldering passion just waiting to erupt if the right serpent happens to pass by.'

'But what about Sophia?' asked Scipioni. 'I said I'd help her out. I promised her.'

'Well, perhaps if the right role can be found for her unique talents . . .'

Scipioni flicked eagerly through a few pages of the Bible, stopped and grinned widely. 'Aha! Here. This is it, perfect!' He spun the book around and handed it to the Pope.

'Are you *serious*?'

'She'd be perfect. You've never seen her fight, have you? The kids love it. Low-slung leather armour, thigh-length strapped boots . . .'

'Yes, yes I'm sure. But it's supposed to be *David* and Goliath.'

'Not very politically correct is it?' tutted Scipioni. 'Doesn't really reflect women's role in modern society, does it? What's wrong with Dana and Goliath, eh? Or Delilah and Goliath? Or Daphne . . .'

'It's David,' insisted the Pope firmly. 'Now, c'mon, back to work. Let's see this without the camel's head.'

Scipioni pressed the 'replay' button and continued his search through the pages of the Bible. There was a part in this for Sophia he was certain. And if he could only find the right one she'd be here by the end of the week, every curve of hers scanned in and digitised, ready for anything he could possibly think of.

In his mind, a shiny, black-carapaced alien licked its slavering lips and advanced towards a semi-naked Sophia, writhing helplessly in the clutches of far, far too many chains.

19:42 The Vatican

On the top floor of a Ligorio designer villa in the wilds of the Vatican gardens, two lab-coated gentlemen of the cloth stared at an elephant. With its trunk raised towards the fine example of Mannerist ceiling work, it stood on its hind legs in the centre of a small lake of milk.

'And just what, precisely, am I supposed to be seeing here?' asked Cardinal Kotonawa, assuming the gentle air of imperiousness which was normally Cardinal Holridge's. He took his eyes off the performing pachyderm and, enjoying playing the Head of the Congregation for Icon Authentication a little too much, he focused a laser-hard stare at the recently ordained lab technician, Father Luigi.

'Hmmmm. Not working,' offered the novice.

'I think I had worked that one out,' tutted Kotonawa in an unnervingly accurate impersonation of Holridge.

'Two minutes.'

'We've already been here ten. How long am I supposed to wait before whatever it is I'm waiting for starts to happen?'

'Soon,' offered Father Luigi, scratching his head and wishing he was doing something he was good at. Like walking on water again. He turned his attention back to the nine-inch porcelain elephant in its petri dish of milk.

Kotonawa made a noise in his throat and, rubbing the small of his back, he stared around the room. Five technicians nursed numerous bits of shiny and expensive equipment, some feeding racks of test-tubes into hungry scientific mouths, others mucking out the waste trays at the back of some gurgling technology. All of them devoted to their particular research project.

A wriggle of pride squirmed in his intestines. Right now he was in charge of all he surveyed and what *he* said went. Well, at least until Holridge returned.

Hiding a smile, he turned his attention back to the nine-inch porcelain model of Ganesh the Hindu elephant god. 'Two minutes, time's up. Now, d'you mind explaining what theological insights you were hoping to get out of dipping porcelain elephants in dishes of milk?'

'Milk,' answered Father Luigi economically.

'I need some more to work on here. I don't recall much in the Bible about milk. Manna yes . . .'

'Milk through trunk,' expanded Luigi and performed a surprisingly graceful impersonation of an elephant spraying gallons of semi-skimmed across the lab. For a moment, Kotonawa wondered if 'elephant spraying milk' was a move he should introduce into his daily t'ai chi exercises. But before he could ask, realisation hit like a forty-ton truck.

'No, no, no. It's the other way round. The elephant drinks the milk,' explained Kotonawa, recalling the spate of cases

176

in 1995 when hundreds of similar statues guzzled gallons of milk before thousands of stunned Hindu worshippers.

'It *drinks* . . . ?' frowned Luigi. Confused, he picked up a sheet of paper written in fluent Hindi and slapped it irritably. Somewhere along the rocky road of translation from Hindi to Italian something, it would seem, had gone a little awry.

Kotonawa helpfully stood the elephant on its head, reset his stopwatch and bent to watch the unfolding miracle. But other things were seeking his attention.

At that instant a couple of motors whirred into life and began hauling open a pair of large corrugated doors at the far end of the lab. Kotonawa raised his eyebrows curiously. He was certain they weren't expecting delivery of any large pieces of equipment today.

Miffed that someone was playing with the doors during a time when he was in charge, Kotonawa tucked his clipboard under his armpit and strode across the laboratory. Preparing for the ancient managerial discipline of 'the tearing off of strips', he stood, feet slightly apart, clipboard firmly in the small of his back, his eyes as cold as long-dead glaciers.

It was a minor miracle he wasn't crushed by Cardinal Holridge as he backed in through the doors waving his hands frantically and shouting instructions to the pair of Swiss Guards pushing a rather heavy trolley down the slope. 'Left a bit. Left. Left! Mind that wall! Mind it . . . Good, good. Now, to me. To me. C'mon . . .'

Cardinal Kotonawa stared open mouthed as a fifteen-foot tarpaulin-covered object rumbled into the lab at a speed which was perhaps just a little too swift.

'Right hand down a bit,' shouted Holridge, jogging backwards. 'Right hand down. Right. Right! RIGHT!' He dived out of the way at the last possible minute.

Twelve feet of lab bench, several dozen test-tubes and a couple of pipettes weren't quite so fortunate. They were written off spectacularly in the ensuing collision.

As the dust and panic slowly settled around the lab, heads began to appear above tables and around chairs, all eyes pointing towards the thing under the tarpaulin rocking gently back and forth upon the trolley. Nervously, Father O'Suilleabhain slid into the lab, unseen.

'What . . . what is *that*?' gulped Kotonawa, emerging from behind a filing cabinet and dusting off his lab vestments.

For a moment, Cardinal Holridge was far from forthcoming with any kind of answer. He was dealing with a pair of trembling Swiss Guards as they backed towards the doors. 'No, I'm sure you didn't mean to crash it like that . . . Yes, brakes on trolleys *are* a good idea, especially when moving heavy loads down slopes . . . Look, don't you worry about it. I won't tell. Your efficiency records are safe with me. Honest. No, *really*. Bye.' And, with the briefest of metallic clangs, the doors slid shut on the two fancy-dressed Guards. In a second, breathing heavy sighs of relief, they were off on their toes, convinced that a certain Papal Secretary would be very interested in hearing all about their little excursion. Very interested indeed.

Inside the lab, Cardinal Holridge cracked his knuckles and, with a suitably theatrical flourish, grabbed at the hem of the tarpaulin. 'Taa daaaaahh!' he fanfared and, with a single sharp tug, revealed what lay beneath.

'What is it?' repeated Kotonawa. 'Where did it come from?'

'Where? Straight out of the sky, that's where. Nyaaaaoooowkaboooom,' announced Father Fintan in what he hoped was the best way of clearing his name of any blame before anyone had the chance to sully it. 'I didn't do it. Really, I didn't. In fact I was nowhere near it when it happened. See, I was down at the quayside minding my own . . .'

'Father O'Suilleabhain. Shut up,' hissed Holridge, more than a little weary of listening to Fintan's similarly themed rantings as they had flown across the whole of Europe.

'Will somebody tell me what it is?' demanded Kotonawa.

'Shiny,' admired Holridge, pulling bulbous faces in the reflective hull.

'I can see that. But I didn't ask what it looks like, I asked what . . .'

'Here's a clue,' interrupted Holridge and, not looking around, he handed his lab manager a small lozenge of alien alloy identical to that which coated the ship.

Kotonawa turned it over in his hands his mouth sagging open in awe. 'This . . . this is for real?'

'Oh yes indeed,' Holridge nodded and continued scrutinising the seamless hull, trying to figure out quite how he was going to get inside.

'But this . . . this is a st . . . st . . .' gagged Kotonawa.

'Star chart?' offered Holridge. 'Is that the phrase you're looking for?'

Kotonawa nodded numbly as he stared at the diamond-laser etchings shimmering on the surface of the metal disc.

'Er, Fintan, would you be kind enough to fetch the good Cardinal a chair?' asked Holridge as the hull's crystal-clear reflection of Kotonawa turned pale and wobbled a little unsteadily.

'They've got tentacles!' whispered the Japanese lab manager and, moments before a suitable chair was forthcoming, he slithered to the floor.

'Hmmm, when he comes around could you tell him that the NASA website might be a good place to find a star map or two,' said Holridge, grabbing a large magnifying glass off a handy bench and starting to examine the hull of the alien vessel in greater detail.

In an ashtray on an insignificant table in the middle of the Piazza Risorgimento, a small gob of chocolate-veined froth lurked miserably. Glistening, it looked up at Agent Oleg Olevski supping at a glass of beer and tried to console itself with the thoughts that there was just no pleasing some people. Too much head, not enough head, bubbles too big, too much chocolate . . . It wasn't easy being the froth on a cool refreshing lager. It was even harder being froth in an ashtray. Pathetically, it dissolved into a small miserable puddle.

Of this passing, Oleg Olevski was oblivious. His mind was currently engaged in dialling a long and complicated number on his KGB-issue 'pocket' telephone. He would the dial around to the stop for the last time and, perching the thirteen-inch long communications device between his shoulder and ear, massaged his finger as the connection was made.

'Good evening, comrade, this is the Borodin Balti House, what is your order?' crackled a voice in a stern Russian accent.

'Good evening. I'd like a 3, two 45s and a side dish of 37.'

There was a vague rustling of papers barely audible above the constant hiss of static.

'Good evening, Agent Olevski,' answered the stern Russian voice, identifying the agent's call-in number. 'Who do you require?'

'Commander Tarka Dal,' answered Oleg feeling faintly embarrassed by the entire attempt at secrecy. If anyone had the intelligence to have devised a way of breaking into his conversation then he was sure they'd have enough nous left over to work out that he wasn't in fact currently ordering a take-away from the Borodin Balti House.

There were a dozen clunks as contacts connected, then a small snippit of *Swan Lake* before a voice barked, 'Report, Agent Olevski.'

Oleg shrugged as any pretence of coversion vanished.

'Information from SS *Denisovitch* correct. Touchdown Vatican.'

'Identification of cargo?'

'As described by *Denisovitch*. Unknown.'

'Conclusions?'

'Insufficient information,' answered Olevski, staring at the walls around the Vatican City. 'Recommend activation of Agent Rublev.'

'Recommendation received and understood. Have a good evening with Jolene. Out.'

Olevski scowled as the connection was severed. Was there anyone who didn't know about his personal life? He shoved his telephone back into a large holster under his arm, stood and headed off towards the opera house and an evening with the daughter of the Canadian minister. A wry smile crossed his face as he suddenly realised that he was under orders to enjoy himself. And, being under orders, this would be on expenses. Suddenly the evening ahead looked even brighter. It had been a long while since he'd had champagne.

As Agent Olevski exited the Piazza Risorgimento and headed off towards the Tiber, deep in a drawer in a desk in the depths of the Vatican a KGB field-issue telephone began to ring. It was answered on the second bell.

'Hello?'

'Agent Rublev, I have a small job for you . . .'

A shady figure in a secretive room pulled out a pad and pen and, under the stony gaze of a pair of cavorting cherubs, began writing.

A handful of knuckles whitened momentarily around a tightening chuck key as a diamond-tipped bit was wound into an overkeen Bosch. The green drill surged with all the amperage of the Vatican grid as Cardinal Holridge pocketed the key and blipped the switch, flexing his power-tool's muscles in preparation. Six inches of high-tensile case-hardened bit spun cheerfully, sending shards of artificial light in all directions.

'Right,' he growled, squaring his shoulders and setting his jaw with a great deal more confidence than he really felt. 'This is it, d'you hear me? This is it!'

Father Fintan looked at Cardinal Holridge and wondered who it was that the Head of the Congregation for Icon Authentication was trying to convince: himself, the humming Bosch in his hands, or the overly shiny alien hatchback squatting motionless on the table in the centre of the underground laboratory. In truth he would probably never find out.

Like a Scots Guard readying his pipes for the skirl, Cardinal Holridge clutched the drill tight under his armpit and advanced on his target. Blips of trigger-happy power surges betrayed his nervousness as he neared the impenetrable surface and lined up.

'This is it,' he reminded himself and squeezed the trigger hard. In seconds, the bit was spinning at a good fifteen hundred revs per minute, hammer action primed and ready. For a brief moment the whining Bosch filled O'Suilleabhain's mind with screaming images of sadistic dentists. But, mercifully, it was only a brief moment. Holridge lurched forward, struck the outer hull of the alien craft and leaned all his might on to that tip of spinning diamond. Whine turned to drumming, teeth rattled in their sockets and the drill began sheeting a shower of pyrotechnics that would have made any Bonfire Night sparkler quiver with envy.

A thin wisp of smoke curled up from the hull and his Holy Shoulders pressed harder. Earthly diamond squealed against alien alloy and suddenly, with a cough of shorting electronics, the Bosch's motor burnt out.

Cardinal Holridge stood choking in a cloud of acrid smoke, cursing. Snarling, he hurled the dead drill across the lab. It bounced to a halt beneath a distant table, next to three fused Black and Deckers.

'Damn that thing!' cursed Holridge with a very unholy look on his face. 'Damn it. Damn it!'

The alien craft shone with a smug air of impenetrability, not a scratch showing from the DIY assault.

'Ahhh, now I thought that might happen,' offered Father Fintan O'Suilleabhain, looking up from the preserved index finger of some ancient saint. 'I knew it would be tough. I knew it.'

'Oh, did you now?' growled Holridge, grabbing another tool from a bench and fitting a full-face welder's mask. 'Well, let's see how it copes with this!'

'I don't think you'll have much joy,' suggested Fintan, watching Holridge stalk across the lab with a screaming angle grinder in his hands.

Cascades of sparks fountained across the lab as the matter of different galaxies met head on.

The Earthly one lost, the angle-grinder suffering the equivalent wear of slicing a hundred thousand paving slabs in three seconds.

'This is not a problem,' insisted Holridge, more for the benefit of his self-esteem than anything else. '*Not* a problem.' The toothless angle-grinder clattered into a corner and he dashed towards a trembling oxyacetylene torch over by a distant cupboard.

One click of his Zippo and a tongue of flame licked from the nozzle. 'Ready for this? Huh? Are you?' he muttered under his breath as he altered the mix to give a searing point of translucent violet. In seconds the flame was licking the hull in a nimbus of intense heat.

Cardinal Holridge's determination only started to flag when his asbestos gloves began smouldering and his visor turned to syrup.

It was then he decided that perhaps a more subtle approach was needed.

'Where are those X-rays?' he shouted. 'Bring them here. Now!'

Across the lab, Cardinal Kotonawa looked up from a computer terminal full of star charts and tutted. 'Find the NASA website, fetch the X-rays. One day he'll make his mind up,' he grumbled under his breath.

'Kotonawa, the X-rays? C'mon, c'mon!'

'Patience is virtue,' mumbled the Japanese one and forced an inscrutable smile in his favourite Shinto manner. He picked up a wad of photographic sheets and headed towards a large expanse of wall-mounted light-box.

'Patience? Hmmmm, that's a virtue I can't afford right now,' cursed Holridge and flicked the lights on. Fluorescent tubes blinked reluctantly into life and showed a neat collage of eight slides making up the now familiar pattern of the alien craft. Sadly it was totally opaque, as black as a Balinese shadow puppet and twice as incomprehensible.

'And what's that supposed to be?' gasped Holridge pointing at the silhouette on the wall.

'X-rays,' answered Kotonawa helpfully.

'No, they can't be. X-rays show the inside of things. You know, details of hinges, locks, clues that'll tell us how to open this thing up.' He squinted closer, searching desperately for the fine tracery of circuits and pipe-work he needed. 'That shows nothing.'

'On the contrary,' announced Kotonawa. Holridge turned, glowering expectantly. 'They show it is useless to peer into spaceships with X-rays.'

Holridge's voice, when it came, was strained through a filter of politeness. 'Thank you for that most enlightening of observations. If you have anything else as useful to add in the near future, please, please don't hesitate to keep it to yourself.'

Holridge whisked a magnifying glass off a suitable table and began peering at the collage of X-ray prints, his nose inches from the wall. 'There's got to be something here. Nothing is that impervious to X-rays. *Nothing.*'

Kotonawa shrugged and, wielding a cross-head screwdriver with the casual ease of a majorette, decided to see precisely how destroyed the four power-drills really were. Maybe, if he could just salvage the brushes from one, the coil from another and . . .

He didn't get very far.

Whether it was the sudden look of alarm that inhabited Father Fintan's face, the way he pointed a trembling finger, or simply the eerie creak of the table which made Cardinal Kotonawa halt in his sandalled tracks he would never be certain, but halt he did. Slowly, sensing that something definitely untoward was happening behind him, he turned. Almost instantly his jaw dropped.

The spacecraft began to move.

Slowly at first, but gaining speed and rhythm, it began to rock back and forth. Beneath it, the trolley creaked objection with every oscillation.

'Stop rocking on your chair, Kotonawa,' hissed Holridge his eyes straining at the wall of X-ray pictures. 'Can't you see I'm concentrating.'

'Er . . . I . . . I . . .'

The spacecraft rocked a little more forcefully, the trolley groaning like a badly maintained four-poster in the company of a pair of over-enthusiastic newlyweds.

'Kotonawa, this is not helping,' growled Holridge over a background of grinding furniture. Father Fintan rubbed a finger around the inside of his collar, watching the oscillations of the shining craft. Unwittingly, he found himself humming Ravel's *Boléro* in a slow and particularly lecherous manner.

'Be quiet.' An artery pulsed at Holridge's temple as he tried in vain to ignore the distractions emanating from behind him.

The rhythm of the spacecraft picked up a few beats per minute and Holridge's concentration snapped. Dropping his magnifying glass he fixed Kotonawa with one of his hardest stares, took a deep breath and spluttered into undignified silence with the anticlimax of a Skoda on a cold morning. His eyes looked past his Japanese colleague and began swinging gently from side to side, captured by the hypnotic motions of the gleaming craft.

'What's it doing?' whispered Holridge, trying his best not to think of quivering Nissan Micras in secluded spots of romantic woodland, windows steadily steaming up as passions overtook ventilation systems. 'What's it doing?'

'Well, it's a spaceship,' began Fintan, almost hypnotised. 'Maybe it's getting ready for blast-off . . .'

Holridge stared at the two Ytterbium Collider Drive exhausts rocking before him. The purple sheen of metal all too recently exposed to exceedingly high temperatures blinked at him as knowingly as panda's eyes.

'B . . . blast off?' he choked and the table ground back its reply. 'You mean like ignition and . . . and . . . whooooooof?' Holridge's arms whirled about his head in a surprisingly accurate impersonation of a NASA shuttle hurling itself into orbit on roiling clouds of solid fuel afterburn.

Kotonawa and O'Suilleabhain nodded, their heads moving in time with the craft.

'But . . . but . . . if that happens then . . .' He stared down the double barrels of the exhausts, convincing himself that, even now, unfathomable technology was pumping explosive fluids up to requisite operating pressures, moments away from a sudden unstoppable eruption.

The spacecraft shuddered suddenly and the gyrations picked up their tempo.

'Run!' shouted Holridge, grabbing Kotonawa by the scruff of the dog-collar and bundling Father Fintan out of the lab ahead of him. As he slammed them shut behind him he found himself wondering just how blast-proof the lab's blast-proof doors really were.

'C'mon, this way, this way!' yelled Holridge, a little disappointed that he didn't have to fight with klaxons warning everyone in a half-mile radius that they were in the middle of a very dangerous 'Red Alert'. He sprinted off down the corridor, heeled around a corner and realised with a spasm of disappointment that he was alone.

Kotonawa and O'Suilleabhain stood, noses pressed to the window, steaming the glass like a pair of fifteen-year-olds window-shopping in Amsterdam.

'Get away from there,' shouted Holridge. 'Run, while you still can!'

Father Fintan stared in through the window, his hips swaying in time with the grinding of the alien vessel, his eyes wide.

And suddenly, just as it looked as if the trolley in the lab wouldn't last another minute, the spacecraft shuddered, seemed to hover in a moment of ecstasy and rocked gently to an oddly satisfied halt.

'D . . . did you hear that?' asked Father Fintan a few moments later as Holridge eased himself around the corner and peered into the lab.

'What? Did I hear what?'

'Well, it sort of sounded like "Ahhh . . . ahh . . . ah . . . ah . . . ahhhhhhhhhhhhh",' answered Fintan.

'Like *When Hally Met Sarry*,' added Kotonawa, in one of his more helpful moments.

O'Suilleabhain nodded and looked at his feet, feeling a blush of extreme embarrassment coming on as he realised quite why the spacecraft had been gyrating in such a rhythmic manner.

Holridge swallowed noisily. 'No! You're . . . you're not saying that . . . that in there . . . in that spaceship there've been two . . . two aliens . . . at it? In my lab?'

'Well, I . . .' began Father Fintan, peeling his eyes away from the floor. 'Love is a wonderful . . . Aaaah, look!' He leapt away from the window and pointed frantically into the lab.

All eyes stared as the atmospheric entry shield on the front of the spacecraft shimmered fluidly and folded back, disappearing into two previously undetectable pockets. Beneath it lay a curved expanse of alien neo-silicate visor which, under normal circumstances, would have been ten times clearer than the finest of lead crystal. Right now it was a bit steamed up. A single purple digit rose dreamily from the floor of the vessel and began wistfully drawing in the thick layer of condensation on the inside of the windscreen.

'Look, it's a . . . a t . . . t . . .!' announced Kotonawa, turning pale and collapsing in the corridor.

Idly the red-wine-coloured tentacle picked out a sequence of drippy letters, scrawled a plus sign underneath and wrote another series of unfathomable letters beneath. Nonchalantly, it surrounded the lot with an anatomically dubious representation of the organ used by certain alien species to circulate any particular bodily fuids essential to life. Oddly, it bore an uncanny similarity to a large clover leaf.

'Er, I think that answers your question,' said Fintan.

20:12 The Vatican

In a small room in the depths of the Vatican, words were flying like distressed puffins whilst several hundred million lire's worth of high-tech computer equipment gnawed on a few terrabytes. Scipioni, the erstwhile director of *Gazan Dolls*, stabbed a finger triumphantly in the middle of the Bible. 'Got it!' he announced. 'This is perfect.'

Pope Angeles barely stifled a groan. 'What is it now?' he asked reluctantly.

He looked at the name on the page again to remind himself. 'This . . . Noah, eh? What about Noah?'

'Yes?'

'It's perfect for my Sophia!' declared Scipioni, his thoughts shimmering with delicious images of his well-upholstered tank commander behind the helm of the Ark. She stood, wrestling with the tiller in full Technicolor, rain lashing her from all angles, her clothing sticking to her in all the right places and a few more besides. With the correct lighting and translucent garments he knew it would be utterly wonderful.

'Oh, no, no, no,' moaned Angeles, head in hands.

'Why not?' snarled Scipioni. 'Why won't you let her play Noah? C'mon admit it, you don't like her do you?'

'It's not that . . .' began the Pope. 'It's just that she's . . . well, face it, she's just not the Noah type.'

'Nonsense! She can captain a ship in the highest of seas. Haven't you seen *Breakfast at Tripoli?* She should have had an Oscar for the way she landed that frigate in complete darkness and right under the nose of the enemy . . .'

'I'm not talking about her no doubt massive maritime skills . . .'

'And she can herd any animal you can name. Two by two, ten by ten, or any other numbers you pick . . .'

'I'm sure she can . . .'

'So what's wrong with her being Noah then, eh?'

'Because Noah isn't, and never will be, a five-foot-six drop-dead-gorgeous Italian babe, that's why.'

Scipioni's face reddened angrily. 'There you go again, making excuses.'

'It's true, look it up in there!' snapped Angeles pointing to the well thumbed copy of the Bible.

'Details, details,' growled Scipioni flicking over the pages at random. 'I'm tellin' you now, Sophia in a wet T-shirt would look ten times – a hundred times – better than any pot-bellied, bearded . . . Aha! What about this Methuselah, then? That's got to be a woman with a name like that.'

'Old guy with a beard,' answered Angeles, shaking his head.

'Er . . . Pontius Pilate? Whoever heard of a guy called Pontius?'

'The whole Roman Empire,' tutted the Pope.

'You're kidding, right?'

'Deadly serious.'

'Well, we're in real trouble here. I mean disaster,' wailed Scipioni, throwing his hands in the air with the gusto for which Italians are famed. 'You said make it look good, right? Make it bring loads of teenagers in. Teenagers don't want to see a film cast entirely from men with beards. They want something pleasing to the eye . . . A bit of seduction . . . A bit of . . .'

'Sophia?'

'Exactly. And the more bits of her the better. See? Now, c'mon, you know she's perfect for Noah.'

'No way,' insisted His Holiness.

'Okay, okay, where does it say Noah's a man, eh?' challenged Scipioni, holding the Bible out to the head of the Roman Catholic Church. 'Show me.'

'Genesis 6:9. Look it up yourself. Then try 6:18 and 7:5 . . .'

Scipioni looked lost, the Bible unopened in his hands.

'That's page six,' offered Angeles. 'About a quarter of the way down. "Noah was a righteous man . . ." See? Then straight across from there. "And Noah did all that the Lord commanded him." Him, you see? It's there in black and white.'

'Ahhh, now, not so fast there,' said Scipioni, his finger alighting under a very baffling sentence, his eyebrows curling with the delight of a defence lawyer who has just found the tiniest of legal loopholes. 'Are you absolutely sure every word in here's right? I mean, that could just be a slip up in translation couldn't it? Him, her, it's easily done.'

'Don't be ridiculous.'

'Well, it says here that Noah was six hundred years old? That's got to be a mistake, surely?'

Pope Angeles snorted, stood and headed for the door.

'Where are you going? I haven't finished yet.'

'Since it's obvious you don't believe the translations, how about you look at the originals. I'm sure Cardinal Holridge would be only too pleased to give you a quick lesson in ancient Hebrew.' With that the Pope slid through the door in a flurry of Versace lounging vestments.

Scipioni was up and on his toes in seconds. He dashed through the door, excitement rising as he saw a glimmer of hope, a slim chance that he could get his Sophia into the Vatican and scanned in. Okay, so he didn't expect to have to learn ancient Hebrew to do it, but hey, she was worth it. She would be so grateful.

Riding whalebacks of mid-Atlantic swell, the USS *Indiscriminate* was steaming furiously towards the Mediterranean. In the privacy of the war room, Major-General Gelding III was venting spleen about how less than pleased he had been with the performance of the short-lived and eponymous Multi-Disciplinary Observation Force.

'I cannot believe it!' he fumed with almost as much vigour as his cigar. 'It was right there in front of us. And they took it away! We didn't even get the slightest glimpse of it!'

'If I may make a suggestion . . .' began Major-General Isenheimer.

'Damn those Cardinals,' ranted Gelding, pacing up and down. 'Never thought they'd be so damned secretive.'

'Ahem. A suggestion?' repeated the Head of Speculative Intelligence.

Gelding whirled on his heel and headed back across the war room carpet. 'So secretive. How in Hell are we going to find out what it is they've got? Can *anyone* tell me that?'

'I have been trying to do that very thing for the last twenty minutes,' said Isenheimer. 'I know precisely how we can get our hands on all the information we require prior to entering Italian waters.'

'Well, come on then. Spill it!'

'Agent Lincoln,' grinned Isenheimer.

'What?' gasped Gelding. 'Activate Agent Lincoln?'

'There's no need. He's already in place. Been inside for years. In fact, this is his fourth Pope,' said Isenheimer proudly.

'Well get on to him,' blustered Gelding, snatching a red telephone off the desk and thrusting it into Isenheimer's chest. 'Dial. Now!'

Safe behind an army of Swiss Guards and a very tall wall, a telephone rang.

'Hello, Agent Lincoln. It is an extremely fortuitous colouring of tie you are wearing today,' fizzed a voice through the earpiece.

'It matches my eyes with utmost accuracy,' answered Agent Lincoln, delivering the identification code with casual efficiency.

'Agent Lincoln, I have a small job for you . . .'

A shady figure in a secretive room pulled out a pad and pen and, under the stony gaze of a pair of cavorting cherubs, began writing.

20:38 The Vatican

Cardinal Holridge and Father O'Suilleabhain peered at the motionless alien craft and, as they had done for the last half hour, wondered what to do next. Much as it hurt his professional pride, Holridge was beginning to have to admit he was at a bit of a loss.

'Is it safe?' asked Father Fintan nervously.

'Judging by the state of those drills, I would say the answer is a definite yes,' mused Holridge, casting a weary eye over the heap of shattered DIY equipment on a bench in the corner. 'Nothing's going to get in there without whatever's in there giving permission, if you see what I mean.'

Father Fintan nodded, his eyes fixed on the ship.

'Hmmm, thus one problem remains,' said Holridge, rubbing his chin. 'How *do* we persuade them to come out?'

'A siege,' offered Fintan. 'They're bound to come out sooner or later for food.'

'More likely to be later,' said Holridge. 'The distances involved in interstellar travel will have ensured that these aliens will have already solved the problem of their nutritional needs. Perhaps even before they lifted off for the first time.'

'Not necessarily,' said Fintan hopefully. 'Maybe their cupboards are bare and they stopped off here to grab a few supplies.' He pointed to the image drawn in the misty neo-silicate screen. 'Maybe that's a shopping list.'

'More likely to be a warning.'

'No, they wouldn't send out a warning like that. There'd be sirens and klaxons and flashing lights.'

'This is not some tacky sci-fi B-movie,' insisted Holridge. 'We're dealing with highly intelligent beings here, I'm certain of it!'

Outside, in a not too-distant corridor, His Holiness the Pope wasn't so sure that he was dealing with an intelligent being at all. He hurried down a corridor of the Papal Academy of Sciences in a flurry of Versace lounging vestments. Hard on his heels was Giorgio Scipioni, red leather-bound Bible tight under his armpit. 'And another thing,' pestered the director, 'if Noah really was six hundred years old wouldn't he, or she, have had more sons? I mean, three in six centuries isn't very impressive is it?'

Pope Angeles whirled around a corner, his teeth grinding.

'And what about grandchildren, eh? All those years and not one to show for it . . .'

With a surge of relief, Angeles caught sight of the very door he had dashed across the entire width of Vatican Hill to reach; the door to the laboratory of Cardinal Holridge and the Congregation for Icon Authentication. If anyone could give Scipioni the answers he wanted, it had to be Holridge. He put on a spurt and lunged for the handle.

He and Scipioni were a good ten feet into the underground lab before the scene hit them. Open-mouthed they slowed to a standstill and looked around.

The guts of three Black and Deckers and a Bosch lay in a

small sacrificial heap on a bench. A toothless angle-grinder and an empty oxyacetylene torch sulked in the corners they had been flung into. But it was the unfeasibly shiny thing on the trolley that really grabbed their attention.

'What . . . what is it?' spluttered the Pope, trying desperately to think of any icon which could possibly look like that.

'Ah, Your Holiness, what an unexpected surprise,' swallowed Holridge, leaping to his feet.

'What is that?' repeated the Pontiff, pointing.

Holridge, somewhat at a loss to know precisely where best to begin, pointed to the Irish priest genuflecting at the papal Nike trainers and said, 'Your Holiness, this is Father Fintan O'Suilleabhain. I guess you could say he's . . . er, responsible for this.'

'Oh, Holy Father,' gushed Fintan excitedly and began smothering the papal ring with hundreds of kisses.

The Pope looked from the top of Fintan's bobbing head to the gleaming craft and, his mind still reeling with thoughts of *Faith: The Final Frontier*, he leapt effortlessly to entirely the wrong conclusion. 'You're responsible for this? You . . . you *made* it?'

Fintan looked up. 'Well, I wouldn't go as far as that . . .' he began but the Pope was away across the lab.

'How did you do it?' asked Angeles, staring awestricken at the gleaming surface. 'Papier mâché? Fibreglass?' He tapped the hull of the alien spacecraft with his knuckle. It rang with the unmistakable tones of alien alloy.

Holridge and Fintan barely controlled the urge to leap for instant cover.

Across the lab, Scipioni's eyes lit up in amazement. In all his years of directing films he hadn't seen quite such a convincing-looking prop.

'All these inscriptions,' enthused the Pope, 'are they based on anything? Egyptian, or Sanskrit, or Hebrew?'

O'Suilleabhain scratched his head and shrugged in confusion.

'You can tell me,' urged the Pope. 'Your trade secrets are safe with me.' Scipioni sidled towards the bewildered Father Fintan, eager to catch any pearls of manufacturing wisdom that may fall his way.

'I . . . I've never seen anything like it in my life,' admitted Fintan.

'Oh, very good. Made them all up? Well, no copyright problems there then, eh? And the shape? Where did you get that from?'

'Er, it just . . . came to me,' answered Fintan, wondering why it was that he was being asked such peculiar questions. It was strange but he almost got the impression that the Pope thought he had perhaps had a hand in designing the thing.

Angeles headed around the back of the craft and stared in ignorance at a pair of Type-23 Ytterbium Collider Drive exhausts. A magical purple sheen of overheating spread around them like chocolate ice-cream on a four-year-old's face. 'Oh, look at those colours. So realistic, but . . .' He turned and fixed O'Suilleabhain with a concerned expression. 'Now don't get me wrong, I like it, I really do, but I think we'll have to lose that for the Ezekiel shots. What d'you think, Scipioni? See, I want to get the feeling that the craft are powered by the Will of God rather than flame-throwers or warp engines, or whatever it was you were trying to show here. You weren't to know, of course. I only decided that yesterday. Still, should only take ten minutes with a can of gold spray to cover that. Well, that and the ring of eyes around them. Er, you can do a ring of eyes, can't you?'

Father Fintan's eyebrows crawled up his forehead.

'Of course you can. Anybody that can make something this realistic could probably knock off something that simple in their sleep. And don't worry too much about the budget, I've already earmarked . . .'

'Make something?' spluttered Fintan, his mind finally catching up with Pope Angeles's babbling. 'You don't think I made that? With my own hands?'

'Well, okay, you probably had an assistant. Holridge, it wasn't you, was it? I somehow got the impression that you were against the whole idea of *Faith: The Final Frontier*. Not turning up like that . . .'

'Against? Me? Er, Your Holiness . . . I went to collect . . .'

'You collected this? For me? Oh, Holridge, thank you!' smiled Angeles. 'Still, that doesn't solve the problem about rings of eyes around the middle of the ship. Now I'm sure we could stretch the Religious Education budget to cover a student from art college or . . .'

'Your Holiness,' began Fintan, feeling suddenly nervous. He wasn't exactly used to contradicting the head of the Universal Church. Well, not face to face anyhow. 'Er, if you think that I had a hand in making that then you are . . . er, how can I say it . . . wrong.'

A look of disappointment slithered on to Scipioni's face.

Pope Angeles raised an eyebrow but continued to examine the far side of the craft.

'Your Holiness, I didn't have anything to do with it,' insisted Fintan. 'This was built by no man's hand. It came from outer space and . . .'

'Yes, yes, and I'm sure you want everybody to believe that's true. I must say it does look convincing enough. But . . .'

'But it *is* true!'

'Oh, nonsense,' tutted the Pope, examining the side for any signs of a door handle. 'C'mon, open it up, I want to see

197

inside. Are there any aliens in there? Which d'you prefer H.R. Giger's beasties or ET?'

'Well, Giger anytime, but what's that got to do with . . .' spluttered Fintan, looking pleadingly at Holridge for support.

'Personally, I'd go for the Giger look too, all black and shiny and deadly. I like that in an alien. Gives me the creeps mind but you can't beat a good shiny black . . .'

'Tell him I haven't a clue what he's on about!'

'He hasn't a clue what you're on about, Your Holiness,' offered Holridge helpfully.

The Pope peered under the curve of the atmosphere-scorched hull and frowned. 'What is this? Some kind of joke? You should know if you put aliens inside or not. Is there something wrong with your memory from sniffing all those fibreglass solvents, hmmm?'

Fintan looked around desperately. 'Your Holiness, I . . . I'd know if there was aliens in there if I'd actually put aliens in there but I really haven't so I really don't,' he blurted and began fiddling with his nails.

'Well, open the door then, and we'll see if your assistant put . . .'

'I didn't have an assistant.'

'Well, at least let me see how you've decorated the inside. Is it all sticky and slimy? C'mon, open the door.'

'I . . . I can't,' whimpered Fintan. 'I don't know how. I didn't make it!'

And for the first time in what seemed to Fintan to be far too long, Pope Angeles stopped grilling him.

It was, however, a temporary hiatus.

'Well, if *you* didn't make it, then who . . . ?'

A heavily pregnant pause settled uncomfortably around the lab. It would have stayed there ages, picking out nursery colour schemes and waiting for the onset of labour, had it not been for the sudden arrival of Cardinal Kotonawa. He burst through the door, waggling a sheaf of printouts. 'I've got it, I've got it!' he declared and, shoving the scattered intestines of four drills on to the floor, he slammed them on to the bench. 'You'll never believe where it came from.'

Holridge and Fintan were over by the bench in seconds as Kotonawa dropped a lozenge of metal on to the bench and began pointing out certain undeniable similarities between the diamond laser-etched star chart on the alien alloy and the laser-printed star charts on the bench. 'Here's the Pleiades cluster. Here's the Horsehead Nebula. And this is . . .'

'Galaxy 3C390.3,' whispered Holridge in a growing state of shock. 'That's incredible.'

'It gets better,' grinned Kotonawa, pointing to a small arrow on the metal disc. 'See that? I couldn't figure what it meant before, but now I'm certain it means "beyond galaxy 3C390.3" '

Holridge swallowed and reached for a chair. 'But that means . . .'

'Yes. That ship came from a region of space which we can see only once in every two thousand years.'

'You mean . . . ?'

Kotonawa, Holridge and O'Suilleabhain stared simultaneously towards the outer reaches of charted space.

'This came from . . . the Star of Bethlehem?' whispered Holridge.

Kotonawa nodded.

'Guys, guys, c'mon this *is* a joke, yeah?' asked the Pope incredulously.

'The NASA website doesn't seem to think so,' said Kotonawa as matter-of-factly as he dared.

The Pope was round the front of the spaceship in a flurry of Versace. 'You've been on to NASA?'

'Well, we had to be absolutely sure of what we had before we mentioned it to you,' winced Holridge, feeling like he was guilty of some sort of crime.

'And what exactly *do* you have here?' asked the Pope.

'Er . . . I believe it's called a First Contact scenario,' offered Holridge, feeling the lino beneath his feet turn into the very thinnest of ice sheets.

'Eh?'

'You know, the first meeting of mankind and his distant extraterrestrial cousins.'

The Pope looked over his shoulder at the interstellar hatchback and began to have the horrible feeling he was beginning to know why the thing looked so convincingly realistic. 'First Contact?' he whispered, mostly to himself.

'We had to get to them first,' explained Holridge, kicking reasonable science in the face of the head of the Roman Catholic Church while he was reeling. 'Er . . . after all who better to say "Hi" than you, Your Holiness?'

'Of course,' agreed Kotonawa. 'Who's to say if we can trust any of the world's governments with something so important.'

'Yes, yes,' rejoined Holridge. 'They'd have this covered up and our distant cousins dissected before we could say Novena. I mean look at the fuss the Americans kicked up in 1947. All that over a crumpled weather balloon. Now, just think what they'd do if they found this?'

Pope Angeles was wearing the type of expression you'd expect of a Pontiff if he'd just found out God was a transvestite and travelled across the outback in a bus called Priscilla.

'And besides,' offered Holridge, 'we had every right to bring them here. They did land on Vatican property.'

Father Fintan nodded in nervous agreement and tried not to think about chapel roof repair funds.

200

Angeles stood in the lab, his head whirling with shock. 'But . . . but . . . how d'you *know* it's really well . . . alien?' he whispered, turning almost as white as his Versace vestments.

Giorgio Scipioni tapped the Pope on the shoulder and pointed to the ship. 'Er, do you know of any Earthly technology that can do that?'

Before their very eyes a seam was starting to form in the gleaming hull, tracing out the shape of a door with the geometric skill of circus-trained mercury.

Pope Angeles screamed, upturned a handy table and leapt behind it for cover.

'What's happening?' squeaked Cardinal Holridge, on the floor behind another table.

The hairline fracture grew to a good quarter-inch and, with a fluid whirring of utterly alien technology, a panel in the side of the craft gull-winged towards the ceiling. Duvets of green-tinged moisture tumbled across the trolley, settling momentarily like liquid cotton wool before oozing away across the floor.

The gull-wing door clicked to a halt and Father Fintan found himself thinking of de Lorean sports cars pulling up outside Monte Carlo casinos. But instead of a deliciously turned feminine ankle appearing at the roadside, heralding the imminent unravelling of a Bond-girl lookalike, a squat purple appendage stomped on to the trolley. Seconds later, it was joined by another two and, before anyone in the lab could move, a six-foot-tall conical alien had jumped on to the floor. It chirruped in an eerily fluid manner, turned and offered a helpful appendage to its mustard-yellow travelling companion.

Kotonawa stared across at the waggling tentacles and, silently making himself a promise that he would never touch sushi again, he collapsed behind a table.

'You Could've Wiped It!'

As a successful example of intergalactic brotherhood and cosmic cosiness, the First Contact scenario in the basement lab of the Pontifical Academy of Sciences wasn't really shaping up to very much. Ten embarrassing minutes had already slithered by without so much as a 'D'you come here often?' or a 'Take me to your leader' passing between aliens and clergy. And, much to Pope Angeles's mounting disappointment, it looked as if many more tens of equally unsuccessful minutes were destined to follow.

He stared across the laboratory, taking in all the relevant details. The three tentacles, the triplet of elephant-like feet, the curiously pursed tube which stuck out the front of what he assumed was their faces – if not, he shuddered to think what he'd been staring at for the last ten minutes. But he was most fascinated by their colours. One mottled in the rich purples of Ribena and Merlot, the other a mousse of English and French mustards fighting for supremacy. Somehow they clashed superbly. Now if he could just get Gaultier to run him up a suit in that purple and have Armani run him up a mustard waistcoat . . . Ohhhh, Heaven.

The taller purple alien trilled and cooed once more with the fluidity and meaning of a skylark in summer and waggled a pair of tentacles in a hypnotic, but extremely baffling manner.

202

'What? What are you saying?' said the Pope, his palms outstretched. 'Look, I'll keep this simple, okay? I'm the Pope. Me. Pope. Head of Roman Catholic Church. Me.' He tapped a ringed finger proudly against his Versace-upholstered chest. 'Supreme Pontiff. Vicar of Christ. Sovereign of the State of the Vatican City. Understand? That's me too. Successor of St Peter. That's me as well. Me . . .'

'Er, Your Holiness . . .' began Holridge nervously.

'Metropolitan of the Roman Province. I'm that too. See? And then there's the Patriarch of the West and . . .'

'Your Holiness. I don't think this is helping.'

Angeles held up an apologetic hand to the aliens and turned on Holridge. 'Not helping? Of course it is. They've got to know who they're talking to,' he whispered.

'But . . . well, I don't think they do.'

'You sure?' gasped the Pope, looking concerned. Stifling a sigh, he turned back to the pair holding tentacles under the shadow of their gull-wing door.

'Hmmm, you have a point.' Speaking slower and significantly louder, he started again. 'Look, *I'm* the *Pope*. Me. Me.' The aliens shuffled back a step. 'The Pope. Head of the Roman Catholic . . . What? Why are you looking at me like that?' He turned on Holridge.

'Because they don't understand a word you're saying,' answered the Head of the Congregation for Icon Authentication.

'Oh.' Desperately, he turned back to the aliens and stabbed his chest. 'Pope? Me?'

'It's no good, Your Holiness.'

'And I suppose you have a better idea?'

'Well, er . . .'

'Great. So how are we supposed to get through to them, eh?'

For a few moments silence filled the lab until suddenly

Scipioni's eyes lit up. He dashed across to the Pope. 'Er, I know it's a bit of a long shot, but why don't you . . .' He ended the sentence by whispering into Angeles's ear.

'You're serious?' asked the Pope.

'It worked on top of the Devil's Tower, it should be a piece of cake for you.'

'But Giorgio, *that* was a movie.'

'Well, how else are you going to get through, eh? There isn't exactly much choice.'

'All right, all right. Let's try it. I want a musician here, now!' he demanded and glared at Kotonawa and O'Suilleabhain. 'Go fetch. Now! There's bound to be one hanging about in St Peter's Square.'

The Cardinal shrugged at the priest and headed off for the door. Fintan's hand was on its handle and twisting as Angeles suddenly barked another order. 'Wait a minute. You, O'Suilleabhain. You're Irish, aren't you?'

Father Fintan nodded warily.

'Well, don't you play anything? All Irish play some sort of musical instrument, don't they?'

'Er, well, I don't know about musical, but I've got this.' He produced an extremely battered and salt-corroded mouth organ from a pocket.

'Can you play that for me?' asked the Pope eagerly.

'Ahh now, I'm not too good at requests . . .'

'I'm not looking for much. Just five notes.'

'Five notes? That won't be keeping anyone entertained for long now, will it?'

'We're not meant to be entertaining them. Just communicating with them.'

'With . . . with this?' Fintan looked doubtfully at his well-sucked mouth organ and scratched his head. Many an hour he had spent blowing on that chunk of metal and never once had he considered that one day it would be used to reach out across the infinite divide of space to touch one of his interstellar brethren. To date the furthest he'd ever reached was to irritate the entire block at seminary.

'Yes, with that mouth organ and the power of music,' declared the Pope, wishing that a documentary camera crew had captured that moment for posterity.

'Now, would there be any particular five notes you're wanting?' asked Fintan, licking his lips and burying the mouth organ in an envelope of fingers. This was going to be an interstellar message with just the right vibrato. 'How 'bout the opening of "O'Rafferty's Pig"?' If it was good enough for Val Doonican . . .' He took a preparatory breath.

'No, no!' squeaked the Pope. 'There's only one set of five notes for a time like this . . . Think!'

Father Fintan rolled his eyes as he thought hard. 'Of course! How silly of me. I should have thought instantly of Chris de Burgh's Christmas classic "A Spaceman Came Travelling".' And, readying himself for his own unique rendition of the sugary chorus, he filled his lungs.

The Pope was across the lab in seconds, the palm of his hand slapping itself across the row of holes. 'No, no, no! *Anything* but that!' The mouth organ wheezed and died with a gurgle. The Pope was staring deep into O'Suilleabhain's eyes. 'Five notes. Root, up a tone, down a major third, down an octave, up a fifth.'

Father Fintan's eyes closed as he ran through the sequence in his head. 'Oh, you mean the *Close Encounters* theme?'

Pope Angeles nodded vigorously.

'Why didn't you say?' Fintan took a breath and launched into a very rough version of the infamous synthesised string patch.

The silence which greeted it was utterly embarrassing. The aliens angled their eye-stalks to look at each other and shrugged an array of muscles above their tentacles.

'Again,' urged the Pope. 'Play it again.'

Six eye-stalks swivelled silently towards Fintan and stared unblinkingly.

'Again, again. You're getting through.'

Fintan licked his lips and blew again. The aliens waggled eye-stalks in all directions, taking in the scene. Had they possessed the necessary musculature they would certainly have been furrowing their brightly hued brows.

Instead, they glanced quickly at each other and, in the blink of an eye, whirled on their feet and slithered back into their craft. With a hiss of alien hydraulics the door slammed shut and the atmospheric seals healed over.

'Oh great, oh great. Now look what you've done,' snarled Pope Angeles, glaring accusingly at Fintan and Scipioni in turn.

'But, I did say I wasn't up to much,' whimpered Fintan, glancing at Holridge and Kotonawa for any offer of support. 'How am I supposed to get through to them if they're cooped up in their ship again?'

'You wanted to communicate,' suggested Scipioni nervously. 'I . . . I think we have.' He smiled thinly.

'And what, pray do tell, makes you think we got anything useful out of that?'

'Well,' hedged Scipioni, 'if ever they do come out of there again, we'll know not to be serenading them with mouth organs. Spielberg was right to use nasty big synths. Ahhh, what a film-maker, so insightful.'

The Pope gave Scipioni one of his most withering looks. 'Damn shame he wasn't available at short notice. C'mon you, we've still got work to do.' In a swirl of Versace he stormed towards the door.

'But what about Sophia?' squeaked Scipioni and turned desperately to Cardinal Holridge. 'Tell me, was Noah a man or a woman?'

'Ahhh, now that depends on which translation you read,' began Holridge before he caught sight of the icy stare the Pope was giving him. 'But . . . but er, all of them agree he's a man. Every one.' He ended on a mozzarella grin and a curtsey.

'Told you,' hissed Angeles and disappeared through the door. 'Now come on!'

Scipioni turned and ran after him. 'Wait, what about Moses? She's perfect for that. I'm tellin' you, they'd be queuing up to go off for forty days hiking with her. I know *I* would!'

'No,' insisted the Pope.

'C'mon, Sophia's perfect for those desert scenes. She sweats so divinely, you know. I tell you she can make droplets of perspiration trickle towards her navel on demand. She'll get an Oscar for that one day, you mark my words . . .'

Scipioni's voice faded down the corridor failing totally to cut any papal mustard.

In the lab, Father Fintan sat on a table swinging his legs despondently. Miserably, he stared at his mouth organ lying in his lap and breathed a heavy sigh. Okay, so he'd be the first to admit that he was nary a patch on the great Larry Adler, but his mouth organ playing had never caused his audience to flee for cover and bolt themselves away out of earshot. Well, all right, so he'd never actually *had* a real face-to-face audience before, but that was beside the point.

'Got any more drills?' asked Cardinal Holridge, rubbing his chin thoughtfully, staring at the gleaming and hauntingly silent spacecraft.

'You've destroyed them all,' said the Japanese Cardinal, shaking his head and looking at the smouldering heap of ex-power tools.

'Hmmm, now maybe if I could get a screwdriver in the gap in the door . . .'

'What gap? It's gone.'

'No, no, I can still see it, I'm sure I can still see it. There . . . look.'

Kotonawa peered through his thick glasses at the exact spot to which Holridge was pointing. The reflection which stared back from the alloy hull was utterly seamless.

However, half an inch to the right of Kotonawa's convex alter ego, a small slit began to appear. It extended itself vertically across the hull, the alloy seeming to melt before their very eyes.

'Screwdriver, quick!' hissed Holridge, holding out the palm of his hand like the most demanding of open-heart surgeons.

'What for?' asked charge nurse Kotonawa.

'Get a screwdriver in there and I can prise the thing wide open.'

'I don't think you'll need to do that. Look!'

The gap widened to a good quarter of an inch and, with only the slightest hiss of extraterrestrial hydraulics, the door arced open again.

'Ha, ha, cracked it,' chuckled Holridge excitedly. 'It was the threat of the screwdriver that did it. Now, all we need to do is wedge it open and . . .'

Suddenly, the doorway was blocked by the two aliens as they slithered into view and jumped on to the floor. Before anyone could move, the purple one planted a four-foot-high tripod in the middle of the lab and his beautiful mustard assistant slapped a curious-looking box on top. It glowed eerily, emitting crackles of static like a badly tuned radio in a thunderstorm. The Merlot-and-Ribena-coloured alien focused three withering eye-stalks on the hissing device and landed a well-aimed tentacle on top. There was a squeal of protest and the hissing stopped.

Holridge, Kotonawa and O'Suilleabhain stared in baffled

silence, wondering what precisely the creatures were intending to do with that strange alien device. Would they be atomised with one flick of a switch? Or would their wills be bent to the service of these brightly hued invaders? Waves of sixties sci-fi paranoia lapped at O'Suilleabhain's toes, sending quivers of alarm up his legs.

Three purple eye-stalks twisted and peered directly at him, looking him up and down in the casually calculating way a butcher weighs up a pot-bellied pig. Much to his concern, the gaze seemed to linger far too long around the tender vicinity of his boxer shorts. Nervously, he felt things contracting, trying to hide. They didn't get a chance.

A purple tentacle lashed across the lab, closed around something and recoiled with a whip-like crack. Fintan screamed and checked the intactness of his anatomy. Much to his relief, there only appeared to be one thing missing.

Across the lab, the purple alien held the mouth organ up to a small orifice and, with vibrato in all the right places, blew a surprisingly accurate rendition of those famous five notes. The mustard-yellow alien leaned forward and cooed a gentle trilling sound at the device on the tripod and, almost instantly, the lab was filled with waves of fluent Russian. A yellow tentacle flicked a switch and, with barely a hiccup, the translation switched continents.

'. . . Фильма астерйск . . . Richard Dreyfuss in this seminal alien-encounter movie which marked Steven Spielberg's consolidation as a director and producer *par excellence*.'

Helpfully, the purple one played the five notes again and tossed the mouth organ back across the lab. It landed in O'Suilleabhain's lap barely missing some of his more tender parts. A smiggot of spittle glistened on the rusty instrument.

'You could've wiped it,' cringed Father Fintan and a strange cooing and trilling filtered out of the translator.

In a flash, the tentacle was back across the lab. It snatched the offending organ and was polishing it vigorously on a small towel grabbed from another table. In a second, Fintan's gob iron was back in his lap, clean and dry.

'You . . . you . . . understood,' gagged the bewildered priest and hoped that no one would ever ask him what the first words said to these visitors from beyond the stars had been. Given time and a stiff gin or five, he was sure he could've come up with something a little more auspicious than those four words.

'Course we understand,' said the purple alien. 'This translator is programmed with over one hundred and fifty thousand different languages.' He patted the odd device affectionately. 'And a stack o' dialects 'n' derivations that would 'ave you really knackered if y' tried shakin' a stick at 'em. Oh, bugger, it's flicked on to colloquial mode, hold up . . .' He nudged a dial. 'That should be of a more formal nature now. Am I correct?'

The three Earthlings nodded, Cardinal Holridge with somewhat more awe than the others.

'One hundred and fifty thousand languages,' he gasped. 'But . . . but why so many? There aren't that many on Earth.'

'There aren't that many in this galaxy,' answered the purple alien. 'It's a weakness of mine, but I hate subtitles.'

The three Earthmen looked at each other and shrugged. 'Subtitles?' asked Holridge eventually.

'Of course, those little things you get across the bottom of the screen that you can't read if there's anything white behind them. Really spoil the enjoyment of a decent film they do. I'm telling you, to appreciate the art house movies of Tau Ceti fully you need a really decent translator. Have you seen them?'

The three clergymen shook their heads.

'Oh, you really ought to. Of course, some of their favourite

210

ultraviolet passages might be a little lost on you, their compound eyes are bit more sensitive to UV. But then you'd know that, wouldn't you?'

'Er . . . we would?' shrugged Holridge, finding it rather difficult to believe he was having a conversation about intergalactic cinema with a six-foot purple alien.

'Well, actually, if I stop and think, I'm not sure I've seen any Tau Cetians here. Have you, dear?'

The mustard-yellow alien shrugged demurely. 'Plenty of others, but not them. No.'

'Hold on, hold on,' spluttered Holridge, scratching his head in total bafflement. 'Are you saying you've been here for weeks, months . . . ?'

'Oh, no, no. We just arrived.'

'Then what's all this about seeing Tau Cetians around here? How d'you know so much about what's going on our planet?'

'You haven't exactly been keeping it a secret. Your TV signals have been scattering all across the universe for decades. But, then, I'm not surprised you'd want to tell everyone. You Earthlings should be proud. It's not every planet that's got quite such a liberated attitude to extra-terrestrials. Not only providing shelter for any alien that passes your way, but you actually give them jobs.'

'Er . . . We do?'

'Oh, Kh'Xandhra, don't you just love them? They're so modest. It must be a way of life for them now. They don't even notice that some of their finest actors in their most popular shows are extraterrestrials.' He turned back to the gathered representatives of Earth. 'Well, now we're here, too. Where do we sign?'

Cardinal Holridge took a step backwards, grabbed Koto-nawa and O'Suilleabhain by the elbows and pulled them towards the door. 'Er . . . I . . . I . . . need to have a word with my colleagues,' he attempted to explain to the creatures from beyond the stars. 'Nothing serious, er . . . formalities, you know. Make yourselves at home.'

'We intend to,' smiled Kh'Vynn graciously and caressed the tentacle of his mustardy beloved.

Across the lab the door closed behind the three clergymen.

In the corridor outside, Cardinal Holridge held his head and tried to make sense of what he had just heard. 'Did you hear that?' he squeaked. 'Did you hear what they said? "Where do we sign?" What's going on?'

'It seems it's not an accident they're here,' whispered Father O'Suilleabhain staring into the middle distance. 'They *want* to be right here. On . . . on a casting couch.'

'Where do they think they are?' gagged Holridge. 'Hollywood?'

'Well, as a matter of fact . . .' began Fintan.

'No, no.' Holridge waved his palms in denial and backed away. 'Nothing crosses the icy wastes of space just to be in the movies. Nothing.'

'Nothing until now,' shrugged Fintan. 'Face it, Holridge, your lab is now full of stagestruck aliens. And, er, until we're finding out quite how they take to disappointment, I would be suggesting we go and find them a suitable casting couch.'

'Are you mad?'

'He does have a point,' conceded Kotonawa uncomfortably. 'After all, if they have the brains to build that spaceship, what weapons have they got stashed away inside?'

'No, no, they wouldn't. This . . . this is the Vatican! They wouldn't just vaporise it.'

'They might be Protestants,' pointed out Kotonawa.

Holridge's face turned pale as he looked over his shoulder into the lab. The yellow and purple aliens waved ostensibly friendly tentacles. Holridge swallowed. 'All right, all right, for the sake of the intactness of St Peter's and the prevention of a major intergalactic incident I will humour them. But, first thing in the morning, we tell the Pope everything. Clear?'

Fintan and Kotonawa nodded.

'Now, go and fetch me a couch. I don't care where you get it from, just make it comfortable. I reckon I'll be spending a long night on it.'

Holridge smoothed down his lab vestments, took a breath and headed back for the door. Seconds before he turned the handle he called down the corridor to the fleeing pair of clergy.

'And fetch me a copy of *The Alexander Technique*. All actors are supposed to need that, aren't they?'

'You're the boss,' shouted Kotonawa and skidded out of sight around the corner.

'But for how much longer,' whimpered Holridge to himself as he pushed open the door and re-entered the lab. His gaze settled on the shiny ship which he was convinced was bulging with thousands of kilotons of the deadliest of weaponry, balanced on the most delicate of hair triggers. He swallowed nervously and forced a smile.

Fifteenth of April. Easter Saturday

06:32 The Vatican

Between the curving columns of the geometrically misunderstood St Peter's Square, a dense sea of bodies rose and fell in a tide of excitement. Amongst the throng, ripples of excitement darted here and there, causing eddies of restlessness, spreading flurries of tangible anticipation. And in amongst this rich trawl of treasures, tantalising inches from dozens of 'inconspicuous' money belts, the slitheriest of

Italian pickpockets were trapped like mosquitoes in setting amber. The weighty crush of those drawn to the Pope's Easter address made the job of the casual thief's getaway impossible.

Six hundred and forty thousand members of the world's public had already gathered in the sweltering heat and waited patiently for a further hundred thousand to pack in at the back after sauntering down the Via della Conciliazione.

High above them, the Pope adjusted his chain and took a quick peek out from behind the curtain. Nervously, he fiddled with his ring.

A third of the way back, an American tourist with a pair of immensely powerful binoculars spotted the curtain twitch and let out a shriek of involuntary excitement. In seconds the crowd were baying for His Holiness, screaming for him to burst on to the balcony way above their heads and deliver to them the undeniable truth.

Precisely which undeniable truth this was they hadn't a clue. They just knew it was true and, er . . . well, undeniable. Over the last few days the Vatican propaganda machine had been buying up prime-time slots on every TV channel on every continent, flashing up cryptic adverts, raising their worldwide profile to create this heaving frenzy in St Peter's Square.

Pope Angeles stepped back from the curtain, turned and stared once again at the pair of aliens standing on the cool marble floor. For a tiny moment he wondered if the 'God Loves *Me*!' T-shirt covering their oddly tentacled torsos wasn't just a teensy bit tacky.

Almost instantly, he dismissed such thoughts, casting them behind him like so many whining devils. They had to wear those T-shirts as a message to the world.

If God loves aliens and the aliens know it, then surely this

214

was the religion for anyone. Grey-skinned and ugly. It doesn't matter. Come. Embrace. Baptise today!

Outside the windows, the crowd was chanting. Baying for the word.

'Okay, boys,' declared Pope Angeles in his most presidential voice. 'This is it. Here we go!' He reached a white-gloved hand out towards the gold doorhandle of opportunity, took a deep breath and . . .

His bedside alarm shattered the dream with a warbling of infernal transistors.

Pope Angeles leapt upright in his Louis XIV four-poster and stared around him in the total confusion of one wrenched rudely awake.

The alarm trilled at him again and for its troubles received a clenched fist on its 'off' button. Angeles leapt out of bed, tugged his Tang-dynasty-style kimono on and whirlwinded through the door, his mind fizzing excitedly.

'Breakfast, Your Holiness?' offered Cardinal Tardi, in the next room, holding out a steaming chocolate croissant as he prepared a stack of paperwork.

Angeles grunted, took the offering and breezed out of the far door in a scatter of crumbs.

'Your Holiness? Your Holiness?' shouted Tardi ineffectually.

Grumbling, he sat on the edge of the papal desk and began dialling numbers into his portable Motorola.

07:01 The Vatican

The darkness which had settled throughout the tiny roomful of computer graphics equipment was shattered in a single flick of index finger. A fluorescent tube coughed into life, banishing shadows in a second.

'Wake up. Wake up!' shouted Pope Angeles striding

215

across the room and shaking Giorgio Scipioni firmly by the shoulders.

'Ohhhh, Sophia, you came for me,' mumbled Scipioni, reaching blearily out and pouting at the Pope.

'Scipioni wake up. It's me. And I've got it!'

The director shook his head in confusion, opened his eyes and pulled his sleeping bag up around his nipples. 'You! What are you doing here? Where's Sophia?'

'Dream on,' said Angeles. 'Now come on. Get up!'

'What? What time is it?'

'Time for a change of plan. C'mon, I've got a new job for you.' He picked up a bulky camera and began looking for the switch. 'Got any film for this?'

'Three spools, yeah, but what d'you want with it? What's going on in that brain of yours?' croaked Scipioni, scratching his head, rubbing his eyes and realising he was desperate for a coffee.

Angeles grinned proudly. 'The answer! Oh, yes. Oh, yes. In fact, if the PR is handled correctly and the unveiling co-ordinated with my Easter address then . . . ohhh yes . . . a few well-placed ads and . . .'

'Whoa, whoa. And once again for the hard of understanding,' pleaded Scipioni, pulling on his jeans self-conciously.

Pope Angeles pulled focus on him through the camera. 'What is the only thing guaranteed to grab the complete, unwavering attention of every teenage youth brought up on *Star Trek* and *The X Files*?'

'Er, those erotic shots of Gillian Anderson and a lecherous alien in *Penthouse*?'

Angeles blushed as he recalled precisely what that horny little grey was up to with a certain undressed FBI temptress. 'Ahem, besides those particular photographs. This is better.'

'A display of Klingon battle lingerie?'

'No, no, what do they *all* dream of?' insisted the Pope, staring at Scipioni, the camera dangling by his side.

'You mean besides being trapped in a lift with Ms Anderson and a pot of massage oil?'

'Yes, besides that,' frowned Angeles, trying desperately not to think of what would happen if it got far too hot in that lift and she had to start peeling off her clothes one by one by one.

'I give up,' tutted Scipioni, shattering Angeles's daydream before the second button of her blouse. 'What *do* they all dream of?'

'Isn't it obvious?'

'Nope,' confessed Scipioni.

'Meeting a real live alien,' enthused Angeles, gathering his thoughts admirably and rubbing a finger around the collar of his dressing gown.

Scipioni's face lit up. 'My God, you're right!' His thoughts dashed towards the unfeasibly shiny spacecraft away across the Vatican and started wishing he was inside and fiddling with a hundred different knobs and buttons, or whatever else aliens used. 'They'd be queuing down the whole length of the Tiber to see them.'

'And while they're waiting, we give them the Good News!'

'What good news?'

'The Good News. The Bible!'

'Oh, yeah. Fine. Whatever.'

'Grab some film and cameras and whatever else you need. C'mon, we've got a commercial to shoot. The world's first ad for a papal address.'

'But, but . . . that's tomorrow,' panicked Scipioni.

'Exactly. No time to waste,' grinned the Pope and whirled off towards the door, his brain fizzing with thoughts of droves of potential converts flocking to St Peter's Square in their eager teenage millions.

217

An ocean-grey Lynx helicopter wound itself up to take-off rotation and stepped into the sky above the Tyrrhenian Sea. In moments it had left behind the deck of the USS *Indiscriminate* and was whacking low towards the knee-cap of Italy.

Rear-Admiral Rosenschmirtz looked down at his saffron robes and sandals and frowned. 'Er, would now be the correct time to fill in a few of this mission's less apparent details?'

'Uh-huh. Such as?' mumbled Major-General Gelding around his ubiquitous Havana.

'Our attire. Are these saffron robes absolutely necessary?'

'Of course,' interrupted Isenheimer, Head of Speculative Intelligence. 'How else d'you expect us to get in there? They're not exactly famous for their open-armed welcome of those in military uniform, you know.'

'But . . . Tibetan monks? I know we've got the right hair cuts for the part, but isn't it just a little bit inappropriate? They're Christians in the Vatican.'

'Are you questioning my orders?' growled Gelding. 'Religion all looks the same. Long robes and muttering. They'll never notice.'

'But what about simple civvies? I'm sure that with the right baseball cap even you could look like a normal member of the public.'

'And you expect them to let us in to where the *real* action is goin' down? Think, man! Look the part, you get the job,' hissed Gelding as they slid over land for the first time. 'They're up to somethin', I'm tellin' you. Somethin' hush hush. Somethin' the Pentagon doesn't even know about.'

'But we have agents for this sort of thing.'

'Agents, pah. Who needs 'em? Would you employ Pierce

Brosnan to make love to your wife, eh?' insisted Gelding. 'It's the same thing.'

'It is?' spluttered Rosenschmirtz, scratching his head in confusion.

Gelding was far from interested in Rosenschmirtz's bafflement. He was peering out of the port window, plumes of excited breath flaring on the glass, memories of action in Nam stirring his loins. 'Aha, there we are. Perfect timing.'

A hundred feet below, a Roman taxi was heading towards a small field and a rendezvous with a certain ocean-grey Lynx. In under an hour the three military types would be just another trio of monks outshining the morning sun, soaking up the Easter atmosphere in the Vatican.

07:33 The Vatican

For the past five hours, Father Fintan had been sat cross-legged on the floor of the underground lab of the Congregation for Icon Authentication, his attention completely enraptured by the two aliens from beyond the stars. His fingers were itching to start gluing any handy boxes of Bryant and May into a perfect representation of the shiny craft before him. All he needed was a few more essential structural details.

'So how did you actually get here?' asked the Irish priest. 'Was it warp drive, or hyperspace, or did you just nip through a handy wormhole?'

Kh'Vynn shrugged. 'I just fired up the Ytterbium Collider Drives and . . .'

'Wow! What are they? How do they work?'

'Er . . . by colliding ytterbium, I guess,' offered Kh'Vynn unhelpfully. 'But don't ask me what it's collided with, I never was much good at mechanics and stuff. Being Third Elected Brother of the Line of the Union of Militia of . . . owww!'

A mustard-yellow tentacle whipped across the side of his Ribena-coloured head and Kh'Xandhra rounded on him. 'You promised you'd never mention our heritage again!' she hissed. 'I don't want to be reminded of our world. We are away from all that, together now. That's all that matters. You and me, together, embarking on a new and optimistic beginning.'

'Oh, my beloved, I am sorry. I didn't mean to remind you of the hatred our families endured for these past centuries. I never meant to mention that enmity, that malignant destroyer of love which drove its way between us like a burning laser-bar, scarring our very hearts in a million tender and vulnerable . . .'

'All right, all right!' squeaked Kh'Xandhra. 'Well, you know now. Don't remind me again. Clear?'

Father Fintan sniffed appreciatively and reached for his handkerchief. But even before he had the chance to dab any embarrassing moisture from the corner of his eye, the door of the lab was kicked open and a clatter of lighting floods burst in.

'Okay, I want that one over there,' barked the Pope, pointing to the far corner. 'Those two in that corner and this uplighter . . .'

'Who's directing this?' hissed Scipioni irritably from behind a trolley sprouting a forest of barn-doored floodlights and associated scaffolding.

Much to his surprise, Angeles found himself beginning to blush in his Tang-dynasty-style kimono.

'What's going on here? Who dares to burst into my lab unnanounced?' spluttered Cardinal Holridge, leaping off the chaise-longue which was standing in as a casting coach and temporary bed. 'Oh, Your Holiness, I didn't recognise you without your vestments.'

'Where are all the power points in this lab?' tutted the

Pope, ignoring Holridge's outburst and waving a cable which trailed from a large piece of readily recognisable cinematic equipment. 'These things don't run on thin air, you know?'

'Er . . . I . . . over there,' spluttered Holridge and hoped he was still asleep and dreaming all this. Across the lab, Scipioni hauled a large floodlight up on a ten-foot tripod, fired it up and banished shadows from a good quarter of the room. In minutes he had hoisted another aloft and cast vast pools of blue halogen light on to the ship and its passengers.

'Er, Your Holiness, may I ask what it is you're doing here?' asked Holridge nervously.

'Isn't it obvious? We're filming. Here, plug that power lead in over there will you?'

At the mention of the 'F' word, the flaps of skin that passed as alien ears pricked up and pointed towards the Pope.

'Filming?' coughed Holridge. 'But, er, how does this lab fit in with *Faith: The Final Frontier*? I don't remember that much science in the Bible.'

Behind him, the two aliens were clutching each other with delight as Scipioni unpacked a chunky Sony Betacam recorder. They had hoped to be screen-tested fairly soon, but this . . . ? It was way beyond even their wildest dreams.

'That idea was yesterday. This is today,' said Pope Angeles helpfully. 'Bring me that VT, will you?'

'But, Your Holiness. Your address, tomorrow, I thought it all depended on *Faith*?'

'My address will be ruined if you don't get a shift on. If we're to catch the networks with a full ad by tonight we can't waste any time. Now get that cable plugged up,' demanded the Pope in a remarkably dictatorial manner. Holridge was obeying before he even realised.

Within minutes, the entire lab was kitted out like a film

studio, snakes of cabling wriggling across the floor, lights heating the place. The Pope settled himself into a director's chair and played with the clapperboard.

'All right Scipioni, it's over to you,' announced His Holiness and chewed his lip excitedly as the small Italian-American shouldered the Sony Betacam. A TV screen lit up on the console in front of Angeles, wobbling shakily as focus blurred into view. 'O'Suilleabhain, get off the set if you don't mind.' He pointed to a space in the lab far out of sight of the camera.

The Pope turned and looked directly at the pair of quivering aliens and spread his palms soothingly. 'Now please don't worry. This won't hurt. We won't steal your souls or anything. Now just stand right there.'

Kh'Vynn looked at his beloved Kh'Xandhra and pursed his triangle of lips into what passed as a wide smile. There was no doubting it, they had definitely come to the right place. In a matter of days they would be getting into real acting, they were sure. But, right now, as their director in the kimono said, they just had to stand there and be filmed.

And so, as Scipioni filled countless frames with close shots of alien skin and cryptic views of their hooves and tentacles, next door, Cardinal Kotonawa was staring at a very different screen showing a host of very different images.

'Oh, my God, no,' he whispered to himself over the hum of a Sun workstation. 'No, that can't be.' A screenful of calculations stared implacably back at him, sure in the knowledge that they were most definitely right. 'But that means . . .' Desperately, he reinputted a host of albedo constants, a flurry of point light source readings and then rescanned the best image he had recieved all too recently from the Hubble Space Telescope. In moments the answer came back on the screen. The Star of Bethlehem they had seen was most certainly not a star. It just wasn't bright enough.

Nervously, dreading the answer, he began inputting the diameter of the planet, added estimates of the depth of any probable atmosphere and then pulled out an ancient mathematical model from the Manhattan Project. Biting his fingernails he ran the calculations. 'Oh, my God. It can't be true. It can't,' he gasped as the Sun whirred to a halt and flashed the answer up before him. Trembling, he pressed 'print'. Holridge had to see this. He just had to.

Next door, Kh'Vynn was still striking poses for the camera. Tentacles lashed around the back of his head as he pouted for the lens. Then he grabbed Kh'Xandhra around the midriff and stared longingly into her eyes, trying to capture the finest moments of romance from a dozen different Hollywood greats. And all the time Scipioni was snatching these moments from the air, nailing them down firmly on to the tape in his video camera, watched by Angeles on the monitor console.

'That's it, that's enough. C'mon let's get editing. Now,' insisted the Pope, looking at his Rolex with mounting concern.

Scipioni glanced at the counter in his screen and flashed off a few more arty shots of the edge of the hull of the unfeasibly shiny ship. With a click, he ran out of tape.

'C'mon, there's no time to waste,' announced His Holiness. 'Leave this equipment here, just bring the tape.'

Scipioni flipped the cassette out of the Sony and dashed off towards the door.

'Wait a minute, you can't just leave all this stuff in my lab, I've got work . . .' began Holridge.

'Somebody'll be round to clear it up,' shrugged Scipioni. 'Sometime! Maybe.'

And, just as a Tang-dynasty-style kimono'd Pontiff

223

breezed out of the lab, dragging a film director behind him, Cardinal Kotonawa entered, looking both extremely confused and rather worried at the very same time. But he had no time for questions. He had too much on his mind.

'And where've you been?' snapped Holridge, glaring at the Japanese Cardinal. 'You're never around when you're needed.'

'I . . . I was busy,' said Kotonawa, eying the pair of aliens warily. 'Er, I think you'd better come outside a minute. I've got some news.'

'Outside? Since when have you ever needed . . .'

'Since when? Since . . . since they arrived,' whispered Kotonawa, trembling and pointing at the aliens from behind a wad of papers. 'I'm really not sure we can trust them.'

Suddenly worried and curious, Holridge followed out of the door.

'The bad news,' began Kotonawa, amazed at the speed with which Father Fintan had dashed back across the lab and started chatting once again with the purple and yellow pair, 'is this!' He handed Holridge the wad of papers densely covered in the indecipherable calculations of albedo points and explosive coefficients. 'Look at it!'

'What's all this? It doesn't make any sense . . .'

'Try this!' Kotonawa pointed to a now familiar printout from the Hubble Space Telescope. 'You wanted to know why the Star of Bethlehem was so dull this time? Well, it's all here in my calculations. They show it's not a star at all . . . but a planet with an albedo of 0.98. It reflects a vast amount of the light that shines on its surface.'

'Er . . . and that's bad news? People make mistakes about stars and planets all the time. It's nothing to worry—'

'Well, take a look at this, then.' Kotonawa pulled out an enhanced image of the same slice of space. But this time the

224

'Star' peeping around the edge of galaxy 3C390.3 was much, much brighter. 'Six hundred million times brighter,' whispered Kotonawa, nervously glancing over his shoulder into the lab. 'And that's exactly bright enough to show up in our sky two thousand years ago.'

'What?'

'And exactly how much brighter a planet would be if . . . if . . . its atmosphere was being engulfed by an uncontrollable nuclear holocaust.'

'Wha. . . ?'

'And those are exactly the right conditions to leave a shattered, dead planet, its surface fused by the unfeasible heat into an almost perfectly reflective glass surface. In short, a planet with an albedo of 0.98. *That* planet,' finished Kotonawa, shaking and jabbing a finger at the Hubble printout. 'That story about them coming here to be valuable members of society, you can't believe it. They're here to colonise our planet because they completely destroyed theirs two millennia ago in a vast and cataclysmic explosion that made a screaming fireball of their planet's atmosphere.'

Holridge stared from Kotonawa to the papers and back again, unable to take it all in at that time of morning. 'Ah . . . and the good news?' he begged desperately.

'Oh, of course, I could be completely wrong,' shrugged the Japanese Cardinal.

07:45 Rome

Sporting only a dozen more scratches and five dents to the front wing from that morning's dash across the Tiber, a Roman taxi slewed to a halt at the Vatican end of the Via della Conciliazione and disgorged a trio of saffron-robed gentlemen. Snatching a several-thousand-lira note from the

Havana-chewing Buddhist monk, the taxi driver floored the distressed Fiat and vanished in a cloud of Michelin.

'Italians,' frowned Gelding as the taxi's progress was marked by screams of irate tourists gathering for tomorrow's address, 'always in so much of a rush.'

'It's the sun-dried tomatoes and extra virgin olive oil,' said Isenheimer, resettling his tangerine-coloured skull cap. 'A deadly mix. When you've gotta go . . .'

'Geez, they never heard of real food over here? American food? What they need is a Big Mac and fries.' Gelding rummaged under his cassock, checked his holster and tightened up the ubiquitous rope around his monasterial midriff. 'C'mon,' he growled, stubbing his Havana on the toe of a nearby statue and slipping it into his pocket. Setting his jaw to grim determination and his eyes to peeled, he marched off across St Peter's Square at double speed. Hidden in plain sight, Isenheimer followed hard on his heels.

For Rosenschmirtz this was all getting just a little too much. 'We're going *in*?' he spluttered, clutching at the statue's toe.

'Of course,' growled Gelding in a very non-Tibetan manner.

'But . . . isn't there another way?' whimpered Rosenschmirtz, wishing he was far, far away from there, nice and safe on the USS *Indiscriminate*, ready to press a button and launch a missile at a distant target. That's why he'd joined the Navy. Things were civilised in the Navy. Any contact with any enemy was done across a decent and respectful several miles of nice safe sea. None of this hand-to-hand, eyeball-to-eyeball stuff. 'Er . . . haven't you people heard of binoculars, or telescopes, or satellites, or . . .'

'There's only one way to get accurate tactical information,' insisted the saffron-robed Major-General, 'and that's to get in, on the ground and sniff it out. C'mon.'

226

And Gelding was off across St Peter's cobbles.

Rosenschmirtz glanced around him and suddenly felt very, very small and, worse, very, very exposed. 'Er, wait for me!' he whimpered and dashed off in a flurry of robes towards a small wooden door which led into areas of the Vatican far from normally accessible to the general public. And certainly never accessible to the general military.

A gaudily uniformed Swiss Guard snapped to attention as the three sunrise-hued monks marched around the end of a colonnade of pillars, prayer wheels at the ready.

'Follow my lead,' hissed Gelding out of the side of his mouth, deftly unclipping his silenced Mauser. Safe in the knowledge that his firearm could inflict far more damage than the Guard's ceremonial pike, he marched onwards. 'Om mani padme om,' he chanted recalling the heady days of the sixties. He reached for the handle of the door.

'Om mani padme hum,' joined in Isenheimer with a feeling of acute embarrassment and fiddled with his prayer wheel.

'*Om* mani padme *hum!*' repeated Gelding as the locked door refused to open. '*Om, Om!*' he scowled at the Guard.

'Er, do you have permission to . . . ?'

Gelding waggled his prayer wheel threateningly a quarter of an inch away from the end of the Guard's nose. 'OM!' he insisted and rolled his eyes.

'Yeah, sure, right away. It's just that they're very choosy who they let in here,' struggled the guard, as he unhooked a large key from his belt.

In seconds, the three of them were through the door and roaming about the private inner sanctum of the Vatican.

Outside, the Swiss Guard wiped a bead of sweat away from under his curly helmet and hoped that no one had seen any of that.

227

Father Fintan O'Suilleabhain sat amongst the snakes of electrical cabling and looked up at the pair of screen-test-happy aliens.

'Aha. What about this one?' grinned the priest, suddenly jumping to his feet and forming the fingers of his right hand into a surprisingly passable replica of the most powerful handgun in the world. 'Okay, punk,' he whispered pointing at an imaginary felon on the floor. 'You're asking yourself, in all that confusion, did I fire six or seven . . . no, no. You're askin' yourself, in all that confusion, did I fire five or six or . . . Oh, forget that bit.' Fintan flashed an embarrassed grin at his audience, then resettled himself into his meanest stance and pointed both barrels of his fingers at the floor. 'What you've got to ask yourself is . . . do I feel lucky? Well, go on, make my day!' he whispered huskily.

'That's easy! Clint Eastwood in *Dirty Harry*,' cheered Kh'Vynn with a ripple of applauding tentacles. 'But I'm not sure the lines were right. Didn't he say something about "I'll be back"?'

'That was Arnie in *Terminator*,' tutted Kh'Xandhra.

'Your turn,' enthused Fintan, looking to the Merlot-and-Ribena-hued creature.

'Er . . . oh, I know,' began Kh'Vynn and took a series of short sharp breaths, inflating his head to twice the size of normal. With a deft series of flicked tentacles he adjusted the translator to subtitle mode and began his charade. 'Ack ack ack ack. Ack ack ack!'

Helpfully, the translator beamed a holographic string of letters into the air.

'Oh, that's too easy. Gimme a massive clue, why don't you?' frowned Fintan as he read the shimmering words hovering in the air above the translator. ' "Nice planet. We'll

228

take it!" I could've got it without the subtitles, you know. I could!'

'Really? It was *that* good?' asked Kh'Vynn's shimmering subtitles, a career in the movies taking a real step closer.

However, before Fintan had the chance to admit that simply standing there and going, 'Ack ack ack' was enough to clinch it as *Mars Attacks!*, Cardinals Holridge and Kotonawa strode in and closed the door.

'We'd like a word with you,' said Holridge, staring firmly at the two aliens.

Kh'Vynn's head deflated back to its normal size.

Holridge took a breath and, with the definite feeling that the thinnest of ice-sheets was currently hovering beneath his slippers, he began. 'It's too early in the morning to beat around the bush so, er, well . . . I'll come straight to the point, shall I? Without any preamble or anything, I'll just come right out, in the open, here now, and, before every-one, er . . .'

'Look, why are you here?' interrupted Kotonawa, a vast wad of papers slung over his arm.

Kh'Vynn glanced a single eye-stalk towards Kh'Xandhra. 'It's like we said. Earth is a great place to be if you're an alien.'

'Better than the place you came from, eh?' pressed Kotonawa. 'Loads more, ahem, *atmosphere* on Earth, is there?'

Kh'Vynn's eye stalk twitched. 'Er, yes, yes. You've got the finest movie industry in the whole universe here.'

'And you feel that perhaps there was something, er, *lacking* back home?' suggested Kotonawa. 'You thought you'd come here for a breath of fresh air, hmmm?'

'Well, it is nice to be able to see stars overhead, yes,' admitted Kh'Vynn. Kh'Xandhra flashed him a stern look.

But Kotonawa was on it in a second. 'And why would you

be unable to see stars overhead, hmmm? Perhaps because you were forced to live your entire lives underground, hmmm?'

Kh'Xandhra fidgeted uncomfortably.

Kotonawa was on a roll. 'And why would you be living underground? It wouldn't have anything to do with a certain immensely destructive war approximately two thousand of our years ago which resulted in the sudden and complete burning of your atmosphere? A burning which, had it not been for the fortuitously timed stockpiling of gaseous purifiers and development of atmospheric synthesiser plants, would have almost certainly ended in the complete destruction of your species?'

Kh'Xandhra's tentacle lashed out of the sky and slapped across Kh'Vynn's cheek. 'You told him! I told you our past was our secret! You spilled it all. The purifiers, the atmospheric synthesiser plants . . .'

Holridge's jaw dropped in speechless shock.

But he wasn't quite as shocked as Kotonawa. 'Er, sorry, I guessed about the gaseous purifiers,' he gulped.

'See, I didn't tell anyone,' whined Kh'Vynn, nursing his reddening cheek. 'It's still our little secret.' He tried a smile.

It didn't have a chance to take effect, for at that very moment Cardinal Holridge found his voice. 'Oh, my God, it's all true. This . . . this madness that Kotonawa forced me to believe. You destroyed your own planet. An entire planet, turned to glass by the actions of one race . . .'

Kh'Xandhra was waving defensive tentacles in all directions. 'No, no. It wasn't us. We didn't do it! You've got to believe us. We had nothing to do with it.'

'You . . . you didn't?' gasped Holridge. 'Really? Honestly?'

'Really. Cross my spleen,' she pleaded. 'It wasn't us . . .'

It was all Holridge needed. He rounded on Kotonawa

prodding at the wads of papers. 'There, look. I knew it! It wasn't them.'

'. . . it was our parents,' finished Kh'Xandhra.

08:33 The Vatican

Acres of mustard-yellow skin slithered past in unidentifiable waves of texture. Synths swirled in quivering vibrato strings. Swatches of Ribena and Merlot blinked in tight edits of contrast. Silhouetted tentacles lashed in low-light graininess to a snatch of industrial jungle. A cluster of clanking chains swung darkly in front of a high-power hand-held spotlight. A flash of unfeasibly shiny spacecraft burst in stark black and blinding white. A hand reached for a light-switch backed by *Psycho* string stabs. Another hand arced out of the sky and snatched the first away. A woofer-bashing voice-over read, 'See it all, tomorrow. The Truth from the people you never thought you'd hear it from.'

A whisker of silence fell in the darkened editing suite.

'Oh, yes, oh yes!' chuckled the Pope, slapping his hands together excitedly and rocking back on the chair. 'Even heathens will sit up and take notice of that. Brilliant. Brilliant. How did you get my voice to sound so deep?'

'Technology,' mused Scipioni, staring at the now blank screen and rubbing his chin thoughtfully. 'But . . . there's something missing,' he whispered to himself.

'No, no. It's got everything. Suspense. Drama. Eye-catching colours and, ohhhh, that voice-over! I never knew I could sound so sexy.'

'That's it!' shouted Scipioni slamming his fist on to several million lire's worth of tele-cine equipment. 'That's what's missing.' The pneumatic delights of all that went by the name of Sophia swam into view, clad in a piece of string with ideas of bikinidom.

231

'Er . . . you've lost me now. I say it's got everything and you say there's something missing. What's not there?'

Scipioni turned and leaned closer to the Pope, his hands spreading wide like the least trustworthy purveyors of pre-owned automobiles. 'You got to trust me on this one, okay? Go with it, you know?'

'Go with what?'

'Er . . . it's a bit hard to explain in a way that would allow you to really appreciate it. Now, if I were to *show* you it . . .' Scipioni let the sentence drift temptingly in the dark air.

'Showed me what?'

'Ahh, now, that would spoil the surprise, wouldn't it?' grinned Scipioni. 'Do me a favour, let me get a couple of bits and bobs and I'll show you a version of this ad that'll blow your little cotton socks clean off.'

'A couple of bits and bobs?'

'Oh yes. I can see it now, you'll have to up the crowd control in St Peter's. Hey, you could even charge admission. They'll be flocking, flocking.'

'What d'you want?'

'A Sea King, fuelled and ready in ten minutes.' said Scipioni. 'I, er, need a few things from my location shoot.'

'Well, I . . .'

'Look, you've already got this version in the can. What harm can I do that, eh?' wheedled Scipioni and somehow barely managed to avoid fluttering his eyelids at the Supreme Pontiff. 'Hmmm? One little teensy-weensy chopper? It's not as if you're using it, is it?'

'All right, all right. Just this once, and just cause I'm in a good mood. I'll inform Vatican 2.' And with that the Pope ducked out of the editing suite happy that for the second time in as many days he was sitting on the most amazing address the entire world had ever seen. Now all he had to do

232

was book ad space on all the major networks, sit back and deliver a killer speech tomorrow.

Scipioni wasted barely a second before he was on the phone to a certain building site in the hills south of there. A site which bore an uncanny resemblance to the main street of the Gaza Strip.

In one of the large trailers beloved of movie-makers the world over, a mobile phone rang. On the sixteenth warble it was answered with an eloquent, 'Uh?'

'This is your early-morning call,' chuckled Scipioni. 'And before you object, yes, I do know what time it is. Look, have you got a pen and paper there?'

Blearily, Stig Folini, the all-too-recently promoted director of *Gazan Dolls*, reached for a notepad and began writing things down.

'. . . and I want all of them, including the spare heads, got that?'

'Yuh.'

'Good. There'll be a nice white helicopter down to pick it all up in about forty minutes. Have everything and everyone out and ready to ship. Clear?' hissed Scipioni excitedly as he completed the list. 'Folini, is that clear?'

'Uh . . . yeah.'

'Excellent.' Scipioni cut the connection and sat back in the editing suite, rubbing his hands with the moisturising oil of heady anticipation.

08:59 The Vatican

For the better part of the last hour the three clergy had listened in stunned silence as Kh'Vynn, the Merlot-and-Ribena-hued alien, had related their star-crossed story. Much to Kh'Xandhra's discomfort he missed out nothing of their past. Like the finest of storytellers he began at the

233

beginning. In this case, the beginning of the end. He spilled it all almost without pausing for breath. The Democracy Wars over two thousand years ago; the planet-strafing swarms of dictatorial Strato-Fortresses trading laser fire with the democratically piloted Tropo-Nihilation Engines; the build-up of volatile ytterbium ion compounds in the atmosphere and then . . . the final battle. One laser bolt too many and the saturated atmosphere caught. Had they not been forced underground years before, the casualties would have been almost incalculable. As it was, it took years for the enemy populations to expand, hiding away from each other, excavating through the surface plates of the planet, digging out new living spaces from the bedrock.

'It wasn't my fault the foreman had given me the wrong survey sheet,' said Kh'Vynn with a covert glance at Kh'Xandhra. 'Okay, so I know he told me not to use a tectonic disruptor on sedimentary subplates, but, when that whole stratum caved in and I peered through that chink in the rock wall, well, I was glad I had. Of course, I didn't know at the time that I was looking into the palace gardens of my democratically selected enemy. I just knew, there and then as the dust settled, that I had found . . .' He looked winsomely at Kh'Xandhra, his eye-stalks moistening. 'Love,' he mouthed.

'You mean, you've eloped?' whispered Father Fintan, chewing moistly on his handkerchief.

'We had no choice,' said Kh'Vynn. 'Of course, we tried everything we could.'

'I'd find any excuse to stroll the gardens down by where he was working,' smiled Kh'Xandhra, barely hiding a blush of pure French full-grain mustard. 'I'd toss him love rocks when no one was looking.'

Fintan raised his eyebrows.

'You wouldn't believe quite how many verses of poetry

she could cram on a chunk of sedimentary subplate. I've still got some of them if you'd like to hear . . .'

'Ohhh, no!' winced Kh'Xandhra, slapping tentacles to her cheeks and blushing deeper.

'What a beautiful story,' sniffed Fintan. 'Shakespeare would've killed to have written that. And it's all ended so happily.'

'Er, yes . . . I guess so,' coughed Kh'Vynn in a far less convincing manner than he had hoped for.

As ever, Kotonawa was on it like a rat on a month-old Camembert. 'Is there, perhaps, something that you're not telling us?'

'What gave you that impression?' Kh'vynn attempted feigning innocence. If this had been a Hollywood screen-test, the diner-waiter circuit would have been beckoning.

'Tell them,' hissed Kh'Xandhra. 'They're our only hope.'

'I don't like the sound of this,' said Kotonawa.

Kh'Vynn fiddled with his tentacles and did a far more passable impression of being exceedingly uncomfortable. 'Er, you know that last battle I was telling you about.'

'The one where both the entire warring fleets of Strato-Fortresses and Tropo-Nihilation Engines were utterly destroyed,' offered Fintan, just to show how much he had been paying attention.

'Ha, is *that* the impression I gave,' mugged Kh'Vynn, beginning for the first time in his life to understand that Earth phrase about sailing close to the wind.

'There's one left?' gagged Kotonawa. 'Is that it?' He pointed to the unfeasibly shiny ship behind them. 'Have you come here to destroy us?'

'Ahem, if I may answer those questions in the order they have been asked,' said Kh'Vynn, trying for presidential calmness. 'No. No, and er, No.'

'What? Then why are you trying to frighten us?' whined

235

Fintan, beginning to wish for a quiet and far less stressful life spent at the bottom left corner of Eire. 'If there are no ships . . .'

'There are two!' interrupted Kh'Xandhra. 'The flagships.'

'It's nothing to worry about,' offered Kh'Vynn, nervously. 'As long as they don't find us then everyone will be perfectly safe. Perfectly.'

'And . . . and if they do?' asked Fintan.

Kh'Vynn raised a pair of tentacles into a shrug. And just to offer even more confidence to the terrified triumvirate of trembling clergy, it was followed by another pair of shrugs.

It was Cardinal Holridge who finally broke the numb silence. 'Look, he's right. There's nothing to worry about. Nothing at all. We're the only people who know they're here. Nobody ever need know. This is our secret.'

'But for how much longer?' asked Fintan, a nervous quiver in his voice. 'Take a look around you.'

Cardinal Holridge looked at the floodlights, the monitoring console and the Sony camera staring unblinkingly in his direction. 'Oh, my God,' he whimpered as the penny dropped.

Invading the Vatican

13:14 Fifteenth of April. The Vatican

A rectangular paperbag flexed its tanned recycled torso languorously and proudly displayed the tattoo which marked it out as having the perfect pedigree thereabouts – it was a Vatican Museum carrier bag. And proud of it.

With only the slightest of rustles it spread itself out in the April sun, angling itself to catch the rays to its best advantage. Three feet away, a bevy of impressionable young sweet wrappers sighed and went weak at the corners. But of such flighty admiration the carrier bag was unaware. Its attention was elsewhere.

A buxom and deliciously assembled package from the Cafe Donatello lay not eighteen inches away. She sunned herself brazenly, wearing nothing but a wrinkled smile and a smattering of lightly greased croissant flakes.

Handles sweating with anticipation, the carrier bag rustled up a final dose of courage and, catching a light afternoon breeze, sidled off across the concrete.

Whether its overtures would have been successful, no one will ever know. At that very instant the swirling downdraft from a heavily laden Sea King helicopter flicked it across the concrete landing pad and pinned it helplessly to the outer Vatican wall. Shrieking, the bevy of impressionable sweet wrappers were whirlwinded into a distant mossy corner. The bag from the Cafe Donatello settled lower behind her sheltering rock and waited out the unwelcome disturbance. She knew from experience it wouldn't last long.

And sure enough, a few seconds later the pilot of Vatican 2 reacquainted the three aviation-grade Michelins with the comforting feel of concrete and shut off the power. Well before the rotors had idled to a halt, things had begun to emerge from the helicopter's capacious interior.

It all began innocently enough, half a dozen bulging trunks stuffed with a variety of costumes, make-up and assorted prosthetics, but as a delighted Giorgio Scipioni sprinted across the helipad, arms outstretched towards his beloved Sophia, a three-clawed foot uncurled on to the concrete. April sunshine glinted off the exoskeleton of its calf, flashed off its solid thigh and positively rippled across the surface of the creature's heavily armoured torso as it straightened up to its full seven foot six. A drool of saliva swung stickily from its overly toothed jaws.

'Bloody 'ell and I thought it was hot back at the location shoot,' complained the alien, its voice muffled inside its head.

'That's my Folini, always complaining,' beamed Scipioni.

'You try wearing this lot for two hours. It's like a sauna in this head,' moaned Folini, barely audibly. 'How much longer do I have to wear it?'

'I just need a few action shots, that's all,' said Scipioni, his eyes lingering on Sophia.

'Action?'

'Yeah, just a bit of running and jumping, you know, the usual.'

'Let's get on with it before I die,' complained the alien, claws perched petulantly on the kind of shiny black hips H.R. Giger would have given his favourite pencil to have designed.

'All right, all right, gimme a few minutes to check focus

and exposure. When I give you the signal I want you come running across that lawn, over that flowerbed and through that archway in that wall over there, right?' Scipioni pointed to a door in a distant chapel. 'I'll be tracking you all the way with the camera over there in the chapel, you know, all jerky documentary style.'

'Yeah, yeah, whatever you say,' grumbled Folini. 'Just make it quick. I've already sweated off three stone in here!'

Wrapping an eager arm around the shoulders of the leather-clad Sophia, Scipioni grinned, led her off towards the chapel and an appointment with a waiting bottle of perfectly chilled Veuve-Cliquot Ponsardin.

Grumbling irritably to himself, Folini kicked around restlessly on the helipad, refamiliarising himself in the art of moving about whilst furnished with two-foot-high clawed heels and a razor-sharp tail.

And so it was that, eyes peeled for anything suspicious, a triplet of saffron-robed monks rounded a corner, stopped in their tracks and hit the dirt behind a suitable rhododendron. Their prayer wheels quivered nervously as they stared at the seven-and-a-half-foot alien practising t'ai chi on the Vatican helipad.

'Oh, my God!' squeaked Rear-Admiral Rosenschmirtz, elbowing himself out of sight. 'What's ... what's it doing? Can you hear it, growling to itself? Oh, God what's going on here?'

'Who cares what it's doing now? Just think what we can do with it!' grinned Major-General Gelding, his faithful cigar hovering inches from a year's worth of leaf litter. 'Isenheimer, you still got your Sea King licence?'

'Er, yes,' admitted Isenheimer warily.

'Great. Okay, men, let's get in there, overpower that thing, lock it in the hold and take off.'

'Overpower it?' whimpered Rosenschmirtz. 'You mean

like grapple with it? No way. Have you seen the size of that thing?'

'Seven foot six if it's an inch. But the bigger they are . . .' enthused Gelding determined to bag the beast he had been chasing across the length of the Mediterranean. Okay, so he hadn't known quite what his quarry had looked like but, hey, a target was a target.

'Of course,' nodded Isenheimer. 'A fine plan. Let the Vatican deny it exists then, eh? When it's safely behind bars in the brig of the good ship *Indiscriminate*.'

'The Vatican?' hissed Gelding. 'Who cares what they say. The only comments I'm interested in are those from the Bioweapons Division!' chuckled Gelding, his thoughts set on impending promotion.

Gelding edged forward on his elbows, straining to see every detail of his proposed run-up, his eyes devouring every hummock and dip, assessing them for ankle-twisting potential. But, just as he noticed a Cafe Donatello paperbag sheltering behind a small rock and decided to skirt a few feet to the right, it all became utterly irrelevant.

Suddenly, the seven-and-a-half-foot creature raised its head, stared into the distance and, as if in response to some covert signal, set off at a furious gallop. It dashed across a nearby expanse of lawn, eating up the distance in a curiously leggy lope, hopped over a decorative flowerbed and, barely slowing, ducked out of sight into the gloom of a chapel.

'Oh, my God,' whimpered Rosenschmirtz, 'did you see the speed of that?'

In the bush, Major-General Gelding began to wonder if it wouldn't have been prudent just to have left this operation to one of the agents stationed thereabouts. It could well have been a bit safer . . .

Under the unblinking gaze of a pair of cavorting frescoed cherubs, Cardinal Tardi glared at the vast map of the Vatican spread on the table before him. Dotted about it were one hundred and fifteen blue-yellow-and-red-striped pins, each representing one of his precious Swiss Guards. Pinched tight between his right thumb and forefinger hovered another.

Tardi's brow furrowed as he once more compared a table of last-known positions with recent sightings and tried to figure what had gone wrong with his beautiful system. It had been developed by his own steel-trap mind over the last few years and involved meticulous planning, extraordinary loyalty and a massive bill for mobile phones. But he knew it was worth every lira for he, and only he, knew exactly where each of the Swiss Guards was positioned at any time of any day of any month of the year.

Except today.

Baffled, he stared at the gaudily striped pin in his hand. 'Where the Hell are you?' he snapped at it. 'And why aren't you answering your phone? You'd better have a damned good excuse SG 105, otherwise . . .' He stabbed the pin hard into the map in the exact centre of the small but very secure section of the Vatican which was dedicated to the punishment of wayward Guards. Of course, it hadn't been used since 1546, but today . . . well, all that might just change. He was in one of his darker moods. A mood caused by the horrible feeling that things just might be slipping out of his control. A mood darkened by the nagging suspicion that there were several dozen loops which he was ever so carefully being cut out of. A mood whose only relief would be the sudden and imminent infliction of extreme discomfort upon any innocent victim who happened to be in the way.

There was a knock on the door and Cardinal Tardi leaned back in his chair. An air of external calm hiding the boiling frustration within, he moved a bright pin on the map, stabbing it into the area which represented his room. 'Come,' he called.

A man in a Michelangelo designer uniform slid efficiently through the door and snapped a crisp salute.

'Found him, SG1?' asked Tardi, without ceremony and without looking up.

'Yes, sir,' answered the Swiss Guard First Lieutenant with a faintly Germanic click of his heels and a swift assessment of Tardi's mood. 'Er, it seems he's just piloted Vatican 2 back on to the helipad.'

'What?' snarled Tardi, spinning in his chair and consulting a meticulously recorded flight register. 'He's just landed? He's not even scheduled to be taking off! What in God's name does he think he's doing taking V2 out without permission?'

'I think you will be able to ask him that yourself,' said the First Lieutenant, edging towards the door. 'It seems he's on his way here.'

Tardi rolled up his sleeves and rubbed the heels of his hands together in an unnervingly businesslike manner. 'Oh, good,' he hissed through banks of gleaming teeth, 'I think I'll enjoy that.'

The First Lieutenant took another nervous step backwards and swallowed as he heard the all-too-hasty approach of flight boots. With thoughts of lambs and premature slaughter uppermost in his mind, he swept the door open and the panting pilot dived in with both feet.

'Ah, SG 105,' declared Tardi from beneath darkening brows and steepling fingers. 'Do, please, come in.'

For the First Lieutenant, Tardi's wolverine politeness was suddenly unbearable. 'Er, if that will be all?' he whispered, backing away through the door, distancing himself from even the remotest possibility of imminent bloodshed.

'Oh yes, SG1, please do go about your normal business,' answered Cardinal Tardi, his eyes unwavering from their focus on the helicopter pilot's throat. 'SG105 and I will be quite all right on our own.'

The First Lieutenant fled, already composing the advertising for a new pilot's position.

In the office of the Papal Secretary, Tardi was wasting no time in the tearing-off of strips. 'It is not your own private helicopter for use on any whim, clear?'

'Yes, sir, but . . .'

'You do not, repeat, *do not*, simply fire up the engines and hop over the wall. Understood?'

'Yes, sir, but, the . . .'

'And as for flight plans and fuel requisitions . . . Do I *have* to remind you of the price of aviation fuel?'

'No, sir, but, the Pope called me up and asked me to go. "Scramble in ten," he said,' blurted the pilot. 'He was quite specific about it. Er, sir . . . are you feeling all right? You look a little pale.'

The crow's feet around Tardi's left eye twitched. 'And what was so important that he had to have you scramble in ten?'

'At first I only knew I had to collect a few things from a set of co-ordinates. But when I saw it climbing into the hold, I couldn't believe my eyes.'

Suddenly a telephone rang in the bowels of Tardi's Louis XIV desk. Staring into the middle distance he snatched open the drawer and clamped the headset to his ear. 'Yes?' he answered automatically and placed himself on the horns of a two-way conversation.

'*Agent Rublev, we're awaiting your report. What's going on?*' snapped the earpiece.

'Er . . . Report?' he answered vaguely, attempting to marshal his thoughts into some sort of credible answer.

The pilot looked at the Papal Secretary. 'That's what I'm trying to do,' he answered.

'*Agent Rublev? What have you found out about the helicopter delivery?*'

'Ahh, the helicopter,' floundered Tardi.

'That's what I'm trying to tell you,' mouthed the pilot. Tardi continued to stare in to the middle distance.

'*Agent Rublev? Agent? Report?*' crackled rough Russian vowels through the earpiece.

Suddenly the pilot grabbed a sheet of paper and began scribbling a message frantically across it.

'*Agent Rublev?*' barked the phone.

In a flurry of paper, the pilot thrust the message in front of Tardi, his fingers jabbing at it desperately.

'*Comrade Rublev! You can be replaced, you know?*' harried the headset.

'Eh, er, I . . .' Tardi stared glassily at the note and started to read it out loud. ' "The helicopter is full of . . . aliens?" '

'*What!*' crackled the Russian on the phone. '*Say again, over?*'

Tardi stared at the note. ' "The helicopter is full of aliens." What the Hell . . . ?' He threw the headset down, slammed the drawer and snatched the pilot around the collar as decades of Tardi's credibility crumbled in the Kremlin. 'What are you doing to me? What's the meaning of this?'

'It's true,' gasped the pilot. 'I . . . I saw it.'

'Saw what? Tell me?' barked Tardi, shaking the pilot hysterically. 'What did you see?'

'There was seven-foot-six of it! Black, shiny, armoured, in my helicopter.'

'And Angeles ordered you to get it?'

Gasping for breath, the pilot nodded.

'Angeles has ordered a lot more besides,' announced Cardinal Alighieri, stepping through the door with his trusty Sony surveillance tape-recorder.

'What? Doesn't anyone knock any more?' hissed Tardi. 'Can't you see I'm busy?'

'All right, all right, if that's more important than finding out precisely what His Holiness has been up to for the past three hours, then feel free, do carry on,' said Alighieri, heading towards a vacant chair.

Tardi looked from the bluing pilot to the cassette machine and back again. Finally he made a decision. Fixing the pilot with a withering stare he whispered in his ear. 'You've got a phone in your pocket. Next time, use it. Now, go!'

He needed no second bidding.

'This had better be good, Alighieri,' growled Tardi. 'I was enjoying that. My shoulders feel a lot more relaxed now.'

'Well sit down, you aren't going to like this.' Alighieri pressed 'play' and the unmistakable sound of a telephone conversation spilled out of the Sony's grille.

'Hello? CNN Advertising Placement?'

'Angeles?' queried Tardi scratching his head. Alighieri nodded as a female voice answered the Pontiff in gushing Dolly Partonese.

'When would you require an advertising slot scheduling?'

'How much for this evening, prime time?'

'I'm sorry, sir, that's all booked. I can offer a slot in three months . . .'

'I said how much for tonight? I need thirty-five seconds between the six pm news and the hair adverts?'

'I'm sorry, sir, that time is fully booked, I can't authorise . . .'

'Fifty thousand dollars says you can shave thirty-five seconds off the news schedule. You know as well as I do nothing happens over Easter.'

245

'*I'm sorry*?'

'*Seventy-five thousand*?'

'*Is that cash*?'

'*Courier delivered. No questions.*'

'What the Hell is that about?' blurted Tardi, his shoulders tensing visibly.

'And there's more like it on here. He's been on to CNN, Sky, all the networks, even the BBC. So far he's successfully placed thirty-two adverts. And all timed to start at six thirty, tonight.'

'Are you absolutely sure?' trembled Tardi.

'You heard it. That's him. I can play you the rest if you think it'll convince you.'

'Have you checked it with CNN?'

'First thing I did,' said Alighieri, with not a little professional pride. 'They flatly denied it, of course.'

'Oh, God. It *is* true.' Tardi tugged open a small cupboard, placed a large glass on the desk and emptied a good three fingers of Smirnoff into it. 'Four days he's been in office and I'm already losing it.'

Cardinal Alighieri nodded almost apologetically. 'But what is he doing? It doesn't make sense. I thought tomorrow was going to be his big announcement for *Faith: The Final Frontier*. What can he possibly hope to achieve with a worldwide advertising blitz at six thirty in every time zone?'

Tardi reached for the vodka and gulped it down in one. 'I don't know,' he wheezed. 'But we've got five hours to find out.' He stood, slowly pushed his chair under its Louis XIV desk and, his crow's feet ticking only slightly, he stared straight at Cardinal Alighieri. 'Remind me,' he said, his index finger jabbing the desktop, 'remind me never to let another Italian-American in. They're just far too headstrong.' And with the first fingers of vodka trying their very best to work at the re-mounting tension in his shoulders, he headed out of the door.

In the covert shade of a suitable rhododendron, a bare elbow jabbed a set of saffron-robed ribs firmly. 'Over there, look!' whispered Major-General Isenheimer and he pointed enthusiastically.

Gelding blinked between a forest of dark green leaves and tutted as, away across the lawn, a black-cassocked figure strolled nonchalantly towards them, swinging his tightly rolled umbrella with a studied air of casualness. 'It's only a verger.'

'I don't think so,' said Isenheimer, professional interest mounting as the mysterious verger sauntered towards the gleaming whiteness of Vatican 2 resting on the helipad.

'Really?' gasped Rosenschmirtz, nervously picking up on the tone of certainty underlining the Head of Speculative Intelligence's words. 'You mean he's an . . . an . . .'

'Agent,' completed Isenheimer proudly.

'Oh, come *on*,' spat Gelding. 'Not everyone who carries a rolled umbrella and wears the type of bowler hat John Steed would kill for is *necessarily* an agent, you know?'

'Oh no? Does it look like rain to you?'

'I'm telling you that's not an agent. It can't be. We're here first,' insisted Gelding possessively. 'Even our government don't know about this.'

'Notice anything about his eyes?' suggested Isenheimer to the more easily impressed Rear-Admiral. 'See the way they stare unblinkingly at the helicopter, devouring every detail of the interior as if searching for the slightest confirmation that it has been transporting non-quarantined animals? Classic signs of a trained agent.'

'Really?'

'That's just idle curiosity . . .' began Gelding.

'*Professional* idle curiosity, years of training . . . Wait, what's he doing now?' whispered Isenheimer, almost vibrating with the excitement of covert operations coursing through his veins. 'Oh, yes. Watch this!'

The mysterious verger paused on the gravel path with a slight crunch of polished heels and, first glancing over both shoulders, he removed his bowler hat. Holding it before him, he began fiddling around inside.

'Oh, watch what? He's just having trouble with his hat lining,' tutted Gelding. 'Happens all the time with mine.'

'You've got a bowler?' asked Rosenschmirtz.

'No. A stetson, but they're pretty much the same. Mine's got a bigger rim and I can't do Oddjob impersonations with it, but really there's nothing in it.'

'That's not hat-lining trouble. Listen,' ordered Isenheimer.

The other two strained their ears above the rustle of leaves in the wind and the distant fighting of Italian car horns locked in battle around the Colosseum. It only took a few moments for them to pick up the click and whirr of tiny shutter mechanisms.

'He's damn near shot off a full reel,' enthused Isenheimer. 'Thirty-four . . . thirty-five . . .'

Agent Etheridge-Willis exposed the last frame, wound it on and tossed his bowler back on his head. In a moment he was strolling back the way he had entered, a verger with a reelful of surveillance 35mm Kodak hidden in his bowler.

'Now d'you believe me?' asked Isenheimer smugly. 'No way was that the action of an innocent verger out for a stroll in the gardens.'

'Could be,' muttered Gelding in desperate denial. 'He might be going off on leave soon, y'know, back home and . . . and, he just took a few snaps to show his pals.'

'You're reaching.'

'Nonsense. It could be true.'

'Wait a minute,' hissed Isenheimer. 'Hmmm, what do we

have here?' He pointed to a diminutive gardener who was pushing a suspiciously clean-looking barrowful of rakes across the lawn. Trying his best to look as if he was far more interested in the state of the grass than he was in the white Sea King on the helipad, he zigzagged his way towards a large flowerbed.

'Japanese?' whispered Isenheimer under his breath and tugged a small notepad out of a hidden pocket in his saffron robe. He ran his thumb down the lettered ears on the edge of the pages and opened it under 'J'.

'Jamaican . . . Javanese . . . Aha.' He stared hard at the field documentation, fixed the features of the crisp photograph in his mind and looked up. 'Yup, that's him. Definitely Agent Sushimi Hiro.'

'But what's he doing?' asked Rosenschmirtz as the diminutive agent stopped in his tracks, cast a wary glance around him and pulled a large bag of white powder out of the bottom of the wheelbarrow. He poured in a few litres of water, shook it industriously and, to the surprise of those watching, emptied it on to the lawn just out of sight behind the flowerbed. Wiping his hands, he pulled a large camera out of the barrow, clicked a vast telephoto lens on to the front and proceeded to blitz off a roll of Fuji's finest in the direction of a certain angel-white chopper.

'This is big,' whispered Isenheimer.

'Er, just how big is big?' asked Rear-Admiral Rosenschmirtz, certain that he would much rather be far out at sea surrounded by the comforting nest of several thousand tons of steel and a few squadrons of deadly missile-laden aerodynamics.

'Big. With a capital "B" and a capital "IG",' answered Isenheimer, his voice quivering ever so slightly with excitement. 'Twenty dollars says that all the major powers have an agent here within the hour.'

'Even the F . . . ?'

'Even the French.'

'Oh, God, it's . . . it's *that* big!' whimpered Rosenschmirtz. Next to him Gelding simply groaned.

Having successfully used up the necessary two minutes for certain chemicals to bind to others, Agent Sushimi Hiro reached down to his feet and pulled a large hard something out of a recently made indent in the grassy surface. Amazed, the three counterfeit monks watched as the Japanese agent placed a perfect cast of a three-clawed footprint into the bottom of his barrow and covered it with a scattering of garden implements.

And so, whistling the latest hit single by virtual pop star Kyoko Date and mucking out his Tamogotchi, Agent Hiro wheeled his barrow out of the Vatican, secure in the warm glow of another mission accomplished.

'The actions of an innocent gardener?' asked Isenheimer, looking at Gelding on his elbows next to him under the bush.

'All right, all right, so the English and the Japanese are sniffing about here, so what? There's three of us.'

'So what?' coughed Isenheimer incredulously. 'Do you have *any* idea how big something needs to be before the English get up and actually *do* something?'

'Er,' hesitated Gelding as he wrestled with a tactical decision. 'Gentlemen, it's time to take this to a higher level. It's time we talked to . . . the President!' He flashed a quick salute in the direction of Washington and pulled a small radio out from beneath his saffron robe. In moments, and much to the relief of Rosenschmirtz, he was arranging a rendezvous with a certain ocean-grey Lynx helicopter.

14:27 Local Space

Out on the thinning edges of Earth's atmosphere, a pair of million-ton spacecraft slammed on their anti-inertia brakes and, with complete disrespect for the laws of physics, slowed to below light speed. The shock waves completely mucked up Sky Sport for a few moments, rattled all the rivets in Mir and baffled an entire settlement of Inuit by setting up strange paisley patterns in that night's *aurora borealis*.

'What d'you mean, "our fault"?' bellowed the mustard-coloured Regal Commander across a broad-band radio signal. 'It was *your* son that kidnapped *our* daughter. And it's a damn good job he doesn't have the common sense to tune a Type-23 Ytterbium Collider Drive for covert manoeuvring. It was a piece of cake tracking him across the wastes of space.'

'Tracking *them*,' came back the equally angry reply. 'She led him on. Nothing but a no-good slut . . .'

'How *dare* you speak about a member of the Royal Classes like that?' roared the Regal Commander, turning ever more towards the darker end of all things mustardy.

'Nothing but a tart, flashing her knees around like that . . .'

A yellow tentacle slammed hard on to the comms console and cut the connection in mid-sentence. 'Prince of Sensors,' bellowed the Regal Commander across the bridge of the vast craft. 'Begin scanning. Weaponry Regent, power up the forward pulse cannons.'

For a brief moment, the lights on the bridge dimmed as power was rechannelled. And as a vast weaponry system began heating, a small port opened in the Strato-Fortress's alloy hull and a shimmering ray of scanning radiation began sweeping across the darker reaches of southern Peru.

'And another thing,' began the Regal Commander again, breaking radio silence, 'if it hadn't been for the innefficiency of your labour forces, none of this would've started.'

'You shouldn't have built your so-called palace so near to sedimentary subplates,' came the rasped reply.

'It was your overbreeding that forced you to have to spread so far. You lot have *no* control!' And the Regal Commander once more severed communications.

'Found them yet?' he snapped at the Prince of Sensors.

'Er, well . . .'

'C'mon, it shouldn't take *that* long!'

'It seems, Your Regality, that something is blocking our sensor arrays. It seems their atmosphere is full of, er . . .' He glanced back at his console. 'Nitrogen.'

'What?' hissed the Regal Commander. 'You mean . . . ?'

'Yes, Your Highness, whilst Princess Kh'Xandhra remains on the planet's surface we cannot locate her.'

'Sir, there is one solution,' offered the Weaponry Regent, quivering with excitement. 'If there was no atmosphere . . . ?' His tentacle hovered over a red button.

'Not while my daughter is down there!' snarled the Regal Commander. 'I don't want a scale on her head hurt.'

'Your Highness, there may be another possibility,' suggested the Prince of Sensors. 'It seems this planet is ringed by a network of carefully positioned manufactured objects. Some of which appear to be large enough to support life and offer accommodation.'

Instantly the Regal Commander's mind was filled with thoughts of some of his daughter's favourite Tau Cetian dramas, the ones that took place on vast shimmering prison arrays of metalwork hovering in space.

'You mean she could be in one of them?' he asked.

'Yes, sir. Any one of them.'

'Well don't just sit there. Get scanning!' bellowed the Regal Commander.

In seconds, beams of investigative radiation was emanating from the hull of the million-ton craft and trying its best to work out what was inside the nearest of several hundred communications satellites cluttering local space.

His face sporting the wide smile of extreme artistic satisfaction, Giorgio Scipioni peeled the final few self-adhesive dots off the backing paper and applied them in a neat line from the backs of Sophia's knees to her deliciously turned ankle. 'There, perfect,' he confirmed and stepped back across the darkened CGI studio to admire his handiwork.

Sophia cast a dubious glance down over her spotted body. 'Okay, so run it by me again. What *exactly* is all this for? You said it had something to do with modelling, right?'

Scipioni nodded cheerfully and rubbed his palms together.

'So, where are the catwalks?'

'Oh, there's no need for anything so primitive. This is *computer* modelling.' Much to Scipioni's satisfaction Sophia's eyes glazed over momentarily at mention of the 'C' word. He knew he had her.

'Oh, I see,' she answered, trying to hide the fact that, patently, she didn't.

'It's motion capture,' answered Scipioni importantly, moving in for complete information overwhelm. 'The computer scans in all those dots and builds up a digitised 3-D model of your every move. No self-respecting action film can do without it these days. It's essential for all those really complicated computer-generated special effects.'

'I know that, I *know*, I'm not stupid,' frowned Sophia. 'But just answer me this. Are you absolutely sure I have to be *completely* naked?'

'Oh, yes, yes, definitely,' enthused Scipioni, rubbing his hands down his thighs.

'Why?'

'Oh, er, it's essential. Clothes get in the way, see? I want to motion capture *you*, er . . . not what you're wearing.' He

253

hurried across to the screen on the Render-Bender and began setting up a frame-filling shot of her.

Sophia's frown deepened suspiciously as she looked down at a small village of white dots clustering into an almost complete pair of double-E cups. 'Are you sure you had to stick all these here?'

'Oh, yes,' grinned Scipioni, licking his lips.

'And why was that?'

'Technical,' he answered and spun around on his swivel stool to face her. 'It's a sad truth but, well . . . as sophisticated as these modelling programmes are, they still can't quite get the exact hang of complex harmonic motion. You wouldn't believe the amount of processing time that's been spent in trying to model the exact swing of womanhood in motion.'

'Really?' whispered Sophia, swinging her shoulders and watching the effect. 'So you *didn't* just stick all them dots on for fun?'

Scipioni tried his best to look horrified. 'Oh, no, no, not at all. That's essential for data collection, that is. Essential.' Biting his bottom lip, he turned back to the screen and typed in a few overly complex instructions. And so it was that, as Stig Folini struggled out of the alien costume in a room next door, Scipioni flexed his fingers and readied himself to digitise the over-pneumatic Sophia.

He didn't get very far. Much to his extreme irritation, the door was flung open. His Holiness Pope Angeles swept in on a wave of Armani and took a stool next to him.

'All right, how's this new edit going?' he asked breathlessly.

'Er, I . . .' Desperately, Scipioni attempted to cover the monitorful of enspotted Sophia. He failed. 'New screen-saver,' he suggested and offered a Parmesan smile.

'I don't want to know,' frowned Angeles. 'What about your new ad?'

'Er, it's coming on . . . coming on.'

'I take it that means it's not finished?'

'A few more hours and I should be ready.'

'That's way too long. C'mon, we'll have to go with the original cut. Bring it with you.' The Pope stood and edged towards the door.

'Bring it? Bring it where?' flustered Scipioni.

'A private screening I've arranged. C'mon. They'll be waiting,' added the Pontiff and ducked out of the editing suite in a whirl of designer vestments.

'Who'll be waiting?' Scipioni called after the sound of retreating Gucci sneakers. 'What private screening? Hey . . . ?'

The silence which filtered back down the corridor failed to cast much light on his volley of questions.

'Er, Sophia, look, I've got to . . .' Limply, he pointed out of the door. 'Just stay there, right where you are, I'll be back. Honest.'

Before the liberally spotted Sophia's snarl could blossom into fully fledged scorn, Scipioni snatched a videotape from a shelf and was away on his toes. As he clattered off in hot pursuit of the Pope he cursed the way things just always seemed to be coming between him and the filming of that oh-so-tasteful multi-tentacled sex scene so essential to the artistic balance of *Gazan Dolls*.

14:55 The Vatican

The sound of confusion rising from the knot of baffled Cardinals filled the corridor outside the Vatican lecture theatre. Each crimson-clad man looked at every other, searching for a clue as to why they had been summoned at such short notice and in such an extraordinary manner. Never in the recent history of the Vatican had the entire stock of Cardinals been brought together at pike-point by the Swiss Guard.

'Is this your doing?' accused the Head of the Congregation for Religious Attire, extremely miffed at having been hauled away from the fine claret which was accompanying his grilled sea bream on a bed of a spinach ragu.

'Of course not,' hissed the Head of the Congregation for Extraordinary Affairs, somewhat unhappy that the enjoyment of his lobster bisque had been prematurely curtailed. 'As a matter of fact I had considered it was your doing,' he sneered as the sparkling Chardonnay in his quarters turned ever more still. 'Is this another emergency meeting to discuss nuns' hemlines, perhaps?'

'If you think that I consider you would have anything constructive to add to that particular debate then I fear you are more than a little mistaken,' growled the claretless one.

'Gentlemen, please, put down your fists,' cried the Secretary for Christian Unity, pushing through the clot of Cardinals, his palms raised.

'Oh, please leave them to it. I might learn something of the ancient art of boxing,' chipped in the Prefect for Catholic Education.

'You might learn to keep your nose out of other people's, ahem, discussions,' threatened the Head of Extraordinary Affairs, carefully sidestepping the use of the word 'argument'. It was a point which had been raised several years ago by the President Emeritus of Propaganda; no matter how it looked to everyone, no matter how it sounded and absolutely no matter how many blows were traded, Cardinals never ever had arguments. *Never.* Honest.

Fifty yards down the corridor both Cardinals Holridge and Kotonawa and a bewildered Father Fintan O'Suilleabhain were being prodded on apace by a sturdy pair of Swiss Guards.

'Mind where you are waggling those pikes,' complained Holridge, up on his toes, his buttocks feeling remarkably vulnerable before far too much ancient weaponry.

'Ah, gentlemen,' said Pope Angeles, emerging from a stairwell twenty feet ahead of them. 'Good of you to come.'

Suddenly, to Holridge it was as if the pikes and the Swiss Guard had ceased to exist. In a flash he was next to the Pope, eyes wide with worry. 'Your Holiness, I need a word about . . . about our, er . . . visitors?' His glance darted nervously about, his pupils terrified tadpoles in a stormy sea of concern.

'It's okay, I will be announcing them to our brethren in a matter of minutes,' smiled His Holiness excitedly.

'Announce them? No!' squeaked Holridge. 'You can't.'

'Oh nonsense, it's the very least I could do. After all, it does seem a little unfair that your colleagues find out at the same time as the rest of the world. I know, it's only a few hours, but, hey, a small privilege is still a perk in my book.'

'A few hours?' wheezed Holridge, scratching his head as he trotted sideways down the corridor. 'But . . . but your address isn't until tomorrow.'

'Ah, yes. The main event. But the ad for it is ready to go this evening.'

'Did you say ad? Advert? As in television? As in pictures of the aliens on everyone's television?' spluttered Holridge, realising that Fintan's conclusion had been right. This wasn't going to be their little secret much longer. The world, and anyone else who happened to be listening, would know that there were aliens in the Vatican. His eyes darted nervously towards the sky, searching for the prying ears of concerned parents.

'What else would I mean?' shrugged the Pope.

'But . . . cancel it. You must. Call a halt to this now before it's too late!' pleaded Holridge, snatching at the Pope's Armani sleeves, terror writ large across across his worried brow. 'They don't know they're here. We're safe for the moment, but if they find out. If they're out there and listening . . .'

257

Angeles stared at the panicking Cardinal. 'Who are out there?'

'Parents!' whispered Holridge, the whites of his eyes showing as he imagined tentacled mothers targeting weapons of mass destruction from low-Earth orbit.

'Cardinal Holridge,' frowned the Pope, removing a pair of white knuckles from his sleeve, 'when was the last time you had a holiday? I really think you should book something. Tomorrow.'

'They're might not *be* a tomorrow! Listen to me! It's the Star of Bethlehem all over again! Zzzzzzzap wooooooof babooom!' insisted Holridge, waving his arms in a surprisingly accurate impersonation of death rays strafing the Earth, igniting the atmosphere and blowing the entire planet to the kind of shimmering cosmic dust that would make Tinkerbell weep.

Pope Angeles stopped suddenly in his tracks, looked the panting Holridge up and down and, in as gentle a voice as he could muster under the circumstances, said, 'Cardinal Holridge, it pains me to have to remind you of something so theologically basic, but, as I know it's not unusual for, say, professors of advanced mathematics to forget how to carry out long division, I shall overlook this slip. Now pay attention. The Star of Bethlehem appeared around Christmas, tomorrow is Easter. Take a holiday.' He wheeled on his feet and strode off into the middle of the throng of Cardinals, ushering them around him like a headmaster calling assembly and sucking them into the Vatican lecture theatre.

Holridge raised a finger of protest, readying himself for an in-depth discussion regarding the slippage of the Julian calendar with respect to the seasons and the subsequent corrections of Pope Gregory, but somehow the rapidly emptying corridor didn't seem like a worthwhile audience. His jaw swung pathetically.

'It might not be turning out as bad as all that,' began Fintan, attempting a limp smile of encouragement. 'Who's to be sure their parents will be recognising them at all? I've heard that TV always makes you look fatter than you really are.'

Holridge stared at the Irish clergyman as he puffed out his cheeks hamster-fashion.

'And then there's places you've been. They are always looking totally different on TV, don't you think?'

Holridge shook his head, turned and reluctantly headed off into the lecture theatre.

'Have you ever considered a career with the Samaritans?' asked Kotonawa.

'No,' said Fintan, his face brightening.

'Don't,' suggested the Japanese Cardinal and followed his brothers in vestments into the theatre as the sound of indignant footsteps and complaining rattled into earshot behind.

'And I'm asking you again, SG 79, who gave you these orders? Who arranged this meeting? Who's been interfering with my Swiss Guard?' snapped Tardi at the Guard herding him and Alighieri down the corridor towards the hastily arranged papal meeting.

'It came from the top,' answered the Guard nervously from under the horizon of his shiny plumed helmet.

'The top of what? Your head, perhaps?'

'It was His Holiness himself,' answered SG79.

'What?' coughed Tardi incredulously, the chains of command swinging even further out of reach. 'But that's not right. It should have come through me. Anything regarding the deployment and usage of the Swiss Guard *must* come through me, that's the way it is.'

'Er, perhaps you were busy?' shrugged the Guard.

'What? I am *never* too busy to give out orders. It should have been my job. How can anyone else ensure that maximal manpower efficiency is maintained throughout the entire operation? It can't be left to chance. Oh no, co-ordination of this level requires the most careful planning, charts, flow diagrams . . .'

'Er, we're here, sir,' observed SG79, snapping a crisp salute and pointing to the door of the lecture theatre.

'What?'

'Ahh, the last two,' called the Pope out through the open door. 'Do come in, we're all ready to start.'

And so, with the distinct feeling that far too many rugs were writhing uncontrollably beneath his feet, Tardi drifted towards his seat at the front of the auditorium. Alighieri closed the door and followed.

Almost instantly the lights dimmed and a single spotlight arced on to the Pope. He stood, gleaming in his Armani vestments and rubbed his hands together eagerly. 'Since the dawn of time, man has been plagued by three little words – Are we alone?' he declared and barely stifled a thrill of delight as he noticed the overdramatic lick of reverb which Scipioni had added to his mic feed. 'Who knows how many sleepless nights have been spent by the more easily worried of our ancestors as they stared into the night sky and asked themselves that question? Well, today I can finally answer that hottest of science fiction chestnuts.'

There was a wave of sharply intaken breaths. They knew this was an extraordinary meeting, but they hadn't realised quite how extraordinary it was going to turn out.

Cardinal Holridge bit his fingernails and shook his head.

'Gentlemen,' continued the Pope. 'It is time to forget about Roswell, time to put aside thoughts of von Däniken, for today is the day that conspiracy theories and cover-ups end. Are we alone? Gentlemen, it is my pleasure to announce the answer is no, not any more!'

Despite themselves every Cardinal stared in amazement as

a large video screen lowered itself out of the roof and crackled into life. With a dramatic swirl of synthesised chords, the screen filled with acres of mustard-yellow skin slithering past in unidentifiable waves of texture.

'Oh, God,' whispered Holridge around a mouthful of nail fragments, 'what has he done?'

Throughout the auditorium Cardinals sat up and paid shocked attention as swatches of Ribena-and-Merlot skin blinked at them in tight contrasting edits. Gasps rippled around the auditorium as the scene changed to stark silhouettes of grainy tentacles cross-cut with gleaming black claws. Six hundred watts of industrial jungle sound-track pounded at holy eardrums as millisecond strobes of light showed an unfeasibly shiny spacecraft. Stabs of *Psycho* strings shrieked insistently as a hand reached for a light-switch. Suddenly the scene shifted to daylight and a shaky hand-held glimpse of a seven-and-a-half-foot crea-ture as it hurdled a flowerbed. And as a shiny claw snatched a hand away from a light-switch a woofer-bashing voice-over read, 'See it all tomorrow. The Truth from the people you never thought you'd hear it from.'

As the lights came up again so the tide of stunned questions rose.

'Gentlemen, gentlemen,' shouted Pope Angeles, his arms raised for calm. 'Welcome to the Dawn of the New Age of the Church! Starting here at six thirty tonight, when that hits the screens of Europe's TV sets you'll feel the shock-waves of wonder.'

'And several other shock-waves too,' muttered Holridge, miserably staring at a very grim twenty-four hours to come. As that ad reverberated around the world, appearing at six thirty in every one of Earth's time zones, it would be terrible. Especially when the Americans discovered they weren't the first to be told.

'You can't show that,' shouted the Head of the Congregation for Extraordinary Affairs from the eighth row. 'There'll be mass panic.'

'Panic?' countered the Head for the Congregation for Religious Attire. 'Nobody'll believe it. I think the only hysteria we will hear is hysterical laughter. Who in their right minds can believe in the existence of aliens?'

A ripple of agreement harrumphed around the auditorium.

'Well, I do,' said Pope Angeles.

On the front row, Cardinal Tardi's head was reeling as he tried desperately to recall the rules regarding the removal of clinically insane Popes.

'And how do I know this with such certainty?' continued Pope Angeles. 'How can I stand here before you and announce with complete confidence that aliens from other worlds exist? Because quite simply, in the best tradition of the ancient apostles, I have seen them.'

The auditorium filled with a discontented murmur.

'And what you have just seen is film of those very creatures. That ad is just a brief taste of what is to come.'

The murmur rose to a concerned hum.

'For tomorrow, at the end of my papal address, I have the honour of revealing those extraterrestrials to the waiting world.'

The hum erupted into uproar.

'Are you mad?' squeaked the Head for the Congregation for Religious Attire. 'The papal address is for spreading good news amongst the peoples, not inducing mad panic.'

'But don't you see?' smiled His Holiness. 'This is the *perfect* Good News!'

'What? Happy Easter everyone, we've just been invaded?'

'No, no. Advanced beings have come to us from on high. They're here, they came to us. Who knows what secrets they have brought with them, ready and willing to share with us?

262

Why, in a single leap they could advance our technological intellect by centuries.'

A wave of begrudging acceptance lapped around the auditorium.

Encouraged, Angeles pressed on. 'They've crossed the vast wastes of space, thus proving they have sure and certain knowledge of cosmology. Their insights into the very nature of the universe must be legion. Gentlemen, they're ahead of us scientifically, what if they're also ahead of us spiritually? What if they're also . . . closer to God?'

A blanket of shock settled across the sea of Cardinals.

'But even if they aren't, it doesn't matter,' enthused His Holiness. 'Just the simple fact that these beings exist is the best news we can possibly give the world. Tomorrow I can sing it loud across the airwaves, I have proof that God exists! Proof!'

Suddenly this was all too much for Cardinal Tardi. 'Whoa, whoa, how does having aliens in the basement prove that God exists?' he asked, voicing the thoughts of the gathered audience.

'My dear Tardi, can you not see it? For centuries we have believed, as an act of faith, that life here on Earth was created by the very hand of God Himself.'

A theatreful of red birettas nodded in agreement.

'But what if life on Earth just happened by chance? Take a few handfuls of assorted organic compounds, throw in a stray bolt of lightning, stir in a bit of chaos and, bingo, by the laws of chance we get a bucket of DNA? What if life here just simply started up one day? Where does that leave God?'

'Oh no,' muttered Tardi shaking his head. 'What have I done? Elected an evolutionist heathen?' Catherine wheels of accusing headlines spun to the forefront of his mind. New Pope Is Darwinist – Official!

'If life on Earth is just a happy accident of cookery then He'd be on very shaky ground,' continued Angeles over the murmurings of unrest. 'But *that's* the Good News! It's *not* accidental! Think about it, gentlemen. What are the chances of a bunch of chemicals just happening to turn into an amoeba? Trillions to one against. Okay, so it might just happen once if you wait long enough. But *twice*? On two completely separate sides of two different galaxies? That's *got* to be a miracle. And who do we know that does miracles?'

For a few uncomfortable moments there was a deadly silence as all present chewed over the irrefutable logic of the Pope's message.

'So . . . so what you're saying is, er . . .' began Cardinal Tardi. 'In a nutshell . . . Aliens exist, therefore . . . er, God exists?'

'Exactly. And what's more, He's far, *far* bigger than anyone ever imagined. Who knows how many other races are waiting for us out there? After all, just look at the number of beetles He made. And not to mention finches. Gentlemen, there's so much out there for us. It's time for the religions of the world to put aside their differences and unite with us under the Christian flag! Now, if you'll just excuse me, I really must dash. There's a few details I've got to iron out with Reuters.'

And in a flurry of Armani he leapt off the stage and dashed up the aisle, fizzes of excitement crackling off his lapels.

No sooner had the door slammed shut behind him than the buzz of random discussion erupted.

'So does that mean God is an alien?' asked the Head of Christian Education, rubbing his temples.

'Of course not,' said Father Fintan. 'He's an astronaut, everybody knows that.'

On the front row Cardinal Tardi sat with his head in his hands, trembling. Four days it had taken for his entire world to begin unravelling. Already his reputation in the KGB was shattered by that unfortunate mentioning of helicopters full of aliens. It was only a matter of time before word spread to the other government agencies he had been cultivating. And the decades he had spent ensuring that Vatican life ran smoothly, the years he had made certain that any of the Popes he had served under had a decent speech ready at all times, all that time he had succesfully foreseen potential *faux pas* and made absolutely sure that they were avoided, *all* of that would be completely wasted if this address was allowed to go ahead.

The world wasn't ready to hear news like that. And it certainly wasn't ready to hear it from the Vatican. It was all too dangerous. All too terrifying. Somehow, this had to be stopped.

He stood and, ignoring the uproar around him, he headed hurriedly backstage towards a chance to save the face of the entire Roman Catholic Church and his reputation amongst numerous governments secret services. Now, if he could just get his hands on that video . . .

15:13 The Vatican

'Why didn't he listen?' growled Cardinal Holridge under his breath as he kicked open the door of the basement lab of the Congregation for Icon Authentication. He glared at the unfeasibly shiny spacecraft sat on the rusting trolley, turned away and hurled himself on to the casting couch. 'I can't believe he's going to do it? Forty-five different TV companies already booked and he's still got hours to go!'

Behind him, a thin line of liquid metal oozed apart and began to open.

'I can see it now,' moaned Holridge. 'Every single home in the world will get pictures of those two aliens beamed straight into the front room.'

'Er, I counted at least three aliens,' mused Fintan, scratching his head and running back through the advert.

'And it's not just the advert. It's the address tomorrow.

You heard him. He's going to show those two off to the world as a finale,' worried Holridge.

'Really? Us?' said Kh'Vynn, catching Holridge's last words as the gull-wing door slid fully open on a sigh of alien hydraulics.

'Oh, yes,' groaned Holridge, glaring at the visitors. 'He's got it all sorted. With the Reuters link-up the pictures'll be everywhere in seconds. CNN, Sky . . . You name it. Crystal clear shots of you and the Pope standing in the middle of a balcony high above St Peter's Square, crowds of onlookers below. A picture in every home.'

'Every home?' squeaked Kh'Vynn delightedly. 'Did you hear that, my beloved, every home will see us!' He wrapped a pair of Ribena-coloured tentacles around Kh'Xandhra's midriff and spun her happily around. 'Oh, my darling, this is even more perfect than I had hoped. Aren't these people so kind arranging all this for us,' he chirruped as he saw them both treading the boards of the world's TV sets as the alien stars of the future. 'Ahhh, interstellar stardom beckons,' he grinned, wriggling his hips in a way that would've made Dale Winton blush.

'Well, enjoy it,' growled Holridge. 'You've got twenty-four hours before . . . Zzzzzzzap wooooooof ba-booom!' For the benefit of the visitors he repeated his uncanny demonstration of sudden atmospheric combustion and instantaneous planetary destruction.

Kh'Vynn's eye-stalks drooped miserably. 'Oh cruel fates,' he whined dramatically, slapping the back of a tentacle across his forehead. 'Paradise found only to be taken so cruelly from us in the moment of our imminent success.'

'How d'you think *we* feel,' snapped Holridge. 'We live here.'

'But why?' asked Kh'Xandhra. 'What have you done to deserve planet-wide destruction?'

'What have *we* done?' coughed Holridge. 'We're only accessories to interstellar elopement! That won't go down too well with your parents, I presume? How will it go? They'll beam you off the balcony and then open fire?'

'Ahhh,' breathed Kh'Xandhra and looked guiltily at her feet.

'Er, have you met our parents?' asked Kh'Vynn nervously, amazed that Holridge had such accurate insights into the way things were quite likely to go.

'Look, it might not be that bad,' suggested Kotonawa, attempting to inject a twinkling of hope into the growing atmosphere of deepening gloom. All eyes turned on him. 'Er, well maybe your parents haven't even noticed you're missing.'

Kh'Vynn shook his head. 'They noticed. It was a little hard not to. Two smashed Security Hovva-Thrusters, a melted neosilicate window with polymarble frame, a stolen ship, numerous infringements of flight regulations including speeding, flying without due care and attention . . . Er, need I go on?'

'It's no good,' whined Holridge. 'Whatever way you look at it, they're fugitives.'

Kh'Vynn and Kh'Xandhra nodded.

'And the penalty for harbouring fugitives?' asked Kotonawa, not really wanting to hear the answer.

'Zzzzzzzap wooooooof ba-booom!' offered Kh'Vynn.

Kotonawa's mind whirled. 'Okay, okay . . . er, so maybe they don't know where they've gone. I mean, the universe is a big place with lots of little galaxies to hide in and asteroid belts and . . .'

'If they don't know where they are right now, they certainly will after every single TV satellite flashes a certain advert into the ether. Face it,' observed Holridge, 'we're doomed. Doomed!'

Kotonawa racked his brain for a glimmer of urgently needed hope, squeezing ever harder as desperation settled over the lab. 'I've got it! I've got it! There's still a few hours left.' He turned to Kh'Vynn. 'Maybe we could just fix your spacecraft and, well, it'll be sad to see you go, but under the circumstances . . .'

'Fix it? And this from a man who daren't lift the bonnet of his Skoda?' hissed Holridge.

'All right, all right, so we get a man in? There must be someone at NASA who could, er . . . all right, forget it.' And the tarpaulin of gloom resettled.

But only for a few moments. Suddenly Kotonawa slammed his fist into his palm and leapt to his feet. 'I've got it! I've *really* got it this time! It's obvious. Been staring me in the face all along!' He took a deep breath befitting a man who was about to make a suggestion which would save the entire world from imminent destruction *and* bring about the happiest of endings. 'It's simple. Let's get the Pope to marry them!'

'What! Are you serious?' gasped Holridge.

'Of course I am! How better to placate a gang of irate parents? Instead of having a daughter stolen from under their noses we'll be able to give them a brand new son. Don't you see, it's perfect!'

'Marriage?' squeaked Kh'Vynn. 'Er, that's a bit sudden isn't it, I mean . . . phew, that's commitment and stuff, isn't it? And . . . and children, yurgh.'

'Males,' hissed Kh'Xandhra. 'They're all the same.'

'All right. Just forget I said anything about marriage, okay,' sulked Kotonawa, folding his arms. 'Just forget it.'

'Er, well it wouldn't've worked anyway,' began Kh'Xandhra glancing up from her feet. 'You see, they'd rather I married something I'd stepped in. My dad's a bit picky about things ruining the Regal Family name. *Very* picky.'

'How picky?' asked Kotonawa reluctantly.

'Zzzzzzzap wooooooof ba-booom!' answered Kh'Vynn.

'That's it then, we're doomed,' shrugged Holridge and wished he had a large supply of tequila to hand. 'Destroyed because of a thirty-eight second advert showing two aliens.'

'Er, that's not actually entirely correct,' said Father Fintan. 'It's a small point I know, but, well, if you're writing epitaphs its better to get it right.'

'What are you on about?'

'Well, there were three aliens in that advert.'

'Two aliens, three aliens, what difference does it make!' shrieked Holridge and made his way across the lab towards a large cupboard stocked with industrial alcohol. Now, if he could just find a few lemons to go with it . . .

'It could make all the difference in the world,' said Fintan, a slight tremor of excitement quivering in his voice. 'Ask yourself this. Where did Scipioni get the third alien from?'

'That's obvious. He's a film-maker, they rustle up things like that all the time,' grumbled Holridge.

'Exactly,' said Fintan. 'Gentlemen, I think I might have the answer. It's a million-to-one shot but, well, it might just work. Cardinals, how good are you with a needle and thread . . . ?'

16:04 Rome

If anyone had asked Cardinal Tardi just how he had managed to get hold of a video of a certain advert then his answer would almost certainly have involved mention of the removal of certain sugar-based confectioneries from pre-school infants.

Having sent Alighieri off to monitor any imminent telephonic communications emanating from the papal phone, and cleared the auditorium on the pretence that the Sisters of Mercy had booked it for a showing of *The*

Sound of Music, he whirled on his heel and carefully secreted himself in a suitable pool of dense shadow. He hadn't needed to wait long before a certain Giorgio Scipioni emerged from a side door and hurried up the aisle, video box tucked under his arm. Barely stifling thoughts of obtaining said video via the expeditious use of a dull object to the back of the director's skull, Tardi held his breath and followed.

In minutes the Cardinal watched as Scipioni ducked into a room deep in the bowels of the Radio Vaticano building, placed the video on a handy chair and, rubbing his hands lecherously, disappeared into a rear dressing room with a cheery, 'Sophia? Hi honey, I'm home. I've come to check on those spots of yours.'

It took just over a minute and a half for Tardi to run off a copy of the advert, drop the original back on to the chair and slide out of the door again.

Right now, having run off copies for all the world governments who possessed good books he wanted to get back into, he turned left in his trusty dark blue BMW and floored the accelerator down a street behind the Canadian Embassy.

In seconds he had slewed the car to a deft handbrake halt between two Fiats and was pulling a Betamax tape out from the collection of other duplicates nestling on the passenger seat. A VHS PAL for the British, NTSC for the Americans and a crisp recordable-DVD for the Japanese. He crossed the street quickly, thumbing his key fob back over his shoulder. Obediently the BMW flashed its indicators and slammed its central locking shut.

Moments later he was at the front door of the targeted house, his fingers working away at the hairpin in the lock.

Up on the third floor, a silhouetted figure hunched over his recently purchased night-vision binoculars and, elbows perched on the windowsill, he watched the activities of a blonde-haired woman in the swimming pool of the Canadian Embassy. Much to the spy's delight she had, as was her early afternoon habit, locked the door and spent the last fifteen minutes cruising the pool in a lazy backcrawl. As usual, her ultramarine one-piece swimsuit lay discarded on the side of the pool.

But, just as she tumble-turned with a glimpse of taut buttock and headed off on another length, a specially loosened floorboard creaked a warning behind him. The agent spun on his heel and, leaving the binoculars on the tripod, he rolled soundlessly behind his aging sofa. He peered through the upholstery button specially fitted with a wide-angle lens, watching the door as he reached for his Walther PPK.

Instinctively, he slithered soundlessly behind his sofa and primed his harpoon gun. If someone had been sent for him, he wanted all the information he could get before finally pulling the trigger on his trusty Walther. Experience had shown him that even the hardiest of spies seemed to want to explain the tiniest of details when they had a three-foot shark harpoon sticking out of their thigh. But, just to be on the safe side, he reached under the sideboard and began peeling the gaffa tape off a handily placed sawn-off Winchester. Casually he made a mental note to remind himself to invest in another harpoon gun.

Across the room, the handle twisted cautiously and, with a groan of hinges, the door swung open.

'Hello, Agent Olevski? You in there?' said Cardinal Tardi as he strode into the room. 'Cooee, anybody home?'

For fifty long milliseconds Olevski had to fight with his trigger-happy index finger. 'Get in here, slowly,' he barked from behind the sofa.

Tardi stepped over the threshold, nervousness written large across his face. 'Er, I come bearing gifts.' He waved a video box and searched the room for Agent Olevski.

271

Sighting the binoculars he strolled across to the window and peered through. The daughter of the Canadian minister drifted nakedly across his field of view.

'What do you want?' demanded Agent Olevski emerging from behind the sofa.

'Brought you this,' said Tardi, holding out the video, his eyes still fixed to the binoculars. 'Moscow said you can transfer it straight to them.'

'VHS?'

'Course not. Betamax.'

'What is it?'

'That's being nosy.'

'And so's that. Get away from those binoculars, that's my surveillance.'

'Hmmm, since when have they spelt that v-o-y-e-u-r-i-s-m?' grinned Tardi as a final flash of buttock marked another tumble-turn.

'I didn't ask for this mission,' protested Olevski.

'It's a dirty job, eh?'

'Gimme that video,' snapped the Russian agent, snatching the box from the Cardinal and heading across to a vast video-player in the corner of the room. 'Oh, you didn't rewind it. Did you know that the vast majority of wear and tear is inflicted on your video by rewinding tapes?' He reached into a small box, pulled out a curious lozenge-shaped device and slid the video inside. 'However, this neat video rewinder solves all of that. By taking care of the mundane rewinding duties it protects my VCR and thus prolongs its life.' It clicked to a halt. 'There!'

Tardi tutted to himself and flopped down on the sofa. Much to his surprise, he didn't flop as far into it as he expected. 'This a new sofa?'

Agent Olevski grinned proudly. 'I have found a great value solution to the problem of sagging furniture. A remarkable rejuvenation, don't you think? And all carried out using Sofa Saver's revolutionary wooden platform construction.'

Tardi picked up the edge of the cushion and stared for a moment at the shelf of plywood printed with a green-dyed double-interlocking S. 'Er, about the video?' he reminded.

'In a moment. I just have to move this amazingly heavy filing cabinet in order to get to the hidden cupboard behind it.'

'Do you need a hand?' offered Tardi as he watched Olevski roll up his sleeves and muscle up towards the heavily laden cabinet.

'That won't be necessary,' he grinned and offered another silent nod of thanks to Agent Etheridge-Willis for introducing him to the delight of the 'Innovations' catalogue. He pressed a pair of index fingers against the cabinet and pushed. With the slightest of sighs it moved out of the way. 'Teflon-coated SlitheriKups placed at each corner of heavy household appliances can ease the strain of moving. *Voilà!*'

Olevski pulled open a large cupboard and revealed an almost spherical object crammed within. He flicked a switch and an array of carefully angled lamps erupted into life, shining on a dozen clusters of solar panels. 'Just give it a few minutes to warm up,' he muttered, pulling a long co-axial cable out of a small panel and fiddling around at the back of the VCR.

'What the Hell is that?' asked Tardi.

'You mean apart from ancient?' tutted Olevski. 'Ever heard of Sputnik VII?'

Tardi shook his head and shrugged.

'Not surprised. It never really officially happened. Bloody Americans stole all the thunder of that by sticking a couple of golfers on the moon. Well, Cardinal Tardi, meet Sputnik VII. My very own satellite up-link to Moscow, courtesy of

Botchnik Technologies. We just piggy-back it on a telephone signal and bounce it straight into Moscow HQ, easy. And if there's not too much sun-spot activity I can even get Sky Movies on it. This video better not be too long, I forgot to recharge the batteries on my mobile.'

'It's only thirty-eight seconds.'

'What? Is it a surveillance tape?' he asked as he hefted his aging telephone out of his coat pocket and began dialling.

'You'll see,' grinned Tardi as he heard the all-too-familiar tones of Moscow Central's receptionist rattling into Olevski's ear.

In a remarkably short time the order came through and Agent Olevski pressed 'play'. The antique Betamax machine clunked mechanically for a few seconds, whirred strangely to itself and then began broadcasting simultaneously to the cream of the KGB and a battered Sony colour portable.

'Oh my God!' whispered Agent Olevski as his screen filled with acres of mustard-yellow skin and the tiny speaker tried its best to keep up with the swirling synths. 'What the Hell is it?'

16:08 Local Space

On the main command deck of the million-ton Strato-Fortress, hovering on the fringes of Earth's atmosphere, the Prince of Sensors shrieked with delight.

'Sir! Your Regality, sir! I have located her!'

'What? Where?' gasped the Regal Commander, leaping to his feet.

The Prince of Sensors pointed to a tiny dot on his screen. 'There! An orbiting station! Look!' he flicked a switch and the main screen on the front wall flashed up images of mustard-yellow skin tightly intercut with shots of purple and unfeasibly shiny spaceships.

274

'Kh'Xandhra! My Kh'Xandhra! And *that* other creature! Navigational Serf, set course. Immediately!'

In moments, banks of Type-98 Ytterbium Collider Drives were hurling the alien craft across the Heavens towards the small chunk of space hardware hovering in geostationary above Italy. Anti-inertia brakes dragged the Strato-Fortress to a halt five hundred yards from one of AT&T's newer and shinier telephone satellites.

'Visual!' demanded the Regal Commander and the wall lit up with a view just off the port bow. 'What? That's it? But it's so small. Oh, my Kh'Xandhra! How dare they confine her in there?'

Feverishly, the Prince of Sensors tuned his instruments, attempting to pinpoint her exact position.

'Communications Minion!' yelled the Regal Commander. 'Get them on. I want a word with them!'

'Sir, 'tis done,' answered the creature at communications efficiently. 'Full band-width and translator engaged.'

The Regal Commander took a breath and stepped up to what passed as a microphone. 'This is the Regal Commander of the Strato-Fortress currently hovering five hundred yards away . . . Oh, sod the diplomacy. You've got my daughter, you have thirty seconds to hand her back!'

There was no response.

'Are they getting this?'

'Yes, sir!' whimpered the Communications Minion.

The Regal Commander turned back to the microphone. 'I repeat, you have thirty of your Earth seconds to return my daughter to me, otherwise I shall be forced to open fire!'

Again, silence was the only answer.

'Is this the ancient tradition of the calling of bluffs?' growled the Regal Commander, marching towards the Weapons Console.

Across the flight deck tentacles were shrugged.

'Give me back my daughter!' shouted the mustardy one and flicked a few power switches. Weapons systems powered up. 'Twenty seconds!'

'Er, sir, I don't know how to tell you this,' began the Prince of Sensors, 'but I've tried on all frequencies, wavelengths and amplitudes and, well, Kh'Xandhra is not on that vessel.'

'What! Do they dare toy with me? Do they have the temerity to play games? Well. Game Over!' The Regal Commander slammed his enraged tentacle on to the weapons console. A flare of hypercharged plasma arced out of a handy nacelle and vaporised several million dollars' worth of communications satellite.

Twenty-two thousand three hundred miles below, several hundred faithful AT&T customers began tapping their headsets against suitable bits of furniture as the lines fizzed, started ranting about the returning of daughters and suddenly went mysteriously dead.

15:15 Florida

Safe in the back of the anonymous grey bulletproof limousine, currently topping a hundred and twenty down a hastily emptied freeway, the President of the United States of America cleared his throat.

'Hmmm, all right, so it's fast but somehow I don't think that's what's gotten you guys so excited. You didn't drag me out of the White House just to show me this. Am I right?'

'Very astute, sir,' fawned the Vice-President and put on his serious face. 'Er, there have been developments, sir.' He looked across at the Chief Scientific Officer of the Pentagon Advisory Committee Regarding Entities of a Non-Earth Origin. 'Show him.'

Professor Olenburger pressed a button in the door handle nearest to him and an LCD screen began showing a recently

276

intercepted screenful of mustard-yellow and purple aliens. 'See it all tomorrow. The Truth from the people you never thought you'd hear it from,' growled a woofer-heavy voice-over and the thirty-eight second snippit of video was replaced with a sea of static.

'What the Hell . . . ? Where the Hell did you get that?' gasped the President, reaching for the drinks cabinet and a stiff shot of Jack Daniel's.

'Private Sputnik VII satellite uplink. Rome to Moscow, sir.'

'Russians?'

'Yes, sir,' affirmed the Vice-President and had to bite his tongue before he mentioned anything about it being blind-ingly obvious it was a Russian communication. Nobody else would be caught dead broadcasting such highly sensitive information via the far from secret-tight Sputnik VII system.

'It's genuine?'

'Yes, sir. Most definitely, sir. Wouldn't have brought it to your attention if I hadn't known it was one hundred per cent Mom's apple pie genuine, sir. Misinformation is the sand in the Vaseline of victory, sir.'

A thrill of pride oozed through the President's ex-military heart as he heard his favourite motto flung back at him with complete belief. 'So, what's it all mean, Professor?' he looked across at the exobiologist.

Sucking his teeth noisily, Professor Olenburger jabbed at the rewind button and spooled the advert back to the start. 'Notice the way this mustard-yellow surface moves,' he began, slipping into his favoured lecturial voice as the video began playing once again. 'See the folds here and the way the light plays across the highlights. Now compare it to this Merlot-and-Ribena-hued surface and you will see that it also behaves in the same manner. The same manner indeed as this tentacular protuberance seen backlit here against dangling chains. Note the feeling of scale offered

277

by the falling drips of a liquid, which, judging by its refractive quality and the general fluidity of its movement, I believe I can safely assume is terrestrial water at an ambient temperature of no less than . . .'

'Professor, er . . . the point?' scowled the Vice-President, understanding perhaps three words out of four.

'The point,' answered Olenburger over the top of his thick lenses, 'is that this video quite clearly shows living entities which have been filmed in a deliberately covert and obfuscative manner utilising a variety of modern cinematic techniques, all of which are currently in vogue amongst manufacturers of low-intellect high-shock sub-sci-fi thrillers.'

The silence which filled the back of the limo served only to amplify Professor Olenburger's tooth-sucking.

'But what's it mean?' pleaded the President.

'Hmmm. Frankly, it is as meaningless as any commercially produced, er . . . commercial.'

The Vice-President shook his head in disbelief. 'An ad? Are you telling me the Russians are using their Sputnik VII satellite system to broadcast advertising?'

'However,' continued the exobiologist frowning impatiently as if at an unruly student, 'unintentionally they have supplied more information than they anticipated. I know precisely where it was made and who made it! Observe!' Professor Olenburger stabbed the video controls and began shuffling the video forwards frame by frame through the shanky hand-held sequence of the seven-and-a-half-foot shiny alien skipping over the flowerbed.

'Oh, my God. Look at that!' gasped the President as the tail rotor of a large white Sea King helicopter edged its way on to the screen. 'It's Vatican 2.'

'Now, if I remind you about the papal address tomorrow . . . ?' said Professor Olenburger.

'Oh, God, of course!' whispered the President. 'It all fits! "See it all tomorrow. The Truth from the people you never thought you'd hear it from." '

Olenburger nodded. The Vice-President shook his head in open-mouthed incomprehension.

'But, they wouldn't dare announce that to the world, would they?' gasped the President. 'What could they possibly stand to gain?'

'Everything,' said Professor Olenburger with not a little admiration for those involved. 'They show the world that aliens exist and, bingo, they prove God exists!'

'Whoa, whoa . . . How?' gagged the Vice-President.

'Miracles and chances and interstellar coincidences,' dismissed Olenburger. 'You want the details, you listen in to his address tomorrow. He'll explain it all after he shows the aliens off.'

'He's . . . he's going to show them off? To the world?' whimpered the Vice-President as the truth began to dawn. 'No, no, he can't . . . Does he have any idea of the panic it'll cause? The hysteria, the riots, the looting . . . Oh, God! We can't let this happen, sir. He'll . . . he'll destroy all we've worked for in the last five and a half decades. Hell, it's the only thing we've ever agreed on with the Russians and the Japanese and . . . Jeez, all of them!'

'Agreed? What have you agreed?' asked the professor, for once interested in something the country's second-in-command had to say.

'We can't tell the general public about aliens. It'll completely destroy worldwide productivity,' insisted the Vice-President. 'Well-known fact, ain't it? You tell the average factory worker that mankind ain't top dog in the galaxy no more, that some goddamned slimy alien is more intelligent than him and he's gonna down tools in a second!'

'And you consider *that* more important than the proof that God exists?'

'Er, yeah,' nodded the Vice-President. 'For an industrial economy . . .'

'Have you forgotten the Flock Coagulation Scenario?' insisted Professor Olenburger. 'Do you not recall my theories and the impact such a revelation would cause? No one doing anything against God, sitting around singing hymns, calling each other "brother and sister". One God, one religion . . .'

'One huge mess,' interrupted the President, shaking his head. 'It'll be like the sixties all over again, only a hundred times worse. Gentlemen, it's our duty to the world to do something about this. To stop it now, before it's too late!'

'But . . . but what can we do?' squeaked the Vice-President, his head whirling in confusion. 'We've got less than twenty-four hours to save the world!'

'Drastic times call for drastic measures.'

'No . . . ? You can't be thinking of . . .'

'We have no feasible alternative. It's dangerous, but they've brought it upon themselves. Gentlemen,' declared the President, his bottom lip trembling ever so slightly, 'I am hereby declaring Operation Desperate Measure in a definite go-mode.'

'Ahhhh, I was hoping you'd say that,' grinned Professor Olenburger as the limousine slowed to a tyre-burning halt and the door was pulled open by a marine in Ray-Bans and full cabbage kit.

'Mr President, your carriage awaits,' added the exobiologist. He pointed across the tarmac to the high shouldered angles of a revving Stealth Fighter. 'Everything is on board and waiting.'

'Well, let's get to it!' declared the President, sprinting off across the Tarmac with a surge of Federal pride.

In minutes the Stealth Fighter was lifting off the runway and, almost invisible to radar systems the world over, was heading towards the knee-cap of Italy on full afterburner.

In a similar limousine two hundred miles due south of Moscow an almost identical conclusion was being reached. Within the next half hour, as the news of a certain advert spread amongst the world's military, over a dozen other final solutions were prodded into various stages of life.

18:26 The Vatican

High on a Louis XIV flame mahogany desk a figure in shimmering white raised his arms and turned into the very embodiment of all that was angelic. All he was missing was a halo. And a couple of wings.

'All ye gathered before me,' he expounded, looking out over seas of devoted faces, 'have come to hear the truth, the one holy truth, the one undeniable . . . Hmmm, nah. Too pompous. Er, all you who have braved the transport systems of this Earth . . .'

Suddenly there was a knock on the door. Pope Angeles looked around nervously, frozen in mid-rehearsal. The door was knocked again. Harder, more desperately.

Angeles leapt off the desk, flung himself on to the matching chair and hastily scattered paperwork across the flame mahogany. 'Yes? Who is it?' he called, trying to sound as calm as a Pope who'd just been innocently doing some admin all afternoon. Honest.

Cardinal Holridge burst in and dashed across the papal office in a flap of emotions and crimson vestments. 'Your Holiness, please don't do it!'

'Do what?' he asked, guiltily moving an unimportant memo over a heel mark on his desk.

'The advert!' squeaked Holridge. 'Please, don't let them show it. The parents will . . .'

'Oh, not that again. I thought I told you to go and book a holiday. I know the Turin Shroud thing didn't work out as well as you wanted . . .'

'No, it's not that!'

'Don't get me wrong, I appreciate all the hard work you've put in to get it all that far, I really do . . .'

'Please, listen!'

'And if it had all been just a little less sciencey, well . . .'

'Your Holiness, don't show that advert, you don't know what it'll do!'

'Cardinal Holridge,' said Angeles with an edge of irritation in his voice, 'it's all going ahead.'

'Look, if it's a case of the address, you've no need to worry. You can give the world this!' He tugged a small pottery elephant out of an inside pocket and waggled it at the Pope. 'This can do miracles. It drinks milk through its trunk and . . .'

'You expect me to show that to the world?' coughed Angeles.

'All right, all right,' pleaded Holridge, dropping the porcelain pachyderm and pulling a pack of cards out of his pocket. 'What about this? Here, pick a card, any card . . .'

'Cardinal!' shouted Pope Angeles. 'It's going ahead. It's out of my hands now!'

'No, no, just get on the phone.' Holridge glanced feverishly at his watch. 'You've still got an hour to stop them. You can stop . . . Why are you shaking your head?'

By way of reply, the Pope flicked a few buttons on his remote and a 42-inch Sony LCD TV unfolded from behind a handy bookcase. A young and impressionable Italian weather girl filled the screen and calmly began her daily six twenty-eight bulletin.

'No!' squeaked Holridge, his gaze flicking from his trusty Timex to the green lozenge showing the time on screen. 'It can't be . . . !' He held his wrist to his ear and looked around the office, bewildered. A marble carriage clock stubbornly showed six twenty-eight. 'But . . .' he began, the ground seeming to shift beneath his feet.

And suddenly his mind whirled back to a certain small island four and a half miles off the coast of Eire. The memory of him winding his watch back an hour shimmered in crystal clarity.

'Oh, God. I didn't reset it! It's all too late,' whimpered Cardinal Holridge, raising a terrified gaze towards the edges of the atmosphere, listening for the sound of powering annihilation engines, and vowing never to cross another time zone in his life.

At that very instant, on the edge of an army barracks outside Dusseldorf, the end of the same weather report was being completely ignored by a pair of expatriated teenagers. They didn't bat an ear at the bored voice-over which followed.

'And coming up after the break we have *Hit Charade*. The show where you, the record-buying public, spot those new releases most likely to be hyped into the charts. This week, with new singles out from The Cure, Placebo and Cardiac Arrest, we'll be asking just what is the future of medicine in modern music?'

And just as every clock in the house clicked over to half past six, the TV screen surged with a uniquely mustardy shade of yellow. Despite themselves, the teenage boys looked up as acres of cryptically filmed alien skin slithered behind glass.

'Hey. What's this?' asked Connor, aged thirteen, as the scene flipped to pools of Merlot and Ribena.

'Boring,' tutted sixteen-year-old Clancy, disagreeing with his brother on principle. He watched in hidden amazement as silhouetted tentacles lashed chains in full Tandy twenty-one-inch glory.

'Looks scary,' grinned Connor as a seven-and-a-half-foot alien hurdled an innocent Vatican flowerbed. 'It's *Alien*!' he squeaked and was instantly on his feet whirring and clicking like a yellow loading machine. 'Get away from her you *bitch*!' he shouted and lashed an imaginary steel backhand across a gleaming Giger brood mother.

'Connor! Language!' yelled his very own mother from the kitchen.

'See it all tomorrow. The Truth from the people . . .' began the TV, but never had the chance to get another word in. Connor had latched on to the magic 'T' word and was leaping to exactly the conclusion the Pope had envisaged. 'The Truth,' he parroted excitedly. 'It's *The X Files*! A new series! Brilliant!'

And the TV went back to rattling on about the essential use of Vitamin pro-5 for deep-seated shiny hair that lasts.

'It isn't,' grumbled Clancy, moodily hurling the NAAFI-bought *Radio Times* at his little brother, having already checked through it. 'Anyway, it's boring. Scully's dog ugly.'

'Gimme that poster then.'

'No.'

And so it was that, along with other incomprehensible adverts, like the ones that promised wings, total protection and complete undetectability but never once showed the slightest glimpse of an F-18 Eagle or a Stealth Bomber, the advert slid into the murky recesses of the back of Clancy's mind.

In an orbit twenty-two thousand three hundred miles above him, it wasn't being so easily ignored.

'That was her. That was my daughter Kh'Xandhra. Did you see her?' shrieked the Regal Commander as he stamped agitatedly around the Battle Bridge of the million-ton

Strato-Fortress. 'I'd recognise her skin tones anywhere. That was her, I know it. Where is she?'

'The signal emanated from a small chunk of space hardware hovering on a bearing of . . .'

'Don't just talk about it! Get me there. NOW,' bellowed the Regal Commander, flapping his tentacles in a state of extreme frustration. Almost immediately a host of Ytterbium Colliders roared into life and shoved the vast craft across space, demonstrating an exquisite manoeuvrability which Mir could only dream of.

Slewing to a halt fifty metres from the offending chunk of dollar-heavy space hardware, the Strato-Fortress powered weapons systems and opened a barrage of hailing frequencies. 'You have thirty seconds to hand over my daughter or suffer the painful consequences!' roared the Regal Commander over a stack of handy frequencies.

There was no answer.

Thirty-one seconds later a screaming arc of hyperplasma was all that remained of one of Rupert Murdoch's finest TV satellites.

'Your Regality, sir,' began the Prince of Sensors as his neck began to feel ever more vulnerable. 'I'm . . . I'm picking up another signal bearing . . .'

'So, they still want to play, do they? Lock on and load the argon lasers,' growled the Regal Commander and the Strato-Fortress skipped off across another short expanse of cold space.

Twenty-odd thousand miles below, on the outskirts of Dusseldorf, a pair of teenagers stared at the screen of static. 'Mum!' screamed Connor. 'The telly's knackered!'

'*Language*, Connor!' answered the kitchen.

A Fistful of Pansies

Sixteenth of April. Easter Sunday

08:27 The Vatican

The pair of statically cavorting cherubs looked down from the ceiling of Cardinal Tardi's office as he surveyed the unfolding chaos in St Peter's Square. He pulled focus on his state-of-the-art binoculars and watched as the final touches were added to a vast area of staging which had blossomed overnight. With a grunt of approval, he placed a precise tick on a list as a dozen steeplejacks swung from various parts of a scaffolding frame and, in response to a host of yelled commands, hauled two hundred-foot screens into position either side of the papal balcony. All along the saint-lined colonnades, technicians from Reuters laid kilometres of cabling, plugged them up to vision mixers and microphone booms and manhandled a variety of cameras into a host of vantage points.

Much to Cardinal Tardi's surprise, and slight disappointment, it seemed that everything was proceeding according to the immensely detailed schedule he had in his hand.

But suddenly his eagle eyes lit up as they spotted a glaring transgression. In a second and a half he had tugged his mobile out of its holster and was dialling furiously, his gaze fixed on the small Fiat van sporting a six-foot ice-cream cone which was nosing its way into the square from the Via della Conciliazione.

On the fourth ring his mobile was answered. 'Good morning. Intruder in sector fifteen!' he said into his Motorola with a thrill of satisfaction.

Behind him, Cardinal Alighieri stopped munching away at a very large chocolate egg which had been stuffed with Napoleon Brandy truffles. He shook his head and stared at the crimson back of the Papal Secretary. Surely he hadn't heard right? Could he really have said 'Good morning'. 'Er . . . Anything interesting?'

'Ooooh, nothing that can't be handled expeditiously,' grinned Tardi as four Swiss Guards appeared from all points of the compass and homed in on the fibreglass cornet of 'Mr Flaky's Itinerant Ice-Cream Emporium'.

' "Expeditiously"?' coughed Alighieri around a large chunk of choclate shell. 'My, we are in a good mood this morning.'

'Of course,' smiled the Papal Secretary power hungrily as the offending van was surrounded, the driver's door wrenched open and 'Mr Flaky' was spread palms down on the roof. Tardi watched as sheets of paperwork were pulled from back pockets and examined.

'What's that?' Tardi asked of his mobile phone 'Of course he hasn't got permission. I'd know if I'd given permission, after all, I am in charge of that sort of thing. No, no, I have not granted a trading licence to "Mr Flaky's Itinerant Ice-Cream Emporium." My signature? Nonsense. A forgery . . . Not to worry, just escort him off Vatican property immediately and that'll be that . . . What? There's no room to park on the Via della Conciliazione? Park him in the Piazza Risorgimento. Bye.'

He stabbed the 'End call' button and playfully bounced

the phone off the seventeenth-century sofa under the window.

'I don't believe it,' said Alighieri with not a little amazement, a fragment of chocolate melting twixt thumb and forefinger. 'Escort him to the Piazza? Are you feeling all right?'

'Oh, yes. Shouldn't I be?'

'Er, well, you and good moods haven't exactly been close lately.'

'I haven't exactly been in charge lately, have I?' grinned Tardi in a way that implied something significant had happened to shift the delicate balance of power in his favour.

'What have you done?' whispered an awestricken Alighieri, chocolate melting down his thumb. 'You've got through to your contacts? They're going to stop the address?'

'Stop it? Oooh, no. Let's just say the message won't be quite as striking as it could have been.'

'What are you going to. . . ?'

'Ah, now *that* would be telling. Come on, I have a Pope and a few dozen procedural hoops for him to jump through.' And so, relishing the thought of an entire day spent ordering Angeles about the place, Cardinal Tardi swept out of his office.

Licking his fingers, Alighieri followed, his mind full of questions.

Outside, in the morning sun, a trio of heavily decorated US officers went with the flow of the gathering crowd. As he pushed a heavily laden wheelchair towards St Peter's Square, Major-General Hiram J. Gelding III's thoughts flashed back to the early hours of that morning and the sudden unexpected red alert status which had echoed around the USS *Indiscriminate*.

'*What the Hell's the meaning of this?*' he had bellowed on reaching the bridge.

'*Incoming, sir,*' the marine at the radar screen had answered as the roar of approaching jet engines had threatened to drown the din of klaxons. Moments later the unmistakable high-shouldered silhouette of a Stealth Fighter had dropped out of the Mediterranean night and squealed to a halt on the flight deck, trailing a parachute.

'*Containment squad!*' Gelding had screamed into a microphone and twenty marines had surrounded the Stealth Fighter, rifles aimed, armed and ready.

'*That won't be necessary,*' the President had announced from the top of the aircraft steps. '*Er, is there a Major-General Gelding here? Do ask him to meet me in the briefing room.*'

Gelding's mind replayed last night's hasty briefing in almost cinematic clarity. The messages of support from the President, the confirmation of his worst fears about the Vatican and, finally, the unveiling of the load on the wheelchair before him: the very heart of Operation Desperate Measure. And before it had all really sunk in, the Fighter was arcing stealthily into the dawning Italian sky and heading back towards the safety of American airspace.

Suddenly Gelding was nudged in the side by Rear-Admiral Rosenschmirtz and his attention tumbled back to the present.

'I said the war veterans' corral is over to your left,' repeated the Swiss Guard on crowd control, waggling his pike at a half-empty area towards the front of the square. 'Er, is he all right?' he asked, indicating the figure in the wheelchair covered head to foot with a blanket.

'Horrific injuries,' whispered Gelding. 'Don't want to frighten the nuns, do we?'

'Er, no, I don't suppose we do,' agreed the Guard and waved them through into the maze of crowd control barriers. 'Enjoy the address.'

'Oh, we will,' grinned Gelding with just a little too much relish. 'C'mon, out of the way. Move,' he barked and assaulted the ankles of a dozen choirboys with the wheelchair. 'Let me through. Coming through. Can't you see we're on a pilgrimage here?'

A hundred yards behind them a small Fiat van sporting a six-foot fibreglass ice-cream cone found an opening and trundled on to the cobbles of St Peter's Square.

09:23 Local Space

High on the bridge of the Strato-Fortress, the Regal Commander stared at a chunk of yen-heavy space hardware, a tentacle tip playing gently over a cluster of red buttons. 'Well, is this another pawn in their pathetic game of cat and mouse?'

The Prince of Sensors pulled every last scrap of information out of the screens before him.

'Well, Your Regality, your daughter isn't anywhere near. . .'

Before the report was finished several dozen weapons arrays had discharged in a searing arc of extraterrestrial destruction.

Twenty-two thousand three hundred miles above the unmistakable peak of Mount Fuji yet another communications satellite suddenly erupted in a blaze of violent plasma and blacked out all the telephone lines across Japan.

'So where is she? Where are they keeping her?' bellowed the Regal Commander hurling himself on to the throne on the bridge. ' "See it all tomorrow," they keep saying. Well, it's tomorrow already! Where is she? Doesn't any of you know?'

The silence which drifted across the bridge fell heavily pregnant and began suffering morning sickness.

'Are you certain that translator is working correctly?'

demanded the Regal Commander, jabbing at a box of electronics with an angry tentacle.

'Er, absolutely,' enthused the Knave of Translation, feeling for his neck.

' "See it all tomorrow." See it where? Where is she?'

'Er . . . they don't say exactly . . .'

Nervous eye-stalks watched as the Regal Commander's cheeks turned gradually towards the hotter end of all things Dijonnaise.

'Er . . . if I may offer a suggestion, Your Highness,' began a custardy-looking minion, squinting up from a monitor screen.

'Yes, yes, what is it?' barked the Regal Commander, advancing menacingly across the bridge.

The Minion in Charge of Translating Alien Broadcasts pointed a tentacle to his screen and, trembling only very slightly, indicated a smiling figure up to his knees in John Innes's finest potting compost. 'Your Highness, the creature you see is one of the indigenous mammals. It would seem they have an overfondness for some of the peculiar vegetative growths which infest the planet's patches of soil and spend inordinate amounts of time cosseting . . .'

'This *does* have a bearing upon my daughter's whereabouts?' growled the Regal Commander, his upper lip twitching.

'Oh, absolutely, Your Highness. Er, if I may draw your attention to this small bedding plant here.' He pointed to the tiny blue-and-yellow pansy nestling in the presenter's hand. Right on cue, Alan Titchmarsh smiled at the camera and continued enthusing about his fistful of pansy.

'. . . which I believe covers every border in the gardens in the Vatican at this time of year. D'you know, now, that's something I'd really love to see someday.' Misty-eyed, he looked at the camera, shrugged and smiled the very smile that had endeared him to a million couch-bound gardeners across southern England. 'Ahhh, well, back to me daffs.'

'And just why are you showing me this?'

The Minion in Charge of Translating Alien Broadcasts pointed to another screen upon which was freeze-framed a picture of a seven-and-a-half-foot alien hurdling a flower-bed. 'Er, if I may direct your Regal attention to this small patch of soil, here.' The minion's tentacle tip circled a clump of freshly tilled earth blooming with the very Italian pansies which so captured the heart of Alan Titchmarsh. 'Perhaps this Vatican place might be a good place to start looking?' offered the minion.

The Regal Commander peered from one screen to the other. He knew he was no expert on Earth-bound plant-life but he had to admit there was more than a passing similarity in the petal structure and colouring which did lead him towards the feeling that . . . 'Set a course immediately,' he yelled, striding over towards the Navigational Serf. 'To that Vatican place. Now!'

And so it was that with its laser cannons at full power, the Strato-Fortress slid out of geostationary orbit, its Type-98 Ytterbium Collider Drives growling at half ahead.

Seconds later, humming the Creature's Republican Hostility Anthem under its breath, the pilot of the Tropo-Nihilation Engine accepted his democratic order and swung the vessel off in hot pursuit.

09:56 The Vatican

High on the saint-lined colonnades which curved out around St Peter's Square, a veritable village of technicians were blissfully unaware of quite how lucky they were that Cardinal Tardi didn't know precisely what they were up to. Three power drills ground masonry bits into the delicate

292

buttocks of numerous saints and secured a collection of fibre-optic cables and satellite uplinks.

'It all happens on that middle balcony over there, yeah?' asked a CNN cameraman, nudging one of the bevy of official Reuters crew and pointing across the growing sea of the faithful.

'Take a guess,' tutted the technician and, head down, he continued checking signal clarity from three dozen different feeds.

'Look, mate, I only asked,' grumbled the CNN cameraman and moodily fiddled with his focus. It was then that he felt the unmistakable prod of a sawn-off AK 47 in his ribs.

'Hand over the camera,' whispered a voice with a heavy Iraqi accent. 'Do it now. Quietly!'

'What? Are you mad? I know you Reuters guys are possessive but . . .'

'Arguing isn't worth it,' hissed the Iraqi agent. 'Nobody will hear the shot over the drills. Now, the camera?'

'Yeah, yeah, take it! Jeez, a guy tries to get a little extra work on the side . . .' The man from CNN handed over his trusty Sony and was clubbed into unconsciousness for his troubles. The Iraqi agent tugged a baseball cap down over his eyes, began fiddling with a variety of meaningless knobs and hid himself in plain sight.

Not ten feet away the Reuters technician made absolutely certain that the six-foot uplift disc was degree perfect.

Suddenly a vast roar of excitement startled every pigeon in St Peter's Square as two vast screens sprang into life either side of the papal balcony. Pictures of the crowd sprang across the pair of hundred-foot screens glowing with the full-colour digital clarity that U2 would have killed for. Spotlights blasted out half-kilowatt pools of light, temporarily blinding the massed ranks of the St Peter's Choral Society gathered on the hastily erected staging. A pair of crossed stereo mics thumped open and, with a cursory tap of a baton, they set about delivering a crowd-pleasing rendition of some of the more popular Latin hymns. Within minutes, a hundred-foot-high soprano was cheerfully deafening the entire congregation.

And, in an ante-room somewhere in the depths of St Peter's, Pope Joshua Angeles's heart skipped half a dozen beats.

'Ahh, the world awaits,' grinned Cardinal Tardi as he smoothed the shoulder flaps of the Pope's ceremonial Versace vestments. 'Are you ready for this?'

'Is there any chance of a quick JD?' whispered Angeles. 'You know, medicinal?'

'You crave alcohol at a time like this?'

'Too right,' confessed His Holiness. 'I'm terrified.'

'Ohh, nonsense. Just relax. Your coronation is simple. Follow my instructions and everything will be perfect.'

'Yes, yes, you're right,' panted the Pope around artificially deep breaths, wishing he'd taken lessons in the Alexander Technique.

'Of course, I'm right,' soothed Tardi. 'I just wish I could be so certain about this address of yours.'

The seeds of doubt germinated quickly in the fertile loam of Angeles's concern. 'My address? What? What's wrong with it?'

'Oh, I'm certain that it will be heralded as one of the more, er . . . *interesting* chapters in Vatican history,' dismissed Tardi. 'Once the fuss has died down, of course.'

'Fuss?'

'I always think it's such a shame pioneers are never recognised in their own lifetime. It would have been so easy for you to have taken good, solid, traditional subject matter for your address, delivered it with complete authority and, well, simply revelled in the complete support of the entire Church for many a happy year.'

'Er, I could . . . ?'

'Still, sex before marriage has been done so many . . . Oh, my Lord, is *that* the time?' declared Tardi, snatching up a gleaming white tiara and crook. 'Come on, come on, we'll be late!' In seconds he was ushering Pope Joshua Angeles out through a small side door and joining the end of a slow-moving conga chain of Cardinals swinging smouldering incense burners.

'Wait, wait, d'you think I should change my add—.'

'Sssh, no time to discuss things now. C'mon, now look solemn,' whispered Tardi, hiding a grin and falling into step behind the line of his crimson colleagues. 'There'll be a camera crew just around the corner.'

And Tardi was right. There was indeed a camera crew lurking at the end of a small high-arched passage just off to the left, and they were on the receiving end of a host of desperate requests.

'*Camera thirty-six. You there? Come in!*' screamed the cameraman's headphones.

'Answer it,' whispered an ex-KGB agent masquerading as a soundman.

'How?' asked the cameraman.

'Tell him!' snarled the counterfeit soundman, kicking at his gaffa-taped Reuters colleague and removing his gag. 'Tell him!'

'Red button on right earph—' A brand new length of silver tape silenced him again as he was hurled back into a pool of dark shadow.

'*Camera thirty-six? Answer me! Are you there?*'

The ex-KGB man pressed the red button. '*Da, da. . .* er, yes.'

'*At last! Now, hold on the procession and keep that focus sharp, we're going global in ten. Okay?*' and the headphone clicked into crackling static.

In a small Portakabin, which was doubling as a studio, a hassled-looking Desmond Lynam received a final dab of silver to his sideburns and was counted in by a heavily stressed director. Ever the consummate professional, Des flicked on his easy smile and welcomed the world to Rome.

'Good morning and thank you for joining us here at St Peter's Square in the Vatican on this warm Easter Sunday, for what promises to be quite a meeting. Later we'll be having a few bars from local lad Luciano Pavarotti, after the . . . er,' he jammed a finger into his ear in the way of sports commentators the world over. 'Well, it seems we're already a few minutes ahead of schedule. Ladies and gentlemen . . .'

'Thirty-six, we're going global. Three . . . two . . .'

'. . . I give you, the papal procession!'

As the pair of vast screens either side of the balcony flicked from an image of a hundred-foot-high soprano being showered with roses to that of the first incense-shrouded Cardinals, a roar of excitement erupted. Mexican waves of delight rippled across the crowd, crashed against the distant colonnade and swept back again.

It was only with an immense effort of will that His Holiness didn't break ranks and start kissing any available baby. Somehow, he marched on slowly, head bowed, his face a picture of solemnity and entered the cool gloom of the Cathedral of St Peter's.

10:27 Local Space

Banks of inertia brakes burst into action and slowed the million-ton Strato-Fortress to a halt on the interstellar equivalent of a sixpence.

'Your Highness, geostationary orbit achieved. We're directly above the Vatican,' declared the Knave of Thrusters.

'About time, too!' roared the Regal Commander. 'Prince of Sensors? Can you find her?'

'Er, not through so much nitrogen, sir . . . Now if we were perhaps a *little* lower?'

'Knave of Thrusters, take us down.'

Immediately a bank of Type-98s belched into life and, in a splendid example of brute force over aerodynamics, the Strato-Fortress sank surprisingly gracefully towards the outer edges of Earth's atmosphere.

10:57 The Vatican

The sound of backsides shuffling on oak pews fell across the inside of St Peter's Cathedral for the fifth time as Reuters went away for another commercial break.

'Is this absolutely necessary?' whispered the still-not-completely-crowned Pope Angeles.

'Oh, yes,' answered Tardi. 'They wouldn't have agreed to the full show without the ad breaks.'

'And what about this?' hissed Angeles, flicking the hastily prepared script before him. 'Isn't this a bit much?'

'They wouldn't go for the Latin. Said it sounded too holy. Besides, nobody understands it any more,' answered the Papal Secretary with one eye on the director crouching behind the pulpit. 'It's all a question of packaging. Give the people what they want.'

'And my address? Have they changed that?'

'No, no, that's still up to you. You can go ahead with it and risk everything if you really want . . . Aha. Time!' whispered Tardi as the director counted fingers down from five. The Papal Secretary stood and stepped into a perfect picture of solemnity. As he took a theatrical breath and opened a large book a dozen cameras sharpened focus on him and a flock of mic booms wheeled around his head.

In the square outside, two one-hundred-foot Des Lynams leaned calmly across a desk and anchored the proceedings with professional slickness. 'And welcome back to St Peter's Square here in the Vatican. Now, if you've just joined us, we've had a terrific morning here in front of a capacity crowd of devotees. Great crowd, great atmosphere and . . . ahhh, we can go now back inside St Peter's Cathedral and join Pope Joshua Angeles for his vows.'

The screen flicked to a tight focus of Cardinal Tardi facing Angeles on his throne. Behind them, columns of light angled themselves into a perfectly moted backdrop in a way that would have made Steven Spielberg proud.

'Your Holiness Pope Joshua Angeles,' asked Tardi, 'do you take this Church to be your holy future life, for better or worse?'

Cringing inside and desperately wishing for the grace and comforting incomprehensibility of the original service the Pope answered, 'I do.'

'In sickness and in health?'

'I do.'

'For richer . . .'

In the depths of the basement lab of the Congregation for Icon Authentication, Father Fintan O'Suilleabhain stared at the twelve-inch colour portable on a lab bench and shook his head in awe. 'Now that takes courage to be sure. Declaring a vow like that in front of the whole world.'

'The whole world?' asked Kh'Vynn, his ear flaps pricking.

'Yeah, simultaneous broadcast. You should see all the cameras kicking about up there, you'd love them. All them cables and microphones, looks just like a film set.'

Kh'Vynn looked at Kh'Xandhra and, just by the slight flush of excited mustard around her knees, he knew that she was indeed hatching similar thoughts.

'Oh, look, look. Here it is! The big moment.'

On the colour portable, and countless other screens around the world, Pope Angeles stood and, disappearing momentarily behind a cloud of incense, he crossed towards the pulpit, every step followed by a cameraman edging cautiously backwards before him. Angeles knelt, bowed his head and, in a criminally simplified version of a tradition dating back centuries, he received the tall three-tiered hat of office. The papal tiara.

Almost too soon, the director tapped his microphone and, precisely eighteen minutes since the last time, Reuters went to an ad break.

Holding on to his new tiara, Pope Angeles looked up at Cardinal Tardi. 'Look, are you sure this counts without the water and the oil and all the other ceremony?'

'Trust me,' whispered Tardi as the procession of Cardinals filtered out of the pews and reassembled in the aisle. 'We can do it again properly tomorrow. Well, of course, that's if you feel up to it after your, er, forthcoming controversial address.'

'Feel up to it? Er, why shouldn't I feel up to it? It's not that bad . . . Is it?' worried Angeles as he was handed his ceremonial crook and shepherded on to the tail of the procession.

'It is not my place to offer value judgements, Your Holiness. However,' he tapped his chest, indicating an inside pocket, 'I have a fully prepared speech, ready to go if you . . . Oh, time.'

The director waved frantically and, somehow appearing utterly seamless to the outside world, screens stopped proclaiming that the vitamin pro-B7/seratogenin hybridised supercomplex is *the* chemical your hair is crying out for and began zooming in on the procession heading outside.

In the densely packed confines of St Peter's Square,

excitement was rising on another Mexican wave of delight. Groups of people erupted into spontaneous bouts of cheering, folk tossed hats into the Italian air and banners waved wildly. But excitement wasn't the only thing rising in the square. The local temperature was merrily shooting up towards the realms of uncomfortable.

A group of the Sisters of Mercy had noticed it first but, putting it down to the thrill of having a new Pope in their midst, shrugged it off and began peeling off the heavier of their cassocks. A dozen students from UCLA dismissed it as their own fault for standing too close to a rack of hot Reuters' electrical equipment and began toasting the new Pope with chilled Budweisers a little earlier than planned.

But nobody gathered between the curling colonnades could possibly have known the real reason for their hot flushes. Of course, chances are that if they'd been informed that it was all something to do with the tight-beam thermal exhaust from three hundred and twenty Type-98 Ytterbium Collider Drives struggling to keep a million-ton Strato-Fortress hovering fifteen thousand feet above their heads, they probably wouldn't have believed it.

Well, you wouldn't really, would you?

11:19 The Vatican

The door to the basement laboratory of the Congregation for Icon Authentication was kicked open and two Cardinals whirled through it in a flurry of crimson vestments and sweat. Father Fintan O'Suilleabhain looked up from the twelve-inch colour TV as Cardinal Holridge sprinted past behind him.

'I saw you,' he cried, excitedly pointing to the TV. 'You were on there!'

'Of course I was on there,' tutted Holridge, hurriedly

300

stripping off his outer cloak. 'Everybody was on there. Damned cameras were everywhere. Everywhere!'

'And then there were all the cables and wires and things,' added Kotonawa. 'It was a wonder nobody had a nasty accident. Still, I suppose that's the downside of broadcasting live to the entire world.'

Kh'Vynn's left tentacle tapped irritably against the bench he was sat on. All this talk of live broadcasts was getting just a bit too much for him.

'There, there, our time will come,' trilled Kh'Xandhra soothingly and stroked his knee. 'We agreed this was for the best.'

A low gurgling emanated from somewhere near the back of Kh'Vynn's throat. 'Best for who?' he growled under his breath. 'Look at them. They don't even want to be seen on TV. It should be us!'

'It will be, my love,' smiled Kh'Xandhra. 'We've waited this long, a few days won't make any difference.'

Cardinal Holridge poked his head and bare shoulders out from behind a large screen. 'Fintan, is the transport ready?'

'Oh, yes, absolutely,' called back the priest, his eyes transfixed by the TV as it already began showing selected highlights of the morning's coronation.

'Well bring it over! Bring it over! We don't have all day, you know.' Holridge disappeared back behind the screen. Reluctantly, Fintan stood and headed off towards a small golfing cart which had been very hastily curtained all around.

From behind the screens the sound of a body struggling into something strange and uncomfortable drifted into earshot. 'Kotonawa, why did you have to make this thing so tight,' grumbled Holridge above the squeak of stretching rubber. 'I can barely get it over my hips.'

' "Hips", he calls it. That is a waistline. And a not insignificant one at that!' answered Kotonawa.

'Are you suggesting I'm fat?'

'If the cap fits . . .'

'It's not a cap I'm trying to get into!'

'Gentlemen, please!' interrupted Fintan, halting the golf cart by the screens and climbing out. 'Your carriage awaits.'

'About time too,' muttered Holridge over the sound of a straining zip grinding ominously shut. In a flash the two Cardinals were in the front seats and the curtains were being tugged around them.

'I still don't see why I can't drive,' complained Fintan.

'Your job is here,' hissed Holridge in strangely muffled tones. 'You've got to keep an eye on those two, just make sure they don't leave here. We can't risk their parents seeing them.'

'Yeah, but . . .'

'Zzzzzapp woooof ba-boooom! Remember?' added Kotonawa and the golf cart pulled away with a whirr of electrics. In seconds it was through the outer door and powering its way up the ramp.

Minutes later a pair of Swiss Guards snapped crisp salutes as it skittered around a tight corner and raced towards them. Wondering only momentarily why a set of full-length curtains surrounded everything, they tugged open the double doors they were guarding and stepped back behind them. Barely decelerating, the golf cart whirred down the last hundred yards of the path and clattered into the corridor.

As the doors shut behind, Cardinal Holridge slewed the laden cart around a corner and skidded it to a halt at the foot of a wide staircase.

'Okay, we're here,' he said as he pulled back the curtains. In the corridor a pair of tentacled aliens clambered awkwardly out of a golf cart and, pausing only to check their zips were straight, they headed off up the stairs.

Outside by the door, one of the Swiss Guards took off his shiny helmet and rubbed his temples wearily. 'Ohhhh, I think I've been out in the sun too long. D'you know, I could've sworn there was a purple tentacle hanging out of the back of that cart.'

'A purple tentacle?' gasped his mate, looking concerned. 'Wow, man, you need a break. It was yellow.'

11:53 The Vatican

Far below the infamous balcony at the centre of St Peter's Square, Luciano Pavarotti took centre stage and, larger than life on the hundred-foot screens, he launched into his trademark 'Nessun Dorma'. Throughout the sea of sweating folk, the more emotional of football fans reached for a host of handkerchiefs and wiped away a tear.

In the wood-panelled ante-room above the world-re-nowned tenor, Pope Angeles's intestines were tying them-selves into the kind of knots that would have even the most ambitious of Boy Scouts trembling in their boots.

'Sit still!' snapped the girl with the eye-liner pencil, pressing the sweating Pope back into the make-up chair and glaring at him.

'I'm . . . I'm sorry. But . . . just listen to that!' he beamed, pointing towards the crowd beyond the curtained balcony. 'What a performer!'

'I can hear him, all right? He's not a patch on Freddie Mercury if you ask me. Now d'you want to look your best, or not?' she growled, tapping the make-up pencil impatiently against her knuckles.

'Well, yes, but, er . . . do I really need eye-liner? I mean, shouldn't I just go out there the way God intended me to?'

The girl sighed wearily and glared at him with the air of a woman who had conquered similar objections on more than one occasion. 'The way God intended, huh? You're wearing vestments, aren't you?'

'Well, yes, Jean Paul Gaultier's finest as a matter of fact . . .'

'I rest my case,' she interrupted and pinned him to the chair with the skill of a professional wrestler. 'Open wide, look to the left and let me and No. 7 do our job.'

'But, but . . .'

His objections were cut off by the sudden eruption of Cardinal Tardi through the door at the far end of the room, Alighieri hard on his heels.

The Papal Secretary strode three feet into the ante-room and stopped abruptly, his face curling into a picture of distaste. 'What is that noise?' He scowled out of the window.

'Pavarotti,' grinned Alighieri, showing off.

'No, the other noise. It's disgusting.'

Alighieri listened to the crowd trying hoplessly to match Luciano's stirring vocal performance.

'The public,' tutted Tardi as a group of German students discovered a surprisingly funky footstomping rhythm and bashed it out for all it was worth. 'Why do they insist on joining in?'

'Ah, Tardi, there you are,' declared Pope Angeles from the far end of the oddly bare room.

'I've told you before, sit still,' hissed the make-up girl. 'Or do you want pink talc all over your Gaultier vestments?'

'Pink talc?' began the Pope before he disappeared in a cloud of that very thing, administered by a large wad of cotton wool.

'Stops your skin looking too shiny in this heat,' busied the girl in a final wave of efficiency. 'There. You're done.' She whisked off the green nylon apron and scurried out of the door to make sure Desmond Lynam's make-up was still satellite standard.

Cardinal Tardi frowned at the coughing Pope and stepped

solemnly up towards him. 'Your Holiness, as has been my proud duty for the last eighteen years, I bring you this.' He unclipped an eighteen-carat gold latch, pulled open a lignum vitae box and bowed. 'Your Holiness, may I present you with your microphone.'

'Oh, that's very kind but you really shouldn't have gone to all that trouble. I've already got one.' The Pope pointed to the curtained balcony and the unmistakable silhouette of a Sennheiser radio-mic perched atop a slender stand, ready to go. 'Those chaps from Reuters are so thorough, you know?'

'I notice they didn't provide a speech-writer,' muttered Tardi at a perfectly calculated volume.

'What was that?' asked Angeles.

'Ohh, nothing,' dismissed the Papal Secretary with a theatrical flourish of his hands. 'Well, nothing that a few years won't heal.'

'I'm not changing my address,' whispered His Recently Crowned Holiness.

Tardi pulled a sheaf of notes out of his inside pocket. 'But this is perfect. Couple of jokes at the start, bit of a moral message, not too heavy, not too limp and then a positive uplifting ending. It can't fail! You'll be the most popular Pope who ever . . .'

But, before Tardi had a chance to thrust the papers into Angeles's hands, a quartet of Reuters technicians burst into the room, two shoulder-toting cameras, the other pair sprouting an array of fill-in spotlights and a fluffy microphone each. With almost military precision they positioned themselves either side of the balcony and reported in via their headsets.

Alighieri watched it all in wide-eyed wonder, sure that last year's address hadn't been quite so adrenaline-rich. And just as he thought it couldn't get more exciting, Pavarotti changed up a key and the door at the back of the room burst open. The cameras and floods swung instantly, pinning and mounting a startled pair of aliens, one a kind of mustardy yellow, the other the colour of Ribena and Merlot.

'Ahhh, there you are!' smiled Pope Angeles, shedding a fine powder of pink talc from his cheeks.

Cardinal Tardi simply pointed at the two creatures, mouth open, silent. Seeing creatures from beyond any known space on a large Sony LCD screen was one thing, but there, right in front of him, in the flesh . . . well, that was quite something else entirely. His bowels writhed nervously as the colour drained from his normally pale cheeks. Desperately, he reached for the back of a handy chair and, panting ineffectually, he tried to steady himself. 'Oh, my God, look at the size of those . . . tentacles!' It was all he managed to say before he slithered to the floor and began reciting ancient Latin nursery rhymes around his thumb. And, for the first time, Pope Angeles began to have some serious doubts that he was really about to do the right thing.

Outside, Pavarotti soared majestically to the end of his fifteen-minute set and, sweating somewhat more than usual, bowed to rapturous applause and the odd hurled rose. Seconds later the headphones of every Reuters technician crackled with a message from their producer.

'*Okay, we have feed, we have an audience, we have . . . Camera thirty-two check your framing! That's better. Okay, everyone, we have a go-mode. Is the Pope in position?*'

'*Check,*' barked a rear-balcony cameraman through his headset.

'*Run VT!*' announced the producer and, in the privacy of the Portakabin below, he stabbed a broadcast-standard 'play' button.

And so, at exactly midday local time, the two hastily erected screens either side of the papal balcony switched to showing acres of mustard-yellow skin. Kilowatts of synth soundtrack echoed across St Peter's Square.

In the middle of the crowd, Giorgio Scipioni shrieked with excitement and bit his sweating knuckles as the biggest screens he had ever seen showed the world his work. Next to him Sophia skipped up and down, perspiring expertly and clapping as wildly as an inebriated aerobics instructor.

Cameras swept the crowd, plucking rapt expressions of wonder from a cluster of nuns, snatching gazes of awe from a flock of convent girls and capturing stray moments which, in their own small way encapsulated the whole spectacle in tiny wordless nuggets.

On the screens a fifty-foot hand reached out towards a forty-foot light-switch. A shiny claw lashed out of the sky and grabbed at the hand. For a moment, the action paused and suddenly a new woofer-heavy voice-over rang out over the entire crowd. 'See it today,' rumbled the effects-laden voice of the Pope. 'The Truth is here, the Truth is now!' Together, in an act of staged intergalactic unity, Sophia's fifty-foot hand and the Gigeresque claw flicked the switch.

Spotlights blasted out from the central scaffolding tower and the screens flicked to showing matching hundred-foot views of the balcony.

Much to the Pope's delight, the crowd went wild with screams and foot-stamping applause. His heart pounding in the depths of his Gaultier-upholstered chest, he snatched five deep breaths, grabbed the curtains and stepped out on to the balcony.

It was then that terminal stage-fright grabbed him firmly by the spleen.

As far as he could see, all across St Peter's Square, right down the entire length of the Via della Conciliazone and along the banks of the Tiber, tiny sweating faces looked up at him through a swirling heat haze, glistening with

ytterbium-exhaust-induced sweat, quivering with expecta-
tion.

He stood, mouth open, trapped between the screaming
urge to dash back inside and grab Tardi's speech and the
overwhelming wish that God had sent him two small furry
aliens instead. The world, he was certain, would be much
happier to accept a pair of Tribbles than the tentacled things
he was about to unleash on them.

But he knew it was too late for him to change his mind. His
public was waiting, they had come, they needed a message . . .

'Oh, God, now I know how Moses felt,' he whimpered to
himself. A thousand kilowatts of amplification broadcast it
all to the waiting audience.

A full ten seconds of intestine-writhing terror followed
before he heard the first ripples of laughter from below. He
stared at the mass of people below, then he turned his gaze
Heavenwards in wonder.

No, it couldn't be, could it? Was this a sign? A snippit of
encouragement from Him?

Whatever it was, it was now or never. Nervously, he
fumbled his speech out from his Gaultier pocket, his hands
trembling as he tried to smooth it flat on the railing of the
balcony. It was then that disaster struck. Sweaty palms,
excessive nerves and a particularly smooth marble surface
all conspired with a stray gust of wind to snatch his carefully
prepared speech out of his grip and whisk it off into the
lower reaches of Vatican airspace.

Dumbstruck, he watched the sheets of double spaced A4
tumble away across the crowd and felt completely and
utterly exposed.

Below him the crowd shuffled restlessly in the mounting
heat. Somehow he sensed that heckling was only moments
away.

'Er, look,' he began, not knowing where he was going,

'you've been watching me all morning and . . . well, I had a speech all prepared but . . . okay, here goes . . . in a change from the traditional, I'd like to introduce you to a couple of guests.' He beckoned frantically through the double doors of the balcony.

'I guess that's you,' whispered Alighieri in the relative safety of the ante-room.

The two extraterrestrials looked at each other, nodded in a strangely wooden manner and, their every movement tracked by the pair of cameramen, they stepped out into the spring Roman air and into history.

'*Oh, my God, look at that!*' squeaked the OB director as his equipment splashed vast images of the two nattily poncho'd aliens on to the screens either side of the balcony. '*All cameras get this. Get all of this!*' he shrieked into his headset, deafening every cameraman under his control. Thirty lenses whirled off the crowd and snapped focus on the papal guests as shyly, almost awkwardly, they waved tentacles at the crowd in what they hoped was a friendly manner.

It was a miracle the entire crowd didn't scream and leg it down the Via della Conciliazione in a blaze of screaming panic.

'*That's it, that's it!*' grinned the director in his Portakabin, looking at a complete wallful of alien-filled screens and a passport to the ranks of OB of the year awards. Behind him the Reuters satellite uplink relayed the pictures to the massed newsdesks of the world. Unknown to him, it also beamed the signal straight into a million-ton spacecaft hovering in geostationary orbit fifteen thousand feet directly above.

On the Battle Bridge of the Regal Strato-Fortress, a large mustard-yellow creature slapped excited tentacles to his cheeks and thrilled at the first sight of his long-lost daughter. 'Oh Kh'Xandhra, my darling. There you are, safe and sound and alive and well and . . .' The Regal Commander paused, blinked and looked more closely at the live feed. He squinted suspiciously at the image of his daughter waving weakly from the screen, growled and snatched the Minion for Health out of his hammock. 'Look at her. Look at my Kh'Xandhra! Does she look healthy to you?'

'Hmmmmm, well, she does look a little peeky.'

'Peeky? That's jaundice that is. She's yellow I tell you.'

'Your Highness, in case you hadn't noticed, she's always yellow.'

'Not *that* yellow. And look at her eyes. Lifeless. Where's the sparkle gone? I tell you she's ill. That damned Kh'Vynn's given her something. Why else would she be wearing that dreadful cape?'

'But, Your Highness, he's wearing one as well.'

'That proves it. He's given her something. That bastard kidnaps my daughter and then *infects* her!'

At that very moment, the Regal Commander wasn't the only one upset by the images of the two aliens on the balcony. Down in the basement lab of the Congregation for Icon Authentication, Kh'Vynn was tapping angrily on the bench.

'Look at that. Pathetic! How do they hope to convince anyone that they're real with such jerky movements as that. Our reputation on the intergalactic stage is going to be ruined if we let this carry on.'

Father Fintan looked across at Kh'Vynn. 'Not necessarily,' he offered helpfully. 'I mean look at Arnie. Who would've thought he'd get where he is today after his acting in *Conan the Barbarian*?'

'Nice try,' sulked Kh'Vynn and reached out towards the off switch. 'But I'm sorry, I can't bear watching this.' The TV crackled into blackness. 'Let's play charades,' he suggested, his mood brightening just a little too quickly. 'Fintan, d'you want to go first?'

'Er, no, no, I haven't got anything in mind. After you.'

Kh'Vynn rolled his eye-stalks as if thinking back through all the magic movie moments he had ever seen. 'Oh, I know . . .' he murmured and, smoothing down an imaginary suit, he stood. 'Er, you need to stand for this one,' he said to Fintan.

'Hmmm, I'm not sure you're supposed to use props.'

'C'mon, stand up. You won't get it otherwise,' insisted Kh'Vynn, pulling the priest to his feet and launching straight into his part. Pursing his lips he looked embarrassedly at the floor and said, 'Look, I'm really sorry about this . . .' He curled his tentacle into what passed as a perfect substitute for a tightly clenched fist.

'James Cagney!' shouted Fintan. 'But I don't know what film.'

'No, no . . . it's not Cagney. Er, look, Fintan, I really am sorry but . . .' Kh'Vynn's fist tightened and arced behind him.

'Ooooh, this is a hard one. I don't know any film starring someone called Fintan.'

'Sorry,' muttered Kh'Vynn, spinning his tentacle and bringing it down hard on the back of Fintan's head.

'Nope, still haven't a . . .' began the priest, before he hit the floor.

'Did you have to do that?' hissed Kh'Xandhra.

'We've got no choice. It should be us up there,' he pointed in the general direction of St Peter's Square. 'This it what we came here for.'

'I thought that was to be with me,' pouted Kh'Xandhra.

'Yeah, yeah, that too. Now come on!' Snatching the translator, he stepped over the unconcious priest and dashed towards the door.

Everyone in St Peter's Square stared transfixed at the hundred-foot-high screens showing the pair of woodenly waving aliens. Well, everyone but the most sensitive that is. They were already on the floor overcome by the mounting heat, the sheer terror or, in the case of those from a more sheltered monastic background, both. But, outside the confines of that small section of Rome, nobody noticed. All cameras were pointing directly at the balcony, snapping up every movement of the visitors from beyond the stars, every curl of rubbery tentacle.

All, that is, except those whose crews didn't hail from the Reuters school of TV journalism. At that very instant a team who would be more at home in the Pentagon than any TV studio were wrestling their way towards the war veterans' corral and a certain Major-General Hiram J Gelding III. A hundred yards to the north, a gang of ex-KGB agents were elbowing nuns aside with the barrels of their Kalashnikovs as they made a beeline towards 'Mr Flaky's Itinerant Ice-Cream Emporium'. High on the colonnade an Iraqi cameraman searched the crowd for his colleagues and, directly below his toes, a clump of what at first appeared to be innocent Japanese tourists suddenly began manhandling industry-standard Sonys out of numerous carrier bags.

Up on the balcony, Pope Angeles cleared his throat. 'Er, as I guess you might have noticed, Kh'Vynn and Kh'Xandhra here aren't quite of this world.'

Half a dozen Carmelite Sisters who had been hoping they had been seeing things fainted quietly as their worst worries were confirmed by His Holiness.

'But there's nothing to be scared of, believe me,' announced the Pontiff. 'They're quite friendly really. There's absolutely nothing to fear from our cousins from beyond the stars.'

Fifteen thousand feet above the Pope's head a mustard-yellow creature chuckled evilly and stroked a bright red button on a charged-weapons array.

'In fact,' continued Pope Angeles obliviously, 'we should actually be very grateful that they've deigned to come here. I know I am. You see,' he fished around in the back of his head, trying to remember the words he had written in the speech which was fluttering away over downtown Rome. 'Er . . . they bring a message.'

The purple-hued alien to his right nodded stiffly.

'For centuries,' continued His Holiness, 'mankind has sat around discussing whether we're all alone in the universe, you know, whether life on Earth is merely the product of chance and a large number of randomly combining chemicals sticking themselves together in a way that just sort of happened to spring accidentally into life.' Deep inside, Angeles wished he still had his script in front of him. He was sure he had made that point better on page two, paragraph three. Below him there was a wave of confused head-scratching.

'Er, well, I know I've wondered about it,' he floundered and wiped at his forehead. 'And the only answer we the Church have been able to offer is to call upon faith; you just have to believe that life is a miracle. But – and here's the Good News – it's not like that any more,' he announced feeling his foot settling on to firmer ground. 'Here, next to me on this balcony, is the living proof that life on this planet isn't a once-in-a-galactic-lifetime never-to-be-repeated special off-chance happening. It didn't just happen. It was planned. By God!'

Right on cue, and just as the Pope had dreamt it, the two aliens slipped off their ponchos and revealed the natty

T-shirts underneath. In crisp, freshly printed letters the alien chests announced the message 'God loves *me*'.

'Look everybody!' evangelised the Pope. 'If these aliens know that God loves them then isn't it time we woke up and realised that he can love us too? Just as much. Religion can be for every sentient being in the entire galaxy! Yellow, purple, grey? It doesn't matter. Come world. Embrace. Baptise today!'

And as the Pontiff's words echoed across acres of dumb-founded ears, an armed posse burst into the Reuters control Portakabin and pointed a collection of deadly handweapons at the nose of the director. In seconds they had gagged Des Lynam, broken into the papal radio-mic feed and begun asking difficult questions. 'You say they're aliens from beyond the stars, but how do we know they're *real* aliens?' boomed several hundred kilowatts of amplification.

'Who's that?' spluttered the Pope, looking around him for any ventriloquists invading his balcony. 'Who said that? How dare you ruin . . . ?' He looked straight down at a flurry of activity as a camera crew hurdled a fence and leapt into the war veterans' corral. Right on cue, Major-General Gelding spun the wheelchair around to face the lens and Rear-Admiral Rosenschmirtz pulled off the full-length blanket which had been covering the figure beneath. Instead of the horribly disfigured war veteran which every-one had been led to believe was there, something more shocking was revealed.

'Are your two aliens as real as Mr Roswell here?' shouted Major-General Gelding through a hastily commandeered radio-mic. On cue the vast screens switched to the feed from the Pentagon camera crew and showed hundred-foot pictures of the classic grey alien as it uncurled and stood, blinking benignly and waving in a stiff but strangely presidential manner.

Up on the balcony, Kh'Vynn looked at Kh'Xandhra nervously.

'Oh my God!' gasped the Pope. 'I . . . I thought we were the first?'

'No way. This creature's been here since 1947,' answered Gelding around his trademark cigar. 'And is now a fully fledged American citizen.' He waggled a passport in front of the camera.

'You mean all that *Men In Black* stuff is actually true?' coughed the Pope, leaning over the balcony.

'Aliens have been here for years!' boomed back Gelding enthusiastically.

'That's brilliant!' declared Pope Angeles. 'Don't you see? This just adds more proof to the existence of God. Three alien nations existing at the same time. A mere instant in the age of the cosmos. That *cannot* be chance! Three alien civilisations!'

'Er, make that four,' announced a roundly vowelled Russian accent through a megaphone. At the far end of St Peter's Square, Agent Olevski wobbled on the roof of a small Fiat van and clung to the large fibreglass cone of 'Mr Flaky's Itinerant Ice-Cream Emporium'. He pressed a series of buttons on a suitcase-sized transmitter and, with only a few seconds' delay and a short blast of static across the screens, he hacked into Reuters local area broadcast network. The left-hand screen began showing live pictures from a Soviet cameraman down by his ankles. A host of Ukrainian choirboys screamed and ran as a nine-foot scaly alien, with claws to match, unfolded itself from the confines of the ice-cream van and rubbed at what passed as the small of its back.

'Five,' shouted an excited Japanese voice as the other balcony screen was hijacked by a beam from a box of state-of-the-art electronics. It began broadcasting pictures of an insectoid creature as it stomped across the top of the curling colonnade towards a terrified Iraqi cameraman. Curiously, it moved in exactly the same way that had made Godzilla famous the world over.

On the balcony, the Pope was jumping up and down in spasms of delight. 'Everyone, look around you! Look at this! It's incredible. The proof has been here all the time! God's hand has worked across the entire universe!'

'Are you sure?' asked the voice of Gelding as he slapped high fives with the slender, fragile-looking grey. 'I mean, are you absolutely certain that what you're seeing now is really the product of a distant planet? Or could it be something a little more, ahem, *terrestrial* in origin?'

'What? Of course, I'm sure,' declared the Pope defiantly. 'It's alive isn't it? It's moving. It's proof of God's work in a distant galaxy.'

'Uh-huh, watch and learn,' grunted Gelding and grasped at the grey's hand. Suddenly with his other hand he lashed a machete out of the sky and hacked at the creature's bony elbow. All those who didn't faint, or reach for suitable places to throw up, screamed and surged forward angrily. 'Look at this!' cried the Major-General revelling in the chaos. 'Wires!' He waggled the obviously man-made arm triumphantly for all to see. 'Silicon Valley's finest animatronics systems!'

'What? What are you doing?' shouted the Pope, feeling suddenly helpless. 'What is the meaning of this?'

But before anyone answered, a roar issued from the vicinity of the Mr Flaky van as a man in full Cossack dress leapt into view and advanced across a rapidly clearing expanse of cobbles. He brandished a vast sword frantically before him, slashing the air in deadly scything curves, threatening the scaly nine-foot monster.

All cameras whirled on to the action, broadcasting it in minute detail on the screens.

'No, stop that. This is *my* address!' shouted the Pope. 'Listen to me!'

Suddenly the beast lurched forward, the Cossack spun wildly and slashed it a deadly gash across its midriff. It staggered backwards, reeled dramatically and, before the entire world, the creature from yet another galaxy split into two grinning circus dwarves. They bowed quickly to the biggest audience they would certainly ever have and cart-wheeled away behind the ice-cream van, leaving their rubberised costume in ragged tatters.

'No, this cannot be!' denied the Pope. 'This is some cheap publicity stunt, isn't it? What are you advertising? Tell me!'

Before he could receive an answer, the crowd's attention was snatched by a strangled scream coming from high on the colonnade. The Japanese insectoid creature was clutch-ing at its head and writhing in full Kibuki agony. Mouth parts thrashed wildly, antennae spun out of control as it fell to its knees in over-acted suffering. Suddenly it screamed a final tortured scream and wrenched its head clean off in a glistening fountain of sushi and tomato.

As fourteen nuns, a certain Iraqi cameraman and a particularly sensitive Monsignor passed out, a well-known sumo wrestler stood and bowed long and low, his insectoid's head dripping raw fish.

'My people,' begged the Pope across the PA system as he desperately tried to regain some degree of control. 'What purpose these tasteless displays were set to achieve is completely baffling to me. I can only guess that perhaps this was aimed at somehow undermining my message to you today. Well, it has failed. My truth, *the* truth, is still intact. Whilst those aliens were nothing more than cheap costumes and puppets, these aliens here upon the stage with me are entirely real.'

317

Kh'Vynn looked nervously across at the trembling Kh'Xandhra.

Pope Angeles turned to the Merlot-and-Ribena hued Kh'Vynn. 'Go on,' he said, 'I know you're real. Tell *them*! Please.'

Fifteen thousand feet above everyone's heads, the Regal Commander of the Strato-Fortress glared at a monitor screen on the Battle Bridge. 'Go on, tell them, if you dare,' he cackled. 'If you *can* without a full vote and three recounts.' He raised his voice to anyone who was listening. 'That's the fatal flaw with those idiot democratic types, they can never make a decision on their own. Now if he'd asked my Kh'Xandhra . . .'

'Er, Your Highness, we have an incoming ship,' announced the Prince of Sensors as the million-ton Tropo-Nihilator swooped in on a superheated plume of ytterbium exhaust.

'And an incoming message, Your Regality,' added the Communications Serf as his Incoming Message Sensor lit up.

'It took them long enough to vote on how to get here. What do they want?' tutted the Regal Commander and the speakers crackled into life.

'On behalf of the duly elected representatives of the Council of War, I, as Comrade Communicator, do ask the following. Are you aware of any communicable diseases which your daughter may have been carrying at the time of her abduction of our Kh'Vynn?'

'My daughter?' bellowed the Regal Commander. 'It is your Kh'Vynn which has given her an as yet unidentifiable ilness. Look at her skin, so jaundiced . . .'

'All representatives of the medical quorum agree that it is our Kh'Vynn who is looking the more unwell, indicating that . . .'

'That he's been ill longer and has given whatever it is to

318

my daughter. How irresponsible. How dare he kidnap her whilst in the grip of a deadly disease?'

'She seduced him and dragged him into the endless wastes of space!'

The Regal Commander slammed his tentacle on to the communications panel in a fit of temper. It erupted into a fountain of sparks. 'How dare they even suggest that?' he snarled. 'One more comment like that. One more and . . . Are laser cannons at full charge?'

'Of course, Your Regality,' beamed the Tactical Serf.

The Regal Commander stared at the tiny screen showing his daughter standing on the papal balcony and listened in on the pleadings of the figure in white. 'Why won't you tell them you're real?' begged Angeles. 'Please, speak to them. Kh'Xandhra?' The aliens looked back at him blankly.

'She's really ill,' growled the Regal Commander. Behind him the Minion in Charge of Health nodded sagely and hoped that he wasn't about to be asked for a diagnosis. 'No daughter of mine would ever refuse a chance to speak to such an audience. Damn that Kh'Vynn. Damn them all.'

On the monitor, Angeles turned back to the crowd in St Peter's Square. 'They *are* real, honest. I've spoken to them. I don't know why they won't . . .'

'Because they can't,' challenged Gelding, waggling his grey's severed forelimb. 'You know as well as anyone that there's no such thing as aliens. They're merely figments of people's imaginations. Substitutes for religion . . .'

'No!' shouted the Pope thinly through the monitor's speaker grilles. 'They're real. I'll prove it!' The Regal Commander watched as he whirled desperately in a flurry of Gaultier vestments, snatched Kh'Xandhra firmly by the tentacles and pulled her towards the balcony. 'Talk to them!'

Shaking her head she backed away.

'Talk!' pleaded Angeles, grabbing her by the shoulders and shaking hard. 'Talk!'

The Regal Commander watched in horror as her head rattled woodenly three times before the hastily sewn stitching holding it on gave up in spectacular fashion. With a sickening wrenching sound Kh'Xandhra's head tore off and revealed the terrified and sweating face of Cardinal Holridge.

The Pope screamed.

It wasn't half as dramatic as the reaction of a certain Regal Commander. He was on his feet and across to the weapons controls in seconds, a vein pulsing wildly at the side of his head.

'My Kh'Xandhra!' he screamed. 'That blotchy purple bastard's killed my beloved Kh'Xandhra! He's given her acute dissolving plague. Kill them. Kill them all!'

And just as the Creature's Republican Council of War passed a motion to engage in sudden military action, the entire weapon systems of the Strato-Fortress opened fire. Laser cannons sliced into the alloy hull, severing power conduits in cascades of sparks. Plasma-pulse rifles ruptured vital superstructures, setting off a whole series of chain reactions which were certain to spell complete and utter destruction within the next few minutes.

But that wasn't going to get in the way of a bit of extreme retaliation.

The Tropo-Nihilation Engine's hyper tasers shorted through a thin cloud bank, ionising vast sections of the Strato-Fortress's outer skin in preparation for the launch of a dozen ion-seeking hyper-gravity missiles.

'Fire?' proposed the Weapons Committee Representative. A unanimous vote carried the motion and a joyous purple tentacle hit the launch button.

On the balcony fifteen thousand feet below, Cardinal

320

Holridge was trying his very best to explain his unexpected appearance in alien fancy dress. 'Look, Your Holiness, you probably won't believe it right now, but . . . er, this *is* for the best. If their parents ever found out that they were *really* here, then . . .'

'Believe me, it would be a real mess. Zzzzzap whooosh . . . ba-boooom!' offered Cardinal Kotonawa from inside a hastily stitched copy of Kh'Vynn. Somehow it lost its impact through the half-inch skin of the purple-painted rubber mask.

'Ask them yourself,' pleaded Holridge. 'They'll tell you everything. You don't have to believe us.'

'Believe . . .' muttered Pope Angeles in a state of shock, his entire address unravelling around him. He shook his head in sheer incomprehension. Where had it all gone wrong? What banana skin of evil fate had brought him to this, to here, high on the papal balcony in front of a world-wide audience, listening to the excuses of a pair of Cardinals in rubber suits? Right now, he should be pressing forward, hammering home his truths, moments away from uniting the entire world in the sure and certain belief that God was alive and well and happily starting life in all corners of the universe. It wasn't really turning out to be the best morning of his life.

'You don't have to believe *us* about the pair of million-ton spaceships that are in orbit,' said Kotonawa muffledly.

'Believe?' whimpered the Pope, his eyes glazing over in defeat.

'I tell you,' offered Holridge, 'it took me a while to believe all that stuff about the complete destruction of an entire planet's atmosphere. Unless I'd seen all the pictures with my own eyes . . .'

'With your own eyes . . .' mumbled Angeles in a low monotone. 'Seen it with your own eyes . . .' Miserably, he looked out over the sea of perspiring faces and sighed as he realised just who had flung Fate's banana skin his way. Mentally he kicked himself for not seeing it earlier. Surely nothing on this Earth could've stuffed him up quite so neatly? 'You got me,' he muttered to himself as he glanced Heavenward. 'They're just not ready for it yet, are they?'

Much to his surprise, a cloud fifteen thousand feet or so above him seemed to flash in silent agreement.

Shrugging and taking a deep breath, Pope Angeles stepped forward and cleared his throat as he addressed the crowd.

'Erm . . . well, I expect you're all wondering what all that was about,' he began in an oddly human tone. 'I bet you're wondering where this "truth" is that I promised you, aren't you? "See it here, today!" and all that. Well, sorry folks, but if you think you're going to get it just by turning up here, it's time I told you, that's not how it works. It hasn't worked like that for two thousand years, why did you think today would be any different?' he said, not entirely sure if he was trying to convince them or himself. 'I mean, face it, most of you didn't exactly put yourself out much to get here. Couple of hours on the bus, overnight on a nice comfy plane. Not really what you'd call suffering, is it? Not really a pilgrimage? And if crawling all the way across India on your bare knees doesn't work, what makes you think a day-trip out here will?'

There was an uncomfortable silence and a complete charter flight of tour operators swallowed guiltily.

'What did you expect? A sign that God exists? A sudden revelatory experience as the clouds part and Charlton Heston appears? Or did you think the sky would explode spontaneously into a million different colours? Well, if that's what it takes to see the light, God bless you.' He turned away from the balcony and, far more round shouldered than he had been when he came out, he trudged into the ante-room and a very dodgy future.

'D'you think that was our fault?' asked Kotonawa through half an inch of muffling purple rubber.

Holridge shrugged uncertainly and closed the door behind them just as another door burst open and Kh'Vynn and Kh'Xandhra spun in excitedly.

'Where are the cameras? Show me the cameras!' gabbled Kh'Vynn through the wonders of his translator. 'I want the world to see us!'

The crew from Reuters stared at them, scowled and glared at Holridge. 'How many more of these things have you got?' tutted a soundman and pulled at one of Kh'Xandhra's tentacle tips. 'Well, they don't fool me. I've got a pair of rubber gloves that feels more convincing than that. C'mon guys, there must be a bar open somewhere.'

'What's that supposed to mean?' whined Kh'Vynn.

Any explanation that might have been forthcoming never left Holridge's lips.

At that very instant, fifteen thousand feet above them, a dozen ion-seeking hyper-gravity missiles struck alien alloy and imploded. The hull of the Regal Strato-Fortress buckled terminally, complex circuitry shorted and one hundred and thirty-two Type-98 Ytterbium Colliders went critical. On the Creatures' Republican Tropo-Nihilation Engine, things weren't much better.

Alarm klaxons blared and hundreds of warning sirens heralded the complete collapse of all superstructural integrity. With a single massive groan a main chassis support beam wrenched itself free and plunged through the dead centre of the weapons generator grid.

And the sky erupted.

A pair of exploding chrysanthemums filled the horizon as two million tons of spacecraft tried their level best to prove

Einstein was right about matter and energy. Sparks and flares spun and streaked across the sky in flaming whirls of elemental colour.

Almost as one the crowd looked into the Heavens above them, their jaws dropping in awe as the words of Pope Angeles rang loud in their ears. And, just as they were beginning to wonder if this was what seeing the light was all about, a shock wave of hyperheated ytterbium exhaust blasted into St Peter's Square, ricocheted along the Via della Conciliazione and flattened the crowds along the banks of the Tiber.

14:05 The Vatican

Two hours later a volunteer nurse in a Red Cross uniform and blue rinse was shaking her head as she watched yet another victim of extreme dehydration down a litre of water.

'But I'm telling you, it's true,' gasped the patient between mouthfuls. 'The sky . . . it just went babooom!'

'Yeah, yeah,' tutted the nurse, smearing a tube of aftersun through his Bruce Willis haircut. 'Staring at it long were you? Straight into the sun?'

'No, I . . .'

'Then where did this come from, hmmmm?' she slapped his cheeks.

'Owww, that hurts!'

'Yes. And so it should. I don't know how many times we tell people to wear a hat and have the right sun-block, but do you listen?' She looked at the heavily decorated breast of his Major-General's uniform. 'You military types never learn. I bet you've forgotten how hot it was in the Gulf War. And you never drink enough. Tourists,' she frowned. 'Next!'

'But it wasn't the sun . . .' began Gelding.

'Next!' insisted the nurse, clenching her fists in a way that would have made any matron proud.

Deep in the underground laboratory of the Congregation for Icon Authentication a strangely sombre mood was hanging around a clump of seven beings and a stack of technology.

'Well, that's that then,' muttered Father Fintan, rubbing at his bruised chin and throbbing head. 'After being involved in this I've got no chance of becoming a Cardinal.'

'Think yourself lucky,' tutted Cardinal Kotonawa, his head sticking out of the top of purple-skinned torso. 'You aren't going to have to put up with the constant sniggering every time you walk into a room.' He struggled once again with a zip that seemed to be rusted shut.

'Luxury,' grumbled Cardinal Holridge. 'That's the end of my scientific career. No one'll believe anything I say, ever again. Especially if it's about aliens.' Miserably, he looked around at the unfeasibly shiny spacecraft and the pair of tentacled creatures chatting away industriously down the telephone. 'What are they up to anyhow?'

Everyone shrugged.

Giorgio Scipioni looked at Sophia. 'Bet His Holiness won't let me get my hands on his Render-Benders any more.'

'After the trouble you've caused, I'd say no way,' she frowned, a couple of white dots still clinging to her earlobes.

Suddenly, across the lab, Kh'Xandhra slammed the telephone down and stomped across the floor. 'That's it, I give up!' she moaned, her voice filtering out from the grille in her tiny headset translator. 'I've tried everywhere and even Paramount don't want me. They say that there's nothing I can teach them about prosthetic forehead technology and besides they've got all the aliens they need for *Star Trek: The Infinite Franchise.*'

Kh'Vynn slouched his way across the floor. 'Same here. I'm beginning to think we'd have been better off heading for

Tau Ceti. At least they have an active alien employment opportunity programme.'

Giorgio Scipioni's right eyebrow pricked up curiously.

'Well, that is indeed that. The future is definitely on the bleak side,' complained Holridge.

'Hmmm, it is around here, sure,' began Giorgio Scipioni rubbing his chin and looking at the scatter of video equipment still littering the lab. 'Tau Ceti, you say, Kh'Vynn?'

'Er, yes, but . . .'

'How many of us can you fit in that ship of yours?'

'Well, seven would be a bit cosy . . .'

'And the equipment?'

'Even cosier, but, not impossible. Why?'

'Hey, Holridge, how long d'you think it'll take to get that thing up and running?' asked Scipioni, pointing to the unfeasibly shiny craft and slipping a far too companionable arm around his shoulder.

'Well, if it's something as simple as a melted inlet, which, if Kh'Vynn's description of the effects of an oxygen/nitrogen atmosphere on non-tepid galactic converters is anything to go by, it could be, well, hmmm . . . Couple of days?'

'What are you and Kotonawa waiting for?' enthused Scipioni suddenly. 'With your brains, Fintan's costume skills, Kh'Vynn and Kh'Xandhra's acting ability, my directorial prowess and Sophia's looks, Hell, Tau Ceti won't know what's hit 'em!'

'Er, can someone give me a hand with this zip?' pleaded Cardinal Kotonawa, his tentacles failing yet again to shift the stubborn piece of metalwork. 'Please?'

'Just one thing?' asked Holridge, ignoring Kotonawa's whining and staring at the pair of creatures from beyond the stars. 'There aren't any time zones in space, are there?'